THE HOMESTEAD ON THE RIVER

ROSIE MACKENZIE

THE HOMESTEAD ON THE RIVER

Copyright © 2019 Rosie Mackenzie

Second edition 2024

ISBN 978-0-6457338-9-1

Ballynastragh Books.

www.ballynastraghbooks.com.au

To Rob, Charlotte, Georgie and all my cherished family.

For all you have given me.

Calcutta, India, 1945

Kathleen Wynn stepped to the edge of the verandah and took a long, cold sip of iced tea. Before her was one of her favourite views in India: the glorious Tollygunge Country Club gardens rolling down to the lagoon thick with water lilies and tall reeds. In the distance she could hear the sounds of a drum and a flute drifting from the servants' quarters.

She turned and smiled as she watched Jessica in her element, surrounded by a group of admiring servicemen. Next to her was a jovial fellow with closely cropped dark hair. Already the red veins on his face suggested he was a heavy drinker. Jessica had pointed him out to Kathleen last week when he'd fallen off his horse at a servicemen's polo match.

'His name is Guy Preston,' she'd told Kathleen. 'His parents made a fortune in jute broking after the First World War. Even if he's a bit of a bore,' she laughed, 'with all the squillions of family money bound to come his way I must say it makes him rather attractive.'

As Kathleen came over to join the group, she saw a stranger standing to one side, watching her. She noticed his blue eyes shaded by thick, feathery lashes and how his hair was blonded by the sun. He was wearing an RAF uniform and the insignia of a squadron leader. She noticed that among his ribbons was a Distinguished Flying Cross. As she sat down next to Jessica, she could feel his eyes upon her. She looked up and for some time they held each other's gaze. It was as if neither of them wanted to look away.

Jessica turned around and waved to the stranger with her half-smoked cigarette in its ivory holder. 'My dear man, how divine to see you.'

Reluctantly he moved his eyes from Kathleen to Jessica. 'And I must say it's a pleasure to see you, Jessica.' He leaned down to kiss her cheek. 'As always you look a picture.'

'And as always you're far too kind,' said Jessica with a beaming smile that showed her perfect white teeth. She took hold of the man's hand and turned to Kathleen. 'Do let me introduce you to Kathleen Wynn… my very best friend. As you can see, she's by far the most ravishing woman in Calcutta.' She gave a laugh. 'Except for me, of course. Not only is she sublime, she's unfairly clever. She's a Hindi interpreter at Garrison Headquarters.' She grinned at Kathleen. 'We grew up together, didn't we, Kate?'

Kathleen nodded. 'Jessica's parents had a place on the Hooghly River at Barrackpore next door to mine.'

'The most romantic stretch of water in India,' he laughed, pulling up a seat next to Kathleen.

'Yes, it was a paradise for us children. My father was a commissioner in the civil service and the house came with the job when he brought the family out from Ireland.' She glanced at the badge on his cap, which he had tucked under his arm. 'Are you newly posted here? If you know the river so well, maybe not.'

'I've been seconded back to headquarters from the Burma front.' He grinned. 'For some reason they seem to think my experience there might help. Perhaps they imagine I'm far cleverer than I am.'

Jessica raised a beautifully arched eyebrow. 'Oh, I very much doubt that.'

'So you'll be here for a while?' Kathleen asked.

'For a while, yes. Then in and out as usual.' He smiled broadly at her. As he did, she felt she'd known that smile forever and an exhilarating thrill tingled along her spine. He glanced at her riding helmet and the leather crop by her side. 'And where did you learn to ride like that?' he asked.

'You saw me ride in?'

'I did for sure. And a fine-looking beast you were on.'

'Are you a rider as well?'

'I've done a fair bit in my time. Enough to know a good seat on a horse when I see one.'

Much to her embarrassment Kathleen felt herself blushing. 'Thank you.'

He looked towards the stables. 'So what's his name?'

'Joker. I come out here to the Tolly and ride him when I can.'

'She's besotted by him,' Jessica laughed. She leant over Kathleen and placed a hand possessively on his knee. 'Now tell me, where are you staying? At the Officer's Mess?'

'Yes, that's right.'

Jessica smiled seductively. 'Well… you know where I am. Make sure you contact me.'

***

Just on dusk the party headed to Pete's old Wolseley to go into Calcutta for dinner at Firpos, followed by a movie at the New Empire theatre, promising to wait for Kathleen as she checked on Joker in his stable. But when she returned to the gravel courtyard the Wolseley was gone and the squadron leader was standing there on his own, his hat tilted rakishly and a smile on his handsome face.

'There wasn't enough room in the car for you,' he told her. 'So I hoped you might like to come with me.' He pointed to a motorbike parked under a spreading rhododendron. 'If you like horseriding, I took a gamble and thought you might like to try this.' He opened an intricately stencilled saddlebag on the side of the bike and took out a leather helmet. 'My head has taken too many batterings for it to matter, but your pretty head… well —'

9

Kathleen took the helmet and put it on, pulling her hair free. Then she ran her fingers along the side of the red bike where the Indian Chief logo stood out in gold. 'It's beautiful,' she said. 'I've never seen one so beautiful.'

'I found her neglected at the barracks. A couple of the other officers and I have kept busy restoring her on our time off.'

Moving the Indian from under the tree, he straddled the seat, beckoning Kathleen to climb on behind him. Glad she was wearing jodhpurs, Kathleen sat astride but wasn't sure where to put her hands, laying them on her knees, then her lap and finally on the side of the bike. Looking up at the clubhouse, she could see a group still sitting on the verandah where lanterns were casting a warm glow on the balustrades. She wondered if anyone was watching them. If so, would they recognise her? In a second it would be back to the Maharani of Cooch Behar, a family friend, whose city residence housed the small flat where Kathleen lived. That's how it worked in Calcutta. Gossip travelling faster than a Bengal tiger in full flight. She could almost hear the Maharani's startled voice. 'Honestly, Kathleen, you really should be careful. Some of these servicemen can't be trusted.'

'You'll have to hold on to me,' he said, gesturing for Kathleen to grab his waist. She wrapped her arms around him tightly. Now one almighty roar filled the air and he edged the bike forward, taking off in a thick cloud of dust. She loved the wind in her face, the feeling her hair was going to blow away from under the helmet, the speed with which the paddy fields and rubber plantations hurtled by; the screeching gravel; the dust. And she laughed out loud when they roared past the marshy grassland and scattered the sleepy buffalo into the safety of the tree-covered hills. No car was ever this noisy.

'What do you think?' he shouted, turning his head for a second.

'It's brilliant. I'd no idea …'

'Hold on. There's a corner coming up.'

As they took the bend, Kathleen gripped his waist even tighter. She could sense the warmth of his body against hers, feel her breasts sinking into the curve of his back. A tingle ran from the tips of her toes to the very top of her head. On that balmy evening when the world was racked by war, she wanted to ride on the back of his motorbike forever.

***

Two days later he turned up at Kathleen's flat. 'Come,' he beckoned with a wide grin, 'let's go see the real India.'

Once more Kathleen climbed onto the back of the motorbike. Soon they were weaving between cars and rickshaws down Chowringhee Street and out through the native village on the outskirts of town among giggling children, cows, goats scavenging through rubbish, pushbikes, beggars, and women in colourful saris. The smell of burning cow dung permeated the air.

'I wanted to share this with you,' he said, turning to Kathleen. 'It's my favourite place in Calcutta.'

Although Kathleen often enjoyed wandering through the market stalls in the native villages, being part of the chaotic hustle and bustle with him made it even more special.

Watching him laugh and joke with the children, she realised she was falling hopelessly in love. Every off-duty moment they could steal they explored on his motorbike, had picnics by the river, went horseriding in the hills, dined at Firpos Restaurant and went dancing at Government House. Wherever they went, Kathleen was happier than she had ever been.

Until the awful day arrived when her world came crashing down, sweeping away that happiness in one fell swoop and breaking her heart. A few years earlier, when her parents were killed in a railway crash on the way to Bishnupur, Kathleen had thought her world had ended. For weeks she had wept with heartbreak and sorrow until the events of the war made her realise there were people hurting far more than she was.

Now, just six months since that magical afternoon at the Tollygunge Club, it seemed she was one of those people. A week later Kathleen was gripped with a fear greater than any she had felt before.

Part One

Kenmare River, County Kerry, Ireland
1963

Chapter 1

'I do love this one,' Alice said. 'Such a good shot of Lillie.'

'There's no way she'll let us use it,' Kathleen laughed. 'You can see her face.'

Kathleen O'Sullivan and her mother-in-law sorted through Kathleen's photographs in the glass conservatory of Rathgarven, a stone manor house nestled in a secluded rocky cove of the Kenmare River in County Kerry. Alice was writing another article for an English magazine depicting country life in Ireland. To accompany it, Kathleen had taken some photographs, which she'd developed in the small darkroom set up off the woodhouse.

Kathleen picked up another picture of her daughter. Lillie was riding her horse Merlin among the apple trees in the walled garden. It was such a lovely photograph with the light filtering through the trees onto her dark hair. Kathleen had taken the shot from behind, as Lillie was adamant she didn't want her face to be in a magazine.

'Maybe this one will do,' she said, handing the photo to Alice.

'The colours are certainly lovely. But it's such a pity we can't see Lillie's beautiful face.'

Another photo Kathleen had chosen was of her eldest son, Ronan, sailing their small yacht the *Daphne* on the river. There was also one of her younger boys, Marcus and Freddie, climbing the oak tree in the front garden, and a scene of the first hunt meet of the season gathering on the gravel driveway in front of Rathgarven, with Maisie, dressed in her best apron embroidered with harps and shamrocks, bringing the hunters a stiff stirrup cup before they headed off. In all there were five photographs. More than adequate for Alice's article, Kathleen thought.

Now her attention was drawn beyond the window to the curve of the river where a red steamer chugged around the point, heading towards Rathgarven's jetty. With a jolt Kathleen recognised whose steamer it was. Most likely it had come down the river from Kenmare Harbour where the Killarney bookmaker TJ Donoghue kept it. He had visited before under happier circumstances when there had been a regatta on the river. She glanced at Alice to see if she had noticed. Fortunately she still had her head over the photographs. What a hide Donoghue had to arrive like this. If he thought he was going to alight on Rathgarven's jetty, he had another thing coming. Rathgarven wasn't his house yet — and never would be, if Kathleen had anything to do with it.

'I'll just pull this curtain across,' she said to Alice, pushing her chair back and moving to the window to block Alice's view of the jetty. 'You'll be able to see more clearly without the sun on the photos. And,' she added, glancing to the door, 'can you give me a moment. Maisie's heading into Sneem. I forgot to tell her to pop into the chemist for me.'

'Of course, dear,' Alice said as she looked at the photographs. 'You certainly have a way of capturing all of Rathgarven's moods. I'm not sure whether I like it wild and woolly best, or ablaze with sunshine.'

'They're both lovely,' Kathleen said, heading towards the door. 'Although I must admit I prefer it sunny.'

Outside, Kathleen flew down the stone steps and across the newly rolled front lawn, through the green wooden gate and across the meadow to the jetty.

'How can I help you, Mr Donoghue?' she called out, as the bookmaker disembarked. A small smartly dressed group stood on the deck behind him.

'Ah, good afternoon, Mrs O'Sullivan,' he said, tipping his flashy trilby in her direction. 'I trust you be well on this grand day.'

'I am, thank you,' Kathleen said, anger tightening her voice.

'That be great to hear.' Donoghue glanced at the group on the deck. 'I was telling these good folks about your lovely Rathgarven. And they persuaded me to let them have a wee peek.' He puffed the cigarette in his hand and looked towards the house. 'Would Mr O'Sullivan be around?'

Although her husband was up in the back field with Danny, the overseer, rebuilding a stone wall that a rampaging bull had barged through yesterday, there was no way Kathleen was going to tell Donoghue that.

'I'm afraid it's not convenient for you to stop off today. We have a large house party arriving from Dublin for the weekend,' she lied. 'Maybe you could give my husband a telephone call and arrange another time.' She glanced at the group standing on the deck of the boat waiting to disembark. 'I'm sorry to be so tiresome. Today's not convenient.' Donoghue's smart sports coat did little to hide the many good lunches he'd partaken of over the years. Lowering her voice, she said, 'Mr Donoghue, I'd be grateful if you could get back on your boat. Rathgarven is not yours as yet. And until it is, the only guests who'll disembark on our jetty are the guests of the O'Sullivan family.'

'Ah. Is that so, Mrs O'Sullivan?' He removed his trilby and smoothed his thick black hair. 'Though I'm sure Mr O'Sullivan would feel differently. It's a pity he's not here.' He stomped his cigarette into the ground with one highly polished brogue. 'In any case I'll happily take my guests further along the river to where I know they'll be greeted more cordially.'

'Thank you,' Kathleen said. 'I'd appreciate that very much.' She glanced at the hawser in his hands. 'I'll hold the rope steady for you until you're back on board and give you a push off.'

'That won't be necessary,' Donoghue grunted. 'I can back out quite easily myself. But be sure to tell your husband I'll be in touch. And be giving him my best wishes.'

'I will indeed,' Kathleen said.

Kathleen watched him reverse away from the jetty, the loud revving of the steamer's engine sounding an angry farewell. Kathleen didn't care. She was glad to get rid of him. Drawing a deep breath, she tried to calm down. Had there been a gun handy, she felt sure she'd have picked it up and taken a pot shot at him. She could imagine the headline in the *Irish Times*: 'Angry Kerry wife shoots leading bookmaker'.

She turned and walked back along the jetty and into the meadow dotted with daisies and buttercups. For a moment she stopped and gazed up at the gabled house of pale grey stone with its wide French windows and the conservatory on the southern side, where thankfully the curtain was still drawn. The late-afternoon sun shone softly across the façade, coating it with a golden tinge. A shudder passed through Kathleen. Rathgarven had been the home of O'Sullivans for generations. It had even risen again after being burnt to cinders in the Civil War of 1922, when Ireland seemed to have lost all reason. How could James have put his family home in jeopardy? It would destroy his mother when she found out. Although Kathleen had only come to live at Rathgarven fifteen years ago, Alice had arrived as the young bride of the late Eoghan O'Sullivan at the beginning of the century.

She was too angry to face Alice yet and went to the drawing room instead. A copy of the *Irish Times* lay on the sofa with a photo on the front page of President Kennedy giving his civil rights speech. Exasperated, she scrunched the paper up and threw it on the dying embers and watched the fire come alight.

James would be furious she had refused to let the party disembark. Well, blow James. He had got them into this pickle and Kathleen was darned if she was going to let Donoghue rub it in her face.

Just at that moment the door opened and James appeared. He was in his work clothes — the worn beige trousers and a bottle-green jumper under a tattered Donegal tweed jacket.

'Donoghue was here with one of his fancy parties,' she said, her voice shaking. 'I told him we weren't receiving visitors this afternoon.' She gazed down to the jetty, now almost hidden by a soft mist. 'Had you any idea he was dropping by?'

James walked over and knocked his pipe into the brass ashtray on the table. 'I'm sorry, darling,' he said. 'I'd no idea.'

'Does he think he owns the place already? Is that why he came? Maybe he told his guests he'd drop in to see how his new country estate is getting along?'

Kathleen paced the room. By the window she could see a robin redbreast playing among the rose bushes in the garden; in the front field the horses grazed unaware. She became still. James was a good, sensible man. Until this happened.

'Why didn't you come and get me?' James asked.

'What good would that have done?'

'I might've been able to persuade him to hold off.'

'Hold off! Oh my God, James! Can you hear yourself?' Kathleen gazed around the familiar room she loved so much. 'How has it come to this?'

James sighed. 'I've told you. If I'd thought it was a risk, I'd never have done it.' He picked up his pipe. 'Lord Fitzpatrick agreed with me that the beast was a sure thing. He himself placed a bet on it.'

'With his buckets of money and that huge estate, Drominderry, he could afford to lose. We couldn't. Not with the amount of debt we're in already.'

'That's true. Still, my darling, surely you'd have felt differently if the darn horse had come in?'

'But it didn't, did it? Nor did the others Donoghue cajoled you into to betting on later.'

'If they had won I would've made five thousand. Think of the new roof we could have put on Rathgarven, the school fees it could have covered… and…'

'Stop, James. Please…'

'Kathleen, I can understand why you're upset. And for that I'm truly sorry. What we've got to do now is try and fix the situation. I'll make an appointment to see Declan at the bank in Kenmare tomorrow. He's sure to give us a loan to pay Donoghue off. And Paddy says we should reap a grand crop of barley in the spring.'

'You may well be right with the barley,' Kathleen sighed, turning her gaze to the lush, green fields beyond the window. 'But you of all people know there's hardly any collateral left. So nice as Declan is, he's unlikely to be able to help. Besides, it's in all the papers that none of the banks are lending to farmers right now.'

'Donoghue's a reasonable man. I'm sure we can come to an agreement. It's a pity you didn't get me when he dropped in. I could've spoken to him…'

'With all those people there!'

'I'd have drawn him aside…'

'Too late now. Undoubtedly he's floating up the river in his fancy red steamer regaling those very same people with our woes.'

'Kathleen, you're overreacting. It's a lovely afternoon and he wanted to pop in to say hello. Nothing more.'

'I think that's highly unlikely, James. And, in any case, he had a hide to bring people with him. That was unforgivable.'

'Yes. I can see that.'

Kathleen touched her hot forehead. 'I think I'll go to my room, I've got a headache coming on. Your mother is waiting for me in the conservatory, perhaps you could tell her I'm suddenly unwell and can't join you for dinner ... Or,' her voice became high-pitched, 'tell her whatever you wish, James.'

***

Fourteen-year-old Lillie tried to read her book in the library next door. The oak-panelled room was lined with overflowing walnut bookcases and sombre portraits of her O'Sullivan ancestors, who gazed down from gilded frames. From her spot in the window seat it was difficult to miss her parents' raised voices. Ma sounded more upset than Lillie had ever heard her. Even more upset than when six-year-old Lillie had invited a group of passing tinkers into the drawing room for afternoon tea. Lillie didn't like Mr Donoghue with his trilby hats, smart suits and fancy ties. She had seen her mother rush down to the jetty the moment he pulled up in his red steamer. Had Ma told him to leave? Was that why her parents were arguing?

Stealthily moving to the door, Lillie peered through the crack. She saw them clearly now: her beautiful Ma, graceful as one of the swans that swam in the cove, wearing a green plaid skirt and a cream silk shirt, her gleaming mahogany hair falling loosely around her shoulders; and Dad, a wiry man with slightly receding greyish hair and Lillie's own slate-grey eyes. Dad placed his pipe in the ashtray and rested his hand on Ma's shoulder, but she moved angrily away. Lillie could see tears in those magnificent hazel eyes and felt like crying herself.

'And all I can say, James, is that it'll be a tragedy if we lose Rathgarven because of your gambling on a horse,' Ma said. 'A tragedy indeed.'

Realising her mother might catch her spying, Lillie jumped over to the bookshelf and pretended to take down a book. Thankfully, she heard the far door in the drawing room open and

20

shut again. Heaving a sigh of relief, she returned to the window seat, now bathed in the last of the late-afternoon sunshine. For some time she sat there, going over what she'd heard. She felt sick in the stomach. Surely what Ma said couldn't be true. Dad couldn't possibly have lost Rathgarven by gambling on a horse. Or had she misheard?

She looked out the window to where Merlin, her dappled-grey Connemara pony, grazed among the wildflowers under the alder tree in the front field. Contented after the long ride to Sneem with Lillie this morning to visit her friend Sheelagh, he lifted his head as though sensing his young mistress watching him. For a moment Lillie let her eyes wander past him down to the cove and across the river to the shadows and curves of the tumbling Kerry Mountains lifting halfway to the sky. To the left, beyond the jetty, there were corn-coloured haystacks in the far field. She and her brothers had helped Paddy stack them yesterday afternoon.

On the small island not far from shore, her younger brothers Marcus and Freddie scampered up the stone steps of the brooding ruins of an old fort. She heard their voices carrying across the water, squabbling, as they always did, driving Lillie and Ronan nuts. She sighed miserably. Before that man Mr Donoghue had pulled into the jetty she had been wonderfully happy. At long last the summer holidays had arrived, freeing her from her boarding school in Cork and stretching out like a scrumptious dream that went on and on.

There would be fishing for salmon with Ronan in the cove she loved so much, sailing the *Daphne,* riding up into the rocky hills or through the tangled woods teeming with fuchsias and ferns and picnicking by the shore where shearwaters, puffins, ducks, gulls and swans swam and pecked between the rocks and seaweed. Sometimes a dolphin might come in from the Atlantic to swim in the cove. Last summer she and Freddie had watched a seal and her pup cavorting there. She loved the never-ending hours of twilight when, if it wasn't too windy or raining, the family would sit out under the oak tree, her parents and grandmother in wicker chairs, Lillie and her brothers sprawled on the grass. Sometimes they would still be there when the mountains turned to a vivid crimson in the last glow of twilight. And for Lillie there would be lazy times of lying on a blanket reading a book under the elm tree listening to the water lapping against the rocks. At low tide it was the pungent smell of seaweed drifting up from the shore she loved. Or if Paddy had just mowed the lawns it was the whiff of fresh cut grass.

Not that she didn't like winter too, when the wind would whistle along the river, whipping up the water in the cove. As a special treat she and her brothers would be allowed to roast marshmallows in the roaring turf fire in the drawing room. Once when it snowed they tobogganed down the hill behind the house on pieces of plywood. In the kitchen was the warmth of the Aga. When Lillie was smaller, she would scuttle down the back stairs to help Maisie with breakfast, relishing the smell of yummy black puddings, bacon rashers, fresh soda bread and Maisie's favourite Blue Grass perfume.

But now Rathgarven might be lost to that awful man Mr Donoghue. Not burnt to a cinder as had happened in the Civil War. Instead, it was crippled by debt and Dad's gambling. She thought of seeking out her much-loved grandmother to ask her to explain what was going on, but she was due to have her afternoon nap. Maybe tomorrow, when Lillie wheeled her down by the water as she often did, she might be able to wheedle something out of her. Surely she must know what Dad had done.

***

After Kathleen left the drawing room James went to his study and rang Declan at the bank. He and Declan had been friends since

22

their days in the sailing competitions at Kenmare Sailing Club. James had only recently managed to get the phone connected at Rathgarven, so he was glad to be able to use it rather than having to go into town to make an appointment. When the exchange put him through to Declan's secretary he made a time for tomorrow afternoon.

He picked up a photograph on his desk that Kathleen had taken of the children on the jetty with their feet dangling in the water. There was a similar photo of James, his friend Finn Malone and James's younger brother Dermot taken when they were much the same age as Marcus and Freddie. James cursed himself for what he had done. How could he have gambled away his family's happiness?

However, after his meeting with Jessica in Dublin last month, he had been desperate. But couldn't he have thought of another way of raising the money to satisfy her? 'James, my dear, dear man,' she had gushed as she bade him farewell at her hotel. 'I know you of all people won't let me down. And I promise if you come good with this, I'll never bother you for extra again.' She had leant forward and air kissed his cheek. 'Of course you won't tell darling Kate. So there's no need for her to know I was over from London and didn't ring her. It worked out well with you and Finn up in Dublin for the Blackrock reunion.' She pulled her coat closely around her slim body. 'I adore that man, ever since I first met him in India. He's such a good friend, isn't he? A great pity he couldn't join us and had to rush off to the Duncans in Galway.'

'They've been friends for a long time,' James said.

'But I believe he's going down to Rathgarven before heading back to Australia.'

'Yes, he is.'

'Well, do give him my love.'

With a toss of her blonde hair she rushed towards the taxi waiting to take her to the airport. 'I do so much look forward to hearing from you,' she called back. 'If I wasn't so desperate I wouldn't bother you. But,' she added with a grimace, 'as you know, regrettably I am. Bye, darling. Keep safe.'

And then she was gone, leaving James fuming. He had no alternative but to give into her demand without disclosing to Kathleen what he had done.

When he'd got home to Rathgarven he'd saddled up his chestnut hunter and gone for a long ride through the woods and up onto the hills where sheep and cattle roamed between the rocks, to try and calm himself down. Down in the bog he waved to his neighbour, Joe Bourke, who was collecting turf with his donkey. But he didn't stop to talk as he normally would.

From when he was a child James had always ridden. He'd started off competing in small horse shows around Kerry, then graduated to larger ones, finally winning first prize for showjumping at Dublin just before the war. Now, like Kathleen, hunting was his great love. Two days after the meeting with Jessica, and having not slept a wink on either night, he had gone to the Killarney race meet. Was it the lack of sleep that had caused him to do what he did? Not entirely, but it had certainly contributed to his poor judgement. When it hit him how much he'd lost, he had gone into Hannigan's Pub with the intention of getting drunk. But after one drink he lost his thirst and had driven home to Rathgarven where he confessed his shame to Kathleen.

With a pang he remembered the first time he had met her. It was at her Aunt Mildred's place, further along Kenmare River. Although he had had a number of girlfriends before, there was something very different about Kathleen. From the moment he saw her he was smitten. Not only by her magnificent cascade of auburn hair and the way she stood so proud and tall, talking animatedly to a friend of his, it was also her wonderful happy, free laugh. As though she didn't have a care in the world. It was a long time since James had heard that carefree laugh.

Now he moved to the cabinet in the corner of the room and poured a stiff whisky. He was about to take a long sip when he looked at his watch. It was only four. Having a drink at this time of day could only make matters worse. Instead, he put the glass down and went to the door. There was still more work to be done with Paddy. When that was finished he would go and see if he could pacify Kathleen. Though he had grave doubts about that. Walking along the hallway he stopped and looked at the portrait of Dermot. What a fool I am, he thought again, holding his brother's steady eyes with his. A damn, stupid fool.

Chapter 2

Ever since she had heard her parents quarrelling in the drawing room Lillie couldn't get rid of a feeling of doom. So the next day when she positioned Grandma's chair at the bottom of the garden so she could look out to the cove and enjoy the splendid, fragrant afternoon, she still felt quite sick in the stomach. Many years before, her grandmother had fallen off her young thoroughbred when out hunting and broken her back. From then on she'd been confined to a wheelchair.

Lillie looked out to where the *Daphne* was tacking across the cove in a stiff breeze. 'I thought you'd like to watch the boys out on the water, Grandma.'

'Thank you, darling. Perhaps you could come back to get me at five. Undoubtedly I'll be in need of a rest by then. Lord and Lady Fitzpatrick are coming for dinner at eight.'

Lillie placed her bare foot on the brake of the wheelchair. She then leant down and carefully laid a tartan rug over Grandma's knees. 'Would you mind if I stayed with you, Grandma?' she asked

'Of course not, darling. I'd love to have the company.'

Grandma picked up her knitting needles and unravelled a ball of wool from the small wicker basket on her knee and cast on a new row of stitches for the jumper she was knitting for Freddie. Grandma had knitted nearly all the children's jumpers. Even Dad wore a number of her creations. And despite it being quite warm, Lillie herself was wearing a pink cardigan Grandma had knitted for her the previous year.

Lillie perched on a small log nearby. She picked up a blade of grass and placed it between her lips. A swallow fluttered from the oak tree onto the meadow and started pecking busily at the dirt.

On the shore a family of ducks and a cormorant nosed among the rocks. After a moment Lillie stood up, removed the grass from her lips and stomped it into the ground.

'Is anything the matter, darling?' her grandmother asked. 'You seem a little on edge.'

Lillie sat down on the log again and played with a craggy knot in the wood. 'It's just that I've been thinking about how things are hard here in Ireland, particularly in Kerry. You know… Farming and all that.' She stopped, not wanting to tell Grandma what she had overheard. 'I mean… what if we lose Rathgarven?'

'Goodness me, my poor, poor Lillie,' Alice said, placing her knitting on her knee. 'You shouldn't be worrying about things like that. Of course we won't lose Rathgarven. Times are tough, there's no getting away from that. Nevertheless, they've been tough before and we've stumbled through. Your O'Sullivan ancestors have been on Kenmare River since the sixteenth century when Eoghan O'Sullivan, who your grandfather was named after, lived at Dunkerron Castle.' She turned to gaze at the large stone statue that rose up from the middle of an ornamental pond in front of the house, surrounded by camellias and rhododendrons. 'And what about when the poor old house was burnt down in the Civil War? It came back from the ashes then, didn't it? So a few financial problems are a mere drop in the ocean compared to all that history, don't you think?'

'Yes… I suppose you're right,' Lillie mumbled with little conviction. 'Even so, what if Dad…?'

'As I said, being the oldest son and inheriting a place like this isn't by any means as great as it sounds. It's not always easy making ends meet. As your father is finding out. While he struggled to make a living here, men like his dear friend, Finn Malone, who I believe is to arrive this afternoon, were able to flit off to India and Australia to try their fortune.' She smiled. 'India was where he first met your mother.'

'Uncle Finn's coming this afternoon?'

Ever since they were little, to Lillie and her brothers he had been Uncle Finn.

'He is. I thought you all knew.'

'Ronan might have. I didn't. But how exciting. I really like Uncle Finn.' Lillie raised a dark eyebrow and shooed a bumblebee away. 'I didn't know he knew Ma in Calcutta.'

'If it hadn't been for that fortunate meeting your father may not have met your mother, would he? And,' she laughed, 'there'd be no beautiful Lillie or your brothers.'

'I suppose so.'

Behind them came the familiar clink of china. Lillie turned to see Maisie walking across the lawn with a large silver tray in her hands.

Jumping up she ran to help. 'Looks like a feast, Maisie,' she said, eyeing a plate of sandwiches and a platter loaded with hot scones. To the side sat a jar of raspberry jam and a pot of fresh clotted cream.

Maisie glanced down to the shore to where the *Daphne* was being hauled up on the bank by Lillie's brothers. 'I could see that lot were on their way in, so I thought I'd kill two birds with the one stone and bring cool drinks for them as well.'

'What a good idea, Maisie,' Alice said. She looked back up towards the house. 'What about James and Kathleen? Are they joining us?'

Maisie shook her head. 'Not this afternoon, ma'am. Mr O'Sullivan be gone to Kenmare, while Mrs O'Sullivan be in her darkroom developing photos.'

'Busy bees, aren't they?'

'They are indeed, ma'am.'

She then placed the tray on a log and left to return to the house.

As Lillie watched Maisie walk across the lawn, she saw smoke curling out of the kitchen chimney where the Aga was purring happily. She took a deep breath and turned around to pour Grandma a cup of tea from the silver teapot. She then handed her a plate with a scone smothered in jam and cream. She poured herself a long tumbler of lemon squash. Her stomach was in too much turmoil to eat anything.

Now Marcus and Freddie arrived, soaked to the skin, leaving Ronan to pack up the *Daphne*. They gulped down most of the scones and sandwiches in a matter of moments and scampered up to the house.

Later, Lillie settled Grandma in her room, adding a piece of turf to the fire and putting the brass fireguard back in place. Then she went to find Ronan. He was out in the back garden hitting a tennis ball against the wall of the woodshed. As well as playing in the rugby team at his boarding school in Cork he had also tried out for the tennis team and had made it as a reserve. He was determined to make it into the team proper when he went back next term.

'Why didn't you come out for a sail, li'l sis?' he asked. 'A bit rough for a mere girl, eh?'

Lillie adored Ronan, who always called her li'l sis.

'I thought I'd keep Grandma company. Besides, with you lot on board, where was I supposed to fit?'

Ronan looked her up and down. 'Yeah, that's a point. Not as little as you used to be, are you?'

'Ronan!' Lillie exclaimed.

Lillie had put on a bit of weight lately, which was giving her the willies. Ma said it was the age she was. Lillie wasn't so sure it wasn't the way she was meant to be. She and Sheelagh, who was also a bit on the chubby side, spent hours poring over magazines looking at diets, but as soon as Maisie took a fresh loaf of soda bread from the Aga and Lillie smelt the rich aroma wafting through the house, any thought of a diet went flying out of the window.

To add to Lillie's woes, Clara, the daughter of her mother's friend Jessica, was coming to stay. So Lillie would feel even fatter — Clara was as slim as a pencil and hugely pretty.

'Are you excited about Clara coming?' she asked Ronan.

'Yeah, it'll be good to see her.'

When Clara had first come to Rathgarven, it had been with her mother. Lillie remembered being in awe of Jessica. When she'd got out of the car, Lillie thought she was a movie star. She was wearing a tailored cream suit with an otter fur around her neck. The otter still had its head attached. Lillie felt incredibly sorry for the dead otter, as she would hate that to happen to the friendly one who lived in the cove. On her head Jessica wore one of the most glamorous hats Lillie had ever seen, the colour of the blueberries in Paddy's garden. But it was her perfume Lillie remembered the most. Long after she left a room, you could still smell the mixture of wild flowers and musk.

'That horrid man, Mr Donoghue was here again,' Lillie told Ronan, trying to share her worries around. 'He came yesterday when you were at the movies in Kenmare. It sounds to me as though Dad owes him a heap of money. He and Ma were arguing.' She fiddled with the collar of her yellow seersucker blouse, which was always itching her neck. 'Did you know Dad gambled? That he's probably lost so much money we might lose Rathgarven? I heard Ma say so.'

Ronan leaned down and picked up a tennis ball. He hit it hard against the wall, making the shed shudder. If Lillie hoped to get some comfort from him she was disappointed. When the ball hit a rough patch on the wall and dropped dead to the ground, he turned around and said, 'It's none of our business, li'l sis. I'm sure they'll work through it somehow.' There was something in Ronan's voice that told Lillie he may have guessed something of their parents' difficulties. 'I wouldn't go worrying too much if I were you.'

'Oh yeah… And what about Mr Donoghue?'

'If Dad owes him money he'll find a way to pay him back.' He hit another ball. 'And, in any case, you probably misheard. Or misunderstood. Besides, you shouldn't have been listening.'

'I couldn't help it, could I? I mean… it's not as though I was standing outside the door to snoop. I was in the library and they were in the drawing room. The door was open a bit. You know how it's always hard to close it properly.'

Ronan shook his head. 'If we're meant to know what's going on, we'll find out soon enough.' He handed Lillie the racquet. 'Here… you have a go.'

'I don't feel like it. And I don't think you're taking me seriously. If you'd heard them arguing I bet you'd be more worried. But go ahead. Keep hitting that tennis ball and leave the worrying to me.'

With an angry toss of her head she stormed up to her bedroom and threw herself down on her bed. Ronan could be infuriating at times. Sheelagh once told her about a family who lived outside Sneem whose father had gambled so much on the races that he lost their house to the bank and they now had to live in a caravan in that hideous caravan park near Killarney. What if that happened to the O'Sullivans? And, if it did, how would Ronan feel then?

***

'And how is the beautiful Kathleen?' Declan asked, leaning his chunky frame towards James. His black suit was spic and span, much like the one James was wearing for this visit to the bank.

'I'm afraid she's not too happy with me,' James said. 'I hate to admit it. But…well… I did a darn foolish thing.'

He confessed how he put money on the horse that had lost at the Killarney Races. How he had hoped it would solve their liquidity problem, which as Declan knew only too well, was not good. He didn't tell him about the meeting with Jessica.

'But the beast had the hide to lose,' James said, sounding a lot more upbeat than he felt.

'Oh! How much did you lose on it?'

'Two thousand pounds. Then when it lost I stupidly kept trying to get it back. Lost more of course.'

As Declan's eyebrows shot up James told him how Donoghue was ready to swoop on Rathgarven. James knew Declan had no time for Donoghue, who had been known to take a vulnerable gambler's last pound without any shame at all, leaving Declan to sort out the mess. Once over a Guinness in Crowley's Bar he had told James how he had had many a broken man sitting in front of him over the years thanks to Donoghue. Little did James think back then that one day he would be the broken man sitting in front of his friend.

Declan went to the window and stood for a moment looking out.

'Why for pity's sake did you do something idiotic like that?' he sighed, turning back to James and beetling his brow. He picked up a pack of Craven A from his desk and knocked one out. 'It be unlike you to take such a risk.'

'Folks had been talking about this horse for weeks. Everyone thought it had no chance of losing. Even Lord Fitzpatrick said as much. On the way back from Dublin a couple of days before the meet I thought it through and came up with the idea. You could have knocked me over with a feather when the darn thing lost.'

'But to keep going…'

They stopped talking when his secretary bustled in and placed the tea tray with a couple of shortbread biscuits on the desk in front of James.

After she had disappeared through the door Declan shook his head. 'A whisky might've been more in order.'

'It might've at that.' James eyed his friend. 'But do you think you can help? If I can get rid of Donoghue and we reap a good crop of barley I'll be able to pay you back.'

Declan stubbed out his cigarette and looked at his friend. 'We got a directive only last week to say all loans over five hundred pounds have got to be approved by Dublin. Things may not be as grim as the 1950s but they're not exactly bubbling. All I can do is put in an application and hope for the best.' He paused and poured James a cup of tea. 'Hopefully within a couple of weeks we should know something. But, James, I have to say it's not a given that they'll approve it. There are many folk in dire straits at the moment who'll go under if they don't get a loan. Some of them with estates far bigger than Rathgarven.'

'All I can ask is you try.'

'Ah, I'll be doing that all right. I'll put you at the top of my list. Unfortunately, my list is one of many around the country. Now,' he said, pointing to the tray, 'are you going to have that cup of tea, or will you let it go cold?'

James picked the cup up and took a long sip. He decided against a biscuit.

'I'll get the application off in the afternoon mail,' Declan said, rustling some papers out for James to sign. When it was all done, he saw James to the door and placed a hand on his shoulder. 'I'll let you know as soon as I hear a thing. In the meantime, do what you can to hold Donoghue off. Once the word gets around you'll be having every darn sod you owe a penny to leaping in for their piece.'

'Don't I know it,' said James. 'Rest assured I'll heed what you say.'

Declan cleared his throat. 'And the other payments…?' he paused. 'You still want to keep that going?'

James sighed. 'Let's talk about it after we hear about the loan.'

As he drove back to Rathgarven along the narrow road that twisted through the woods beside the Kenmare River, the waves rolling in from the Atlantic pounding against the rocky shore, James wondered what he would do if Declan didn't come good with the loan. Apart from everything else it would break his mother's heart if he lost the family home. He could remember so well the last time her heart was broken. His younger brother Dermot had caused it to break. And in a way it had never really mended.

His family home stood tall and proud in the late-afternoon sunshine as he swung the car in through the gates, and James felt more anguish than he thought possible. He knew Declan well enough to realise there was a definite question as to whether he could get him out of the pickle he was in. Chapter 3

Lillie put the phone down and went to find her mother. She knew she was in the kitchen getting ready for tonight's dinner with Lord and Lady Fitzpatrick, who owned Drominderry House on a large estate ten miles away. Lillie really liked Lady Fitzpatrick with her mass of steel-wool hair and jolly laugh. She always dressed as though she'd just come in from working in the bogs. She wasn't so sure about Lord Fitzpatrick, who had a flushed, pillowy face and dreadful teeth. But as he always brought boxes of chocolates for her and her brothers she pretended she liked him.

In the kitchen her mother was at the sink chopping up potatoes. 'Have you decided whether I can go to the dance at

Kingdom Hall tomorrow, Ma?' she asked. 'Sheelagh just rang. She's going.'

'She may well be,' Kathleen said, turning around and scraping the potato peels into the bin for the chickens. 'However, your father and I have decided you're far too young to be going to dances.'

'Ma! I'm fourteen. The same age as Sheelagh.'

'I'm quite aware of that,' Kathleen said, picking up a carrot to peel. 'Now if you don't mind I've a lot to do to get ready for tonight's dinner. Maisie's laying the table. I said I'd finish up here. And Uncle Finn will be arriving shortly. So as far as I'm concerned that's the end of the matter.'

'But Ronan's going.'

'Ronan will be seventeen in a few months.' Kathleen wiped her hands on her apron and stood with her hands on her hips. 'Now off you go and finish getting your room ready for Clara's arrival. Last time I glanced in there it looked like a jumble sale.'

Lillie shook her head and flounced out of the kitchen. It wasn't fair. She really wanted to go to that dance. In the hallway she passed the photograph of her mother in a sapphire-blue ball gown with her hair up in a chignon. Lillie knew it had been taken in Calcutta, and normally she liked it, but right now she wanted to take to it with the scissors.

'So what will I tell Seamus Flaherty if he's there?' Sheelagh asked, when the exchange put Lillie through from their new phone on the landing. 'If you're not allowed to go.'

Seamus was a boy Lillie had fancied for ages. Just last week at the end of the school term there had only been one spare seat on the bus from Cork, which happened to be next to Lillie. Normally Sheelagh sat with her, but her father had picked her up the day before.

Heaving his bag and tennis racquet up into the luggage rack, Seamus had sat down and flicked his ginger hair back off his forehead. Normally Lillie wasn't so keen on gingerish hair, though on this boy it looked kind of cute.

'Hope you don't mind me sitting here?' he asked, eyeing her from behind lashes as thick as hollyhocks. 'Never seen the bus so crowded.'

'No, of course not,' Lillie said, moving over to give him more room.

'I'm Seamus,' he said. 'Seamus Flaherty.'

'Lillie. Lillie O'Sullivan.'

After Lillie got over her shyness at having him sitting next to her, they chatted companionably. He told her how he lived on a dairy farm out towards Castlecove. He was one of five children, four boys and a girl. He was the eldest and had won a scholarship to Glenstal Abbey at the beginning of high school. He hoped to be a writer.

'Like Brendan Behan?' Lillie asked, as the bus rounded a steep corner.

'Something like that.'

'He's a real hellraiser!'

He laughed and Lillie thought it was a lovely, fun laugh. 'But he's a darn good writer. I'd give a quid to be able to write like him.'

'I've never read anything of his. My brother Ronan has. He read *The Borstal Boy*. He said it was really out there.'

'It's that all right.'

When the bus had chugged down the steep winding road and pulled into Sneem, he grabbed his bag and tennis racquet and handed Lillie her own bag.

'Thanks a lot,' she said, sad they were going their separate ways.

He paused and threw her a smile. 'You going to the dance at Kingdom Hall on Saturday?'

Lillie felt herself blush. 'I'd have to ask my parents if I can.'

'Well, if they'll let you go, I'll see you there. Otherwise I might catch you around sometime.'

'Yeah. You may well do that,' Lillie said.

And, as Lillie watched him jump down from the bus in front of her, she felt her heart race. Did it mean he fancied her? Or was he only being friendly?

Now she was unlikely to find out. 'Tell him I'm not allowed to go,' she said to Sheelagh down the phone. 'My parents think I'm too young.'

'You're the same age as me.'

'That's what I said.'

Ma called up the stairs. 'Lillie… come on down. Uncle Finn's driven in.'

'I've gotta go,' she said to Sheelagh. 'Uncle Finn's arrived.'

She hung up and looked out of the window. Uncle Finn stood by his car, which he must have hired in Dublin, wearing beige trousers, a checked shirt and a sports coat. Instead of a tie like Dad always wore, he was wearing a cravat. He was talking to Freddie, who was holding his pet tortoise, Mandrake. Much as she loved Uncle Finn, she felt so cross with her parents she didn't feel like being sociable. But if she didn't go down she'd get into trouble.

'Gees, look at you,' Finn chuckled, his eyes crinkling in his bronzed face on seeing her step out of the front door. 'You get more like your lovely mother every time I see you.'

'You think so,' Lillie said, moving forward to receive his kiss on her cheek. Despite how miserable she felt she was chuffed he hadn't seemed to notice she'd put on weight. 'It's wonderful to see you, Uncle Finn.'

Finn sighed happily. 'And it's great to be here breathing in this fresh Kerry air with a whiff of the mighty Atlantic.'

Although Lillie thought you wouldn't call him fat, Uncle Finn was solidly built. His warm blue-grey eyes twinkled in fun above a slightly Roman nose and his mouth looked as though it was always about to break into a smile. He talked with a mixture of an Irish and — Lillie presumed — an Australian accent. His mop of coffee-coloured hair had definitely got more grey in it since Lillie had last seen him.

At that moment Marcus and Hugh, the Fitzpatricks' grandson, scampered down from their perch in the oak tree where they had been playing with their bows and arrows and rushed across the lawn, almost knocking Lillie flying in the rush.

'Are you staying long, Uncle Finn?' Marcus asked. 'I'll take you out and show you where the best salmon are biting if you like.' He grinned, showing a gap in his front teeth. 'I caught a huge one off the point yesterday. Maisie said it was the biggest she'd seen in ages. We had it for supper…'

'Stop skiting,' Lillie broke in. 'You're always doing that.'

Finn chortled. 'Crikey, if he caught the biggest salmon Maisie's seen in a heck of a long time he's allowed to skite. And, as a matter of fact, I plan on spending every moment I've got on that glorious stretch of water. And with you lot on holidays, no doubt I'll have plenty of company. Now,' he rummaged around on the back seat of the car and drew out a stuffed toy kangaroo and a wooden boomerang. He handed the kangaroo to Freddie and the boomerang to Marcus.

'Sorry, young man,' he said to Hugh, ruffling his hair. 'I didn't know you'd be here.' He then took the boomerang from Marcus and showed them how to throw it so that it came back.

'Wow!' all three boys said at once.

When Marcus gave up in frustration, Hugh had a go, also without much success. Then Freddie put Mandrake on the ground and had a try.

'It's too hard,' he said, stamping his foot furiously after running to retrieve the boomerang, which had dropped to the ground near a hydrangea bush a few yards in front of him for the third time.

'It takes practice,' Finn said, 'before you can throw like the natives.'

'Are they black natives like in Africa?' Hugh asked, eyes wide.

'With fuzzy hair?' Freddie jumped in.

'They don't have fuzzy hair, but they're certainly black.'

At that moment the front door opened and Ma came out wheeling Grandma. Beside them was Ronan. After they had greeted Uncle Finn, Lillie saw him smile at Ma. 'I brought you a present as well,' he said. 'You too, Lillie and Ronan.' He glanced at her father who had just driven up and come over to join them. 'Nothing for you, old man. I reckoned you've got all you want with this lovely family. But I did bring something for you, Mrs O'Sullivan,' he said to Grandma, bounding over to his car.

A moment later he was back with a scarf for Grandma, a shiny leather whip for Lillie — which went a long way to improving her mood — and a book on sailing for Ronan. Lastly he handed Ma a package.

'You shouldn't have done that,' she said.

'I found it in a record shop in Grafton Street. Open it.'

When Ma unwrapped the paper, Lillie saw it was a Buddy Holly record. One of Ma's favourite artists. The singer had died five years ago and Uncle Finn must have known how sad Ma had been.

'You're very kind,' Kathleen said, leaning forward to give Finn a kiss on the cheek. 'Trust you to know how much this'd mean to me. Thank you.'

'Ah, it was nothing.'

Lillie looked at Uncle Finn. If she was being honest, much as she loved Dad, Uncle Finn was better looking and more fun, too. Then, she supposed, he didn't have the responsibility of running a struggling estate like Rathgarven and feeding and educating four children. Finn flitted in from Australia to go fishing and visit his best friend and his family, so it was easy for him to seem carefree.

Would Ma tell him about that man Donoghue visiting? And how Dad owed him a small fortune? Lillie doubted if Ma would, for that would be disloyal.

But would Dad tell his good friend what he'd done?

****

After dinner that night Kathleen, James and their guests retired to the drawing room where Finn entertained them on the harp as they sat around the roaring fire. James always thought it incongruous that his burly friend was such a master of the strings. Tonight he played 'Danny Boy', one of James's favourite ballads. James watched his friend's face as he sang, illuminated by the darting flames. Age had not been unkind to Finn; although his face was lined and burnt by the harsh Australian sun, he had gained a ruggedness that suited him. Finn should have gone back to Australia a week ago but had stayed on in Ireland to attend the funeral of his favourite cousin in two days' time in Cork. James knew Finn wasn't looking forward to this. Finn, an only child, was devastated that his cousin, who'd been like a brother to him, had taken his own life. Furthermore, at the funeral he would come face to face with his estranged father.

Before the war Finn had worked on his uncle's rubber plantation near Calcutta. When the war broke out, like a number of Irishmen, despite past political differences he volunteered to fight with the British forces, and enlisted with the Duke of Cornwall's Light Infantry. Following the huge losses at Tobruk in 1942 his battalion was disbanded and he returned to India. After the war he worked his passage on a liner to Australia, where he found a job as a roustabout on an outback cattle station in the Northern Territory. He fell in love with Australia and worked up the courage to write to his family in Cork to tell them he wouldn't be returning home to study law and join the family law firm. His father was furious and told him he was wasting his life. From then on he had disowned him. This spurred Finn on to make a success in Australia, where he now had a horse stud, Eureka Park, in the New England district of New South Wales.

James remembered so well when he had first met Finn. It was on the train from Killarney to Dublin, where he was going to boarding school at Blackrock College. After the train stopped in Cork, he had seen the hunched figure of a boy about the same age as himself standing alone in the gangway between two carriages in a howling wind. If the train was crowded, schoolboys weren't allowed a seat. When James joined him, Finn took out a pack of cigarettes.

'Here, have one,' he said, shoving the pack at James.

And it being so cold, James had taken the cigarette even though he had never smoked before. It turned out Finn, who had the largest feet James had ever seen, was starting at Blackrock as well. They worked out they would probably be in the same class. From that moment on they were as thick as thieves, and Finn spent many school holidays at Rathgarven. Even then Finn and his father didn't get on, so he preferred to visit Rathgarven rather than go to his parents at Cork. When he was in India, Finn wrote to James most months, and when he came back to Ireland he would come down to Rathgarven to stay, or James would meet him in Dublin. In later years they would meet up with Dermot if he was in Dublin on leave.

Now watching him play the harp James thought of Finn's cousin, who had left a wife and three children behind. It made him consider his own situation. No matter what dire straits James had got himself into, he would never be able to abandon his family by taking his own life. He looked across to Kathleen, who was watching Finn as he sang. It was a long time since he'd seen her relax like this. There was no way he could spoil her night by telling her his doubts about the loan from the bank. In any case, it was still possible the bank might come up with the money. Yet, even if that happened, James would still have to work out how to make the repayments.

Later that evening, after the Fitzpatricks had made their farewells, James and Finn walked down the drive in the cool, crisp air to shut the gate behind their car.

'I gather Hugh's going to keep living with them for a while,' Finn said.

'Yes, his parents have a second posting with Irish Rubber in Malaya. Probably won't be home for a couple of years.'

'Just as well the Fitzpatricks are there for Hugh, then.'

James nodded. 'I think they regard him as their own now.'

'And the older brother? Charles, isn't it?'

'He's gone to Malaya to his parents. Unlike Hugh, he prefers the heat of the tropics to freezing cold Ireland.'

'Can't say I blame him. So, how are things with you, my friend?' Finn placed his hand on James's shoulder. 'Jessica still giving you trouble, eh?'

James sighed. 'Yes. And more, I'm afraid. Much more. Urgent this time.'

He told him about his meeting with her at the Shelbourne.

'Jesus,' Finn, said, shaking his head. 'What a bloody shemozzle!'

'I know. We left it that I'd get in touch with her by end of the month.' He leant down and picked up a piece of grass, wet with dew. For a moment he fiddled with it. 'Of course I can't tell Kathleen.' He sighed deeply. 'And to make matters worse I stupidly bet on what I thought was a sure winner at the races, hoping that might make enough money to give to Jessica without putting any more strain on Rathgarven. Placed rather a lot on the darn beast. Lost, of course. Tried to get it back on later races. Made it worse. Now I've got Donoghue, the bookmaker, on my back as well.' He sighed even more deeply. 'If I don't come up with some money, not only will Jessica make good her threat, we also have a good chance of losing Rathgarven.'

'Christ, mate. Why didn't you tell me?'

'I've been in a bit of stupor over it. Not quite sure what to do. If it was only Jessica I might have been able to raise that amount. But with the money I lost to Donoghue… Well, that compounds it considerably.'

Finn cleared his throat. 'What if I was to pay Jessica off for good? Get her off your back?'

James shook his head. 'Thanks, old boy. There's no way I can take that sort of money from anyone. Let alone you.'

They paused when they came to the green painted fence around the meadow. As they leant over the top watching the moonbeams shine over the cove, James could feel the fresh salt air on his face; it was low tide and he could smell the seaweed.

'Things are going well out at Eureka,' Finn said. 'I'd a good windfall the other day. Young foal sold for a record price.' He grinned. 'And besides, I'm quite fond of Jessica. Even knowing what she's done to you over the years.'

'Thanks, Finn. But this is my worry, not yours.'

'Listen, mate. I'm not going to let her hold you over a barrel like that. What I'll do is go and see her when I'm in London on the way back to Australia. Leave it to me. I'll pay her something. Blowed if it'll be all she demands. Still, it'll be enough to sort her out. You can pay me back later. And what about this man, Donoghue? Is there some way I can shut the bastard up as well?'

James thought for a while. If he could get Jessica off his back that would be something. For he had grave fears what would happen if he didn't continue to give her money. It was a risk he couldn't take, as Finn knew only too well.

'If you went to see Jessica,' he finally said, 'and — between us — you could get her off my back, that would help.'

Finn gestured towards the house. 'Despite how much you love this place, have you considered throwing it in? It's been one heck of a struggle ever since you took over from your father. This Kerry land may be God's kingdom but as we know it can be hard land to make a living from. As I said, I'm doing well in Australia. In fact, there's more work than I can cope with on my own with the present manager. What I need is a business partner who knows something about horses. Someone I can get along with. Someone I can trust.'

James gulped. 'Are you suggesting I sell up Rathgarven and come and join you?'

'Just a thought, mate. Could solve your problems and give you a whole new lease of life. Kathleen and the kids might even like it. I'd move into the manager's house. Leave you lot the homestead on the river. It's called the Peel. Bloody good stretch of water.' He glanced back at Rathgarven. 'It mightn't be this sort of homestead, but it's not a bad place at all. If you were to sell up and pay off Donoghue you and the family could make a new start.'

'In Australia?'

'Many Irish have.' He chuckled. 'Including your good friend, Finn Malone.'

'And what about my mother?'

'She's a strong woman. She'd cope.' He paused. 'She might even come herself.'

James shook his head. 'Thanks all the same, Finn. If you could see Jessica, I'll try and handle Donoghue. It'd break my heart to leave Rathgarven. Kathleen's as well. Not to mention my mother's. And, of course, Ronan has always thought it'd be his one day.'

'He might be glad not to have the noose of debt hanging around his neck.'

'The economy's sure to have improved by the time he inherits.'

'Ah. But in the meantime you've got to hold onto the place. Anyway… the offer's on the table if the bank doesn't come good.'

'Thanks, Finn,' James said. 'I'll remember that. And thanks a million for taking Jessica on. That's a huge weight off my shoulders. As soon as I can I'll fix you up. Rest assured I will. Now,' he added, glancing up to house and the light in the main bedroom, 'we'd best be heading inside or we'll never be up early in the morning. I know Ronan and Marcus want to take you fishing at dawn.'

'Ah, I be looking forward to that.' He paused. 'And the next day is the funeral.'

'Your cousin was a troubled man.'

'Silly bastard. What fool would want to go kill himself like that, particularly with a family? Bloody selfish act if you ask me. Leaving his mess for others to sort out.'

'And you'll talk to your father?'

'Not if I can help it. But let's not be maudlin. Not on a grand night like this.'

James sighed. 'Thanks again, Finn, for your kind offer.'

'Ah. It's nothing at all. Go to your beautiful Kathleen. You're a damn lucky man.'

James nodded. 'And don't I know it.'

Finn pulled a photograph of a dog from his wallet. 'This is the only being I've got waiting for me back at Eureka.'

Finn was an alcoholic. He could go for months without a drink, then something would set him off and he'd go on a bender. His wife, Dawn, had put up with it for years before she finally moved to Sydney, leaving Finn at Eureka Park on his own, although she had written to James and Kathleen to say that her friend Winifred Black was going to look in on him. *Winifred's very caring*, she wrote, *so I know she'll keep an eye on him.*

James glanced at the photo of Finn's dog. 'He looks happy enough.'

'Dingo's his name. Bloody loyal friend.' He put the photo back in his wallet. 'Now then… you head on up. I'll enjoy this fine Kerry air a little longer.'

As James walked back to the house he thought how lucky he was to have Finn as a friend. And to have Kathleen waiting for him. When he entered their bedroom she was sitting at her dressing table brushing her gleaming hair.

He walked over and kissed the top of her head. 'A great evening, darling,' he said. 'I believe the Fitzpatricks had a grand old time. She's a card, isn't she? And he's always good for a laugh.'

'It was fun, wasn't it? I think Finn enjoyed himself. It's great to see he's not drinking.'

'I think he's finally got it beat this time.'

'Let's hope so.' She looked at him in the mirror. 'So how did it go with Declan?'

James waited a moment before answering; what he was about to say was far from the truth. 'It went well. We should have a loan through before too long.'

'Oh, that's great. And I'm sorry for getting annoyed yesterday. It's just that Donoghue makes me curdle inside. He's so darn smug.'

James went over to the bed and sat down. He took off his tie, then leaned down to undo the laces of his brogues. 'I'm sorry I wasn't here to meet him so you didn't have to confront him on your own.'

'I've been thinking,' Kathleen said, turning around. 'You know how I sometimes do Hindi interpreting for the Indian Embassy in Dublin. I thought I'd write and see if they have any more work. It'd be great to have the extra income, even when the loan comes through.' She smiled. 'I know how hard you slog trying to keep our heads above water. And that to do what you did you must have been desperate to get on top of things. So the least I can do is try and help a bit more.'

This made James feel even worse. He went over and wrapped his arms around her. 'Darling, we'll be fine. Honestly we will. I'm so sorry I did what I did. And you're quite right that it was a desperate attempt. Even so, I should have thought it through more. But it seems it will all end well.'

If only he could be sure of that.

Chapter 4

After they had seen Finn off on his way to Cork, Kathleen, Lillie and Ronan drove up the steep winding road to the station at Killarney to meet Clara. Kathleen had thought of trying to put her off — she hadn't felt much like entertaining another person in the house just now, let alone the daughter of her great friend. If Clara was to get a hint of the difficulties they were in at Rathgarven, Kathleen felt sure she would relay it to Jessica. And Kathleen couldn't bear the thought of Jessica feeling sorry for her. But now that things seemed so much brighter, Kathleen was looking forward to seeing Clara after all.

'Thank you, Lillie, for getting your room ready to share with Clara,' she said, shifting gears as they reached Moll's Gap, the narrow pass with the view over the towering purple of Macgillycuddy's Reeks that she never tired of.

'I made lots of space in the cupboard as I bet she'll have heaps of great clothes as usual.'

'She doesn't have that many,' Kathleen said.

'She has a lot more than me.'

'Jessica probably has more money than we have. And Clara's older than you as well.'

As they passed Lough Leane, the largest of Killarney's magnificent lakes, Kathleen glanced at Ronan as he sat beside her. He seemed quieter than usual. Clara had been coming to Rathgarven since she was five years old. She and Ronan were great friends, which Kathleen knew sometimes caused Lillie immense jealousy. Was Ronan worried that now she had turned seventeen Clara would find her childhood playmate dull compared to her London friends?

When Clara stepped down from the train at Killarney, Kathleen hardly recognised her. Last time she had seen her she had seemed a mere girl. Now she was a beautiful young lady dressed in a tartan skirt with a red jumper, silk stockings and dark blue patent leather kitten heels. Her long blonde hair was loose around her shoulders and there was a hint of rouge on her cheeks. She's like a rose that's burst into bloom, Kathleen mused fondly.

Kathleen thought back to when she was that age. Surely she'd not been as grown-up as Clara? She remembered how her much-loved Aunt Mildred had taken her out of her dreary Dublin boarding school and down to Bewleys' tearooms to celebrate her birthday. In some ways it felt like yesterday. In other ways it felt like another world, so much had happened in between.

Now Lillie rushed ahead to give Clara a hug. Kathleen knew her daughter had spent an age deciding what to wear to the station. Ronan, on the other hand, had feigned indifference, though Kathleen could have sworn he'd taken more time with his appearance than he had in quite a while. He moved forward to take Clara's suitcase. Normally they'd slap each other on the back and before long be exploding in fits of giggles. But now they stood looking awkwardly at each other, neither seeming quite sure what to do next.

Kathleen moved forward and took Clara in her arms. 'How lovely to see you, darling.' She stepped back and gave her an appraising glance. 'Goodness, how you've grown… and so pretty.' She looked her up and down. 'I adore that skirt and red jumper.'

'Thank you, Aunt Kathleen,' Clara said in a voice that seemed more polished than before. Although Kathleen's children spoke well, there was a definite Irish lilt to their accents. Clara's clipped English voice, with her beautifully pronounced vowels, could have come straight from the Queen's own mouth. 'Mummy bought them for me in London. I wasn't sure. If you like them, well, they must be all right.' She gave a satisfied sigh. 'It's so wonderful to be here. Thank you so much, Aunt Kathleen, for having me.'

To Clara they were always Aunt Kathleen and Uncle James.

'Darling … you don't have to thank me,' Kathleen said, putting an arm around her. 'We love having you here.'

As they headed back down the steep road in the Austin to Rathgarven, Clara said, 'There's something magical about these mountains. I always think the waterfalls and rocks look as though they're in a painting.'

Kathleen nodded. 'Yes. I remember when I first drove this road. I thought it was almost ethereal with the mist hovering over those peaks.'

'And Kerry's the only place I've seen so many purple foxgloves.'

A little further on, when they came to Ladies View overlooking the huge expanse of the Killarney Valley, Clara giggled. 'I still think it's funny that it's called that.'

'Well, do you know why?' Kathleen asked.

'Because Queen Victoria's ladies in waiting liked it so much,' Lillie piped up. She turned to Clara. 'Anyway, tell me about school. Is the food as awful as ours is at the convent?'

'It's ghastly. What about yours, Ronan?'

'It's not too bad. But nothing like Maisie's.'

'I can't wait to see her. Paddy, too. And what about Marcus and Freddie? I bet they've grown.'

Since Clara was eight years old she had been a boarder at Jessica's old school, St Margaret's in Bushy in the south of England. Kathleen had been horrified when she heard Clara was to go to boarding school at such a tender age, and wondered how Jessica managed to foot the bill. But she then decided it was probably far better that Clara had the stability of St Margaret's rather than being in India with Jessica as she darted from one romance to the other. Jessica had told Kathleen recently that Clara and Jessica's present husband, Phillip Danville, didn't get on.

Never having met Phillip Danville, Kathleen was unable to say whether Clara's dislike was warranted. Still, having known Jessica for as long as she had and knowing her taste in men, she was inclined to think that Clara's opinion might be correct. Kathleen had always been extremely fond of Clara. In some ways she regarded her as another daughter, and that was one of the reasons she was so keen to keep the friendship with Jessica alive. There were parts of Clara that were like Jessica, such as her love of life and carefree manner. But Kathleen suspected she had a much more sensible head on her shoulders than Jessica ever had. Even when they were children playing by the Hooghly River in Calcutta, Jessica was always coaxing Kathleen to misbehave. Whether it was to run away from their ayah or hide behind the bushes and jump out and frighten the life out of one of the unsuspecting houseboys. And as they grew up, she was forever telling Kathleen to get 'with it'.

'Honestly, my sweet,' Jessica would say, puffing on her cigarette in its long ivory holder, 'you really are such a bore sometimes. There must be an impulsive, romantic streak somewhere inside that sublime head of yours. You've got to open the window and let it fly out and play.'

Yet, Kathleen had often thought since, when I did let that streak fly out, look what happened.

Kathleen wondered if Clara got the sensible bits of her make-up from her father. But who Clara's father was remained a secret Jessica had never disclosed. All Kathleen knew was that Clara wasn't the daughter of either of Jessica's husbands. When Jessica had found out she was pregnant, she had dragged Kathleen to the far end of the verandah at the Tollygunge Club to tell her the news and swear her to secrecy.

'Whose baby is it?' Kathleen had asked, aghast.

'God alone knows.' Jessica looked down the verandah to where their group of friends were laughing and drinking cocktails, finally settling her gaze on the rather dull, extremely wealthy and ruddy-faced Guy Preston, who had a cigar in one hand and a glass of whisky in the other. Kathleen had noticed how he gazed at Jessica adoringly. 'But,' Jessica had whispered behind her pretty hand, 'don't you think Guy will make a great father?'

So on a bright, sunny morning, with Kathleen as bridesmaid in a daffodil-yellow dress, Jessica married Guy Preston in Calcutta's St Paul's Cathedral. Even though it was wartime, there was a lavish reception afterwards in the glorious gardens of the Tollygunge Club. Beside the lagoon, turbaned waiters handed the guests gimlets in glasses that sparkled like the huge diamond on Jessica's finger, before lunch was served on the wide verandah shaded by blinds of woven bamboo. As Jessica got a dreadful case of dysentery and then malaria not long after, it was considered that these two illnesses caused Clara's early birth. To the day that he died, Guy Preston (who, unhappily for Jessica, lost most of his money investing in a friend's jute plantation) believed he was Clara's father. And Clara believed it, too. It was only Kathleen who knew Jessica's secret. And even she only knew half of it.

'Here we are,' Kathleen said, pulling up in the driveway at Rathgarven as Marcus and Freddie rushed out to meet Clara. 'Dinner will be at seven-thirty. In the meantime, why don't you take Clara upstairs and settle her in, Lillie? Our darling Maisie's made your favourite chocolate mousse for pudding, Clara.'

'Yummy, yum!' Clara said, patting her stomach and sliding out of the car with the others. 'At school I often dream of that pudding.'

'Well, you go on up with Lillie and we'll meet later in the conservatory. Alice will be there. She's so looking forward to seeing you.' Kathleen checked her watch. 'When you're settled in maybe you can all go for a walk around the cove. Work up an appetite.'

After they'd gone upstairs Kathleen went to the library and took out some notepaper and began to write to the Indian Embassy. Even when the loan did come through from the bank it would be good to have some extra money coming in to help with the repayments. Although the embassy didn't pay much, Kathleen enjoyed the work. If she could build it up more it would give her great satisfaction. She also thought she would try to do more with her photography. Surely some other publications, like *Horse and Hound*, must pay for good photographs. When she finished writing the letter she put it in an envelope and took it out to the hall table to post in Sneem tomorrow. Hopefully she would get an answer before too long.

***

Clara stayed at Rathgarven for two weeks. During that time she went riding with Lillie and sailing in the *Daphne* with Marcus and Ronan, or sometimes just with Ronan. At other times Ronan, Lillie, and Clara went salmon fishing, with Lillie and Clara chatting nineteen to the dozen.

'Honestly, you two,' Ronan would laugh. 'How do you expect me to catch a fish if you keep scaring them away with all that talk?'

She spent ages with Freddie playing with Mandrake, showing him how to tie a string in a hole in his shell to stop him wandering when they were out walking, reading him stories and laughing with him over comic books. Marcus showed her how to use a bow and arrow. But the person she spent the most time with was Ronan. When Lillie was helping Maisie in the kitchen, he would take Clara out fishing on her own. Like Lillie she would take a book and sit there for hours on end. Even if Lillie wasn't

53

tied up they'd do things together, like rowing over to the island or going for long walks through the woods.

One wet and cold morning with the wind howling through the trees, Lillie found them both in the library looking very cosy. When she walked in, it was as though she had disturbed them. Clara was wearing a pink twin-set, which Lillie hadn't seen before, and she had her hair in a high ponytail with a red ribbon tied around it. She and Ronan were playing scrabble with their heads bent over the board. Lillie sat with them for a while, but they seemed so companionable together she decided to leave them be. She couldn't help feeling a stab of jealousy. Ever since Clara had come to stay, Ronan had seemed wrapped up in her world. Even though he'd only had a few lessons from Uncle Finn, he seemed to be able to play a number of tunes on the harp by ear. One afternoon Lillie stopped outside the library door and heard Clara singing as he played. That night after dinner he played 'Molly Malone' for the family by the fire in the drawing room and Clara sang the words beautifully. Looking at them together Lillie felt another stab of jealousy, for she wasn't in the slightest bit musical and it was a bond that Ronan and Clara shared.

'I think I'm at my very happiest when I'm at Rathgarven,' Clara said one night as they were getting ready for bed. 'You're so lucky, Lillie, to live here all the time.'

Lillie wondered what Clara would think if she knew how her beloved Uncle James had gambled away so much money the family might be in danger of losing Rathgarven.

'Yes, I know I am,' she said.

As Clara stood at the window in her gorgeous silk nightie with the soft moonlight washing over her face, Lillie felt downright dowdy in her checked flannelette pyjamas. She wished her hair was blonde like Clara's, rather than her own boring dark brown, and that her eyes were a startling blue, instead of the gloomy colour of a school slate. And that she was tall and slim like

Clara was, rather than feeling small and dumpy. Even though envy was a sin that could get her a whole decade of the rosary in the confessional box, she couldn't help herself. She plonked down on the bed and flicked through a copy of *Honey* magazine, which had an article about a new group called the Beatles. Sheelagh had given Lillie the magazine, which a friend had brought back from England. Probably a nail in Sheelagh's coffin as far as Lillie's father was concerned — James was sure to think magazines like that were a waste of paper and corrupted the mind.

'You ever heard of that group?' she asked Clara, showing her the page.

Clara looked at the photo. 'Sure have. Everyone at school's talking about them. I like Paul the best.'

'You can have it to read,' Lillie said. 'I've got a book.'

'You sure?'

'Yeah. Go ahead.'

'Wow,' Clara exclaimed a few minutes later, thumbing through the magazine. She held up a page with a picture of the Ronettes. 'What fabulous beehive hair.'

Talking of beehives made Lillie think of Sheelagh, who often did her hair that way. Last night Lillie had spent ages on the phone to her, gossiping about the dance. Lillie was still annoyed with her parents for not letting her go. And she was even more annoyed when Sheelagh told her that Seamus Flaherty had been there. And he had asked Sheelagh for a dance.

'He's a good sort,' she'd giggled down the phone. 'Real cute.'

'Did he ask where I was?'

'No. Why should he?'

'Because… I told you. He asked me on the bus if I was going.'

'Bet he was being friendly. That's all.'

As Lillie held the phone to her ear she hated Sheelagh nearly as much as she hated her parents.

Even now, with Clara lying on the next bed, she hadn't forgiven any of them. And she was also annoyed with Seamus Flaherty. The least he could have done was ask about her.

'I'm going to sleep now,' she said to Clara, deciding not to read her book after all. 'Turn the light off when you've finished reading.'

'Sure.'

Lillie nestled down between the sheets. As she lay there she felt tears threaten. *If only I was as old as Clara I would have been allowed to go to that dance. And I would have danced with Seamus Flaherty.* What's more, if she was older maybe Ronan would take her seriously, rather than spending all his time with Clara, which was really starting to give Lillie the pip. In a way she couldn't wait for her to go so she could have her brother to herself again.

*****

At the end of the two weeks when they all drove her to Killarney station, Clara was almost crying as she kissed each of them goodbye.

'I don't want to go,' she said miserably. 'I'll miss you all so much. That dreadful school in England's too awful to think about.' She looked pleadingly at Kathleen. 'Couldn't I stay here with you? I promise I'd be no trouble.'

'If only you could, my darling,' Kathleen said. 'But remember, there'll always be a room at Rathgarven waiting for you. During the holidays, that is.'

Lillie watched Marcus and Freddie give Clara a huge hug. Now Lillie did the same, and realised that despite being jealous of the time Ronan spent with her, she would miss Clara after all. Finally Ronan moved forward and gave her a kiss on the cheek. As he stood back they held each other's eyes for a long moment before turning away in embarrassment when they saw the rest of the family looking. There's something going on between them, Lillie thought. This was confirmed when Ronan was the quietest Lillie had ever known him on the drive home.

'You okay?' she asked as he sat next to her in the back.

'Yeah. Why?'

'Nothing. You seem quiet, that's all. Are you carsick? This winding road sure makes me feel queasy.'

'Lillie, people don't have to talk all of the time.'

'But it's so dull if people don't talk,' Freddie piped up from the front.

'Ronan misses Clara, Ronan misses Clara,' Marcus chanted.

'Oh be quiet, Marcus,' Ronan fumed, looking out of the window. 'How would you know anything?'

'Now, now,' Kathleen said. 'We'll all miss Clara, but there's no need to fight about it.'

***

Lillie and Ronan resumed their pattern of taking the rowboat out and fishing together. One cold misty morning Lillie pulled her line in and tried to untangle a knot.

She looked up at her brother. 'Do you think Clara's pretty?'

Ronan fiddled with the rod he was holding and prepared to cast. 'Yes. Why? Don't you?'

'She really likes you. You can see it in the way she looks at you. Do you like her?'

'Lillie!'

'Well, do you like her?'

'Of course I like her. It's as if she's one of us. More or less.'

57

'No… I mean do you *really* like her? Wanting to kiss her? That sort of liking.'

The colour rose in his cheeks. 'Hand me that rod of yours and I'll undo the knot. You've worked yourself into a real twist there.' He laughed. 'Not just with your line.'

And that's as much information as Lillie got out of Ronan about Clara. Even so, she suspected she'd hit the nail on the head.

Ronan and Clara *had* kissed and that's why he had gone beetroot.

Chapter 5

When Kathleen picked up the mail at the post office in Sneem she was excited to see she had an answer from the Indian Embassy offering her more translations. The man who usually did the majority of the translations had had a heart attack and was taking sick leave. There wouldn't be a huge amount more work, however there could be a steady trickle. Enough to at least help with the housekeeping. She parked her car under the beech tree at Rathgarven and hurried through the pelting rain to find James and tell him. As it was too wet to work outside, he was doing bookwork in his study. When she opened the door and saw him at his desk, she got a dreadful fright at how grey he looked. It was as if he had aged twenty years since she had last seen him and she wondered for a second if he, too, hadn't had a heart attack.

'James, what is it? Is it your mother? Is she ill? Or one of the children?'

'No,' James said, trying a small smile. 'None of that. Sit down and I'll tell you what's happened.'

Perching on the upholstered chair by the side of the desk, Kathleen looked at him anxiously.

'The bank has refused our loan,' he said. 'Declan rang. The poor man was devastated.'

Kathleen felt an icy shiver run down her spine. The elation she'd felt when she read the letter from the embassy disappeared in a flash and a feeling of total desperation took its place.

'Oh my God! No,' she cried. 'How could they? You seemed so sure. I thought it was just a formality.'

'There was always a doubt. I didn't want to tell you.'

Kathleen got up and began to pace. Outside, the rain was lashing the gravel driveway and the trees twisted and turned in the strong wind. In the cove, the waves beat heavily against the shore. Kathleen knew what this meant. There was no escaping it: they would lose Rathgarven.

She tuned to face her shattered husband. 'You should have told me there was a doubt.'

'I kept putting it off, hoping I was wrong.'

'Do you think Donoghue got to them? He wants Rathgarven come hell or high water. I bet he has every bank in Ireland in his back pocket. Half of the bank managers probably owe him money — he's supposed to be one of the biggest bookies in Ireland. And you of all people know how us Irish like to gamble.'

This was a mean barb, but Kathleen couldn't stop herself.

James came over to her and placed his arms tenderly around her. 'I'm so sorry, my darling,' he said, kissing the top of her head. 'So terribly sorry.'

Kathleen smiled thinly. 'I know you are.' She gave a huge sigh. 'Oh James, what in heaven's name will we do?'

James took a deep breath and Kathleen felt his body shudder as he tried to control his emotions. 'We've no other option than to settle the debt we owe. I've been sitting here thinking it through. We could try to sell, but it would take time in this market. The same with the cattle, which are bringing practically nothing. If we don't do something soon Donoghue will declare us bankrupt.'

'He can't.'

'He can if we can't pay the debt I owe him. I got a letter from his lawyers this morning saying he's prepared to take over the other debts we owe to the bank, so long as we hand the title of Rathgarven over to him pretty much straightaway.'

'How does he know we owe the bank money? Did Declan tell him?'

'I told him as much when I lost that bet to him and he demanded payment. I asked for time so that we could try and come up with the money some other way. He refused point blank.'

'What a blackguard he is.' She swallowed what seemed like a huge boulder in her throat. 'Surely we can't owe him and the bank all of what Rathgarven's worth.'

'There'd be a bit left over. Not much, but maybe enough to tide us over in the short term if we rent something else.'

'But what about your poor mother? It'll kill her to lose Rathgarven.'

'I know.' James bit down on his bottom lip. 'I'll need to tell her before she hears gossip.'

'Now?'

'Yes. There's no point in putting it off. It'll only make it worse.'

Kathleen looked at his distraught face. Despite what he'd done, she felt for him. After all, this was his family home. The home that was eventually to go to Ronan.

'And Ronan?' she asked, trying to control her despair. 'How will we break it to him that he's lost his ancestral home?'

'I'll tell him on my own. I'm the one who lost it for him. The one who's destroyed our lives.'

'Oh my God, James, what will become of us? Where will we live?'

'I really don't know,' he said, blinking hard and moving to the window so she couldn't see his face. But then he seemed to pull himself together and turned around. He picked up his pipe from the desk, filled the bowl and lit it. Standing there with the pipe in his mouth, he took a few long, deep puffs before putting it down again in the ashtray. 'There is one possibility that could save us. But I've no idea how you'll feel about it.'

Kathleen looked at him anxiously, trying to read his face.

'Finn offered me a partnership at Eureka Park.'

Kathleen eyes opened wide. 'You're joking. You mean go to Australia?'

James nodded. 'It was just a thought. When he offered it to me I was horrified, like you are. But sitting here now, I could see no real alternative. He says there's a manager's house, which he'll move into, giving us the homestead. It's on the Peel River, which he says is a lovely stretch of water. As I said we'd have a little left over from here… just enough for our boat fares and to get us started. A way to get back on our feet.'

Kathleen shook her head in disbelief. 'How can we move to Australia with all the children? And leave your mother here on her own?'

'Maybe she'll come with us.'

'I think that highly unlikely, James. Even if she wasn't in a wheelchair.'

'When we talk to her we can see.' He paused, looking towards the door. 'Have you any idea where she is right now?'

'I saw her in the conservatory as I drove in.' She sighed. 'Imagine her reaction, James. She saw the place burnt down in the Civil War. Saw it rebuilt. And now this.'

'She'll be bound to know there's something wrong. She'll pick it up in a second. And be furious if we hide it from her.'

'You've decided already, haven't you? To take up Finn's offer?'

'I don't see what else we can do.'

He seemed so broken Kathleen found it difficult to be angry with him. Even so, the thought of leaving Rathgarven so overwhelmed her she couldn't think straight.

'I need time to think, James. It's not a decision I can make in an instant.'

'Kathleen, if I could see an alternative, I'd grab it. From where I sit we have no option.'

'Even so, you can't expect me to agree instantly.'

'No, of course not.'

Kathleen looked at her watch. 'The least you can do is give me an hour or so before we talk to your mother.' She shook her head. 'I just need to be on my own, James. I'll go upstairs.'

Without waiting for him to answer, she walked out and shut the door. At the bedroom window upstairs she gazed across the meadow where her beloved hunter, Tolly, was sheltering from the rain under an elm tree, and beyond that to the river and the mountains. Angry tears rolled down her cheeks. Despite its dreadful weather at times, Kathleen had grown to love this place more than she imagined possible. She had first set eyes on it just after the war, and as there was still petrol rationing James had driven her here with the pony and trap. She had thought then it was beautiful, despite it being the middle of a freezing cold winter and the trees and flowerbeds being bare. Even though the ivy wasn't sprouting and the walls of the house were stark and grey, she had felt a huge sense of having come home. To think it would no longer be her home, and the home of her children, was incomprehensible.

On the other hand, if she was hurting, James must be hurting so much more. And it was with James that her loyalty should lie. Perhaps it was time for him to make a new start. Although he loved the place, Rathgarven had been a millstone around his neck for a very long time. Even before this had happened with Donoghue it had been a constant struggle to keep on top of things. Neither of them was getting any younger. Maybe a new start in Australia, away from the Donoghues of this world and constant money worries, was what they both needed. Besides, there really was no alternative. Although she was dreading the scene with Alice, James was right that the longer they left it, the worse it would become. Alice was no fool. She must have realised before this there was something going on. She knew finances were tight. In fact she had offered to help with some of the money she got from her articles. James and Kathleen had refused point blank, for they knew how much she liked having her own money. Not that it was a great deal, anyway; it would have been a mere drop in the ocean compared to what they owed the bank. And that's before James went off on a tangent at the Killarney Races.

She stepped over to her dressing table and took out a handkerchief, wiped her eyes, and went downstairs. James was still at his desk in his study.

'I don't suppose there's any alternative other than to go tell your mother now,' she said. 'So let's get it over with.'

James sighed and rose to his feet. 'Thank you,' he said, going to her. 'I know it's not easy for you, but I can really see no other way.'

'Then you can find Ronan,' Kathleen said, looking away. 'I don't envy you that task. I fear he'll be very angry.'

They found Alice sitting in the conservatory writing. She looked so peaceful that Kathleen was loath to destroy that calm. For a moment she thought of shying away. But as soon as Alice saw them she beckoned for them to sit down. She gave them both a warm smile and placed her notebook on the table beside her.

'You two look as if a tsunami's about to rage in from the Atlantic to wipe us all out.'

Something nearly as bad, Kathleen felt like saying, but instead looked at James.

'Nothing like that, mother,' he said. 'All the same I'm afraid I've got some bad news.'

When he told her what had happened, Alice sat for some time without saying a word, looking out of the window at the raindrops on the trees. To Kathleen the silence was far worse than if she'd exploded in an absolute rage.

Finally she turned to them. 'When I saw that man, Donoghue, pull up at the jetty the other day I thought there was something going on. I've known him since he was a young boy. He was a scallywag then. He still is.'

'You saw him?' Kathleen asked.

'I did. And saw you go down and shoo him off.'

'It was my fault,' James said. 'I should have been more careful. There's no one else to blame.'

Alice looked at Kathleen's distraught face. 'That's quite true.' Without a hint of reproach she added, 'Well, there's little point in crying over spilt milk, is there? But,' she asked, turning back to James, 'tell me, where do you plan on taking your family to live?'

James told her about Finn's offer and how he hoped she might come with them.

Alice was silent again. Eventually she nodded. 'I think the offer Finn has given you is hard to refuse. It really is the only way out for you. To stay here and see Donoghue take over our home would be too soul destroying.' She turned away and Kathleen could see how hard she was trying to stop herself from weeping. 'Thank you for your offer for me to come with you.' She looked at them. 'All the same, I'm far too old and set in my ways to consider moving. Besides,' she added, touching her wheelchair, 'I have this encumbrance.' Then she smiled, although Kathleen could see it was forced. 'As it turns out I was thinking of having a change of scenery for a while anyway. You're aware I've a little money put aside from my writings, so I'll be very happy to go to a private hotel in Dublin.' She tried a smile again. 'I know it won't be forever. You'll be sure to make your fortune in Australia and then you can all come back. Now,' she said, picking up her fountain pen to indicate the meeting was over, 'you'd best go and find Ronan and tell him what's happened.' It was then that Kathleen could see the tears Alice had tried so valiantly to repress watering her eyes. But there was no way she was going to let James and Kathleen see her cry.

'Go,' she said firmly. 'Go and find him, James. It's best you tell him how he no longer has a home to inherit. That you lost it in a gambling bet.'

Her voice sounded so wretched that Kathleen not only felt sorry for her, but also for James. She wondered if his mother would ever forgive him for what he had done. Or, for that matter, if she could.

Chapter 6

Ronan was in Paddy's prized walled garden, collecting fallen Granny Smith apples for the two pigs in the sty. He shooed the chickens away and smiled as he thought of the letter in his pocket that had arrived from Clara this morning. She had written it the day she got back to London, and told him how she missed him dreadfully and it was pouring rain outside.

So different to that glorious day under the mulberry tree with you.

It was one sunny afternoon when they had pulled the rowboat into a clearing further along the shore from Rathgarven. They picked mulberries from the giant tree in the middle of the clearing until their lips were so red from the luscious fruit that Clara fell about laughing.

'We look like a couple of clowns,' she gasped.

'Here,' Ronan said, wiping his own lips with a handkerchief. 'Let me wipe your mouth.'

After he had sat down beside her and gently wiped her lips, she leaned over and kissed him fully on the mouth. Although it was only a small kiss, an exciting tingle had passed through Ronan's body, setting it afire in a way that frightened him.

Clara leaned back and looked at Ronan with a wicked grin. 'Gosh, I shouldn't have done that, should I?'

'Why? I really liked it.'

'Do you want to do it again?'

'Yes please.'

This time he held her in his arms and when their lips met he knew that as long as he lived he would never forget that moment. The next day they kissed again; after they'd searched the rocks and seaweed on the shore for treasures that had drifted in from the ocean, they had taken the rowboat across to the island and sat in the ruins of the old fort looking down the cove. As he kissed her, Ronan realised that although he always loved Clara from when he was a little boy and she first started coming to Rathgarven, he had now fallen very much *in* love. So when she left to go back to school in England, he missed her dreadfully. She was his first thought in the morning and his last at night. And every time he played the harp he could hear her melodious voice singing along with him; see her beautiful eyes locked on his. He couldn't wait to see her again and hold her in his arms.

Oh, Ronan, I miss you so very much. I'll beg Mummy to let me come to Rathgarven for the next holidays, the letter said. *In the meantime don't you dare go kissing any other girls. If you do, I'll know for sure.*

As he was happily thinking about all this, he saw his father approaching.

'Ah, there you are, Ronan,' James said.

Ronan threw him a smile. 'The pigs love these Granny Smiths.'

'They do indeed.' His father paused, kicking his heel into the ground. 'Before you go to feed them, there's something I need to tell you.'

Ronan thought he looked worried. Mind you, he often looked worried. Ronan knew there were problems with the economy which were affecting Rathgarven. And that his parents were concerned and sometimes had words about it. After Lillie had told him about that man Donoghue coming around, he wondered if there was some truth in what she'd overheard. However, Dad had seemed less worried since Uncle Finn's visit, so he had put it out of his mind.

'Sure,' he said, throwing an apple into the bucket.

James beckoned him to come and sit beside him on the stonewall. Once seated, his father waited some time before speaking. He took out his pipe, patted the tobacco down and lit it, then coughed nervously a few times.

'Are you okay?' Ronan asked.

'I'm not sure how to tell you this.' His father paused again and Ronan could see he was searching for words. 'Nevertheless there's no easy way. Unfortunately, we have to sell Rathgarven.'

Ronan's eyes widened. 'What do you mean? Why would we have to do that?'

'Well, as you know, the economy is not great here at the moment.'

'But we're muddling through, aren't we?'

His father sighed. 'In a way.'

He then told him how, hoping to make matters better, he had bet on the horses at the Killarney Races and lost money to the bookmaker, Donoghue. And how, as a result of that and what they already owed the bank, Donoghue had threatened to bankrupt them.

'You've gambled Rathgarven away?' Ronan spluttered. 'To that man, Donoghue?'

'I took a risk. It didn't pay off.'

'But why on earth did you take that risk?'

'It seemed a good idea at the time. As I said, I thought it could help our financial situation.'

Ronan moved over to the apple tree and picked a fallen apple off the ground and held it a moment before hurling it into the bucket. He couldn't look at his father. Good old Lillie had been right. Donoghue had been here because their father had lost money to him.

'Does Grandma know?' he threw over his shoulder.

'Yes. We told her a little while ago.'

'She must be devastated.'

'Naturally she is. And for that I'll never forgive myself. Or for losing your inheritance.'

'And Ma?' He turned around. 'What about her?'

'As you can imagine, she's very sad.'

'Sad! She must be a lot more than sad...'

'Yes. But your mother's a strong woman. And I think she understands what I was trying to do. Improve the situation. Though it backfired, that's for sure. She's being extremely understanding. Now, I am asking that you be understanding as well.'

Ronan shook his head. 'So what happens now?'

'We'll make a new start.'

'Where?'

'Australia.'

Ronan gasped. 'Why Australia, for heaven's sake?'

His father explained how Uncle Finn had made him an offer, and he and Ma had decided to accept it.

'So it's all been decided on.'

'More or less.'

Ronan felt like asking why his father had bothered to tell him at all if it was a foregone conclusion. What was the point?

'We wanted to tell you first,' James said, as if reading his mind. 'You're the one it will affect the most. For that I'm truly sorry.'

Ronan could see tears in his father's eyes. He knew he was hurting, but Ronan couldn't bring himself to console him. All he could think of was how this would affect his grandmother. His mother. And Lillie, Marcus and Freddie. While he had always thought Rathgarven would be his one day, he was not naïve. He knew it could end up being a millstone around his neck, but he had always thought he would be able to work through that. Particularly if the economy improved, which it was bound to do. Now he was never going to be given that chance because his father had taken it into his head to make things better by gambling on the horses. And had made matters so much worse. Worse than anyone could imagine. Clara's beautiful face flashed before his eyes. So many times she had told him how lucky he was to live at Rathgarven, how much she loved to visit. And it was here at Rathgarven where Ronan had fallen in love with her.

'I think I'll go down to the jetty, Dad,' he said, salty tears stinging his eyes. He didn't trust himself not to cry in front of his father, so instead he added, 'before I say something I'll regret.'

'Ronan…'

'No, Dad. Not now.'

He left his father standing there and walked through the gate, carefully shutting it behind him. As he traipsed through the grass in the front meadow to the jetty, tears stung his eyes. At the jetty he sat with his feet dangling in the water and placed his hand on the small wooden rowboat tied up next to it. He loved to take the boat out fishing in the cove, but it was hard to accept that soon he would be unable to do so, and he wiped his eyes with his sleeve. Despite his father's explanation, he couldn't imagine what had possessed him to do such a thing. Ronan knew he had the odd flutter. But to blow so much money that they lost Rathgarven…? What the hell was he thinking? It seemed so out of character Ronan thought James must have been drinking. But his father wasn't a big drinker. Uncle Finn was a different matter. If it had been him who had done such a thing, Ronan could understand — he was known for going on a bender. To think they were all to be uprooted and taken to Australia to live on Uncle Finn's property was beyond belief.

He thought of Clara again. What would she say when she could no longer come to Rathgarven? And Ronan would be on the other side of the world. She was bound to meet someone else and forget about him. If he were older he would tell his parents he was staying in Ireland. As it was he had no choice but to go with them.

The jetty emitted a loud creak as someone stood on the boards, and he turned to see his mother walking towards him. Often he and Ma had talked of how he would one day own

Rathgarven, and how he might have a horde of little children running around in the woods and cavorting among the rocks on the shore the way he and Lillie and his brothers did, and play in the ruins of the old fort on the island and fish for salmon and have their own ponies…

'I can see you with the most beautiful wife in the world,' Ma would laugh. 'Hopefully a very rich one who can help with the upkeep of Rathgarven.' Now that dream was smashed irreparably. But if Ronan was hurting, Ma must be hurting even more.

She came and sat beside him and rested her head on his shoulder. 'Oh, Ronan, darling, darling, Ronan. I'm so sorry. And I know Dad is too.'

'Why did he do it, Ma?' Ronan asked, placing his hand on her head. 'Why for God's sake did he do it?'

Kathleen sighed. 'I've no idea what got into him. Except he thought it was going to make things better. As it turns out he's made them so much worse.'

They looked out over the cove as a flock of wild geese flew low over the water.

'Don't be too hard on him,' Kathleen said.

'But what about Grandma? What will she do?'

'We'll work it out.'

Ronan kissed her forehead and stood up. 'And you? What about you? You love it here, don't you?'

She smiled. 'Of course I do. But as long as we're all together I can be happy anywhere.'

Ronan wasn't so sure that was the truth. But if she saw him hurting the way he was right now, she would feel so much worse about it all. It was best she didn't see that. 'I think I'll go for a row,' he said, looking at the rowboat.

His mother glanced up at the dark clouds hovering overhead. 'I don't like the look of those clouds, there's bound to be more rain. And possibly another storm.'

'Don't you worry, Ma. I'll head over to the island.'

'Even so…'

'Ma, I'll be fine. You go back up to the house. Otherwise you'll get wet if it starts to pour.'

'Well, take care,' she said. 'And don't stay on the island too long.'

'I won't. You go on up now.'

Kathleen stood up. 'If you're not back in an hour I'll start to worry.'

'I'll be back.'

But once Ronan got to the island, he climbed up to the ruins and sat on the stone windowsill and looked out over the river to where the clouds raced across the water. He remembered last time he was here. The sun was out and Clara was laughing as they built a small fire in the remains of the fireplace. He felt her letter in his pocket and tears stained his cheeks. He picked up a piece of charred wood and broke it in his hands, the soot staining his skin. He remembered how he and Clara had played hopscotch, drawing the squares in the dirt with a piece of charred wood like this. How they had kissed. Not just once, but many times. They had been so happy. How could that happiness be thwarted so soon? He looked across the water to the grey mass of Rathgarven brooding under the dark clouds. To think it would no longer be in the family was too dreadful to comprehend. If it weren't for Ma he would spend the night out here to try and come to terms with it all without having to look at anyone — particularly Lillie, who was bound to know there was something wrong. But Ma would worry and Ronan didn't want her to have more worries than she had already.

Down on the shore it was difficult to work out where the black clouds met the even blacker water. He got in the rowboat and was halfway between the island and the shore when the wind came up ferociously. Suddenly Ronan no longer had control of the boat. A huge wave broke over the bow, soaking him. The waves were so big it was impossible to keep a straight course as he rowed. Fear gripped him now. What if he couldn't get back to the shore? What if he got swept out to the middle of the river? Then out to the Atlantic? Now an even bigger wave hurtled towards him. Before he had a chance to do anything it picked up the boat and Ronan was hurled into the freezing water. As he surfaced, spluttering, he saw the capsized rowboat drifting away.

No! No!

Over and over he was dragged under until he had trouble breathing. Terrified, he realised the current was taking him further out. He could feel his lips quivering. Please, please, he prayed, let someone see me out here. Clara's laughing face flashed before his eyes. It wouldn't be Australia that would take him away from her, it would be death.

'Help, help,' he shouted, waving his arms frantically in the air, praying that there might be someone watching on the shore.

***

Kathleen saw the wind strengthening. Ronan still wasn't back and she began to worry. She grabbed James and the two of them went outside to look for him. As soon as they got to the meadow they could see the capsized dinghy. Not far from it they could see Ronan in the water and hear him calling for help, his arms thrashing the air.

'Oh my God,' Kathleen gasped. 'He'll drown.'

'I'll go to him,' James said, racing to the shore. 'Hold on, Ronan!' he bellowed across the water. 'I'm coming!'

James was a strong swimmer, but Kathleen wondered how he would get to Ronan. The current could race in the cove, and huge waves rose and fell. She rushed after him and stood on the shore in the pouring rain as he striped to his underpants, leapt in the water and battled out through the waves. Kathleen's heart was beating nineteen to the dozen. Only last year two youths had lost their lives in the river when their dinghy had capsized. Despite it having been a summer's day like today, the water had been freezing cold. It was hyperthermia that killed them before they could get to the shore. Dear God, she prayed, let James get Ronan to safety before that happens to him.

'Dad's coming, Ronan!' she shouted, holding her hands to her mouth. 'Dad's coming! Hold on!'

Watching Ronan struggling to stay afloat as James tried to swim towards him put losing Rathgarven into prospective. If they got through this without losing Ronan, Kathleen promised herself that she would never complain again about what James had done. She would willingly support their move to Australia. When her parents had died in that train crash in India, she had thought she would never know such sadness again. But she had experienced worse. What if now she lost both her son and her husband? James *had* to bring Ronan in safely. She watched him close the gap, but then a huge wave overpowered him and he disappeared under, came up and went down again. She couldn't even see Ronan. She glanced towards the house to see if any of the children were looking out the windows. Thankfully they didn't seem to be — they would be scared out of their wits. She thought of going to find Paddy, then remembered he was in Sneem. And there was nothing Maisie could do at this stage. She thought of jumping into the water herself, but what if she, too, got washed away?

As she stood helplessly on the river's edge, a wave broke over her and soaked her even more. When she wiped her eyes she saw with relief that Ronan and James were making their way towards her. She wasn't sure who was pulling whom, but they were together, and although they were making slow progress, they were closing the gap to the shore. As they got closer she could see that James was pulling Ronan, who was lying on his back. Oh my God, was he dead? Then she remembered her training during the war: if you wanted to rescue someone in the water it was best to get them to lie on their back, put your arm around their neck and drag them doing a sort of dog paddle. Please, please let this be the case here.

As they got closer, James could stand up in the shallows. Kathleen called out, 'Is he all right?'

James didn't answer and just kept wading in, dragging Ronan onto the shore. Eventually he lay him on the grass and turned him on his side. As Kathleen kneeled beside him, Ronan opened his eyes and spluttered, water spouting out of his mouth. His skin was blue from the cold but he was alive. James was also blue and shivering. Kathleen was shivering so much herself she found it difficult to make her lips work in order to speak.

'Ronan,' she asked, touching his cold skin. 'Ronan, speak to me. Are you okay?'

Ronan gave her a small smile. 'I think so.'

'Try and get your breath,' Kathleen said. She looked at James, who was breathing heavily. 'You too.'

Ronan looked up at his father. 'Thank you,' he gasped. 'I would have drowned if you hadn't got to me.'

It was then that Kathleen burst into tears. 'You silly, silly boy. You should have stayed on the island.'

Ronan levered himself up onto his knees and then stood up shakily. 'I thought you'd be worried if I didn't get back before dark.'

'Not nearly as worried as seeing you floundering in that water.' She glanced at James, who had picked up the clothes he had strewn on the shore. 'Now let's go on up to the house and get you both into a hot bath.'

James ran a hand through his sodden hair and smiled. 'I think that sounds like a very good idea.'

As Kathleen walked between them she swore she would never take either of them for granted again. More than ever she was determined to be by James's side, no matter where they ended up living. Her gratitude to him for saving Ronan outweighed any hardship that might be in store.

Chapter 7

Later that evening, when her parents told the rest of the family what was to happen, Lillie rushed upstairs and lay on her bed weeping. She became so angry she could no longer cry and instead began to pace the room, stopping every now and then to look out the window at the river she loved so much. How could her parents have let it come to this? And what about Ronan? Everyone knew Rathgarven would one day be his. Plonking herself down on the bed again she pulled the pillow over her head, hoping she'd be able to blank out everything. She was still there when Maisie came up to entice her downstairs for supper.

'Thank you, I don't want anything,' she muttered from under the pillow.

'You've got to be eating something,' Maisie said, leaning down and putting her hand on Lillie's back, patting her softly.

'Do you know what's happened?' Lillie asked, lifting the pillow slowly from her head. 'What they've done?'

Maisie nodded. 'Your mother said you're selling Rathgarven and moving to Australia. That your father was offered a good job there with Mr Finn Malone.'

Lillie was about to tell her what she thought had really happened with that man Donoghue, then thought better of it. Instead, with tears tumbling down her cheeks, she said, 'How could they leave you and Paddy like that?'

'Ah,' Maisie said, giving Lillie a clean handkerchief from her pocket to wipe her tears. 'Paddy and me, we'll be fine. And I've no doubt at all that you'll all be back before we know it. Things are tough in Ireland right now. They'll get better one day, that's for sure.'

'But we won't have Rathgarven to come home to.'

'There'll be other places.' Maisie forced a smile. 'And how lucky are you! Off to the other side of the world. To Australia, the land of sunshine and opportunity. Now that's one place I've always had a hankering to go to. Quite jealous I am. You'll be seeing those kangaroos jumping about willy-nilly and koala bears clinging to gum trees. Like in those brochures I be seeing. Not to mention being able to swim on those sunny beaches. Unlike the freezing cold ones here. Now,' she added, running her hand through Lillie's hair and brushing away the tears from her cheeks, 'what's say you come down to the kitchen and I be making you some bacon and eggs. Your favourite?'

Lillie shook her head. 'Thank you, Maisie, I'm really not hungry.' She tried to raise a smile. 'Besides, I feel so fat and horrid.'

'There's nothing wrong with you, Lillie O'Sullivan. You're feeling sorry for yourself, that's all. Why not pull yourself together and go down and tell your parents you're happy to be going on this great adventure. It can't have been easy for them to make that decision.'

'I'm not happy to be going. And I can't pretend, so I want to stay here in my room.'

'Well, young miss, if you get hungry later on, you know where to find me.'

Maisie let herself out, leaving Lillie lying on her bed staring at the ceiling. She would miss Maisie so much. And Paddy. Though it would be Maisie she would miss the most.

Half an hour later Lillie heard a knock at the door.

'Can I come in?'

Lillie didn't answer, so her mother opened the door and stepped into the room. She sat down on the end of the bed, where Lillie was now fiddling with a blue rosette she had won with Merlin at the Kenmare show the previous year. Kathleen handed Lillie a photograph she was holding. It was of a laughing Uncle

Finn in front of a timber homestead with a tin roof and huge verandahs on all sides. Set amidst tall eucalypt trees, the house seemed to have a lovely garden.

'This is the homestead at Eureka Park.'

Lillie took the photograph, glanced at it quickly and put it down on the bed.

'I don't care what it's like.'

'You've got to look on the bright side, my darling,' Ma said, placing her hand on Lillie's shoulder. 'You always tend to err on the dark side of things.'

'What bright side could there possibly be? I love Rathgarven. I'm not leaving. I saw you make short shift of that Donoghue man. So, Ma, please don't tell me you're pleased he's going to get it.'

'Pleased doesn't come into it.'

'Dad owes him money, doesn't he?'

'What makes you think that?'

Lillie waited a while before answering. 'I heard you and Dad fighting that day when you got rid of Donoghue.'

'Oh!' Kathleen said. 'Did you now? Well… first of all, he is Mr Donoghue to you. And you best not let on to your father that you heard what you did. Nor anyone else for that matter. We've received a good offer from Mr Donoghue. And with things so bad on the land here in County Kerry, we accepted his offer so we can move to Australia. Do you understand me? Much as I may not like it, and have grave fears about it, I've made up my mind to make the best of it. And Finn's very fond of us all. Now,' she added after a long pause, 'let me explain what's going to happen in Australia.'

'I don't want you to explain.'

'Well, I'll tell you all the same.' Her mother took out a map of Australia and pointed to a red dot marking the small village of Gullumbindy in New South Wales. 'Eureka Park's ten miles out of Gullumbindy.' Kathleen fiddled with the map on her knee and gave a small smile. 'After numerous jobs on huge stations around Australia, including the Northern Territory and far north Queensland, Finn saved enough money to put down a deposit on three hundred acres outside Tamworth, which he's turned into an excellent horse stud.' She stood up and placed the map on the chest of drawers, then went to the window. As she gazed out, she wrapped her arms around her body and gave a shiver. 'You forget how many cold, grey days there are in Ireland.' She turned back to Lillie. 'At least it should be warm in Australia.'

'I like the cold,' Lillie said.

'When I saw photos of that rambling homestead on the banks of the Peel River,' Kathleen continued, coming back to the bed and looking at the photograph lying on the eiderdown, 'where we'd be going to live, I could see the sense in the proposition… and a possible way out of what's happened here at Rathgarven with the awful economy. Finn has assured us,' she went on, as Lillie stared at the photograph, 'that within a short time we'll be able to make enough money in Australia, with Dad's share of the profits at Eureka Park, to maybe in due course come back to Ireland and buy something else.' She smiled. 'And if that happens I promise it'll be on Kenmare River.'

Lillie picked up the photo and fiddled with it. 'It's so unfair. I'll miss everything about here. And I'll have to make new friends. Sheelagh will forget me in a few days. And it'll be so hard fitting into Australia when we're Irish.'

'Half of Australia's Irish,' Kathleen said, raising a smile. 'The Irish have been going there since convict days. And I'm sure you'll have no trouble making new friends. Think of it as an adventure. That's what I'm trying to do.'

'What about the snakes? They're sure to kill the lot of us.'

'We'll pray to St Patrick to protect us.'

'Clara will be sad she can't come here any more. And what about Ronan? He'll really miss her.'

'We'll all miss her. But maybe she can come to Australia when we're settled. That would be a great adventure for her.'

Lillie could see that despite her attempts to be positive, Ma was hurting as much as she was. It would be hard for her as well. At least Lillie and her brothers could try to find new friends at school. Ma would be stuck in the middle of nowhere on her own, apart from Dad, who sounded as though he would be busy running the horse stud with Uncle Finn.

'Now can I get you some supper?' Kathleen coaxed. 'Or will you come down and sit by the fire with Dad and me? Your grandma's there, too.'

Lillie didn't feel she could face Grandma. Surely, despite what her parents said, she must be devastated.

'I'm fine. Truly I am.'

'What if I send Maisie up with some scrambled eggs?'

After a moment, Lillie nodded. 'I'll go down to the kitchen and make some myself.'

But before she did that she went and rang Sheelagh to tell her the dreadful news. Not that they had lost Rathgarven to that awful man Donoghue. But that they were selling up like other farmers were doing and moving to Australia, the land of opportunity.

'So you're not going back to school in Cork?' Sheelagh exclaimed. 'Jees, Lillie, what'll I do without you? What's more it seems the whole of bloody Ireland's on the move. That fella Seamus Flaherty's off to Canada. His parents had to walk off their dairy farm.'

'How do you know that?'

'I bumped into him in Kenmare. And no, he didn't ask after you if that's what you're thinking.'

'Why would I think that?'

'Because it's so darn obvious that you fancy him.'

'What's the point of fancying anyone in Ireland? As you say the whole place is on the move. Whether they like it or not.'

And with that she burst into tears and hung up the phone.

*****

In a way Lillie wished they had to leave the next day, however it turned out *Mister* Donoghue had given the family a month to vacate Rathgarven. Each day she woke up and saw the river and the mountains, and each day Merlin and the other horses in the meadow seemed sadder than the last. Hopefully if she wasn't here anymore she might feel better. The worst thing of all was watching her parents and Grandma going on as though life was normal. No matter how much Grandma was hurting, she never said a bad word against her son. Yet she must know what he had done. If Lillie felt so sad about leaving Rathgarven, she couldn't begin to imagine how sad Grandma must be.

When Lillie sought her out under the oak tree where she was sitting with her knitting on her knee, all she said was: 'Australia. Now that's a country I've always wanted to see. You're a lucky girl, Lillie O'Sullivan.'

'Well, why don't you come with us?'

'Because, my darling, I'm far too old. Besides, Ireland is my home. And I know you lot will be back before I can say Jack Sparrow.'

She had picked up her knitting needles and started to knit busily. It wasn't long before tears dropped onto the cable-knit jumper she was making for Freddie.

Lillie put her head on Grandma's shoulder and let her pat her, as she'd done ever since Lillie was a little girl.

'There, there,' Alice said. 'We're a couple of silly, sentimental old fuddy duddies, aren't we? Now, why don't you go and get us a nice cup of tea and some of the wonderful chocolate cake I smelt coming from Maisie's kitchen a little while ago. It should still be warm with the icing melting, just as I like it.'

After she brought out their afternoon tea, Lillie thought how much Grandma would miss this house. She wondered about the awful time in the Civil War when the original house was destroyed. She had never really asked Grandma about it, but now that they were going to lose Rathgarven again, she wanted to know more.

'Tell me about the fire that burnt the old house down,' she asked, throwing her grandmother a small smile. 'It must've been so scary for you.'

'Indeed it was,' Alice said, putting down her teacup. 'Would you really like me to tell you?'

'Yes, please.'

'Well, I was hiding with the boys in a disused wine cellar under the garage when I first heard the soldiers coming. We'd been warned and had taken some of the valuables from the house, including some of the paintings, in there with us. Unfortunately we'd no time to escape. First of all we heard the sound of horses' hoofs, then the stealthy footsteps, the crash of glass and then the crackling of a fire.'

Lillie shook her head, imagining the terror her father, uncle and grandmother must have felt.

'Your grandfather, you see, wasn't with us. He was a newly appointed senator in Dublin — negotiating a peace treaty with England, which De Valera refused to accept. Part of the policy of his anti-treaty forces was the destruction of any of the 'big houses' of the newly appointed senators they could lay their hands on. Unluckily, Rathgarven was regarded as one.'

'So it was just because Grandpa was a senator?'

'Well, ultimately it turned out to be a mistake.'

'How do you mean?'

'As you know many of the families around the Sneem and Kenmare area are O'Sullivans. And Catholics like us. It would seem that when one of the anti-treaty men realised it was Rathgarven to be burnt down, he sent an emissary, a messenger that is, to try and stop it. He was too late. The fire had taken hold.'

'How awful. But how on earth did you get out?'

'We waited until the morning, well after the last sound of horses' hoofs went down the avenue and the flames had died down. I crept out of the garage, leaving the boys in the cellar below. Straightening myself up, I heard a crunch of gravel. As you can imagine, my heart nearly stopped. I turned around and saw a soldier, gun raised. In that instant I thought I was dead. Then do you know, the strangest thing happened. The soldier lowered his gun and walked towards me. When he got closer, he gave me a sad sort of smile and said, "Mrs O'Sullivan?"

'I stood there dumbfounded before I recognised him. I think it was the colour of his eyes. Like a field on a spring day. I remembered those eyes from when he was a little boy.

'"Kevin Byrne?" I asked.

'"'Tis that indeed," he said.

'You see, he was the son of Moira Byrne, a wonderful member of our staff who'd been with us for many years at Rathgarven. She'd only recently died. He told me how he was the emissary sent to stop the burning. When he realised he was too late he was so devastated he waited behind to make sure there was no more pillaging. And to see what he could do to save anything. He didn't know we were in the cellar until I crept out and he saw me.'

'That's incredible,' Lillie exclaimed.

'I'm not sure how he ended up with the anti-treaty forces. That was the sadness of the conflict. Often one brother fought with the pro-treaty forces, another with the anti- treaty forces, each trying to kill the other. Young as the men were, I doubt they knew the significance of it all. And I've no doubt some were bullied into their allegiance.'

'Imagine if that was Ronan, Marcus or Freddie.'

'Yes,' Alice said. 'It was an utter tragedy.'

'Do you know what happened to the soldier?'

'I never saw him again after that day when he handed me the chalice he'd saved from the ruins. The one that sits on the mantelpiece in the drawing room. Every time I look at it I think of him. He helped me get the boys out of the cellar and then arranged for us to take shelter in a neighbour's house until your grandfather came down from Dublin. After that we moved to Dublin until the new house was built. I owe that young man a great deal.'

'Golly,' Lillie said. 'We all do. How old do you think he'd be?'

'Let me think. What are we now —1963? Probably in his early sixties. He couldn't have been any more than late teens then.'

'I wonder where he is?' Lillie mused. 'It'd be fun to know.'

'Alas, I've no idea.'

'You'd think the Fitzpatricks' Drominderry House would have been more likely to be burnt. It's a much bigger house.'

'And of course they are regarded as Anglo–Irish, their title dating back to King James the First. Rathgarven was very unlucky. As was Derryquin Castle, next to the Parknasilla Hotel.'

This story made Lillie even sadder about losing her family home. Not wanting to let Grandma see her cry, she packed up the tea tray and took it out to the kitchen, where Maisie was getting dinner ready. One look at Maisie and the tears flooded down her cheeks. Before Maisie could see, she rushed outside and went to the stable to get Merlin's bridle. She saddled him up and went for a long ride up behind Rathgarven to the hill where she loved to gallop. From the top was a wonderful view of the Kenmare River and the Kerry Mountains. Dismounting, she sat on the ground and held Merlin by the reins. Sensing her sadness, the pony nuzzled her face. Although one day she would outgrow Merlin, Lillie couldn't imagine life without him. She had owned him since she was ten years old and had promised Freddie that he could have him when she became too big.

Now what would become of Merlin?

Chapter 8

Kathleen was talking to Maisie in the kitchen when the phone rang. It was the exchange putting through an international call: Jessica, who Kathleen knew was in London.

'I just wanted to say thank you for having Clara to stay,' she said down the crackly line. 'She does love coming to you at Rathgarven.'

'We adored having her, as always.'

Kathleen decided to bite the bullet and tell her they were moving to Australia. And that Clara wouldn't be able to come to Rathgarven anymore.

'You're what?' Jessica shouted, making Kathleen hold the phone away from her ear. 'Moving to Australia? What on earth would possess you to do that? Honestly, my sweet, they're not far removed from convict days over there. What's James thinking of?'

Despite the risk of Jessica feeling sorry for her, Kathleen explained how things were so bad on the land in Ireland that they were selling up and moving to Australia. She then told her about Finn's offer at Eureka Park.

'He's going to work for darling Finn?'

'No, he's going into partnership with him.'

'Oh, is he?' Kathleen heard her clear her throat. 'Finn came to see me on his way back to Australia. He didn't say anything about it to me then.'

'Finn came to London?'

Another long pause. 'Yes. Maybe he did it on the spur of the moment and didn't mention it to you. No reason he should really. But tell me, my sweet, what am I supposed to do with Clara during the holidays? If she can't come to Rathgarven?'

Kathleen shook her head in annoyance. Trust Jessica to think of herself before anyone else. Kathleen was so incensed by her selfishness she said there was someone at the door and she had to go.

'And besides, Jessica, this call must be costing you a fortune. We've already had two extensions.'

'Really! I didn't notice. Anyway, my dear girl, you make sure you take care. As I told you, they're a rough lot out there in the colonies.' Kathleen heard her sigh loudly down the phone. 'Surely there must have been an alternative to James dragging you to the other side of the world. All the same, give the darling my love, won't you? He and Finn are such good friends, aren't they? I do so hope working together doesn't spoil that friendship.'

Kathleen wondered about Finn going to see Jessica in London. But then again, she knew Finn would have to fly out of Heathrow. And he was fond of Jessica. So why wouldn't he see her? But she was so angry that Jessica could only think of what she would do with Clara during the school holidays that when she put the phone down she decided to finally do what she'd been putting off for too long: she would attack the attic.

A short while later she stood in the attic and took a deep breath. It was worse than she remembered. There were old carpet scraps, broken pieces of furniture and standard lamps, plus loads of family memorabilia. There was the wooden rocking horse with the shiny black mane that all the children had ridden and now had a broken leg. There were the china dolls that Lillie had long since discarded, some with eyes missing and others with broken arms and legs. Marcus and Freddie had taken it in turns to disassemble them to see how they worked.

Kathleen looked around. She didn't know where to start. In a way she supposed it was good that they had this move, for surely it would make her throw out bits and pieces that should have been thrown out years ago.

'Put it up in the attic,' had been her answer when anyone asked where something should go. 'I'll sort it out later.'

Well, later had now come. James had told her to make two piles: the small amount they could take to Australia, and what was to be thrown out. Donoghue was to give them a pittance for the furniture, which broke Kathleen's heart, but there was no way they could afford to ship any of it to Australia. She had already marked a few small pieces for Maisie and Paddy and wiped tears away when she looked at the rest, which Donoghue would get. Alice, who held onto the hope the family would return one day and be grateful for some familiar objects, had insisted on the family portraits, paintings and the harp, which had been there since she was a young bride, going into a storage depot in Killarney. A few small things, like the chalice that was saved when Rathgarven was burnt down, would go into a safe deposit box with the bank in Kenmare.

Kathleen was depressed to see the 'throw-out pile' growing and growing. But there was no other option, as she threw a fur coat, which had been devoured years ago by a frenzy of moths, onto the pile.

'I've no need for it any more,' Alice had said, handing it to Kathleen, when she and James had returned from their honeymoon in Tipperary. 'James's father gave it to me when we were first married. You'll look heavenly in it.'

Kathleen had worn that coat so many times, particularly that first winter at Rathgarven when snow had covered the ground and Paddy had to hitch a sled behind the workhorse to clear a path to the front door. She had been devastated when she went to get it out one winter and saw what the moths had done, and refused to throw it away. So into the attic it had gone. Next to the fur coat was a sapphire-blue ball gown Kathleen could remember wearing to a ball at Government House in Calcutta. That too went into the throw-out pile.

She looked at the black and gold money tin, which had ceased to hold money long ago and was now full of treasures she'd saved from her Indian days. There was a paper fan, a colourful bangle, a jewelled hair clip and a pair of earrings. There was also a bundle of papers with a rubber band wrapped around them. It had been years since Kathleen had read those pages, yet she knew the words off by heart. All the same, she pulled the rubber band off and opened the first sheet and held it before her eyes. As she read, tears threatened and she wiped her eyes.

> *... As I write to you now, I imagine you by the river reading this letter. I can see you lying on the rug we used to lie on under our very own sun — listening to the birds in the trees, the flow of the rapids over the smooth brown rocks, the fish jumping. I can even smell you, my darling. Or is it the aroma of newly mown grass, honeysuckle, and jasmine that brings you so much closer to me?*

Kathleen recalled those moments by the river so well. Above all, the day before he was first sent back to Burma. How they had made love for the first time. Gently at first and then with such passion that it took Kathleen's breath away. It was as if their souls had lifted from their bodies and were flying with the birds high in the sky, singing out their joy and love. Kathleen had never known such happiness could exist.

> *... Every morning when I awake, I know that it's a day closer to when I'll see you again. That's the only thing that keeps me going. And your photo I have nestled close to my heart.*

> *... I awoke last night, my darling, and saw your face framed within the window, your skin pale against the full moon, your hair dancing in the reflected light. Reaching*

out to take hold of your hand, I realised you were not there, and an emptiness filled my being like no other I've experienced. It was almost worse than when I said goodbye to you and tears rolled down my cheeks.

Stop now, Kathleen told herself. She couldn't.

... Tonight is a beautiful night. All is peaceful. Despite this I'm full of melancholy.

... Remember, my special one, that no matter where you or I are in this funny world of ours, you are forever in my heart. I'd give anything, my darling, to hold you in my arms and run my hands through your lustrous auburn hair. If only I could hear your laugh... I would settle for that.

She remembered the day he had taken her on his motorbike through the village. How she had photographed the children and laughed with them at their antics. How he had sat a small boy called Sanjay on his bike. How he had twirled Kathleen around and kissed her passionately there and then, making the children skip with joy. How they had gone to the river again and made love.

Kathleen placed the pieces of paper down on her lap. Should she burn them? She'd thought of it many times. Surely now was the time to do it. Particularly if she was to make a go of things in Australia. She would take them down to the drawing room fire. No one would be there now. James was out helping Paddy with the cows and the children had gone into Kenmare with Maisie to see a film.

But when she went downstairs and knelt by the fire she couldn't bring herself to burn those memories. They would go in the bottom of her steel trunk for Australia.

***

A week later Donoghue and his family came to Rathgarven to learn the ropes. Kathleen didn't want anyone here except for James and herself. So she asked Maisie to take Alice and the younger boys along to Parknasilla where the boys could explore the tangled woods and the ruins of Derryquin Castle while Alice had afternoon tea with Lady Fitzpatrick in the hotel's lovely drawing room overlooking the gardens rolling down to the water. Lillie had gone for a ride on Merlin and Ronan was out in the cove fishing in the rowboat, which they had managed to rescue from where it had got wedged between rocks downriver after his accident. The oars were missing, of course, but luckily Paddy had managed to resurrect another pair from the woodshed.

When Donoghue drove up in his pretentious shiny black Dodge, Kathleen thought of hiding in her darkroom next to the woodshed. But she couldn't let James go through this on his own. So she put her shoulders back and went to the front door to greet them.

'Welcome to your new home,' she said with a tight smile to Donoghue and his wife, who was dressed to the nines in a floaty, full-skirted dress that looked more suited to the social whirl of Dublin than rural County Kerry. Beside them stood their two children, a boy and a girl of about ten and twelve.

'Thank you, Mrs O'Sullivan,' Donoghue said, lifting his trilby. 'It be a sight for sore eyes to be seeing you again.'

It was all Kathleen could do to be civil. 'Would you care to come to the drawing room?' she asked standing aside to let them in. 'Maisie will bring tea.'

'That'd be grand if we could,' his wife said. 'If it not be too much trouble? For it must be terribly sad to be leaving such a place as this.'

Your husband could have prevented it, Kathleen felt like saying, but instead forced a smile. 'It will be a great wrench after all this time.'

As she served them afternoon tea, their two sulky children stared vacantly out the window at their new country estate, which seemed of little interest to them. Kathleen looked at James's strained face. To know this family would now be the custodians of Rathgarven would be enough to turn most people's minds, let alone the mind of the man who'd lost it in a gambling bet.

There had been a piece on page three of the *Irish Times* just two days ago headlined 'Leading bookmaker buys County Kerry estate'. The article described how Donoghue and his family had purchased a considerable holding, Rathgarven, on the shores of the Kenmare River in County Kerry, which had been in the O'Sullivan family for generations.

> *The O'Sullivans are reportedly moving to New South Wales, where Mr O'Sullivan is to become a business partner with a fellow Irishman, Finn Malone, a prominent horse breeder, at his stud Eureka Park in the New England area.*

When Kathleen saw this article she had scrunched up the newspaper in fury and thrown it in the fire, then grabbed her overcoat and gone for a walk down by the shore. She picked up a handful of stones and hurled them into the cove. It was two hours later, after catching her horse, Tolly, and riding through the woods and galloping up to the rocky, gorse-covered hills she loved so much, before she could bring herself to go back to the house.

Donoghue now checked his flashy watch. 'I be having a meeting back in Killarney in a couple of hours, so the sooner we can look around the better.'

'Of course,' Kathleen said. 'Let's start in the kitchen.' She looked at Mrs Donoghue. 'I gather you're bringing your own help, all the same you might like to have Maisie show you around.'

'Ah, that won't be necessary. I be leaving the kitchen to Nora. The main part of the house will do fine.'

'Oh, very well then.'

As they walked around the house, with Mrs Donoghue oohing and ahhing, and the children looking blankly, Kathleen thought she really would lose it. Somehow she managed to keep it together until they were at the front door again before James took them to look at the gardens and drive them around the estate.

'Goodbye,' she said, standing on the front porch. 'I hope you're very happy here.'

Mrs Donoghue stepped forward. 'Ah, indeed we will. And may you enjoy your new life in Australia. Never been there myself, but I hear it be devilish hot.' She looked down the hallway. 'Tis a grand home you've sold us, Mrs O'Sullivan,' she added.

Sold? Had stolen, more likely, Kathleen thought bitterly.

'If you're half as happy as we've been living here, you'll be fortunate,' she said, trying to control her emotions, and turned away in case they could see the tears in her eyes. Going back inside, she shut the door and leaned against its cool surface. More than ever she was pleased that she and James had found good homes for all the horses and, as yet, despite the children's begging, they hadn't replaced their beloved labrador, Saffron, when she had died of old age earlier in the year. To think of that family having their animals was too much to bear. After some time she wiped her eyes with her sleeve. I've shed enough tears, she thought. I've no energy to shed any more.

Instead, she went to the kitchen to see what she could plan for supper. The family's second last meal at Rathgarven.

***

It was dull and overcast on the day Grandma left Rathgarven for her hotel in Dublin, where she was to meet up with a woman called

95

Bette, who was to be her companion and carer. Yesterday Lillie and her family had gone as usual to Sunday mass at St Patrick's in Tahilla, and Father Downey, the parish priest, had farewelled them from the pulpit.

'May we wish the O'Sullivan family good luck on their journey to Australia. God be with them on their travels.' Lillie saw him look at Grandma. 'And we wish Mrs O'Sullivan all the best in Dublin.'

Lillie wondered whether, if Father Downey knew why they were leaving Rathgarven, he would be so generous in his wishes.

Afterwards the women of the church put on a morning tea and Lillie said goodbye to Sheelagh, who was going to Cork the next day to start back at school.

'I'll miss you so much,' Lillie said with tears in her eyes.

'You lucky thing, going to Australia,' Sheelagh said. 'You make sure you write and tell me all about it. And don't you dare forget me.'

Now with all Grandma's suitcases in the back of the car at Rathgarven, Ma wheeled her out the front door. Beside them was Dad, who had such a sad look in his eyes that, despite her anger at what he had done, Lillie felt sorry for him. She looked at Grandma, who as usual was stoic and trying to make the best of things. She even had a small smile on her face. As had Ma. Lillie had a feeling that if Ma allowed that smile to disappear she would break down. Beside Lillie stood Ronan, Marcus and Freddie, who was doing little to stop the tears running down his cheeks. A little further off were Paddy and Maisie. It was almost as if it was a funeral and everyone was standing around to farewell the coffin. But of course Grandma wasn't dead. But would she die before Lillie and her family ever saw her again?

Now Grandma opened her arms and beckoned Freddie over. Within a second he was by her side. First of all he held Mandrake up to say goodbye, then put him on the ground and held

Grandma tight with his tiny arms. He laid his head on her shoulder and tears fell onto her coat.

'I'll miss you so much,' he spluttered. 'I wish you'd come with us.'

'And I'll miss you, darling,' Grandma said. 'But what an adventure you've got before you, you lucky boy.' She looked around the rest of the children. 'What an adventure for all of you.'

She then beckoned Marcus over. Lillie could see there was no way he was going to blubber. Instead, he leant down and gave Grandma a kiss on the cheek and moved away. Now Grandma asked Ronan to come to her. Like Marcus, he wasn't going to show his distress, nonetheless Lillie was sure there were tears there waiting to flood out. She watched him lean down and kiss Grandma. And watched Grandma put her hand on his shoulder.

'You make sure you look after your brothers and sister. Particularly,' she chuckled, 'make sure you keep those ghastly snakes away from them all.'

Ronan smiled. 'Of course I will, Grandma.'

Lillie saw him turn his head and he moved away, standing with his back to everyone. She was sure now that he was crying. And as Grandma held out her hand for Lillie, she too burst into tears and rushed over.

'Now, now, Lillie,' Alice said. 'No more of that or you'll flood the river before I even leave.'

Lillie wiped her eyes. 'I love you, Grandma.' She leant down and gave her a hug and a kiss. 'I'll miss you so much.'

'Well, make sure you write to me often,' Alice said. 'And I'll write to you often as well.'

Before Dad helped her in the car, Maisie and Paddy came over to say a final goodbye. This was too much for Lillie, who turned away.

'Come on, Freddie,' she said. 'Let's take Mandrake down to the gate and wave Grandma goodbye from there.'

Lillie thought this was better than standing around blubbering, which was bound to upset Grandma. But as the car drove past them at the gate and disappeared down the avenue, she burst out crying again. Then looking at Freddie's heaving body, she wiped her eyes and pulled herself together.

'I'm sure Grandma will be okay,' she said, kneeling down and putting an arm around him. 'She told me she's quite looking forward to going to that hotel.'

'But she'll miss us so much,' Freddie sobbed.

'I know. And we'll miss her too. But there's nothing we can do about it. And Grandma wouldn't want us to be too sad.' She patted Mandrake. 'Why don't you and Mandrake come down and talk to Merlin with me?'

'Are you sad he's going to the Fitzpatricks? He's going to be Hugh's horse now.'

'Yes, but Hugh said he'd look after him for me. And I know he will.'

'What about Ma and Dad's horses? They'll be sad too.'

'They've gone to nice homes. Ma said so. Someone they know through hunting.'

'Do you think Paddy and Maisie will like working for the Fitzpatricks?'

When the Fitzpatricks heard that the O'Sullivans were moving to Australia they had offered Maisie and Paddy jobs at Drominderry House.

'I know they like Lord and Lady Fitzpatrick a lot, and of course they really like Hugh.'

Freddie clutched Mandrake in one hand and Lillie's hand in the other as they walked through the front meadow to find Merlin. 'Will Paddy look after Mandrake properly?'

'I'm sure he will. Particularly if you leave him a sort of care box with instructions and a sample of all his favourite foods.'

'What if we hate Australia? It's a long way away if we want to come back,'

'It'll be a lot different to here. And much warmer. So we should be able to swim more. There's lots of beaches and Ma said there's a lovely river in front of the house at Eureka Park… and Uncle Finn will be looking forward to us coming…'

As she went on trying to cheer Freddie up, Lillie found that she was cheering up a bit as well. She pulled her coat around her against the stiff breeze. Even though she would miss Rathgarven and the Kenmare River dreadfully, if it was warmer than here maybe Australia wouldn't be that bad after all.

Part Two

From the open sea to Australia

1963

Chapter 9

Lillie stood on board the boat that would take them to the Tilbury Docks in London, where they would board the Orient liner, SS *Orcades* for Australia. She stood with her back to the Dublin docks, unable to look. When Ronan joined her, he did a very uncharacteristic thing and wrapped an arm around her shoulder.

'Turn around, li'l sis,' he said, trying to sound jovial. 'Say goodbye. You don't want to think later that you turned your back on Ireland.' He laughed, but it had a sad twinge to it. 'I promise you that within five years I'll bring you home if you want. I promised Grandma I'd be home before I turn twenty-one.'

'I'm coming home long before five years. Grandma will be getting so old by then. I promised her I'll come back as soon as I get my first job and can pay for my passage. I'll leave school early and start working.'

'Be it as you like. Remember my offer, though. One day you might regret not accepting it.'

Lillie looked at him standing there, trying to be so blasé. 'And what about Clara?'

'What about her?'

'She'll be sad she can't come to Rathgarven anymore.' She paused. 'To see you.'

Ronan looked out to sea and Lillie thought he suddenly seemed very sad. 'She'll miss us all,' he said, turning around.

'Did you write to her to tell her what's happening?'

'Yeah. I gave her Uncle Finn's address to write to.'

'Oh. Did you tell her what *really* happened? I mean… not the version that we're supposed to tell everyone.'

'Lillie, that's the *only* version. Forget the other one, okay. Accept what's happened. There's not a darn thing we can do about it. So we might as well make the best of it.'

'Holier than thou, St Ronan,' Lillie whispered meanly in his ear. 'Trying to see the good in everything!'

But as she said it, she thought Ronan was probably right. There was nothing they could do about leaving Ireland and going to Australia, so she might as well try and do what he said and make the best of it. She looked along the deck to where Freddie was playing with another boy and doing handstands. Sad as he was to leave Rathgarven and Grandma, he seemed to have forgotten already. If only Lillie was seven years old and could forget like that.

Twenty-four hours later, after spending the night in a hotel at Tilbury Docks, the family was ensconced on the *Orcades* heading down the English Channel. Surprisingly, Lillie found that she loved shipboard life, particularly the sound of the waves and the gentle movement of the huge vessel through the water. She was given one of the top bunks, which meant she could spread her things out. With the curtain pulled around, she even had some privacy. She enjoyed playing quoits and shuttlecock with Ronan, as well as swimming with him and her younger brothers in the pool on the main deck. Not that flying was an option because it was so expensive, but coming by ship and stopping off at ports along the way gave them a chance to adapt to life away from Ireland. When they were in a port she sent lots of postcards to Sheelagh and her other friends at school and to Grandma, Maisie and Paddy. She even sent one to Clara and wondered if Ronan had as well.

Now as she looked over the railings on the deck and saw the Western Australian coast come into sight, she couldn't believe how quickly the trip had gone. She would be sad to leave the *Orcades*, as all the crew were so friendly and she would miss them heaps. Standing beside Ronan she held onto her yellow spotted sunhat in the strong breeze.

'The first sight of our new land, eh?' Ronan said. 'I bet there's many an Irishman who's said that over the years.' He brushed his mass of wind-blown hair out of his eyes. 'Impressive, eh!'

Pulling her sunhat down against the scorching sunshine, Lillie laughed and wiped the perspiration off her top lip. 'Dad was right about one thing. It sure is hot.'

Freddie rushed up to them. 'What you think, young Fred?' Ronan asked.

'It's exciting.' He grabbed Lillie's hand. 'Isn't it, Lillie?'

Looking at the coastline getting closer and closer, she squeezed his hand tight. He was right. In a way it *was* exciting to see the land that was to become their new home.

***

Two weeks later, after a rough crossing of the Great Australian Bight, and stopping overnight in Melbourne, where due to an industrial strike the passengers weren't allowed off the ship, Kathleen stood on the deck in the midst of her family as the *Orcades* steamed along the coast towards Sydney Heads. What struck her more than anything else was the colour of the sky, a wonderful clear blue spreading to eternity. Leaning over the starboard railings, she could see long stretches of white sand with tiny specks swimming off the shore. Behind one beach there appeared to be a shopping strip and masses of brick houses with red tiled roofs, then the occasional block of flats, and one or two taller buildings. Another passenger had told her she'd often swum on Bondi Beach, famous around the world for its huge stretch of white sand. Kathleen peered closer. Was that beach Bondi?

With the movement of the ship Kathleen wasn't sure if the photograph she was trying to take would come out clearly, so instead she lined the children against the railings and took a photo of them. Years on it would be interesting to look back and analyse each child's emotions: Freddie's and Marcus's wonderment etched all over their glowing faces, Ronan's quiet intent and Lillie's wariness — though Kathleen noticed she was also quite excited.

And if someone were to take a photo of Kathleen? In years to come what would people see in her face? Would they spot what was beneath the surface? Or would they see a woman of a certain age, nervous, yet caught up in the excitement of the moment? And what about James? She gave her husband a small smile, then went over and squeezed his elbow.

'Ma look! Up there,' Ronan said, pointing to a white stone lighthouse on the top of a headland at the entrance to Sydney harbour.

As he lifted his arm a letter fell out of his pocket. Hurriedly, he picked it up and put it back but not before Kathleen recognised Clara's handwriting. She thought of saying something, then decided not. But it was funny that he should carry a letter from Clara around with him. He really must be smitten. Poor Ronan. If Clara did by chance end up anything like her mother, he had a tough road ahead of him.

Soon the *Orcades* turned left, pointing her huge bow into the harbour. Now Kathleen could see real excitement in Ronan's brown eyes, and she reached out and hugged him close. As the ship moved slowly through the water Kathleen stood with her eldest son and her husband in a tight embrace.

Of all her children Kathleen felt Ronan would find it hardest to adjust. At an age when boys were likely to bully, he was the one who would have the most difficult time settling into a new school in a new country. Aside from anything else his accent would set him apart. Girls were somehow kinder. Kathleen felt sure that Lillie, despite her misgivings, would fit in well. And Marcus and Freddie would bamboozle their way into anyone's life, refusing to believe they weren't liked.

'Well, my darling,' she said to Ronan. 'There's no going back now, is there? And I must say it does look impressive.'

Ronan gave a bright smile, which went a little way to reassuring Kathleen that he had put the sadness of losing Rathgarven behind him.

'It sure does look incredible,' he said. 'Take a look at that blue water. Irish seas often seem so grey and dismal. Not that I'm being disloyal. It's kind of how it is.'

Further on there were mansions with lush gardens rambling down to the harbour, some had a jetty at the bottom and a glossy wooden cruiser tied up alongside. It looked so very different to Ireland. Peering through the black binoculars James had given her as a birthday present, Kathleen was sure that despite the ship's engines, she could hear the screech of the red and blue rosellas and the white cockatoos perched in the branches of the trees. Lowering the binoculars, she picked up her camera and took a photo.

'Ma! Ma!' Freddie called excitedly. 'Look over here!'

Kathleen turned and saw the bridge, a massive steel crescent spanning the harbour, with a riot of rainbow spinnakers sailing underneath. She wasn't sure at first whether the bridge was beautiful or ugly. It was certainly impressive.

'Do you want to perch your camera on my shoulder?' Lillie asked. 'It'll steady your arm and make it easier to photograph — sort of like a tripod.'

'What a good idea!' Kathleen said, leaning against the wooden railings and lifting her camera onto her daughter's shoulder. Eyeing the huge steel bridge through the lens, she decided it *was* beautiful after all. She wondered if the ship would go under the bridge, but before they reached it a large tugboat edged the ship to what she later discovered was the

Woolloomooloo Finger Wharf, and weighty knotted ropes were lowered to the men down below. Further on an excited crowd waved banners and bright red, white and blue streamers and there was a band playing.

'Jeepers… Look at that,' Freddie called out, rushing to the railings to peer down. 'Marcus, come quickly. It looks like a carnival.'

For Kathleen it was difficult not to get caught up in her sons' excitement.

Chapter 10

The first inkling Lillie had that things weren't as they should be was when they disembarked into the huge iron shed on the wharf and Uncle Finn wasn't there to meet them.

'I'm sure he's on his way,' her father tried to reassure her mother. He ran a white handkerchief over his forehead. 'He's probably caught up in a traffic jam.' He looked at his watch. 'If rush hour's anything like it is in Dublin, it's probably bedlam out there.'

A few minutes later Ma looked around anxiously. 'Perhaps we should get a taxi to the hotel? Maybe you misunderstood his letter, James.'

He rifled through his coat pocket, took out Uncle Finn's letter and read it out aloud.

I'll be there at the docks to meet you with bells and whistles. I'll ring ahead and find out what time the boat gets in. Can't wait to see the lot of you.

'Sounds clear to me that he'd meet us here.' He folded the letter up and put it back in his pocket. 'So don't panic.'

However, after another sweltering half hour passed, James went to the phone box in the corner of the terminal to try the only number he had for Uncle Finn, the one for the homestead at Eureka Park.

When he came back he told them the switchboard had attempted to get through but there was no answer. Lillie could see the tension around her mother's mouth and the worry in her eyes.

After a further ten minutes, her father went outside to have another look around on the off-chance that Uncle Finn might be there waiting and hadn't been able to get a park.

'Probably the best thing is to do as you say and go to the hotel,' he said to Kathleen when he came back and had found no sign of him. 'Perhaps he forgot that he wrote he'd be here at the docks and is waiting there for us at the hotel. Wondering where we are.'

Ma nodded. 'Please God you're right.'

Half an hour later they were in two taxis driving through the city, the streets chock-a-block with honking, jockeying traffic. The driver of the taxi Lillie was in told them there was a burst water main so they would have to go a roundabout way to get to the hotel. Lillie didn't mind as she could see more of the city, even though she was crammed in the back with Freddie on her knee.

She stared out the window at the tall buildings, some of which seemed to almost reach the sky and blocked the sun from the street. Every now and then there was an entrance to what looked like a railway station where masses of people jostled and shoved each other. One imposing building they passed with the name Mark Foy's in gold writing on it, had a marvellous window display of furs and shoes from Paris. Around the next corner was a massive billboard advertising Taubman's paint and another for a Frank Sinatra concert, which Lillie pointed out to Ma, as she liked Sinatra.

'I don't see any trams,' Freddie complained to the taxi driver as he wriggled on Lillie's knee and peered out the open window. 'I thought there would be some here.'

'Sorry, mate. The last one finished up a couple of years ago.'

'Ah gees,' Freddie said. 'I really would've liked to ride on one. We didn't have any in Sneem, but I saw a movie on the ship with one in it.'

When they stopped at a pedestrian crossing, Lillie saw that the younger women's skirts seemed to be shorter than in Ireland. She loved the jeans one girl had on, rolled up at the bottom. Many of the older women were dressed in suits and most wore hats, as did the men. Now they were passing a cinema with a life-size poster of Audrey Hepburn in *Breakfast at Tiffany's* and another one for *West Side Story* with Natalie Wood. That was a movie Lillie would kill to see, she loved Natalie Wood and dreamt of looking like her. It would have been ages before either of those movies came to Kenmare, if ever.

Sheelagh would tell her that was one advantage Australia had already. *'See I told you it'd be fun. Wait till you meet the fellas.'*

Shortly, the taxis pulled to a halt outside the Australia Hotel, a grand building of polished granite with fancy Greek-looking columns in the centre of the city. The family poured out onto the footpath and stood beside their luggage before a friendly porter came and loaded everything onto a trolley. Lillie eyed her family's somewhat tattered belongings and then glanced at the grand entrance to the hotel. It didn't seem like a good mix.

'My God,' she said to Ronan, looking at the dishevelled state of Freddie and Marcus's clothes and their hair standing on end. 'Talk about country bumpkins! They probably won't let us in.'

Yet, as the porter pushed the trolley through the gleaming door, he acted as though this sort of confused Irish family arrived on the hotel's doorstep every day. Inside, Lillie gazed in wonder at the bustling lobby and the magnificent ornate staircase climbing to what she imagined would be the most heavenly rooms. Around her was a sea of polished wood, black marble and glimmering glass with intricate silver etchings of birds and trees splashed over the surface. She'd never been to the much-talked-about Shelbourne Hotel in Dublin, but she doubted it was as grand as this. And the people lounging in plush armchairs amidst potted palms, smoking and sipping cocktails or cups of tea, appeared as if they were part of a glitzy movie set. Some of the women were in glorious outfits with snazzy shoes and jaunty hats, reminding Lillie of how Clara's mother dressed. And the men were so dapper in their dark suits with hankies poking out of their pockets; others wore sports jackets with cravats tucked around their necks, much like the ones Uncle Finn often wore.

Everywhere Lillie looked she could see herself in a mirror. Compared to the people around her she looked drab. She couldn't help noticing that Ma didn't appear out of place at all as she stepped over to the reception counter with Dad. Lillie saw her as one of the women sitting around in one of the lavish chairs might. It was the way she had of putting an outfit together: the stylishly cut skirt, the red scarf around her slim neck, the tortoiseshell slide in her auburn hair.

Lillie stepped over to join them at the counter, and found it impossible to believe what she was hearing. No booking had been made in their name. Or Finn Malone's name.

'And I'm so sorry,' the pretty receptionist said to her father, 'the hotel's completely booked out, being a long weekend. There's hordes of people here from the country — so I reckon most of Sydney will be full up.'

'There must be some mistake,' her father exclaimed in despair, his voice now slightly shaky. 'Mr Malone assured me he'd made a booking for us. He was to meet us off the *Orcades*. He must have been held up. He's told me he stays here often when he's down from his horse stud at Gullumbindy.'

'Oh yes,' the receptionist said. 'I remember Mr Malone well. He often stays with us. But,' she went on in a worried tone, looking in the ledger again, 'I'm afraid he hasn't made a booking for tonight, sir.'

'When did he last stay here?' Ma asked.

The receptionist gave a cheery smile. 'We were only saying last week that he hasn't been down for quite a while.' She smiled. 'He's one of our favourite guests.' She pointed over to a bar in the far corner. 'There's a harp in there. He often plays it. He sings really well too. Great Irish songs. But also some Aussie bush ballads.'

'How long is "quite a while"?'

'Oh my,' the receptionist said, raising an eyebrow. 'I'd say it was at least six weeks.'

Lillie's father took a deep breath and looked around at Ma, then Lillie and her brothers. 'Are you sure you have no rooms at all? As you can see, there's rather a lot of us.'

'Sorry, sir. We've got absolutely nothing.'

'Could the dates have got mixed up? Maybe he booked yesterday. Or tomorrow?'

The receptionist shook her head of neat-as-a-pin brown curls. 'I thought that too, sir, so I checked. I'm so sorry… we really don't have any booking from Mr Malone at all.' She gave a sympathetic smile and ran a hand over her sun-bronzed forehead where, despite the huge fan overhead, beads of sweat glistened. 'If there was anything I could do, rest assured I would.'

She eyed Ma's distraught face. For a second they held each other's gaze. 'If you wait here for a moment,' she said, 'I'll try a couple of the other hotels in the area.'

Golly, Lillie thought, her heart sinking. What if no one's got any rooms?

A while later the receptionist returned to the counter, shaking her head again. 'I'm afraid, sir, the only rooms I could find for such a large group are in a boarding house in The Rocks area, not too far from here. I've tried everywhere else I could think of. Another receptionist's aunt owns this establishment. It isn't fancy, by any means.' She smiled sympathetically. 'At least it'd mean you'd have a roof over your heads for the night.'

As it was now nearly 7.30 p.m., she urged them to take it. 'In fact,' she went on, smiling now, 'when I told Mrs Gatenby, the lady who owns the boarding house, what had happened, she insisted on getting her husband to make a couple of trips in his ute to collect you. She'd hear of nothing else.'

After her parents agreed to this arrangement, Lillie went over to Ronan, who was sitting with Marcus and Freddie, and told him what was happening. 'Ma looks as though she's going to cry. And Dad doesn't look much better.'

'I'm not surprised,' Ronan said, shaking his head. 'Seems like a complete botch-up.'

As Lillie sat down beside them she was really angry with Uncle Finn. How could he have let them down like this?

***

An hour later Kathleen and her family were ensconced in the ramshackle, and not altogether clean, Parkway Lodge in a quaint area of winding streets, terrace houses, pubs and milk bars near the Harbour Bridge.

When Kathleen discovered the dining room had closed for the evening she looked at James in despair. 'But we've got nothing to eat.'

James sighed. 'I'm sure we'll work something out.'

Fortunately, Mrs Gatenby, with her wispy peroxided hair, kindly sorted out the food problem by setting off down the street to a busy café with Ronan and Marcus in tow. There she got a huge helping of fish and chips wrapped in newspaper and a large bottle of ginger ale, which she refused point blank to take any money for.

'This'll do you until breakfast in the morning,' she told Kathleen, while winking at Freddie and Marcus, 'when these young larrikins can help me make a batch of pancakes.'

Freddie's face broke into a huge grin. 'Can we?' he said with glee, jumping from one foot to the other. 'Pancakes are my very favourite. Maisie always lets me lick the bowl.'

'Well now, young man,' Mrs Gatenby said, leaning down and patting him on the head, 'I don't know who Maisie is, but a decent bowl-licker's what I've been missing all these years.'

After she had left, Kathleen laid out the newspaper on a small trestle table on the verandah off one of the dormitory style bedrooms the children had been given. Dragging a few rickety camp chairs across the uneven floorboards, she placed them around the even wobblier table. Everyone helped themselves hungrily and Marcus and Freddie scuttled to the corner of the verandah where they sat, legs crossed, with a pile of hot potato chips balancing on pieces of newspaper on their knees; a paper cup of ginger ale by their side; wide grins from ear to ear.

'What the heck are we going to do now?' Ronan asked, licking his fingers, as he wrapped the oily newspaper away at the end of the meal. 'If Uncle Finn never shows up then what?'

'Of course he'll turn up,' James said. 'The Australia Hotel knows where we are, so when he arrives, he'll come around here. I'm sure there was some mix-up about the booking, that's all. Perhaps he got his dates confused.'

'But no one's set eyes on him for ages,' Lillie threw in.

'He's probably been busy getting the place ready for us,' James said. 'That's why he hasn't been seen around.'

Moving to the edge of the verandah, Kathleen leant on the railings and looked down on the tree-lined street below where smoke curled from the chimneys of a row of terrace houses. In the distance she could hear the siren of an ambulance or a fire engine. Across the road a group of men seemed to be playing a game of cards around a makeshift table on the footpath under the glow of a street lamp; a couple of dogs loitered in the gutter close by.

'I wonder how reliable he really is, James?' She turned to her husband. 'I mean, we know nothing about his life here in Australia, do we? Apart from what he's told us.' She paused, noticing Ronan and Lillie looking on anxiously. 'Ronan, would you and Lillie mind going to check that Marcus and Freddie aren't destroying the place?'

When they were on their own again, Kathleen gave a deep sigh 'Do you think he's gone on a bender, James? Is that why he seems to have disappeared into thin air? I know we thought he'd given up drinking years ago. And he attends AA meetings. But let's face it… that's why his marriage broke up, isn't it?'

'Kathleen, that was years ago,' James said, his voice clipped. 'The man hasn't touched a drop in ages. Besides, you saw him at Rathgarven. He wasn't drinking then. You don't think he'd be where he is with a successful stud if he's a drunk?'

'We're only going on what he's told us. What if none of it's true? What if there's no horse stud? No house?'

'Everyone knows he's got a horse stud and doing well with it. It was even in the newspaper.'

'You know as well as I do you can't rely on what the newspapers write. In the very same article they wrote about Finn and his successful horse stud in Australia, they wrote that Donoghue bought Rathgarven, making it sound as though it was a normal, everyday sale. Not that the scoundrel had refused to give you time to come up with the money you owed him. Like any decent man would do. Despite me going to see him after the banks refused us a loan to pay him off.'

James looked both alarmed and annoyed. 'You went to see him?'

Despite having promised herself she would go along with James's plans to come to Australia, Kathleen had decided she had to make a final attempt to get Donoghue to see reason.

'Your mother and I discussed it. I'll tell you what he said. It was my husband's debt. And my husband had to pay up like a man.'

'You shouldn't have interfered,' James said. 'Not without telling me.'

'Well I did, didn't I? And there's nothing you can do about it now.' She was so upset she couldn't stop her outburst. 'The best you can do is find Finn. Otherwise, not only have we lost Rathgarven, we've nowhere to go.' She raised her voice. 'What if we've come all this way and —'

James stood up. 'Kathleen, you're getting yourself worked up. You know as well as I do that it was at his suggestion — not ours — that we spoke to his accountant before making the decision to come.'

'I know,' Kathleen said, her voice raised in angst. 'What if that was all a cover...'

'For goodness sake, Kathleen! The poor man's probably sick, had an accident or got caught up somehow. Let's not make him into a roaring alcoholic and criminal. In any case, what good would it do him to bring us all this way if there's no job? Think of it, Kathleen. Why would he do that?'

'All I know is that we're here, on the other side of the world in a dilapidated hotel, probably crawling with redback spiders, not to mention rats. Marcus and Freddie are running bedlam around the corridors, and your eldest son and daughter are totally bewildered. It's not exactly what I'd in mind for our first day in our new land.'

James placed his hand on her shoulder. 'We're getting ourselves in a state. I'm sure after we have a good night's rest, things will work out in the morning. There's bound to be an explanation. If Finn doesn't answer the phone or turn up tomorrow, we'll somehow head up to Tamworth and go out to Eureka Park. If he's not there he's bound to have left the house open for us.'

'You really think so?'

'In any case we can't afford to stay on here.'

There was a long silence, punctuated by the sound of traffic in the street below. 'I suppose you're right,' Kathleen said, trying to be calm, even though she felt like screaming in exasperation.

'There doesn't seem to be much else we can do.' She moved towards the door. 'In the meantime I'd best get those young ones to bed or we're sure to be booted out of here.'

As she headed down the stairs to find Marcus and Freddie, Kathleen told herself to get a grip on her feelings. Fighting with James was not going to achieve anything. That Finn had let them down wasn't really James's fault. Kathleen knew only too well that Finn had his demons. Had those demons taken hold of him again?

Chapter 11

The next morning James awoke before the rest of the family. He crept down the stairs and went out into the street as dawn was breaking. At the kerb he lit his pipe and took a long, slow draw. Despite being exhausted last night, he had hardly slept at all for worrying about Finn. He had a feeling Kathleen hadn't slept much either, for he had heard her tossing and turning in the small bed by the window.

He checked his watch. Just gone six. What time would the switchboard open at Gullumbindy? It was unlikely it would be before seven. Knocking his pipe on the heel of his shoe, he decided to go for a short walk down the street. Across the road he could see the milkman going about his rounds, and a little further on was a bread van. Otherwise the street was empty. The houses were not unlike some of the terrace houses in Dublin, two storeys with verandahs top and bottom and a small courtyard to the front. Many of them looked to be worker's cottages, some more loved than others. Although it was no excuse for what he had done at the Killarney Races, not for the first time he wished he could tell Kathleen about Jessica. But if he did and Kathleen confronted her, as she was sure to do, Jessica would make good on her promise. A promise Finn had told James she had reiterated to him when he had gone to London to pay her off.

'She'll never bother you again,' Finn had told him when he phoned from London before he left to fly back to Australia. 'She's assured me of that. But she did say, and I quote, "If darling Kate gets a hint of it then all bets are off and, I'll have no choice but to tell the whole world what I know." So as long as you keep Kathleen out of it, you can forget about Jessica and her demands.'

James had never really taken to Jessica, finding her melodramatic. The life she had envisaged for herself had fallen flat and for that she was determined to make others pay, without taking into account her own foolishness. He was indebted to Finn for what he had done and couldn't wait to see him in person to thank him.

He had walked for close to an hour before he used the key Mrs Gatenby had given him and found her in the kitchen preparing breakfast for her guests.

Wiping her chubby hands on her apron, she took an aluminium kettle from the stove and ran it under the tap strapped to the wall with a piece of string. 'What about a cuppa?' she asked cheerfully. 'I'll make us a fresh pot.'

'Thank you. That'd be wonderful. I was hoping I could trouble you to use the telephone. Do you think the switchboard at Gullumbindy will be open yet?'

When they'd arrived at the hotel last night, Mrs Gatenby had wanted to know the whole story as to why the family was left stranded at the Australia Hotel. She had suggested James and Kathleen try ringing Finn again then and there, but when James tried, the switchboard in Gullumbindy had closed down for the night.

Mrs Gatenby looked at the black clock on the mantelpiece. 'Most of the country switchboards open early. It's worth a try, anyway.' She placed the kettle back on the stove. 'When you've done on the phone, the water will have boiled.' Whipping a box of matches from the pocket of her apron, she lit the burner. 'What about your good lady? Reckon she could do with a nice cuppa as well?'

James nodded. 'I'm sure she would. I'll take it up to her when I come back.'

He made his way along the dark hallway to the tiny office where a black telephone sat on a table between two bookcases overflowing with magazines, old newspapers and an arrangement of dried hydrangeas covered in grey dust. It took a few tries, but when he finally raised the Gullumbindy switchboard, the operator told him she'd tried ringing Finn again.

'I tried him last night, too. A friend was after him. Not a squeak.'

When James got back to the kitchen Lillie was up and was talking to Mrs Gatenby about Ireland.

'Still no answer at Eureka Park,' he said, as they both stopped talking and looked at him. 'The operator has tried quite a few times.'

'Where could he possibly be?' Lillie asked anxiously.

'I really don't know. But there's sure to be an explanation. And thank you for this,' he said, to Mrs Gatenby, picking up the cup of tea she had waiting for him.

Upstairs, Kathleen was awake and going through her handbag looking for a comb. He handed her the tea and told her what he'd found out.

'The operator says it's unusual for Finn not to tell her if he's going away,' he added. 'Normally he'd pop in and ask her to hold the mail.' He sat down on the chair near the window. 'She wondered if the river crossing on the road out was flooded as they've had so much rain. Even so, she hadn't heard of anyone else being cut off.'

'What if he's had an accident?'

'I'm sure someone would have found him. If it was a road accident the police would have reported it. And if it was out at Eureka Park he did say he had a stud manager. He would have known.'

'True.' Kathleen sighed. 'I never for a minute thought of this happening. But I tell you what, when we do find him, I'll give him a good piece of my mind. Worrying us like this.'

'I'm sure there's a reasonable explanation. In any case I'll ring the hotel again. If there's no news there, I think we should do what we agreed last night. Head up to Tamworth.'

'There's not much else we can do, is there?' Kathleen said, running the comb through her hair.

'We always knew we'd have to buy a second-hand car. That'll need to be a priority now.'

'Yes it will.'

'We can send the luggage by train.'

When James rang the Australia Hotel there was still no news. Scratching his head in consternation, he rang the telephone exchange in Gullumbindy once more. Surely there must be a hotel there where the family could stay for a few nights if Finn didn't turn up and they couldn't get into the homestead.

'There's the Telegraph Hotel,' the operator said. 'Hold on and I'll try that.'

A couple of minutes later she told him the hotel was full. 'There's the picnic races. When I explained what's happened, Mrs Hogan, who owns the Telegraph with her husband, insisted you stay in their house down the road from the pub. Sometimes they use a few of the rooms as overflow from the hotel anyway. Now,' she added, sounding chuffed she'd been able to help, 'I'll put you through to her.'

Five minutes later it was sorted out. The family would go to Gullumbindy and stay at the Hogans' house until James got hold of Finn. Or they went out to Eureka to see if they could get into the homestead. Now he would have to find a car. He hoped Mrs Gatenby would be able to help point him in the right direction.

***

Lillie was delighted when Mrs Gatenby suggested that Ma take her and her brothers swimming at Bondi Beach while Mr Gatenby took Dad out to a place called Parramatta Road to look for a car.

'One of my lodgers said he'd drop you off and pick you up. He's going to see his sister at Coogee,' she said.

120

Lillie could see the relief in her mother's eyes that they would be getting out of the boarding house for a while. 'Thank you,' she said. 'It would be wonderful for the children to see an Australian beach.'

'On a sunny day like today there's no better place to be,' Mrs Gatenby said. 'Now,' she beckoned to Lillie, 'come on down to the kitchen and you can help me make some sandwiches. You can have a picnic on the beach.'

'Can I help?' Freddie asked.

'You certainly can, young fella.'

A few minutes later she was bustling around in the kitchen telling Lillie to get a knapsack out of the cupboard to put the sandwiches in.

'Is it a good beach?' Freddie asked. 'With lots of waves?'

'One of the best.'

An hour later, as Lillie stood looking out to the surf on Bondi Beach, she thought Mrs Gatenby was right. She had never seen such so much white sand. It seemed to go on forever. Even though it wasn't quite summer and it was a work day, it was crowded with people, some under bright umbrellas, others paddling on the shore or surfing in the tumbling waves. There were deeply tanned life guards bulging with muscles, who sat on tall seats like tennis umpires' chairs, and lots of vendors going around selling ice creams and soft drinks. Most of the girls wore two-piece swimsuits, which immediately made Lillie feel dreary in her one-piece. She saw Ronan eyeing them off and even Marcus's eyes were out on stalks. Out on the water a group of fellas were riding the monstrous, breaking waves on long surfboards. Lillie didn't know how they had the nerve go out so far when she just knew the sea was teeming with huge, man-eating sharks.

'I'll sit here,' her mother said, placing the knapsack and towels Mrs Gatenby had loaned them down on a wall running alongside the beach. 'Marcus, you and Freddie stay in the shallows; Ronan and Lillie, don't go out too far. Mrs Gatenby said there's a rip that can drag you out.'

When Lillie had a go in the surf she got dumped by the waves and all the sand went down her woollen swimsuit, scratching her breasts and getting stuck in her belly button. After a couple of goes she decided it wasn't for her so she sat on the sand and let the waves wash over her feet. Soon Ronan came and joined her. Further along the beach Marcus and Freddie were building sandcastles in the wet sand.

'So what do you think? she asked Ronan.

'About the beach? Or about being left high and dry by Uncle Finn?'

'Both.'

'Well, the beach is great. But God knows what's happened to Uncle Finn.'

'Do you think he's gone on one of his benders?'

'Something's happened to him, that's for sure.'

At that moment a girl walked past in a skimpy two-piece.

'She looks a bit like Clara,' Lillie said. 'The same long blonde hair.'

'The hair maybe. But not much else.'

'I wonder what she's doing. Maybe there'll be a letter at Uncle Finn's place if we ever get there.'

Ronan nodded. 'Yeah, you never know.'

'It's funny thinking we mightn't see her again. Forever.'

Ronan used his finger to draw a circle in the sand. 'Even though we wouldn't have seen her until the holidays it's odd being on the other side of the world and her in London.' He paused and looked out to the sea. 'No doubt she'll forget all about us before too long.'

For the first time in her life Lillie thought Ronan was talking to her like a friend, rather than a younger sister. Although she had never really fancied anyone, apart from Seamus Flaherty on the school bus, she thought she knew how her brother was feeling.

'I don't think she'll forget,' she said, touching him on the arm. 'Maybe she'll come visit and...'

Before she had a chance to say anything more, Freddie came bounding up and dropped a handful of sand on her head, rubbing it into her hair.

'Freddie,' she screamed. 'You're a pest.'

Ronan stood up and grabbed him and took him out into the water and dropped him into a wave, making him scream and splash furiously, as Freddie couldn't swim that well. But Ronan was there to catch him. Watching Ronan, Lillie felt sorry for him. Not only had he lost Rathgarven, which rightfully should have gone to him, and despite his refusal to admit that he was smitten by Clara, he obviously thought about her a lot.

Chapter 12

Lillie put her hand to her mouth. She could hardly breathe and thought she was going to be sick. She leaned out of the window, but the wind was so strong it made her feel worse.

Since 5.30 this morning she had been sitting in the back seat of the Holden, which Dad had purchased from a very nice second-hand dealer. Her parents and Freddie were in the front and Lillie was squashed next to the window beside Marcus, with Ronan on the other side. They drove across the incredible Harbour Bridge, through leafy suburbs, and left the chaos of the city behind as they crossed a wide river. Now they were deep in the heart of the countryside. Every now and then they came to a small town; some had pubs, shops and cafes advertising meat pies and fish and chips on the main street. And like in Ireland there was usually a church, often with a school next to it.

'Move over,' she hissed to Marcus, whose knees were spread out over the seat. She gave him a nudge in the ribs. 'You're taking up more room than Ronan. And you're half his size.'

'Ouch,' Marcus snapped, kicking her heel with his foot. 'It's you that's taking up all the space. And you always get the window.'

'I *am* the girl.'

'And?'

'You can change when we get halfway,' Ma scolded, 'so please stop bickering.'

Lillie thought how different the countryside was to the rich green fields of Kerry, where the roads were so narrow and steep, winding through towering mountains, bogs, stony fields and thick woods. Stone walls and hedgerows would block the sight of many of the fields close to the road. Here she could see miles of flat land and barbed-wire fences instead of walls. And there were millions of gum trees, some of them looked as though their trunks had been painted white and others painted black. The blossoms on the wattle trees were bright yellow, not unlike the colour of the gorse at home. Mrs Gatenby had told her that even though the drought had broken up north, parts of New South Wales were still in the midst of it. And, true enough, the land outside the car window was sunburnt, dusty and dry, the sheep's wool a dirty shade of khaki. By a dried-out waterhole (Ma told her they were called dams in Australia, and fields were called paddocks), the willows looked as though they were screaming out for a drink. Every now and then there was a farmhouse with a galvanised water tank sitting on wooden stilts beside it. Often the houses were sort of dumped in a bare paddock, the only trappings being telegraph poles and farm machinery spread among clumps of thistles nearby. Very occasionally there was a posh-looking homestead with a well-watered garden, tall leafy trees and thick bushes, or a long tree-lined avenue that Lillie was sure would lead up to such a place. Further on it was obvious a bush fire (something farmers in Ireland never had to worry about) had been through burning everything. In one paddock the carcass of a dead sheep was being picked at by crows; in another was the charred remains of a farmhouse — a brick fireplace, an old bath and a pile of distorted tin the only hint it had been someone's home.

'My God!' she said to Ronan, who was staring vacantly out of the window. 'It looks like Hell has been through. And the land's so flat, except for those brown hills in the distance.'

'It's probably what the veldts in Africa are like,' he muttered. 'Minus the elephants and giraffes.'

'What about the kangaroos?' Freddie demanded. 'Shouldn't they be hopping around everywhere?'

'Keep your eyes peeled,' Ma said. 'You're sure to spot some soon.'

But much to Lillie and her brothers' disappointment, there were no kangaroos or wallabies to be seen anywhere. Further on, her father pulled the Holden over to let a couple of stray sheep go past. Ahead of them a stock truck was pulled up to a grassy ramp behind a barbed-wire fence, and a bunch of sheep were being loaded on to it. The sheep on the road must be two that had got away. Not for long. A black-and-white border collie came bounding through the fence, yelping and snapping at the sheep's hind legs until they turned around and bolted back through a hole in the fence to join the others.

'Jeepers creepers,' Freddie exclaimed. 'Imagine a dog doing that.' Then he spied a stockman, riding a horse and cracking a whip at the sheep. 'He looks like the Lone Ranger in my comic book!' Next to the fence was a man dressed in a khaki shirt and wearing a bushman's slouch hat with corks hanging down over his face. 'Get a look at that hat,' he gasped. 'Can I have a hat like that? Please, please.'

'We'll have to see,' Ma said.

There wasn't much traffic now, except for a few rattling trucks overtaking them, leading Ronan to complain if they didn't speed up they'd be spending the night sleeping in the car.

'Better be safe than sorry,' Dad said.

No sooner had he said that than they had to slow down as a school bus pulled up in front of them to let a group of schoolchildren get off near a railway crossing. One of the children ran out in front of the bus without looking, causing her father to brake hard, sending everyone flying forward.

'For heaven's sake be careful, James!' Ma shrieked. 'You could've killed him. Us too.'

'It wasn't Dad's fault,' Ronan barked. 'How the heck did he know the kid was going to run out?'

He sounded so cross that Ma gave him a stern look. Lillie had never really heard him snarl at her mother before, so she thought what was happening must be really getting under his skin. Ma now handed around some sandwiches and a bottle of warm lemonade and paper cups.

'Yuk,' Freddie grimaced when he took a sip of lemonade. 'It tastes like it's been in the oven. And these sandwiches are all soggy.'

By the time they finally arrived at Gullumbindy everyone's nerves were on edge. Even Lillie and Ronan were niggling at each other. It seemed to be a small village, not as big as Sneem but bigger than Castlecove. There were a couple of churches, a tiny school, a hotel, a post office attached to someone's house, a corner store, a sort of café and about twenty houses that Lillie could see; there were probably a lot more she couldn't see. Whereas in Sneem the houses were all stone or brick, these seemed to be built of a mixture of materials — stone, brick, wood, tin or a sort of plaster.

Dad turned into a laneway and pulled up in front of a house surrounded by derelict old cars, lorries and tractors that looked as though they had just been dumped there. Later Lillie would discover that Mr Hogan, who her father told her owned the Telegraph Hotel on the corner, salvaged spare parts from the wrecks, which he sold or used to repair other people's vehicles. The wooden house needed a good coat of paint and the tin roof was badly rusted and seemed to be lifting in parts. As she stumbled out of the car with her brothers, Lillie imagined the horror on Maisie's face if she were with them now. Grandma would surely faint in shock at the sight of the O'Sullivan's new home, even if it was only temporary. Sheelagh would gape in astonishment and exclaim: *Jesus, Mary and Joseph, is this where you're going to live? Tell me you're joking!*

Lillie was sure that's what Clara would say as well.

Whether it was the result of the long trip, or the sight before her, Lillie's eyes watered up. She tried to blink the tears away and quickly glanced at Ronan, who was running a hand through his hair and looking sort of stunned. She then eyed Ma and wondered what she was thinking. But, as she stepped out from the car, Ma's face gave little away.

Now the front door of the house burst open and a woman, who Lillie presumed was Mrs Hogan, came bustling out.

'Hello there,' she called, rushing down the path to greet the family. She was tiny with a happy smile and tightly curled dark hair speckled with grey; her dress was a sensible navy blue and she wore black lace-up shoes and white socks.

Lillie's father moved forward to take Mrs Hogan's hand and introduced himself. 'And this is my wife, Kathleen.'

'You poor mite,' Mrs Hogan greeted Ma, false teeth clacking. 'Being let down by Mr Malone like that. I can't imagine what the man was thinking of. Not picking you up when he said he would. And not answering his phone.' She gestured towards the road they'd just driven. 'And that trip's the pits. You must be all dead on your feet.' She looked around and went over and gave Freddie's ear a gentle pull. 'Including you, young fella.'

'My name's Freddie,' Freddie pointed out, looking dazed and rubbing his ear with one hand and shooing flies away with the other.

'You can shoo all day,' Mrs Hogan chuckled. 'Those flies have a mind of their own. And your face and mine is where they want to be. Get used to the critters is what I say.' She then turned to Lillie, who was standing back. 'And you… the only girl among this fine-looking lot.' She glanced towards the house. 'It ain't much, but it does the job. What's more there's plenty of room for you all to bunk down.' She looked at Marcus and Freddie with a grin on her weathered face, the skin reminding Lillie of the overripe passionfruit she'd stolen from Mrs Gatenby's fruit bowl yesterday. 'There's a load of space to kick a footy around,' she added, beckoning for the family to come inside where she had afternoon tea waiting. 'My Bill picked your luggage up from the train station earlier on. Now he's outta town doing a final job. He does fencing and odd jobs in his spare time.'

'He shouldn't have troubled himself to pick up the luggage, Mrs Hogan,' Lillie's father said.

'Ah, it was nothing. And the name's Martha.'

'Thank you, Martha. You're both very kind.'

Following Mrs Hogan down the garden path onto the front verandah, Lillie saw a couple of vinyl lounge chairs pushed up against the wall. And at the far end was a clothesline strung between the timber posts with what looked like Mrs Hogan's knickers hanging out to dry. Inside, the living room had a ceiling of pressed tin with a pattern of flowers, and was furnished with a three-piece lounge which had a few holes worn in its covering. In the centre of the room was a chunky coffee table with flowers etched into the glass top, which was chipped around the edges. A cocktail cabinet of the same dark, shiny wood, and with the same etched glass, stood in the corner with lots of photographs on the top. There were more photographs on the walls, including studio portraits of young children in their Sunday best and one of the family together. A portrait, which Lillie thought had to be the Hogans outside a church on their wedding day with Mrs Hogan very fancy in a flowing cream dress and long veil and Mr Hogan looking incredibly stern in a dark suit and tie, took pride of place over the fireplace.

At the back of the house was the kitchen, where Mrs Hogan had tea set up under a damask cloth on the laminex table in the centre of the room. When she removed the cloth, Marcus and Freddie stared in awe at the chocolate cake covered in thick icing. Even Lillie sighed at the sight of the curried egg sandwiches and the huge jug of lemonade, which she hoped was cold.

'Now get stuck into it,' Mrs Hogan coaxed, beckoning them towards the table. 'It's all got to be eaten. Or it'll go to the chickens or Mrs Batchelor's pigs down the road.'

'You've got chickens here?' Freddie exclaimed in delight. 'I love chickens.'

'We sure do, champ. It can be your job to feed them and collect the eggs. They live in the hen house up near the dunny.' She pointed up the back paddock to a small wooden building with a gravel path leading to it. 'At night you'll need to take a torch for the dunny. And be careful to watch out for snakes.'

Ma looked confused. 'The dunny?'

Mrs Hogan laughed. 'The toilet.'

It was only then that Lillie noticed Ma's face seemed to crumble. But in a second she composed herself and gave Mrs Hogan a small smile as she glanced at the table laden with food. 'You're so very kind to have this waiting for us. It's what we need after that long trip.'

'Ah, not at all. Now come, tuck in. Then I'll show you to your rooms. No doubt you and your hubby will want to head out to Eureka to see what's going on after that. You can leave the children here with me.'

'Thank you,' Ma said. 'I'd be good to sort out what's happened with Finn as soon as we can.'

After they had devoured afternoon tea Mrs Hogan showed them where they would be sleeping. Marcus and Freddie were in one room, Dad and Ma in another and then there was one for Lillie. Ronan was to be in a sleep-out off the back verandah. The rooms were sparsely furnished with iron beds covered in chenille bedspreads. Next to the beds were wooden bedside tables. In the corner of each room was a wardrobe.

'We used to use these as overflow from the hotel,' Mrs Hogan said. 'Not too much these days. People complained they had to use the outside dunny. And, as you can see, it all needs refurbishing.'

Ma smiled at her warmly. 'It all looks just fine.'

Lillie wondered what her mother really thought. Compared to Rathgarven these bedrooms were like prison cells. All Lillie could hope for was that Uncle Finn would turn up and take them out to Eureka Park as soon as possible. And wouldn't he be embarrassed when he realised he'd forgotten they were coming?

***

Having received directions from Martha, Kathleen sat in the car beside James as they drove along Wattle Creek Road towards Eureka Park. After seeing the Hogans' house in Gullumbindy, she hoped more than ever that they would find Finn at home. She was amazed how much greener it was here than it had been further south, where she had been stunned by the harshness of the dry paddocks and burnt-out bush. Here there were rows of tall poplars and other English trees interspersed with gum trees, wattles and telegraph poles, and sheep and cattle grazed contentedly. Every now and then there was a gate that looked as though it would lead up to a homestead. Beside each gate was a letterbox, some made out of old milk urns, and occasionally there was a windmill, which James told her were there to pump water from the dams to the houses.

'Finn said the dams sometimes empty right out. It's hard to imagine after all this rain, but in the height of summer I'd say it looks quite different.'

When they pulled to a stop at Eureka Park's gate, Kathleen looked up at the sign. She remembered Finn being so proud when he'd written to them in Ireland, boasting.

What do you think? This is what I've called my bonzer piece of Aussie dirt.

'Lucky there was no padlock,' she said when she hopped back into the car after opening the gate. 'And if Finn hasn't locked up, it probably means he's here.'

'Not sure that they'd lock up much around here. A bit like at Rathgarven.'

'Maybe you're right,' Kathleen said. 'It seems a long way out of anyone's way.'

As they drove up the track between the post-and-rail fences, Kathleen gazed around at the paddocks, which were abundant in long grass and beautiful stands of trees with many of the wattles a vivid yellow. 'It certainly looks like a good parcel of land Finn's got here.'

In the centre of each paddock was a small dam surrounded by thick reeds. And in the corners were shelters with corrugated tin roofs for the horses.

'It's odd there's no horses,' Kathleen said.

'Maybe he's got them in the yards.'

Further on they drove up a steep hill. Once over the crest, Kathleen saw the river in the distance and on its bank what appeared to be the homestead she'd seen in the photograph. It felt so strange to be looking at it in real life. To the right was what looked like the home paddock, and some timber buildings with iron roofs sprawled across the land next to a thick copse of trees that ran down to the river bank. Presumably those buildings were the stables. Next to those there were yards and beyond that tall poplar trees surrounded an exercise ring. Still there was no sign of any horses.

When they got up to the homestead Kathleen's heart sagged. Although it had a certain charm, with a pitched iron roof and wide verandahs on all sides, much to her horror it looked run-down and neglected, nothing like the photograph at all. Even the garden surrounding it was overrun with weeds and thistles.

'Are we at the right place?' she asked James. 'Looking like this?'

James sighed. 'I'm afraid it is.'

Kathleen was startled to see a dog sitting outside the fence. Its fur was matted and it had a pathetic look to its eyes. It was so skinny Kathleen could see its ribs.

'Oh, how sad,' she sighed. 'He must be a stray.'

James pulled the car to a halt under a wattle tree and they got out. Gingerly the dog stood up and came over to them. Leaning down James patted it on the head. 'Dingo?' he probed gently.

With the mention of the name the dog wagged his tail and his eyes lit up.

'Dingo?' Kathleen exclaimed. 'Finn's dog? You said he showed you a photo of him at Rathgarven.'

'He looked nothing like this in the photo. But I think it's him all right.'

Glancing around, Kathleen expected to see Finn walk up. But the dog was so unloved, surely there was no way an owner would have let him get like that. A huge feeling of foreboding struck her. How had the dog ended up like this? She kneeled down and patted it on the head. Although he looked so dreadful she could see that his forlorn eyes were kind and gentle.

'Where's your master, little fella?' she asked, scratching the dog's ear. 'What've you done with him, eh?'

After a moment James cupped his hands to his mouth and called out: *'Finn! Are you there?'* The only response was the shriek of a galah in the gum tree behind the horseboxes. He shouted again. *'Finn! Where are you?'* All around them was an eerie stillness that sent a shiver down Kathleen's spine. The stables looked empty and there was no sign of life at all, apart from the dog. Not far from where they stood a white Ford truck was parked up against a shed. They went over and looked inside. On the dashboard were an empty packet of cigarettes and a box of matches. A few tools and a broken bit of a bridle and a set of reins lay on the floor.

'The keys are in the ignition,' James said. 'He must be around somewhere.'

They walked over to the homestead. Although the garden was hugely overgrown, beautiful trees surrounded it. And it was in a glorious spot looking down to the river. Kathleen followed James through the wrought iron gate and down a gravel path bordered by purple lavender hedges. A couple of wicker chairs were pushed back against the wall of the wide wooden verandah and there was a cane dog basket in the corner.

James banged on the door. Nothing. He tried the handle. The door opened and he called out. Still nothing.

'Should we go inside?' Kathleen asked, trying to peer down the hallway.

'Let's go and see if we can find him first. He might be down at the stables or out in a paddock.'

Although Kathleen was keen to look inside the house, she thought James was probably right. If Finn had forgotten they were coming and the house was in a mess he'd be upset if they stumbled into it without him here. Moving back down the path she saw the dog standing outside the gate whimpering. When she went through the gate he moved in the direction of the river. Every now and then he stopped and looked back.

'It seems to me he's trying to tell us something,' she called out to James. 'He keeps looking at the river.'

'Perhaps Finn's down there fishing,' James said, coming alongside.

A few minutes later, Kathleen marvelled at the magnificence of the scene before her as she gazed down on the river: the sandstone cliffs, the weeping willows almost touching the water, the pebbly beach shaded by trees. On the bank opposite cattle had come down to drink, churning up mud and dropping cowpats everywhere. They looked so contented. Fat, too. Next to where the cattle drank, a flock of white cockatoos picked at the dirt.

Once Finn had told her: 'The darn cockatoos eat anything in sight. Those and the bloody roos are the scourge of us blokes on the Aussie land.'

In time she would probably grow to dislike the cockatoos. Looking at them now they added to the tranquillity of the scene in front of her. Somehow it made her feel less distraught at having lost Rathgarven to Donoghue. Picking up a stone she threw it down to the water and heard it plop. Now the dog padded along the bank ahead of them. James and Kathleen kept up with him until they came to a fence. The dog squeezed through, turned to them and started to bark.

James said, 'He definitely wants us to follow.'

They climbed over the fence and trailed him along the bank. They must have gone for about five hundred yards when the dog veered right and scrambled up to the top of a ridge. Again he turned around and barked. James and Kathleen clambered up after him, Kathleen glad she was wearing a pair of trousers. The dog padded on and they tried to keep up. Then he stopped. James and Kathleen came alongside him and Kathleen realised they were on the edge of what looked like an old mine shaft. There were pieces of rusting equipment spread around and the hole was partly encircled by a falling down barbed-wire fence. She could feel her heart beating and the dreadful foreboding she'd felt when she first saw the dog in front of the homestead came back more strongly than ever. She peered down into the hole. It was as dark as a cave and she couldn't see a thing. The dog gave a pathetic bark and looked down.

'What do you think's down there?' Kathleen asked uneasily.

'Only one way to find out,' James replied. 'There's a wooden ladder on the side. You wait here. I'll climb down and take a look.'

'God, James. Are you sure? The ladder might be broken. Besides, it's probably crawling with snakes and spiders down there. You don't think we should try and get someone to go with you? What if you can't get back up?'

'Don't worry,' James said, peering into the blackness and shooing a blowfly away. 'I'll be careful.'

Chapter 13

James put his foot on one rung of the ladder and then the next. Although it wasn't far down, he wondered if Kathleen might have been right and he should have got someone else to come with him. When he got to the bottom he put his foot on the ground and looked around. There was a dreadful smell of decay. Worse than if the place was just the deserted entrance to a mine shaft. Maybe there was a dead animal down here, and the scent had been dragging the dog back. When his eyes adjusted to the dim light, he thought he might be right. Up ahead he could just make out a lump of something on the ground. He came closer. Unable to make out exactly what he was seeing, he pulled his lighter out from his pocket and flicked it on. With horror he jumped back.

There was no mistaking that the lump on the ground was the remains of a human being inside what looked like a pair of moleskin trousers and a faded blue shirt. On the corpse's feet was a pair of leather boots. As he stared at the size of those boots, James suspected in an instant whose they were. He took a deep breath to steady himself. Please, please God don't let it be so. Then he noticed the rifle lying on the ground. It was a John Rigby. Finn had a John Rigby. Peering more closely at the body he could see there was an obvious shot wound to the front of the head. The reality of what had happened to his friend hit him with the force of an avalanche. He thought he might keel over.

Finn had climbed down into this mine and shot himself in the head. Why, oh why would he do that? He grabbed hold of a rough piece of wood protruding from the wall to steady himself, all the while staring in horror at the scene before him.

James remembered the day Finn had bought that rifle the last time he was in Ireland. It was the day he was leaving. They had gone into Killarney to see a friend who owned the gun shop before Finn drove to Cork for his cousin's funeral.

'What you think, young James?' Finn had chuckled, holding the rifle up to his eye. 'Should be able to shoot a few roos with this, eh.'

'Looks like it could kill more than a few roos,' James had said.

As he remembered that conversation, James felt hot, sticky tears on his cheeks. He lifted his hand to wipe them away. The gun Finn had bought that day had killed more than a few kangaroos; it had killed James's best friend. By his own hand. For there was no doubt at all in James's mind that lying here at the bottom of this godforsaken mine was Finn Malone.

James tried to get a grip on himself, knowing Kathleen was waiting at the top of the shaft. It was then that he noticed a few whisky bottles by the side of the corpse, and he put together what had happened. Finn had started drinking again and in desperation had ended up here to put an end to his woes, imagining in his addled brain that there was no other way to stop his dreadful affliction. James crouched and went to put his hand on his friend's head, then pulled back. It might contaminate the scene for the police. Instead he buried his face in his hands and wept. After a few minutes he took a deep breath to try and control his emotions. He pulled out a handkerchief and wiped his eyes. What words could possibly explain to Kathleen what he had found down this godforsaken mine?

After what seemed like one of the longest and most desperate climbs of his life, he finally dragged himself back to the top of the mine and stood up, patting the whimpering dog on the head. He looked at Kathleen's beautiful eyes, eyes that would soon be wet with tears. He went to her and put his arm around her shoulders, then steered them to sit down on the log nearby. He told her what he had found.

'No! No!' she shrieked, her eyes wide in horror, her lower lip quivering. 'There's no way it can be him!'

'Regrettably, it's him all right. You only have to see how the dog's behaving. Besides, I don't know anyone else who'd wear a boot as big as that and have a John Rigby rifle the same as his. I was with him when he bought it in Killarney last time he was over. He reckoned you couldn't buy anything like it in Australia.'

Kathleen gaped at the mine in dismay. 'How could he?' She grabbed hold of James and clasped him close. Tears poured down her face onto his shirt. 'Why would he do something as stupid as that? Why?'

'Surely,' James muttered, looking at his wife's distraught face, 'if he'd waited until we got here, we could've sorted his problems out.' He looked at the dog, which was whimpering pitiably. 'I'm sorry, old fellow. So very sorry.'

'You poor wee mite,' Kathleen sobbed, leaning over and caressing the dog's ears.

'He was so fond of that dog, it's hard to work out why he'd leave him like this.'

Totally inappropriately a kookaburra started to laugh in the gum tree above them, its shrill cackling reverberating across the water.

'He must have been desperate.'

'He didn't do it near the homestead,' James said. 'Maybe he was worried you or one of the children might find him on your own.' He took a deep breath. 'He's been my friend for so long I can't imagine not having him around. And,' he said, glancing away and back again, 'your friend too.' He pulled Kathleen close. 'I'm so sorry, darling. So very sorry you had to be here to discover him like this.'

'Can I go to him?'

James shook his head. 'It's best you remember him as he was. Not how he is now. That image would remain in your mind forever. It would erase the image of the fun-loving fellow with a heart of gold that we both knew.' He lifted his hand and wiped a tear from Kathleen's cheek. 'That's how we should remember him. Both you and I. And the children.'

'What about wild animals? Surely they'll get to him.'

'I'll let the police know straightaway. They'll organise to take him to the morgue.'

Kathleen nodded slowly. 'Yes. I suppose that's best.' She rested her head on James's shoulder. 'I'm so sorry for you, darling,' she sobbed. 'So very sorry.'

'As I am for you.' James sighed and looked back towards the mine. 'I must admit I'm loathe to leave him here like this. But despite it seeming like a clear case of suicide, with alcohol surely the cause, the police will have to do their investigations.'

He pulled a handkerchief from his pocket and handed it to Kathleen to wipe her tears. Then he took it back and wiped his own eyes. As if they were cemented to the log they sat and stared at each other in shock until Kathleen sighed. 'It's the total pointlessness of what he's done. That's what I can't understand.'

James gave her a small smile. 'All I can say is I'm glad Dermot's not here to see what's happened. He and Finn got on so well. He'd be devastated.'

'Yes,' Kathleen said. 'He would, wouldn't he?'

'The three of us spent so much time together when we were young… and...'

'I know… And Jessica's sure to be shattered as well. She was so fond of him.'

James stood up and moved away. He stared past the mine to the far hills. Please don't bring Jessica into this, he felt like screaming out loud. If only Kathleen knew how Finn had paid that woman off for him when he was last in London. Got her off James's back. What better sign of a friend was there than that? He took a deep breath to expunge Jessica from his mind. If only it was that easy.

'Come,' he said, turning around and beckoning for Kathleen to go with him, 'there's nothing else we can do here at the moment. We should head back to Gullumbindy and report what we've found to the police.'

Reluctantly Dingo followed them back along the bank, down to the river, and up again to the Eureka Park homestead. Now what James had thought was going to be their new home took on a totally different appearance. He glanced at the empty stables and wondered what would become of it all now. Had Finn sent the horses away because he knew what he was going to do? James felt guilty for even thinking it but he also wondered how he could provide for his family without a job. Or even a home to live in.

He opened the back door of the Holden and gestured for Dingo to jump in. At first the dog refused, but then relented. James held the front door open for Kathleen, then reversed away from the homestead and drove miserably down the long driveway to the front gate. As he shut it behind them, he muttered his thoughts aloud.

'What a waste,' he said, kicking the dirt with the heel of his boot. 'What a damn stupid waste.'

***

James drove in silence as they made their way back to Gullumbindy, lost in his thoughts. Beside him, Kathleen was doing the same.

When they got close to town, she put her hand on his knee. 'Oh James… He must've been in such a dreadful state to do something like that.'

'Yes,' James said. 'He must've been. Or so drunk he didn't know what he was doing.'

141

'I wonder what set him off drinking again.'

'God knows. It doesn't take much to set an alcoholic off. Could have been anything.'

'And we're unlikely to ever find out,' Kathleen said. 'I wonder when Dawn's friend Winifred was out there last. Remember Dawn said she had asked her to keep an eye on him when she left for Sydney.'

James shook his head. 'We don't even know how to contact Dawn.'

Kathleen nodded. 'True. Finn said she'd moved a few times in Sydney.'

James parked the car in the dirt parking lot in front of the police station. Kathleen turned to him. 'Do you want me to come in with you?'

'No. You stay here. This is something I need to do on my own.'

Slowly he got out of the car and made his way up the few stone steps to the front door of the red brick building. Inside was a lone policeman, a gangly fellow with closely cropped dark hair wearing a uniform. He was perched on a high stool on the other side of a tall wooden counter.

'G'day,' he said to James, standing up and leaning on the counter. 'What can I do for you, mate?'

When James opened his mouth he found no words came out.

'You okay, cobber?' the policeman asked, looking at him worriedly.

'Yes,' James finally said. 'Yes, I am. It's just that I've got some very sad news.'

He then told him who he was and what he'd found out at Eureka Park.

'Blimey,' the policeman exclaimed, running a hand over his sunburnt forehead. 'Tell me you're joking.'

'I wish more than anything I *was* joking.'

The policeman, seeing how distressed James was, went out the back to fetch a glass of water.

'Thank you,' James said, holding the glass and taking a long drink. 'It was the shock, that's all. So unexpected.'

'I can imagine that, mate. I'll get another bloke over from Quirindi. That's the nearest back-up. And we'll head straight on out.' He paused. 'Can I drive you somewhere?'

'My wife's outside waiting. But thank you all the same.'

In the car James slumped down in the seat and looked into Kathleen's anxious eyes. 'He's going to get another fellow to come over from the town of Quirindi. Then they'll both head on out. No doubt they'll be in touch.'

Back at the Hogans' house, Marcus and Freddie were playing hopscotch outside and Lillie and Ronan had gone for a walk to the milk bar to get a milkshake. Bill Hogan had arrived home and was on the verandah waiting for them with Martha. He was a tall angular man with weather-beaten skin and eyes faded from days in the harsh Australian sun. Beside him was a cattle dog who started to bark when he saw James and Kathleen with Dingo in tow.

'Enough of that, Ned,' Bill said, putting his hand on the dog's collar.

He had an open, friendly face and James immediately took to him when he threw him a warm smile, making the deep creases around his eyes scrunch like corrugated cardboard.

'G'day mate,' he said holding out his roughened hand. He then smiled at
Kathleen. 'How you be, Mrs O'Sullivan?' He looked from her to Dingo, who was panting heavily. 'Where'd you get this mutt from? Looks a bit like Malone's.'

When James told him what they had found out at Eureka Park he and his wife looked aghast.

'Bloody hell, mate,' Bill said.

'I'm so sorry,' Martha added, rushing over to put an arm around Kathleen. 'What a dreadful shock you must have got.'

'What would the bastard do something like that for?' Bill said. 'Particularly when you were all arriving.'

Martha sighed. 'What was the man thinking?'

'He must have been desperate,' Kathleen said. 'Really desperate.'

James nodded. 'It looks as though it was the drink. Perhaps he was so disappointed with himself for giving in to temptation he thought it was the only way out.' He paused. 'His wife Dawn wrote to us when she first separated from Finn and said a friend of hers, Winifred, was going to look in on him. I wonder when she last went out.' He paused. 'Do you know a Winifred?'

'Winifred Black. Of course. She used to help out in the corner store, but I don't think she's there anymore. And I haven't seen her around lately.' She looked at Bill. 'Have you seen her, luv?'

Bill shook his head. 'No, as a matter of fact I haven't. Maybe she's away.'

'A nice lady,' Martha said. 'Married to a no-hoper, but there you go. God knows what she sees in him.' She let out a long sigh. 'Come, I'll get you a cool glass of ginger ale, this is just too much to take in.'

After pouring them a glass each from the fridge and glancing anxiously from James to Kathleen, she sighed again. 'Lordy me… What the dickens will you do? I mean… With no job? And no house of your own to live in?'

James waited a while before answering. 'I have no idea. No idea at all.'

Bill came over and placed his hand on his shoulder. 'Why don't you come on down to the pub? I'll buy you a beer. You must be crying out for one by now.'

'And I'll make you a cup of tea,' Martha said to Kathleen.

'The ginger ale will be fine,' Kathleen said. 'But you go along and have a beer, James. If you don't mind,' she said to Martha, 'I might have a short rest while the children are out and about. Gather my thoughts before we tell them what we found.'

'Of course dear. I'll occupy them if they come back inside.'

***

Down at the Telegraph Hotel, which Bill told him was originally built in 1867, James sat at the polished wooden bar and Bill introduced him to the bartender, a man called Barney, who sported a thick moustache and a sunburnt, jolly face and poured them each a beer.

'To the soul of Finn Malone,' Bill said, lifting his glass. 'He was a bloody good bloke.'

James nodded wretchedly, seeing his forlorn reflection in the thick glass mirror behind the bar. 'He was indeed. Such a waste.' Then James used a word he hardly ever used. 'A *bloody* sad waste.'

'It's that all right, mate. Mind you, it's your family you've got to look out for now.' After a moment he placed his hand on James's shoulder as he looked around the room. 'How do you fancy running this pub for a while? Until you work out what to do. If you're good enough for Finn Malone to want you as a partner in his horse stud, you're good enough for me.'

James followed his gaze. Despite the wooden flyscreen on the door, the room was buzzing with flies. At the end of the bar a rowdy group of men in mud-splattered work gear smoked roll-your-owns, guffawing and cursing and downing beers straight from the can. In Ireland if you went to the pub the least you would do was put on a clean shirt and drink from a glass. 'Run *this* hotel?' he said to Bill in disbelief.

'That'd be it, mate. It only has half a dozen rooms. Old Barney's due to go on leave for a couple of months. He virtually runs the place on his own. Well, there's a girl that comes in and does the rooms late morning and comes back again in the evening to waitress in the dining room. And Nancy from down the road does the cooking. Her son's looking for a job so reckon he could help you handle the bar.'

James shook his head. Never in his wildest dreams had he thought he might end up running a pub. Besides, where would the family live? When he voiced his concerns, Bill gave him a lopsided grin.

'Well, that's the point I was getting to, mate. The missus is due to go down to Sydney for an operation next week. Woman's business. We'll stay with her sister. After that I said I'd take her on a holiday to our daughter up on the Gold Coast. You could stay on at our place while we're away. Reckon we'll be gone up to a couple of months. And, as I said, with Barney away you can work the bar and keep an eye on this place for me. See what happens after that. I'd pay you fifteen quid a week for working the bar and keeping an eye on things.'

James took a breath. Although Bill's offer was one of the most generous acts James had ever come across, he had no idea what Kathleen would think. Or the rest of the family, for that matter. But what choice did they have? Even if it was only for a short time, this was an opportunity they had to take. Obviously they couldn't go and live at Eureka Park. Now that Finn was dead a hold would be put on his estate. To go back to Sydney was not an option. And going back to Ireland was out of the question with the little money they had.

'What you've offered is extremely kind,' he said to Bill. 'Would you mind if I took a little time to think it over? Talk to Kathleen?'

'Not a problem at all, mate. Being Irish I presume you're a Catholic — why don't you go on up to the church on your own for a while? It's the one up the hill behind the hotel. Come to terms with your loss… remember your mate. I'll go on back to the house and see how everyone's getting along. Maybe I could take the young blokes down to the river to do a spot of yabbying before dinner?'

'Thank you,' James said. 'That would be wonderful.'

Without going back to the Hogans' house, James walked up to the small wooden church on the hill. He sat alone in the back pew with his head on his hands, trying to comprehend what had happened. If only they had got here a little earlier. Not that they could have afforded it, but if they'd flown, rather than come by ship, perhaps this would never have happened.

It goes to show how you think you know someone so well, James thought miserably, when you really don't know them at all.

He stood and moved towards the altar; he picked up a white candle and lit it with a match from the box beneath the brass candle-holder. Placing the candle in one of the holders, he lifted his eyes to the altar.

'To you, my dear friend,' he said, tears streaming down his face. 'The best friend a man could ever hope for.'

He knelt and said another prayer for the repose of Finn's soul.

As he traipsed back along the road to the Hogans' house, he thought of Kathleen. She'd be as flabbergasted as he was by Bill's kind offer. Yet in the end she was pragmatic about it.

'There's nothing else we can do, is there?' she said when he told her. 'Not unless we want to be out on the street.'

And James had to agree she was right.

***

147

Under a clear blue sky, to the sound of a lone piper playing Finn's favourite Irish ballad, 'The Wearing of the Green', Kathleen stood with her family as Finn's remains were lowered into a grave under a towering jacaranda. She watched the purple blossoms floating on the soft breeze as they dropped onto the ground where she stood. She put her arm around James's waist and lay her head on his shoulder. Tears streamed down her face. Ronan stood stoically beside her, holding Freddie by the hand. Lillie and Marcus stood next to them, their faces grim and sad.

Kathleen watched Father Fogarty, the affable parish priest with his shock of red hair, say a prayer over the grave. At first he'd been loath to go against the Church's teaching that a person who'd committed suicide could not have a Catholic service.

Then he'd relented. 'Sure now in Ireland it would not be possible,' he'd said to the Hogans, Kathleen and James as they stood in the living room of the presbytery. 'But, ah… We're not in Ireland now. And when all's said and done who are we mere mortals to deny the poor man such a send-off? I spoke to the bishop and he's kindly given me a dispensation to conduct a short service, though I'm afraid we can't be giving him a requiem mass.'

At the graveside Kathleen thought of the first time she had met Finn. It was at a dance in Calcutta, not long before the war, when Finn had been working on his uncle's rubber plantation a short way out of town. Kathleen and Jessica had been there together, wearing the new tulle dresses their ayahs had made for them. Jessica's was lemon, Kathleen's green and white. She even remembered how her shoes were covered in the same green material. The girls were home from boarding school and it was the first dance either of them had been to. Jessica had taken one look at Finn standing on the far wall, smoking a cigarette and looking brazenly across the room to where the girls stood.

'Take a peek over there,' she whispered to Kathleen behind her hand. 'The dishy one wearing the blue shirt. If I stare at him long enough, do you think he'll ask me to dance?'

However, much to Jessica's annoyance it was Kathleen Finn asked to dance.

'Finn Malone from County Cork would be mighty grateful if you'd give him the honour of this dance,' he had said, giving a wink with his mischievous eyes and making Kathleen blush from the tips of her toes to the top of her neatly coiffed hair.

Now as she stood grieving under the jacaranda, she remembered his laugh. His love of life. His magnificently profane sense of humour. The way his face creased with glee when he got a reaction to his wickedly risqué jokes. For the rest of those school holidays and the following two years, after Jessica and Kathleen had left school and were living back in Calcutta permanently, the two girls had hung out with Finn and his friends, horseriding, playing tennis and partying at the Slap and Tollygunge clubs. It was then that Kathleen discovered he was a heavy drinker. Although she and Finn were never romantically involved, he was one of the best friends she had.

Poor, poor Finn. So totally without pomp or pretence and so incredibly generous, offering James a partnership when the family was in difficulties. A vision of Finn playing the harp at Rathgarven flashed before her eyes and she had to blink hard. Kathleen had always thought it bizarre to see larger-than-life Finn playing the harp so beautifully with his big workman's hands. She felt dreadful that she had been so cross with him, thinking he had let them down. She should have known there was no way he would have done such a thing deliberately. Although if she was brutally honest, what he had done now was letting them down in the worst possible way. If it hadn't been for Dingo, Finn might still be down that mine, and no one would have any idea of what had happened to him. All she could imagine was that his brain had become so addled he hadn't thought through the consequences — that James and his family would be stranded without a home, and James without a job. If only the family had got to Gullumbindy earlier, they could have stopped him. That thought would haunt Kathleen for the rest of her life. As it was sure to haunt James.

Finn's ex-wife, Dawn, came up for the funeral, having seen the death notice the funeral directors had put in the *Sydney Morning Herald*. Kathleen could quite understand what had attracted Finn to her. She was small in stature with shiny brown hair that fell over her face in unruly curls. She had a strong face and piercing blue eyes that looked as if they had seen their fair share of sadness, not least of which would have been the breakdown of her marriage to Finn and his untimely death.

'If he sent the horses away like that, he must've had suicide on his mind for a while,' she said to Kathleen and James as they sat on the verandah of the Telegraph Hotel after helping the Hogans and their staff clear up after a rowdy wake for Finn. She gave a huge sigh. 'But why would he do himself in when you were coming?'

'It does seem strange,' Kathleen said.

'Maybe he didn't send the horses away,' James said. 'Perhaps they got out after he did the dreadful deed.'

'Wouldn't someone have found them?'

'Perhaps they did and they have them in a paddock somewhere. Or they've sold them off.'

Dawn pulled out a handkerchief from the sleeve of her navy blue cardigan and blew her nose. 'He used to ring me from time to time. And sometimes send me money, even though I didn't want to take it. I was always at him to make it up with his father. I know how much his poor mother must've been hurting. She promised her husband that once Finn refused to go back to Ireland to join the family law firm she wouldn't contact him again.' She gave a deep sigh. 'I never should've left him. He begged me not to.'

Kathleen shook her head vigorously. 'No one's to blame. For whatever reason, it was Finn's decision to do what he did.'

James turned to her with a strange look to his eyes. 'What if it wasn't suicide?'

Kathleen looked aghast. 'But you've been in to the police again. They said it definitely was suicide.'

'It's just... well, I find it hard to believe Finn would kill himself like that. He often went on about his cousin shooting himself. What a selfish act it was. Leaving his family to sort out the mess.'

'But when Finn decided to do what he did he must've been so drunk he didn't think that through. All those whisky bottles!'

'Even so...'

Kathleen looked at Dawn. 'You were married to him. What do you think?'

'Drink drives a lot of people to do things they wouldn't normally do.'

Kathleen turned to James. 'Are you saying it might have been an accident?'

'Not necessarily.'

'What then?'

'I honestly don't know.' He sighed. 'I suppose I'm clutching at straws. Unable to imagine him being in such a state as to do something like that. As we all know Finn was an alcoholic. But he wasn't a maudlin one, was he?'

'No,' Dawn said. 'It was more what he would do. Spend up big when we didn't have the money. And sometimes he wouldn't come home at night but roll in drunk in the morning. I was never sure where he'd been. Then again, when he was sober he was the kindest and most loving person in the world. You only had to see how many came to his wake to know everyone who knew him liked him, particularly the women, but he didn't have affairs that I know of.' She paused. 'I think I wrote to you that I asked my friend Winifred here in Gullumbindy to keep an eye on him for me, to go out every so often to see if he was okay. She adored him.'

Kathleen nodded. 'Yes, I remember. Martha and Bill said they know her.'

'I was sure she'd come to the funeral, but when I went to the corner store where she normally works they said she wasn't working there anymore. So I went around to her house, but…' She paused and gave a small cough, 'Her husband said she was in bed with a bad case of influenza. He wouldn't let me in to see her in case I caught it. I must admit I've never liked the man. A real heavy drinker. I can't understand why Winifred ended up with him.'

'That's what Martha Hogan said.'

'Yeah. She'd know all right. With her and Bill owning this pub and all that.'

'Will you try to contact her again before you go back to Sydney?'

Dawn shook her head. 'They don't have the phone. And I'm catching the bus early in the morning to get the train from Tamworth back to Sydney. So I'll have to give it a miss.'

'Can't I drive you to the train?' James asked.

'Thanks all the same, but I've already got my return bus ticket. And I like the bus. Gives me time to think.'

Kathleen stood and went to the edge of the verandah and stared out at Gullumbindy. Oh Finn, she thought. How could you have done what you did? Surely there must have been an easier way out. And I don't mean to be selfish, but had you thought about us? She looked back at James puffing on his pipe and Dawn sitting beside him. What does the future hold for us now? It's all very well for us to live in the Hogans' house and look after the hotel.

Still, even you must know, dear, dear Finn, we can't do that forever.

Chapter 14

The day after the funeral Martha Hogan took Kathleen back down to the Telegraph to give her a run-through. In the dining room the tables were covered with red and white tablecloths with salt and pepper shakers and bottles of tomato sauce and mustard placed in the centre. Some of the chairs looked as though they had seen better days and the flooring was scuffed in parts, however, like the bar area with its wood panelling and paintings of the Australian bush scattered around the walls, it had a warm, friendly feel to it.

Out the back Martha introduced her to the cook, Nancy McGuire, whose cheerful face was as red and shiny as the tomatoes in the cane basket on the kitchen bench. With her hair roughly pushed under a net, she was readying tonight's roast.

'Welcome,' she said, wiping her hands on her butcher's apron. 'I heard what's happened to you and your family. A darn shame it is.'

'Thank you,' Kathleen said, taking her hand. 'It is a dreadful shame.' She paused. 'But I'm told you know this place like the back of your hand. I must say I'm glad about that.'

Nancy chuckled. 'Been here long enough. If I don't know what's going on by now, there's something gone amiss.' She seemed so down to earth and friendly that Kathleen immediately took to her.

Upstairs, the guest rooms were furnished with heavy polished timber pieces and the beds covered in brightly coloured chenille bedspreads. On the top of each dressing table was a vase of dried flowers. Beside each bed was a small wooden table with a copy of the bible. Although the rooms looked a bit worn out from years of use, they seemed as clean as a whistle. By the time they came downstairs again with Martha chatting nineteen to the dozen and telling her what to look out for, Kathleen's mind was like a bog of peat on a rainy day, thick and mushy. All she could think of was what they would do if the staff walked out and left the O'Sullivans to run the place on their own.

Just then James came to join them and Kathleen threw him an anxious look.

'Don't be so worried,' Martha chuckled. 'The two of you'll handle it — it's a piece of cake.' She handed Kathleen a notebook with instructions on how everything worked, and showed her where the phone numbers were for suppliers, the electrician, the plumber and anyone else they might need. She patted Kathleen on the back. 'I reckon you'll do a bonzer job. Now,' she said to James. 'Come… I'll hand you over to Barney. He'll show you the workings of the bar. As Bill's told you, Nancy's son's available to help if you get busy. He fills in from time to time as it is. I reckon he's there now, waiting to meet you. You head along to the house, love,' she said to Kathleen. 'I'll be back there shortly.' She beamed an encouraging smile. 'And don't you go worrying your pretty head any more about managing things. As I said, I'm sure you and your hubby will do a cracker of a job.'

Kathleen took a deep breath. Even with Nancy McGuire and the others here she had grave doubts she would do a cracker of a job at all. Nonetheless, she would just have to roll up her sleeves and make the best of it. She would need to summon greater reserves of strength than ever before. For some reason the harsh conditions in Calcutta during the war flashed into her mind. She could imagine Jessica's amazed reaction. *My dear, sweet thing, what have you gone and got yourself into? And that house you're living in's nearly as bad as a shack in the slums of Calcutta.* Kathleen brushed a fly away that had got in through the open door. *And those ghastly flies! Lordy lord, am I glad it's you and not me.*

***

When the Hogans finally left for Sydney in a cloud of dust, Lillie watched as Ronan and Dad took Marcus and Freddie outside to stack the wood they had helped Mr Hogan chop the day before. She couldn't believe how their life had changed now that poor Uncle Finn had killed himself. When her parents had told her what had happened, she had been dumbfounded and found it difficult to sleep for nights on end, imagining him down that awful mine shaft, having shot himself like that. She also worried herself sick about what would happen to her family now that her father had no real job and they had no house of their own.

In the kitchen she filled up the kettle and took it over to the stove. 'Would you like a cup of tea, Ma?' she asked her mother.

'That would be wonderful, darling.'

After they finished their tea she and Ma spent the rest of the day moving some of their things into the bedrooms the Hogans had vacated, unpacking and doing a shop at the local corner store, which they discovered was overflowing with everything from sweets to garden spades, bags of potatoes, jars of Pond's cold cream, gossamer hairnets and even kerosene lamps.

On their return to the house, she went to the kitchen to poke the gum logs in the fire-box under the boiler. If this went out there would be no hot water for the bath. To wash clothes, the boiler in the outside laundry had to be lit and the water piped into the wringer washing machine. Once the clothes were washed they were hung on the wire line strung between two trees.

'There's nearly always a breeze,' Mrs Hogan had told them. 'And if it rains you can hang them on that line running the length of the verandah.'

That night as Lillie sat on her bed, she wrote a long letter to Sheelagh telling her all about it, though she doubted very much that Sheelagh would believe half of what she was telling her. The worst thing of all was the huge insects that flew in and out of the rooms. As she wrote to Sheelagh, one landed right on her head and she leapt up, shooing it away with her jumper.

Yuk, she wrote. *They're disgusting.*

The next night, when she went to get into bed, there was a huge hairy spider on her pillow.

'Ronan!' she screamed. 'Come *now*!'

When Ronan rushed in he looked at the spider and laughed out loud. 'You idiot! It's a harmless huntsman.'

'I bet you wouldn't be so blithe if it was Clara who was so scared.'

Ronan shook his head. 'I don't think Clara would carry on like that.'

'Oh yeah?'

He picked the spider up and put it outside. 'It's the ones with red backs you've got to worry about. A bite from one of those nasty critters and you're dead.'

'Thanks a lot.'

Later that night Lillie had to go to the loo. She grabbed the torch off the kitchen bench and gingerly made her way outside, keeping an eye out for snakes. Once she reached the dunny at the end of the path she shone the torch around the toilet pan. Ronan had also assured her that's where the red-backs liked to hide and that they *loved* to come out at night. She was sure one sat on the back of the wooden toilet seat. Grabbing a piece of toilet paper, she swished it around. She was so terrified a spider might bite her on the bottom she could hardly do her business. She would have to make sure she went to the loo before it got dark, so she wouldn't have to go later. But it wasn't just the snakes and spiders she had to watch out for. There were lizards and goannas, too, who liked to sunbake on the rocks near the fence in the back garden. They looked like snakes, all slithery and slimy, but had legs and supposedly weren't poisonous.

Ma told her that Nancy McGuire over at the hotel had said the big snakes were often harmless, and it was the little ones that were the most deadly.

'And,' Ma added, 'Nancy said they're the hardest to spot, because they can hide in such tiny spaces… like the box where the hens lay their eggs in the chicken coop, or even in trees, where they can strike as you walk past.'

'Gosh,' Lillie exclaimed, her eyes popping out like marbles. 'We better warn Marcus… And especially Freddie. He said it's his job to collect the eggs.'

Every time Lillie thought of the many things that could kill her and her family, it made her quiver all over like one of Maisie's jellies. There were so many creepy-crawlies, and the crickets that never seemed to go to sleep, chirping day and night. And there were huge red anthills with the biggest ants any of them had ever seen.

One morning Freddie came running inside screaming his head off. 'Help, help… I've been bitten by a snake,' he hollered, holding his big toe and jumping up and down squealing, 'I'm going to die, I'm going to die.'

Lillie felt the blood drain from her face. This was one of her worst nightmares.

After her mother got over the shock she hastily tied a bandage tightly as a tourniquet around his calf. 'This will stop the poison spreading up your leg,' she soothed Freddie.

She then told Lillie to hold the fort with Marcus — Ronan and Dad had driven across to Quirindi to get supplies for the bar.

'I'll rush him down to the doctor. Fortunately it's Tuesday and he does a visiting surgery today.'

Lillie was so relieved when they came back half an hour later and Ma told her the doctor had said it was a bull ant, not a snake after all.

'Well, it sure as eggs hurt,' Freddie spluttered, seeming put out that he hadn't been the first one in the family to be bitten by a snake after all.

As she looked at him sitting there on the table, swinging his legs back and forth, Lillie thought how she would have been inconsolable if Freddie really had been bitten by a snake and died. She adored her little brother so much she couldn't imagine life without him.

She went over and gave him a kiss. 'Well, I'm mighty glad it was only a bull ant.' She pulled his hair. 'Silly idiot, you scared the wits out of Ma and me.'

'I knew it wasn't a snake,' Marcus put in.

'How, smarty-pants?'

'Because he'd be dead by now.'

'Thank you, Marcus. That's really helpful,' Ma said. 'Now… both of you go outside and play while Lillie and I prepare dinner. And make sure you watch out for snakes. And,' she chuckled, 'bull ants, too.'

***

It was Lillie who'd persuaded the Hogans to let them bring Dingo into their home.

'Well, we can't be leaving the young fella to fend on his own, can we now?' Mrs Hogan said. 'What he needs is a family to look after him. Besides, we'll be taking Ned with us. And a house without a dog ain't much of a home.'

And so it was that Dingo became part of the family. Soon he perked up and started eating heartily. Much to Lillie's chagrin, it wasn't her he followed around and wouldn't let out of his sight; it was Dad and Ronan he shadowed.

In the meantime Ma told her that Dad was putting out feelers to try and find another house for them to live in and he was also looking around for a job. But houses were hard to find and there seemed to be no jobs around either.

However, one morning when they were making a batch of scones, Ma said, 'Father Fogarty is going to spread the word throughout the diocese for something. Mrs McGuire told me that's how it often works. So I'm sure something will come up before the Hogans return.'

'Has Mrs Hogan had the operation?'

'Yes. And it was a success. They're still going on up to Queensland to stay with her sister.'

As it seemed they would be living here for a while, Lillie helped Ma try and make the house feel more like home. First of all they took all the rugs outside and beat them with a stick to get rid of the dust, then they washed the curtains and filled what vases they could find with wildflowers from the garden and rearranged some of the furniture.

'We can put it back as it was when the Hogans are due home,' Kathleen said. 'For us it works much better this way.'

Lillie felt all they could hope for was that the holiday in Queensland dragged on for the Hogans. Otherwise her family would be out on the road. Not like a family of tinkers, but a family of Aussie drovers drifting from one campsite to another. Though without any stock. All of a sudden she felt homesick. Not only for Rathgarven and Grandma but also Maisie and Paddy, and most of all Sheelagh and her other friends at school. Would she ever make any friends here? Maybe once she started school she might meet some nice girls. Ronan must be lonely for his friends as well — not that he said much. But sometimes she found him sitting on the back verandah, looking vacantly across the back paddock with Dingo by his side. Only last night she had found him reading a letter, which she thought was from Clara, as she recognised the handwriting. When she asked him if it was, as usual he told her to mind her own business and go find something to do rather than annoy him. So she had left him and gone to help Ma get dinner ready.

When they had first gone to Sunday mass at the small wooden church on the hill, Lillie was sure the whole congregation was watching them with curiosity, particularly as Ma looked so much more elegant than the other women. Her mother always dressed for mass. Today she was wearing a tweed skirt, a cream blouse and a fitted green jacket. On her head she wore a smart hat with a shamrock brooch pinned on the side. Dad of course was wearing a suit and tie and Lillie's brothers wore ties as well. Lillie wore a grey skirt with a matching jacket and a pink pill-box hat that used to belong to Ma.

After mass, the congregation gathered outside the church for morning tea, where there were sandwiches and scones. Marcus and Freddie ran around playing with a few other boys, and Lillie had to admit that everyone was very friendly and welcoming. Well, nearly everyone. As she and her mother were talking to Father Fogarty near the front door of the church, a woman came out after everyone else had moved outside.

'Lovely to see you, Winifred,' Father Fogarty said to her.

When the woman had moved out of earshot, Ma asked him, 'Is that Winifred Black?'

'Yes, that's her.'

'I wonder when she last saw Finn Malone. I believe she was to look in on him from time to time when his wife left.'

'Ah, is that so? Winifred,' he called out to the woman, who turned around. 'This is Mrs O'Sullivan and her daughter, Lillie, just arrived from Ireland. Mrs O'Sullivan and her husband were friends of Finn Malone. Mr O'Sullivan was to go into partnership with him. She wondered if you had seen him recently before he died.'

Mrs Black shook her head. 'I'm sorry. I really must rush. I'm expecting my sister to ring from Melbourne.'

And with that she hurried out of the churchyard.

'Sorry about that,' Father Fogarty said. 'Apart from having to rush off, she didn't look too well, did she?'

'Dawn did say she wasn't able to see her when she was up for the funeral because her husband said she had influenza. Maybe she's still suffering.'

'Could well be so,' Father Fogarty said. 'Anyway, maybe you can ask her another time. You're bound to see her around.'

The next week Marcus and Freddie started at the one-teacher school set in a paddock next to the church. It only went up to sixth grade. As it was near the end of the school term, it was decided that if the family was still living in Gullumbindy, Ronan and Lillie would wait until the new term before starting school in Tamworth. From Ireland Ma had written to St Dominic's for Lillie; for Ronan she had written to the Christian Brothers, who Uncle Finn had told her were a 'grand lot', unlike some of the other Christian Brothers' schools, who were known for mistreating students. A couple of the Irish brothers had even got a Hurley team going in the district and Uncle Finn had played a few games with them. Both schools had agreed to take the O'Sullivans, but had also agreed it would be better for them to start in the New Year.

Lillie offered to go in with Marcus and Freddie on their first day, as Ma was needed in the hotel. The girl who normally cleaned the rooms had a doctor's appointment and Ma had to take over as there were guests arriving later that morning. And Dad was tied up with a salesman selling spirits for the bar. But both her parents had taken the boys to the school last Friday to meet the teacher and look around. When she got there, Lillie was amazed at how tiny the school was. It was much smaller than her convent primary school in Sneem. There were fifteen students all clustered into one classroom, sitting at wooden desks with hinged tops. The names of the children who'd sat at them over the years were carved into them. The teacher, Mr Sloane, taught all six grades. A tall, gangly stick of a man, he was dressed in a dark blue, slightly grubby woollen jumper, a not altogether white shirt, a blue tie and a pair of grey flannel trousers that barely covered his bony ankles. On his feet he had a pair of clunky brown shoes that badly needed a polish. When he greeted Lillie and her brothers she noticed the blue eyes behind his thick tortoiseshell glasses looked tired. His hair stood on end and he carried a cane, which he waved threateningly at the students when he wasn't using it to point to the blackboard. To Lillie it seemed as though he'd had one too many years teaching rowdy schoolchildren and certainly wouldn't put up with any nonsense.

Freddie took one look at him and declared, 'I don't need to go to school in Australia. I know all I want to know.'

So in the end, Lillie sat down with him for the first morning and through the lunch hour, where they perched on a log of wood under a gum tree and ate the tomato sandwiches Ma had made them that morning, sharing the crusts with the magpies and a lone horse tied to the fence under a tree, which Lillie thought must belong to one of the students. When she left Freddie after lunch he had tears in his eyes. But when she went with Dad later to pick him up, he seemed much happier and Marcus said he himself had had a bonzer day.

'I didn't get caned,' Freddie announced with relief. 'One of the big boys did. He squealed like a pig.'

Lillie tweaked his nose. 'What did he do to get caned?'

'He pulled one of the girl's pigtails and made her cry. It must've really hurt. She cried for ages.'

'Couldn't have hurt that much,' Marcus scoffed. 'Not as much as being caned.'

And once again Marcus and Freddie started to squabble until Dad put an end to it.

Lillie wondered what her own school would be like. Would the nuns cane the students like Mr Sloane did? Or would they be kind and gentle like Lillie's favourite nun at the convent in Cork? Although she was keen to start and make new friends, she was nervous that the girls had all known each other forever and might make her feel like an outsider because she came from Ireland and spoke differently.

Chapter 15

Ronan was lying on his bed in the sleep-out listening to Bobby Darin singing 'Multiplication' on his transistor radio and reading a letter he'd got from Clara last week. No one knew he'd got her letter; Ma had asked him to go down and check if there was any mail at the post office and Clara's letter was on the top. On the way home he'd stopped off at the small deserted playground and sat on the wooden swing to read it.

How incredible to think when you read this you'll be in Australia. I still can't believe your parents sold up like that and took you all over there. It must have been so sudden — when I was with you at Rathgarven no one mentioned you were thinking of doing that. When Mummy rang and Aunt Kathleen told her what was happening, Mummy said she couldn't work out why your Dad would do such a thing. Oh, Ronan, I'll really miss Rathgarven and I think of you and the last time I was there all the time. I hope you do as well. All I want is for you to kiss me again. For you to play the harp and me to sing. Every time I think of us I get a warm, fuzzy feeling inside. But how can we be together again when you're way over there and I'm here in dreary England? Mummy hasn't gone back to India and is giving me the heebie-jeebies by insisting I go to all these fancy house parties so I can meet the 'right' people. Mind you, I think it's more her who wants to meet those boring, stuffy types, hoping it'll give her a step up in the world. I know I shouldn't be so mean, but she really is the pits sometimes. Not like darling Aunt Kathleen. You're so lucky to have her as a mother.

Ronan was annoyed with Clara's mother. He'd always thought she was pushy. This proved it. And he was jealous of those 'right people'. Not only would they be rich, unlike the O'Sullivans, he was also worried Clara might fall for one of them. He touched his lips, where Clara's lips had been. To think of her dancing with a lot of toffy fellas irritated him no end. And what if one of those fellas kissed her the way he had kissed her? And gave her a warm, fuzzy feeling just as he had? If she were here now it would be so much easier to cope with everything after Uncle Finn's suicide.

When his parents had told him Uncle Finn had shot himself, Ronan was flabbergasted. But as he knew Finn had had a problem with drink he supposed it wasn't beyond belief. Even so, he must have been desperate to do what he did and Ronan felt sorry for him. And sorry for Ma and Dad, to lose a friend like that. Over and over he asked himself what would happen to them now that they were stuck here with no proper job for his father and no house of their own. He knew Australia would be different to Ireland. But living here was like living on a different planet. There were parts of it he really liked, such as fishing for yabbies in the river, going up to the scrubby hill behind the village and shooting rabbits with Mr Hogan's gun, and cooking on the makeshift barbeque he'd made out of stones in the back garden. It was certainly hotter than Ireland but the flies were a pain. And he missed his friends from school. Here in Gullumbindy there were hardly any boys his own age and even those few who did live here were at school all week. To fill in the time he did odd jobs around the place, chopping wood for both the Hogans' house and the hotel, and he was thinking of putting a notice up in the corner store to say he'd mow people's lawns for them. In one way he couldn't wait to start school up in Tamworth. Then at least he might meet some fellas he could be friendly with. He also missed playing rugby, and while he hit the tennis ball up against the garage wall, it wasn't the same as having a court to play on.

So he was pleased when his parents called him into the living room one night after dinner and told him he was starting school the next week. 'I went to see the Christian Brothers in Tamworth when I was there this afternoon,' his father said to him. He lit his pipe and took a puff. 'As Finn said, they seem like a grand lot. And the boys looked happy enough running around and playing rugby. After they heard what had happened with Finn they made a place straightaway for you, rather than waiting for the New Year. As it's a fair way to come home each night and you'll no doubt have after-school activities, like rugby, it's probably better to stay in Tamworth during the week. Come home at weekends.'

'So it's a boarding school?'

'No. But the head brother told me about a family who have a boy at the school. They have a spare room and would like you to stay.'

'So I'd board with another family?'

'Yes,' his mother said. 'Dad's going up again tomorrow, so you can go take a look. By the sounds of what they told Dad you'd be in the second last year of high school. So it won't be for long. I'd come but that young girl who does the cleaning at the hotel rang in to say her mother's sick and she can't come in till later tomorrow. Lillie and I will have to clean the rooms in the morning, as there's a full house tonight and tomorrow.'

'We'll need to leave about nine, as I want to be home to be in the bar by five,' James added. 'Nancy's son will run it until then.'

Ronan wasn't sure what he thought about living in another family's house, but it seemed as though he didn't have much choice.

'So it's all organised then?'

'In the circumstances it seems for the best.'

His mother smiled. 'If you really hate it we can try and arrange something else.'

'I'm sure it'll be okay.'

But as he walked back to the sleep-out he wished it was a boarding school and he didn't have to live with another family. What if he and the other boy didn't get on? There wasn't much he could do except to go along with it.

***

At nine the next morning he and his father set off for Tamworth.

As he drove, his father asked, 'Have you heard anything from Clara lately? I was wondering about her and Jessica.'

Ronan glanced at his father. It was unlike him to inquire about Jessica. Even when Clara was staying with them at Rathgarven he hardly ever mentioned her name.

'I had one letter. They're still in London. Clara said her mother's getting her to mix with the "in crowd".'

'Oh is she? That'd be Jessica all right.'

'You're not that keen on her, are you?'

James hesitated. 'Your mother likes her. That's the main thing. I must admit I find her a bit over the top. And spoilt. Luckily Clara seems nothing like her at all.'

Ronan had to agree: Clara was very different to her overbearing mother.

'Maybe Clara's more like her father,' he said.

'Could well be so,' James said. 'I never met the man, so who knows.'

When they arrived at the school, they pulled up under a gum tree out the front. It was a brown brick building built around a central asphalt playground. Some of the students looked as though they were going on an outing in their blue blazers, long grey trousers and straw boaters. Others were kicking a football around and a few were sitting on narrow benches eating from their lunchboxes. For the first time in his life Ronan felt shy; much shyer than he had on his first day at school in Cork.

He got out of the car and walked around to join his father, who was knocking his pipe against his heel.

'Well,' James said. 'What do you think?'

'Looks okay.'

As they walked to the front door, Ronan's heart beat hard against his chest. What could be worse than starting at a new school where everyone else knew each other? At least in Cork it was the beginning of the school year when he had started and there were a number of other new students starting as well. Here he would be the only new one.

Inside, they were met by Brother Michael, a middle-aged man with short dark grey hair dressed in a flowing black robe with a tassel around his waist.

First of all he asked Ronan a number of questions about his studies in Ireland, then he said, 'Being nearly seventeen, you should probably be in the class between the Intermediate and Leaving Certificates. So that's where I'll slot you in and see how you go. But come,' he added, 'I'll show you around and introduce you to some of the boys.'

When they went out into the playground he was introduced to a couple of the boys who would be in his class, including Dave, who was the son of the family he was to billet with, who appeared a decent enough bloke. Many of the students seemed to have heard he was coming and despite his thoughts to the contrary, they did their best to make him feel at home, asking about Ireland and if he played rugby. By the time they left, Ronan felt he might fit in all right after all, although sure as eggs there'd be one or two boys who'd give him a hard time.

When they were back in the car, James looked at him anxiously. 'Appears a nice enough place.'

'Yeah it does, doesn't it?'

'Now,' he continued, placing his hand on Ronan's shoulder, 'let's go grab a bite of lunch. Then we'll head around to the Thompson house. Mr Thompson will be at work but Mrs Thompson will be there.'

They parked in the main street of town, which was lined with tall trees, and found a milk bar selling takeaway food. At the counter they each ordered a hamburger with the lot and a bottle of lemonade, which they took back to the car; James had decided they would eat their lunch down by the river.

'Those weeping willows across the water remind me of the part of this river below Eureka Park homestead,' he said, as they sat on a timber bench under a Casuarina tree.

'Have you been back since you found Uncle Finn's body?'

'No. The police have closed the whole place up while things are sorted out, like his will and such. Besides… what's the point? It would just make me lament what could have been. No, we're better to try and make a new start. That's why I've got feelers out for another house. And a job.'

Ronan took a bite of his hamburger and chewed slowly, watching a family of ducks swimming on the river. Downstream a man was fishing out of a small wooden rowboat, making him think of his rowboat at Rathgarven. He shook his head to try to dislodge the image.

'And if neither turns up?'

'Thankfully we've a roof over our heads for the time being. And I still have a bit of money left over from the sale of Rathgarven and the furniture, together with what the Hogans are paying us.' He scrunched up the paper bag his hamburger had been in. 'Now when you've finished eating we'll have a quick drive around town before we head to the Thompsons.'

To Ronan Tamworth appeared to be divided into two. On one side of the main street below the lofty hill the houses seemed much older and were mostly brick or sprawling weatherboards with wonderful rambling gardens and lots of tall trees. The other side of town seemed to be less affluent, with the houses and gardens not so grand. As it was school time there were few children playing in the streets, but here and there grown-ups stood in their front gardens gossiping with their neighbours. All in all the streets were much wider than in Ireland. And there were different sorts of trees and thick colourful bushes.

They easily found the Thompsons' house with its neat garden. Mrs Thompson greeted them at the door. Her hair was greying and she wore a blue twin-set and a pleated tweed skirt.

'So this is Ronan,' she said with a welcoming smile.

'We're very grateful for your generosity in having Ronan stay,' James said. 'It's more than kind of you.'

'Dave will be delighted to have the company,' she replied.

'I met him up at the school,' Ronan said.

'I'm sure you two will get on like a house on fire.' She laughed. 'Nonetheless… so you won't be on top of each other, we've given you a separate room. Our eldest son, Andrew, normally sleeps there, but he joined the Navy last year. It'll be good to have someone in the room again. Come and I'll show you.'

The room was at the back of the house with a view through to the clothesline. It was obvious from the posters on the wall that Andrew was a rugby fan, which made Ronan feel at home.

'Does Dave play rugby too?' he asked Mrs Thompson.

'He certainly does. Why? Do you?'

Ronan nodded. 'I did back in Cork.'

'Well there you go, you've got something in common already. Now,' she said, pointing to the living room, 'let's get you a cool drink. And,' she added, glancing at Ronan's father, 'a nice cup of tea for you, Mr O'Sullivan.'

'Thank you,' James said. 'That would be very welcome.'

Later, as they drove home, Ronan thought that although Dave seemed nice enough, and so did his mother, it would be quite strange living with another family. An Australian family.

Chapter 16

The following Friday evening Kathleen was helping out in the hotel's dining room. A group of women had come in for a quick meal before going to play bingo in the village hall, and a woman, her husband and little son came in and sat down at the table in the corner. Kathleen didn't mind helping out in the evenings as long as Lillie was at home with Marcus and Freddie. It gave her a chance to talk to the local people, who were all so friendly and full of sympathy for the O'Sullivans' predicament. It turned out the couple with the young son she was serving had a sheep station out of town and were waiting for the school bus from Tamworth to bring their daughter back from St Dominic's, the school Lillie was to go to.

'The school rang the post office to say the bus has been delayed with engine trouble,' the woman said, 'so we thought we might as well fill in the time here while we're waiting.'

'Our Lillie's to start at St Dominic's in the New Year,' Kathleen said, pouring her a tumbler of lemonade and her husband a beer. She explained how they had not long arrived from Ireland and the school suggested they leave it until the new term for Lillie to start.

'Oh. How old is she?' the woman asked.

'Fourteen.'

'The same as our Deb.'

Kathleen poured the little boy a glass of milk. 'It'd be great if they could meet before Lillie starts next term,' she said eagerly.

'Well, I've got to go through to Quirindi tomorrow. Why don't I see if Deb can come with me? I can drop her off and they can get to know each other.'

Kathleen smiled. 'That would be wonderful. I'm sure Lillie would love that.'

And so it was agreed that Deb would be dropped off at ten the following morning.

'Ma!' Lillie exclaimed when Kathleen told her what she had organised. 'How could you? I bet the last thing Deb wants is to be saddled with the new girl.'

'If you don't get on, you don't have to take it any further. But it'd be nice for you to know someone when you start.'

'I suppose so,' Lillie said reluctantly.

The next morning at ten Deb and her mother arrived at the front door. 'I'll be back about 11.30,' she said, giving Deb a kiss. 'Have fun.'

Kathleen thought Deb was lovely; she had a bubbly personality and shiny brown hair with a deep fringe, which fell over mischievous deep-set eyes. She was a good two inches taller than Lillie and possibly a bit slimmer. No matter how Lillie tried, she still carried a bit of extra weight, which Kathleen knew annoyed her no end. At first Lillie was shy, but after a few minutes with Deb chatting nineteen to the dozen, she seemed to relax.

After Kathleen saw them off to Allen's tiny milk bar next to the corner store, which served ice creams, lemonades and milkshakes to its customers at its Laminex tables, she went to the kitchen. As she listened to the country and western singer Slim Dusty on the transistor, she looked through the mail that James had picked up from the post office. Yesterday there had been an aerogram from Alice, who said she was settling into the hotel, but missed them all enormously and hoped it was all working out with Finn.

I'm still doing my writing, but rather than writing about country life, I'm writing about living in a private hotel in Dublin. I try to make it a bit humorous. The magazines seem to like it. I got a little bit of money last week from one and have sent a parcel by sea mail for the children at Christmas and enclosed a couple of my articles. Do hope the parcel arrives safely.

This reminded Kathleen that Christmas was only a couple of months away. Would they still be living here when it came around? Although they had a little money left, and they were getting the small wage from the Hogans for looking after the hotel, she worried that they would soon be scraping the barrel. How would she be able to buy the children any Christmas presents? Would James have found a job by then? A house? When the Hogans came back they would be more or less out on the street. The thought of it kept her awake at night, as she knew it did James, too. Although they were both sad for what Finn had done, at times Kathleen was dreadfully angry with him. She and James had decided not to tell Alice about his death at this stage. When the family were settled somewhere, that would be the time to tell her. Otherwise she would only worry about them. In any case, they were loath to tell her, or anyone else back in Ireland for that matter, that Finn had shot himself. And to say he had just died would be a lie. As far as Kathleen was aware it hadn't been reported in any of the Irish newspapers. Even if it was, they would never reveal it was suicide. She had no idea whether Finn's parents knew their son was dead.

Kathleen desperately missed Ronan now he was billeted with the Thompsons, but she was happy he was getting a good education. On Sunday evening when they had dropped him off at the Thompsons she had met both Mr and Mrs Thompson and their son Dave, and took to them all enormously, so she was confident he was being well looked after. When he'd phoned on Tuesday he'd said he was enjoying school and had already made a few friends in addition to Dave, who he really liked. He had even had a game of rugby that afternoon and had signed up for a tennis game. Kathleen cherished all her children and liked to think she had no favourites, but deep down her eldest held a special place in her heart that no one else could touch. That was one of the reasons she'd been so upset when James had lost Rathgarven — it should have gone to Ronan. Although times in Ireland were hard now, who knew what it would have been like when Ronan took over.

Idly she picked up an aerogram and realised it was addressed to her. She glanced at the postmark. India. She smiled; she should have recognised the handwriting. She grabbed a knife and slit it open.

Dearest Kate — Only Jessica called her Kate.

Well, how goes it all? How's the big adventure in the outback of the colonies? I'm dying of curiosity and can't wait to get your first letter. I got your postcard from Naples. It looks as frenzied as Calcutta. How is James getting on? And the divine Finn? Has he turned James into an Aussie cowboy yet? And how about my darling Lillie? And of course Ronan and the little ones too?

I was sad to leave Clara in London and come back here to stinking hot Calcutta. I tried to get her invitations to the best sort of parties while I was there. Although she went to some, I don't think her heart was really in it. Silly girl. She is so grown up now, isn't she? Seventeen going on twenty. But she does look beautiful. It's a bit like watching an orchid come into flower.

Phillip's business is battling, as ever. And of course money is desperate. Nonetheless we still seem to be at one ball or cocktail party after another, which really tests my wardrobe. Last night we went to a reception for Lord Mountbatten at Government House. I must say I find him

If only you knew, Kathleen thought. She wished with all her heart that Jessica was here with her now and they could sit down and have a girly gossip. That Jessica could hold her in her arms and tell her everything would be fine, like she'd done in India just before the war ended, when Kathleen's world had come crashing down. And before that when Kathleen's parents had died; it was Jessica who had been there for her, helping her through the heartbreaking funeral and afterwards. So, much as she annoyed Kathleen at times, she had to admit she had been a good friend over the years.

But Jessica wasn't here with Kathleen. Jessica was in Kathleen's cherished India. Without warning Kathleen's mind slid back to the Tollygunge Club in Calcutta all those years ago when they were trying to pretend things were normal during the war. The fateful evening when Jessica had introduced her to the squadron leader in their midst. Kathleen remembered his face, how the soft

Indian light caught his cheekbones, how she blushed when her eyes locked with his and every part of her body flamed with desire. She remembered each treasured moment of their time together, the motorbike rides, the feel of his body warm against hers, his breath upon her cheeks when he turned to her and smiled, his eyes aglow with fun.

Stop this silly reminiscing, she told herself, refolding Jessica's letter. She made herself a cup of coffee and gazed out of the window as she drank it, watching the washing flapping in the breeze. The Second World War seemed so far away from where she stood now. In reality it wasn't even twenty years ago.

She went to her bedroom and opened the bottom drawer of the dressing table, where she kept the money tin she'd brought from Rathgarven. The key was in her make-up bag where she kept it. She was about to open the tin and once more look at the letters inside, but something made her stop. It felt disloyal to James.

She remembered when they first met. She had been surprised when James came up and introduced himself at her Aunt Mildred's place on the Kenmare River all those years ago, before the war.

'James O'Sullivan,' he'd said. 'I believe you know my friend Finn Malone in Calcutta.'

'Finn Malone. Of course.' Kathleen had paused and given him a smile. 'I don't suppose you've been to Calcutta to visit him? Otherwise I might've met you.'

James shook his head. 'I'm afraid I've been rather tied up here in Kerry. Keeping the home fires burning, you might say.' He looked at her empty glass. 'What if I fill that up for you and we can have a chat?'

The next time she had seen James was when she had come back to Ireland after the war had ended. The night he asked her to marry him was still vivid.

'Thank you, James,' she had said. 'You're very kind.' She gave him a small smile and shook her head. 'But I'm afraid I'll have to turn you down.' She had looked across to the window where the full moon was rising over the cove. 'You, of all people, know why.'

It took a week for James to finally convince her to be his wife. It was the day after she had been to see Rathgarven and fallen under its spell. As it was so soon after the war and rationing was still in force, they decided to go up to Dublin and get married there, rather than have a large wedding in Kerry.

Now, making an effort to bring her mind back to the present, she finished her coffee, washed the cup under the tap, checked the loaf of soda bread in the oven and went outside to get the washing off the line. She wondered how Lillie was getting on with Deb. She hoped they would become friends, for she imagined Lillie was missing her friends back in Ireland. Particularly Sheelagh. As she was about to go inside, over the side fence she caught sight of a woman walking down the street towards the post office. She was wearing a tartan skirt and a navy blue pullover. Even with her head bowed, she looked familiar.

Kathleen went to the fence and called out. 'Winifred?'

The woman turned her head for a second and Kathleen waved.

'It's Kathleen O'Sullivan. I saw you up at the church when we were talking to Father Fogarty.'

Kathleen thought she might ask her in for a cup of tea. But Winifred kept on walking. Kathleen was going to call out again, then stopped. It was obvious that this friend of Dawn's didn't want to know her. So she let it go and went back inside to fold the washing.

***

'I like your dress,' Deb said when she and Lillie had settled at the Laminex table by the window in Allen's milk bar. They were the only people in there, apart from the woman behind the counter who was wiping the benches. 'Did you bring it from Ireland?'

Lillie glanced down at her pink seersucker dress, which she'd always quite liked. Until Clara had come to Rathgarven in her latest fashions from London. After that she'd thought it was dull and boring.

'Thank you,' she said. 'I think Ma got it in Killarney. There was quite a good shop in the main street.'

'I live in jeans,' Deb said, patting the stone-washed jeans she was wearing. 'Not much point in wearing a dress out where I live.' She laughed. 'Don't think I even own one, apart from my school uniform. Oh... and a couple Mum makes me keep for mass.'

'Is your parents' sheep station very big?'

Deb nodded. 'Thousands of acres.'

'You've got to be joking!'

'No.'

'Sounds like it's the size of the whole of County Kerry where I come from.'

At that moment a couple of girls parted the plastic strips that hung in the doorway to keep the flies out and entered the milk bar. One of them was wearing a short flouncy floral dress like one Lillie had seen in a magazine. The other one wore a pair of jeans similar to the pair Deb was wearing. She also had a check shirt a bit like Deb's.

'Hiya Deb,' they both said at once, before heading to the counter. 'Good to see ya.'

'Hi there,' Deb replied. She leaned over and whispered to Lillie, 'They go to St Dominic's. The one wearing jeans is okay. The other one's a real bully.'

Lillie tried to get another look at the bully's face as she heard her order an ice cream and lemonade. But she had her back to her so she couldn't see.

'So do you like school?' she asked Deb. 'I can't wait to start. I'm getting really bored at home, especially since my brother Ronan's started at Christian Brothers in Tamworth. He's away all week.'

'School's sort of okay. Some of the nuns are great, others are a bit weird.'

Lillie fiddled with her straw in the aluminium milkshake container.

'I wonder if I'll be in your class.'

'I reckon if you've come from another country they won't know what class you should be in so you'll have to sit an exam.'

'Really! I hadn't thought of that. I wouldn't have a clue whether Ireland's as up to date as Australia. Do you do Latin? We had to.'

'Yeah. And I hate it. *Amo, amas, amat…*'

'I know. God knows when we'll ever use it.'

When the other girls had got their orders and were walking out they stopped at Lillie and Deb's table.

'They're putting on a screening of *Jedda* at the church hall tonight,' the one in the jeans said to Deb. 'You going?'

Deb shook her head. 'Mum and Dad have visitors coming over. In any case I can't imagine they'd want to drive me in unless they want to see it.'

'I'll tell you what it's like. It's supposed to be really good.'

'That'd be great,' Deb said.

'See ya back at school on Monday,' the other girl said, eyeing Lillie.

Lillie thought she was hoping Deb would introduce her. Either Deb had forgotten her name or she didn't want to.

After they'd gone Lillie giggled. 'She does look a bit as though you wouldn't want to get on the wrong side of her.'

'Yeah. She's a real bitch. I knew she wanted me to introduce you, but,' she grimaced, 'if I did that she'd want to know the gory details of what happened to Mr Malone. Soon it'd be all over the school. She's that sort. A real gossip. So's her father. He's often drunk out of his mind. Her mother's okay though.'

'Well, sounds as though I need to stay clear of her.'

'Yeah. I would if I were you.'

'Anyway,' Lillie said, finishing the last of her milkshake, 'if there's another good movie on at the hall here in Gullumbindy sometime soon maybe you could spend the night at our place.'

Deb smiled. 'That'd be great.'

As they strolled back along the lane a little while later, Deb asked her if she missed her friends from school back in Ireland. And if she'd had a boyfriend.

'Not really. I met this fellow on the school bus, Seamus, who I really liked. He's migrated with his family to Canada. Things are so bad in Ireland. That's why we had to come here.' Which, Lillie supposed, was in a roundabout sort of way the reason her family had come here. 'What about you? Have you got a boyfriend?'

'I like a fellow at the Christian Brothers who I see on the school bus. But I don't reckon he even knows I exist.'

Lillie smiled. 'Bet he does.'

'I'll point him out when you start school.'

And as they waited on the verandah back at the Hogans' house for Deb's mother to arrive, Lillie really hoped that Deb would come and stay the night sometime. It would be great to have another friend to talk to, like she did with Sheelagh. Deb was nothing like Sheelagh at all, but Lillie liked her a lot.

Chapter 17

James was in the bar polishing glasses when he took a phone call.

'Can you start next week?' It was the manager of a farm machinery outlet in Quirindi. 'You'll be selling our Massey Ferguson tractors. It'll involve a bit of travelling around the local properties.'

James sighed with relief. This place was one of many he'd applied for a job. He had been worried sick about what would happen when the Hogans came back. Despite what they were earning from the hotel, money was running short and what they had brought from Ireland would soon be whittled away. There was hardly a moment in every day when he didn't fret about the future. Hardly a minute when he didn't think of what he'd done in losing Rathgarven. And how desperate Finn must have been to do what he did, leaving James and his family high and dry. James had feared that if he couldn't find a job around the district, the family would need to move somewhere else. He had been loath to contemplate that move with Ronan having started school up in Tamworth and Marcus and Freddie ensconced at the local school. This job offer could alleviate things considerably.

'Give it some thought and ring me in the morning,' the manager said. 'We'd like to have you on our team.'

'I could do it along with running the bar until the Hogans get back,' James pointed out to Kathleen when he found her in the dining room laying the tables. 'During the week the bar is never busy through the day. Maybe you and Nancy's son could cope. And with two incomes we'd be able to look around for a house to rent.'

'But those long hours will kill you,' Kathleen said, placing a knife and fork down.

'Nothing else might come up.'

'I'm sure the offer will still be there in the morning.' Kathleen picked up a serviette and folded it in two. 'Maybe we should talk about it overnight.'

James nodded. 'Yes, that's not a bad idea. I told him I'd ring first thing.'

Kathleen smiled. 'It's great that he's offered it to you, James. I'm very proud of you.'

As he walked back to the bar James did feel a bit chuffed. He'd never really applied for a job before as he'd always worked at Rathgarven. And even though this job wasn't offering much in the way of pay, it was a start. Back at the bar he saw a blue car pull up out the front of the hotel. A man wearing a dark suit and carrying a brown leather briefcase got out and came into the bar.

'Mr O'Sullivan?' the man asked as he approached. 'I was told I would find you here.'

'Yes, that's me,' James said.

'Could I have a moment of your time?' The man held out a hand. 'Colin Towers is the name.'

'How do you do,' James said, taking his hand. 'How can I help you?'

'Does your wife happen to be around? It'd be good if I could see you both together.'

'She's in the dining room laying the tables.'

'Are there other staff here?'

James looked at his watch. 'They won't be in for an hour or so. But what's this about?'

'It'd be best if I could talk to you together.'

James looked confused. 'About what?'

'Finn Malone.'

'Finn? What about him?'

'I was his lawyer. As I said it might be better to talk to you and your wife together.'

It was obvious that he wasn't going to say anything more without Kathleen being present so James beckoned for him to sit down while he went to find Kathleen, who slipped off her apron and smoothed down her hair. 'I wonder what on earth he wants. You'd best show him in.'

'You see,' Colin Towers said as few minutes later, pulling some papers out of his briefcase and putting them on the table where the three of them sat, 'Mr Malone came to see me a while back. He asked me to draw up a will.'

'Oh!' James said. 'Didn't he already have a will?'

'No, and it'd been worrying him.' The lawyer fiddled with his papers. 'He said if he'd dragged you and your family all the way out to Australia and something happened to him, he wanted to make sure you were looked after.' He paused and gave an awkward cough. 'You were aware he had a drinking problem?'

James and Kathleen glanced at each other. 'Yes, we were,' James said. 'But what's that got to do with things?'

'Mr Malone was an honest man. He told me that much as he tried not to give in to the drink, sometimes he went on a bender and didn't know where he'd been or what he'd done. He was nervous something might happen to him when he was — well, how would you put it? — without his faculties. And you'd be left stranded, so to speak.'

He picked up a couple of pieces of paper and handed them to James, pointing to a passage on the front page. 'Perhaps if you read this it'll explain matters.'

Both Kathleen and James looked to where his finger pointed.

In the event of my death I bequeath the property Eureka Park and all its stock, buildings, outbuildings and machinery, to my good friend James O'Sullivan. I also bequeath to James twenty thousand pounds so that he can

James was too stunned to say anything. His heart beat hard against
his chest and for a second he thought his head might explode.
Beside him Kathleen took a huge breath and let it out again. She
lifted her head and stared at the lawyer, her eyes wide in
astonishment.

'I don't believe it,' she spluttered. 'When did he write
this?'

'When you told him you were coming to Eureka Park.
Perhaps when you've had a chance to digest it we can talk it
through.'

James held the piece of paper in his hand, reading it over
and over. Like Kathleen, he found it difficult to fathom what he
was reading. Surely Finn would have left his assets to a member of
his family? He may have fallen out with his father and have no
siblings, but what about his mother? Had he totally disregarded
her? Or did he think his parents had enough money of their own?
Was this his way of getting back at them for more or less
disowning him when he wouldn't study law and join his father's
business? Was it some sort of joke?

'What about Finn's parents?' he finally asked when he felt
he was in some sort of control of his emotions. 'I would've thought
he'd leave his estate to them.'

'He told me they are well looked after. You may already
know that Mr Malone's grandfather was a wealthy man.'

James nodded. 'I knew he was well-off.'

'When he died he left Mr Malone's parents a large sum of
money, as well as the house they live in at Cork. Mr Malone got

none of that. Whatever he's made has been entirely of his own doing.'

Colin Towers played with his Parker pen, taking the top off and putting it back on again. He cleared his throat. 'A while back Mr Malone took himself to a clinic for alcoholics in Brisbane run by the Catholic Church. He was determined to try and cure himself before you arrived. He told me that before he went he'd sent his horses to a good horse stud belonging to a mate of his north of Scone. He said he'd get them back when you came.'

'Oh. So that explains why there were no horses,' Kathleen said.

'Yes,' the lawyer said. 'He reckoned he gave the manager notice before he went to Brisbane. Said there wasn't much point in having him around if there were no horses and you were arriving shortly.'

James nodded. 'I see.' He placed his hand on Kathleen's knee and looked at the lawyer. 'Did he appear to be drinking when he came back from Ireland?'

'Yes he did.'

'Oh!'

'Before he went he reckoned he'd given up for good. Had it beat. Even so, he told me he'd gone to see an old acquaintance in London on his way back here who enticed him to have one drink. And I wouldn't have to tell you what happens when an alcoholic succumbs to one drink.'

James felt the breath disappear from his lungs and a cold shiver ran down his spine. Was it Jessica who had enticed Finn to have a drink? Jessica, who loved to drink nearly as much as Finn. Often when she came to stay at Rathgarven, she would retire to bed quite tipsy, having helped herself continually to the drinks trolley. She has so much to answer for, he thought. Then again, so did he — allowing Finn to go to her in London to do his dirty work, instead of doing it himself.

'Jessica said he'd popped into see her,' Kathleen said. 'But surely it wouldn't have been her who gave him a drink. She knew he was an alcoholic. It must've been at a club or something.'

'Yes,' James said, trying to hide his anger, despite his fears. 'You're probably right.'

'One of the reasons he chose the place in Brisbane,' Colin Towers said, 'was because he was allowed to take his dog, Dingo, with him.'

There was a long pause before James put the piece of paper back down on the table and picked up his pipe. He filled it and took a long draw. 'He must have been up in Brisbane for quite a while for Eureka Park to get so run-down. It sounds as though he was in a bad way.'

'He was there for a month after he came back from Ireland. I must admit, once his wife, Dawn, left Eureka Park, he seemed to lose interest in the upkeep of the place. Batching on his own, he let the house and grounds go. I went out there a couple of times and could see it deteriorating. Doesn't take long in this part of the world for things to go downhill. Mind you, he was meticulous with his horses.' A pause. 'He wrote me a letter from Brisbane, saying he was progressing well and would be home soon, and he'd come into the office to sign some documents to do with his tax. I'd been after him to do that. I imagine he hadn't been back at Eureka Park long before —' He stopped talking and fiddled with the lid of his briefcase. 'Before he did himself in. He never did come to see me.'

'Didn't the police try to contact you when he died?' Kathleen asked.

The lawyer nodded. 'I've been away bushwalking in the south-west of Tasmania. I run a one-man show. When I got back, I soon realised what had happened. I've had a few interviews with the police since then.'

'Do they know about this?' James asked, eyeing the document on the table and putting his pipe down in the ashtray. He had a dreadful thought: would he be accused of Finn's murder? Of making it look like suicide so he could inherit?

'Indeed they do. They suggested it was up to me to tell you. They didn't feel it was any of their business.' He smiled. 'I presume they didn't think you'd done your friend in for the money. It appears he was well and truly dead before you arrived at Gullumbindy.'

James stood up and went to the window. Dingo, who always followed him to the hotel, was lying in the sun fast asleep. Not far from where he lay a cockatoo pecked at a fallen apple. James took out a handkerchief and wiped his eyes. He felt an agonising sadness for his old friend. Then an incredible anger rose up within him, threatening to choke him. He wanted to literally wring Jessica's neck. After what she had told him at their meeting at the Shelbourne about what she had done in India, he was surer than ever that she could have enticed Finn off the wagon. Even going to Brisbane to dry out in time for the family to arrive hadn't worked. In the end the demon drink had got its own shocking way.

It was nearly forty years since James and Finn had first met on that train on their way to school. And never once had there been a cross word between them. The many times when Finn was at his worst, he never abused James, even when James sometimes tried to take his car keys away from him when he thought he had had too much to drink.

'Should we not be downing another wee drop before we hit the road?' Finn would chuckle, patting James on the back and beckoning to the barman.

When James would tell him he'd had enough to drink and finally coax him home in his own car, the next day Finn would thank him for looking after him. 'Ah, you're a good man, James O'Sullivan. Why you put up with a drunken sod like me would be anyone's guess. But make no mistake, I be looking out for you. The same as you be looking out for me.'

And in the end that is exactly what Finn had done, leaving James his most treasured possession.

James took a deep breath and returned to the table where Kathleen and Colin Towers sat watching him. He picked up his pipe and fiddled with it. Sad as James was for what had happened to Finn, he couldn't help feeling relieved that now there was a way out of their situation. Feeling guilty for those thoughts, he turned to Kathleen and put an arm around her. He rested his lips on the top of her head and let his tears fall onto her lovely hair.

'Finn …' he began, but could go no further.

'I'm sure all of this takes a bit of getting used to,' Colin Towers said. 'Particularly under such sad circumstances. What's say I head back into town and you come and see me in the morning.' He took out a black diary. 'Shall we say ten?'

James looked at Kathleen. 'Ten sounds fine,' she said.

The lawyer stood up and James saw him to the door.

When he came back into the room, Kathleen was still sitting with the will in her hand.

'I can't believe what's happened,' she said, handing him the will. 'It's too much to take in.' She sighed. 'You stay here… I'll go to the kitchen and make us a cup of tea.'

'A cup of tea sounds like a good idea.'

When she returned with the teapot, Kathleen said, 'We could use the money to buy something else in Ireland. It wouldn't be as good as Rathgarven, but I'm sure we could find something suitable.'

James was in a quandary. If they did sell up and return to Ireland they would be closer to his mother. Then again, wouldn't that be letting Finn down? After all, he had specifically mentioned that the twenty thousand pounds was to be used on Eureka Park. And would it not be better to put that disaster with Donoghue behind them? Start afresh? What better way to do that than in another country, away from the memories of what had been lost?

Should there be any chance of getting Rathgarven back he might feel differently, but that was such a remote possibility he put it right out of his mind. If they took over Eureka Park and made it into a thriving business, that would allow the family to return to Ireland to visit from time to time. And his mother would understand his decision.

He looked at Kathleen. 'I think we owe it to Finn to at least give it a go at Eureka.'

'But you know nothing about running a horse stud.'

'I can always learn. Maybe the fellow who's looking after the horses at his stud can teach me a thing or two.'

Kathleen smiled. 'You'd really like to give it a go, wouldn't you?'

James nodded. 'Yes. I think I would. Still, if you feel strongly against it, I'm prepared to bow to your wishes.'

Kathleen picked up the teapot, poured a cup and handed it to James. 'We're here now in Australia. To go back would be sort of giving in, wouldn't it? So why don't we have a shot at it? See how we go. If it turns out to be too much we can always relook at it then.'

James smiled at her. 'The homestead's in a great spot by the river, isn't it?'

'Yes it is,' Kathleen said. 'And with lots of work I'm sure we can make a lovely home for the family.'

'It'll all be a huge challenge. But I think we're up to it.'

Kathleen nodded. 'I wonder what the children will make of it.'

'Let's mull it over. Tell them tomorrow when Ronan's home from school.'

'That's probably a good idea,' Kathleen said. 'We might have second thoughts during the night. In the meantime you'd better let that man know you can't take the job he's offered you.'

'Yes,' James said. 'I'd best do that.'

Sitting with her brothers in the kitchen after dinner the next night, having been dragged from the telephone where she was talking to Deb, Lillie gasped when her parents told her what had happened. 'You've got to be joking. We own Eureka Park? All of it?'

'Yes,' her father said. 'It would appear so.'

Lillie wasn't sure what she thought of that. Over the last few weeks she had held onto the hope that if things were really bad here and Dad couldn't get a job and there was no house to live in when the Hogans came back, they would have to go back to Ireland. Now they owned Eureka Park they would definitely be staying in Australia.

'So we don't have to live in someone else's house forever,' Freddie exclaimed in excitement. 'We've got a home of our own.'

'We do,' Ma said, casting a glance at Ronan, who sat quietly at the end of the table. In fact he was so quiet Lillie wondered if he'd heard what Dad had said. Or was he thinking the same thing as Lillie? *There goes any chance of going home to Ireland.*

'What's the place like?' Marcus asked, as if he was trying to play it cool.

'It's on a river with lots of trout and other fish,' Ma said. 'And although there were no horses when we went out there, we believe they're away being looked after at the stud of a friend of Uncle Finn's. We can get them back.'

Again Ma looked at Ronan, who was playing with the salt and pepper shakers.

'I can't believe Uncle Finn left it all to us,' he said, lifting his head. 'I mean, no matter what the lawyer told you, it seems as though he'd planned it all, knowing he was going to die.'

'But he didn't know he was going to die,' Freddie pointed out.

Lillie was about to say, 'Yes he did,' when she remembered her younger brothers didn't know that Uncle Finn had killed himself.

'Maybe he had a premonition,' Ronan said.

'What's a prem.. on.. iten?' Freddie asked.

'A feeling that something was going to happen to him,' Ronan said. He glanced at his father. 'Sad as it is that Uncle Finn has died, it sorta gets us out of a sticky situation, doesn't it? I hope one day I've got a friend like that.' He paused. 'So when can we move in?'

'When the Hogans get back,' Dad said, standing up and putting his hand on Ronan's shoulder. 'As I said to Ma, it'll be a challenge. Nevertheless, if we all put our minds to it I'm sure we can make it work.'

Half an hour later Lillie found Ronan sitting on the edge of the back verandah with Dingo lying beside him.

'So what do you think?' she asked, plonking down beside Dingo. 'I asked Ma why they wouldn't sell Eureka Park and go back to Ireland. She said they want to have a go here.'

'It sounds as though the decision's been made, doesn't it? At any rate I'm going back to Ireland by the time I'm twenty-one. So it doesn't really matter to me what they do.'

'Don't you like it here? You said you'd made some friends at school and played rugby.'

'I know. That's not the point. I promised Grandma I'd come home by the time I'm twenty-one. I'll finish school and go to uni or whatever. Then I'll get a job to save my fare up.'

'You'll need a good job to earn that sort of money.'

'I'll make darn sure it happens. You wait and see. In any case… what do you make of it all?'

Lillie picked up a stone and played with it in her hand. She then threw it over into a bed of scraggly lavender where she heard it plop onto the ground. 'I'd rather go back to Ireland. But that's not going to happen. So I guess I'm looking forward to living at Eureka Park. I know it's run-down and all that. But as Ma says it does have a nice river in front of the house. There's even a sort of beach where you can swim. Ma also said we can tie a rope to a tree to jump into the water.'

'We had that at Rathgarven.'

'But we don't have Rathgarven any more, do we? Anyway, I'm going to go ring Deb and tell her what's happened. I think she'll be really pleased that we're staying here. You'd like her. She's good fun. I don't like her as much as Sheelagh yet. But at least she's a friend. Someone to talk to who's not crabby like you often are.'

With that, she patted Dingo on the head, got up and went inside, leaving her brother sitting on the verandah. As she walked towards the phone she was excited. They mightn't be able to go back to Rathgarven, but at least now the family had a place to live. And Eureka Park did sound quite nice.

***

Ronan watched Lillie go inside. When his father was to be a partner with Uncle Finn, he had held onto the hope that once they made a bit of money they would all return to Ireland and buy another place. That was unlikely now. He still found it strange to be living in a different land. Much as he tried not to, at times he still hankered for Ireland and the school friends he had left behind. And at times he felt a bit like a square peg in a round hole at school here.

After one boy took to him on the rugby field trying to knock his teeth out and called him a *goddamn paddy* he soon worked out, after giving the fellow a piece of his mind, that if he spoke with an Aussie accent he would fit in better. So he started speaking with a twang when he was at school. He found that

194

helped. There were a couple of Italian boys and two Greeks, but they'd been there since they were kids so spoke with broad Australian accents and seemed to get less hassle.

But it wasn't all bad. He and Dave had quickly become good friends, and Dave often stood up for Ronan if he was in a scrape. Ronan repaid him by taking a lashing with the leather strap for the cigarettes found in Dave's school satchel, telling the head brother he had put them there. If it had been proved that Dave had cigarettes he would have been expelled, as it was a third offence. At the Thompsons' place they hung out listening to records or throwing a ball around in the back garden, or they might wander down to town to get an ice cream or milkshake at Fitzroy's milk bar. Mrs Thompson even made him a cake for his seventeenth birthday, which his family celebrated the next weekend with a picnic to a swimming hole along Quirindi Creek.

Just yesterday Dave asked Ronan to come out to his uncle's sheep and cattle property in a couple of weeks' time.

'He needs some help mustering the sheep and branding the cattle. Would be good if you could come. I'll show you what to do.'

Ronan looked forward to that. When he left school he thought he'd like to study something to do with the land. Now, as it turned out, the O'Sullivans would have their own property here in New South Wales. What would Clara make of that? He touched his side pocket where Clara's latest letter rested.

Are they being nice, or absolutely ghastly to you at that school? And is the family you're staying with still treating you well?

In Australia he felt so remote from her. Clara had her life in London. And with Uncle Finn leaving them Eureka Park, it seemed more than ever that Ronan had his life mapped out for him here in

Australia. Ronan had seen Uncle Finn drunk on a few occasions, but he'd always seemed a happy drunk, singing at the top of his voice and playing the harp. To think he'd become so gloomy as to actually kill himself made Ronan very sad.

And now they were going to go and live in his house, run his stud and virtually take over his life. It was such a peculiar situation that it took a bit of getting used to. For a moment he sat there, playing with Dingo's ears.

'Now you can come back to your home at Eureka Park,' he said to the dog. 'How about that, my friend?' When Dingo looked up at him, wagged his tail and licked his hand, it was almost as though he understood.

Ronan took out Clara's letter. Although it was a bright, breezy letter, reading it again Ronan worried that she was holding something back. She didn't even mention what she was doing outside of school. What she did say was that her mother had come back to England again and was renting in the centre of London, which she thought was terrifically expensive and she didn't know how she could possibly afford it.

> *She and Phillip seem really unhappy, so that's probably why she's back here. But God knows who's paying Mummy's rent. Maybe she's got a rich lover hidden away somewhere. Wouldn't put it past the old girl!*

Ronan folded the letter up and went inside to his bedroom, where he placed Clara's letter in the top drawer of the chest, alongside her other letters. And as he did, he too wondered who was paying Jessica's rent. Surely she was a bit old to have a rich lover supporting her? Then again, knowing Jessica, maybe she wasn't.

The next weekend Ronan went with his father to take a few things out to Eureka Park and have a look around. Although it would be a while before Uncle Finn's will would be settled, the lawyer had arranged for the family to take possession. It felt both odd and sad to be walking around a dead man's home. But Ronan had to admit, although the place had been let go, it was certainly a good parcel of land. Ma and Dad had been right — the homestead was in a great spot overlooking the river. He could imagine catching a few fish there quite easily. Although it was nothing like Rathgarven at all, he could see the family living there. But they sure would need the twenty thousand pounds Uncle Finn had left them to get it up to scratch.

Part Three

Eureka Park
November 1963 to December 1966

Chapter 18

Goodness, not more bottles, Kathleen thought to herself as she came across three more empty whisky bottles in Eureka Park's pantry. The pantry was the last room she had to tackle. Since the crack of dawn she and Lillie had scrubbed the floors, knocked down spiderwebs, swept up mouse droppings, shaken and washed the curtains, polished the furniture and taken the rugs outside and beaten the accumulated dust out of them. They'd also cleaned out the cupboards and the fridge, which was crawling with maggots. James was meanwhile tackling the sheds and the garden.

'Yuk, Ma… It looks as though Uncle Finn hasn't cleaned the place for years. Probably not since Mrs Malone left,' Lillie said as she carried another load of rubbish out to the bonfire James had made near the sheds.

'Maybe he'd been going to get someone in to do it before we arrived. And… well, it all became too much for him.'

'And then he started drinking like he did.'

'Yes.' Kathleen sighed, as she brought in the curtains to put them back up. 'I can't believe how much dust came out of these. I don't think they could've been aired in years.'

'Why don't we have a break after I get rid of this rubbish? Then I'll help you put them back up. Lucky, lucky Ronan is all I can say, missing out on all of this.'

'He'll have to do his share when he gets here on the weekend.'

'And Marcus should be helping.'

'I know, but quite frankly, darling, I'm happy to have him and Freddie out of the way down by the river.'

Kathleen slumped into one of the old armchairs on the verandah. James had wanted to take them to the tip, but Kathleen had said she would cover them in canvas and they would do just fine. She gazed out over the garden, which she was looking forward to getting under control. Was this spot where Finn had sat, nursing a whisky and deciding to leave all he owned to the O'Sullivans? What had been going through his mind when he made that decision? Surely by that stage he must have had a premonition of what he might do to himself if he couldn't overcome his demons. Kathleen felt tears fill her eyes and she lifted her hand to wipe them away. When he was at Rathgarven Finn hadn't been drinking at all that Kathleen was aware of. Or had he been drinking in Dublin before he came down to Rathgarven and they didn't know? Even when he went to Hannigan's Pub in Killarney with James, James told her he only had a bottle of ginger beer. She patted the wooden arm of the chair fondly. The hardest thing she and James had had to do was going through Finn's belongings. Keeping some things, throwing others out. She could have cried when James held up one of Finn's jackets.

'I was with him when he bought this Donegal tweed at Brown Thomas,' he said. 'He must've had it for twenty-odd years.'

'Will it fit you?'

'I'm not sure. I'll try it on later.'

Kathleen doubted he ever would, but it could remain in his wardrobe as a reminder of his friend.

Now James came up to the verandah and slumped down in the other chair. He put a hand out to her. 'You must be exhausted. You and Lillie are doing a great job.'

'It was certainly a mess. But at this rate we'll soon have it in order.' She nodded towards the neglected grounds, 'And we'll have that garden in order before we know it with the flower beds a riot of violets and petunias.'

James smiled. 'We certainly will. Paddy will be proud of us.'

'Poor Maisie would've had kittens if she'd seen the inside before we got stuck into it.'

When Kathleen had first seen the state of the interior of the homestead, she'd had grave doubts whether they could ever clean it up. The smell of rotting food was horrendous and the flies had found a hole in the flyscreen in the open living room window. The sound of their buzzing was like a lawnmower running at full throttle. Even so, today she and Lillie had started to make headway, and she was beginning to see what a lovely family home it would make.

'Thank you, darling,' she said as Lillie came out carrying three glasses of water. 'Dad was saying what a great job you're doing.'

Lillie sat down on the edge of the verandah, cradling her glass. 'Although parts are yukky yuk… like the fridge, it's quite fun seeing it come to life.'

Kathleen had to agree. Later, when they had hung the curtains in the living room, Kathleen and Lillie went to see how Marcus and Freddie were getting on and were greeted by Dingo, who shook himself all over them before scuttling off down the bank again.

'Thanks a lot, Dingo,' Lillie cried. 'Now I'm soaked.'

Kathleen smiled and gazed down on the water, which was the colour of a field of ripe corn in the late-afternoon light.

At that moment Freddie came rushing up the bank, screaming and holding onto his head. 'That horrid black and white bird's chasing me. It tried to fly off with my hair.'

Sure enough, a magpie was chasing him and diving onto his head.

'You must've gone near its nest,' Lillie admonished him. 'Deb said they do that if you disturb them. They think you're going to steal their young.'

'Well how the billyo was I supposed to know there was a nest? It's not as though there was a signpost.'

Kathleen and Lillie burst out laughing and scrambled down to the river where Marcus was throwing sticks for Dingo to retrieve.

***

Kathleen and James decided on bedrooms: Lillie would have the room out the back, off the verandah. At the other end of the verandah would be Ronan's room. Marcus and Freddie would have the one in the middle of the house and James and Kathleen took the lovely bedroom at the front, which had a window seat looking out onto the garden. The manager's cottage would be a sort of sleep-out for guests. That's if we ever have any, Kathleen thought.

That night, when Ronan had returned from the Thompsons for the weekend, they all sat around the pine table in the kitchen with the fuel stove in the corner now alight. They had managed to get the fridge going first thing that morning, and now James opened it and got out a bottle of Hunter Valley riesling. Kathleen knew he'd been saving it for this occasion, when they were all gathered together at last in their new home. He poured the wine into two glasses and gave one to Kathleen.

'To our new home,' he said, holding his glass in the air. 'We may have a few hard times ahead, but here's to our future at Eureka Park.'

'Hear, hear,' the children and Kathleen chorused.

'And,' James added, 'to our dear friend Finn, who has given us so much to be thankful for. And a huge thank you to the Hogans, who came to our rescue.'

'Mrs Hogan looked really well when they came back yesterday,' Lillie said.

'I think they thought we'd done a good job looking after the hotel,' Kathleen added. 'Particularly your father.' She laughed, eyeing James. 'Mrs Hogan said the locals will miss you no end.'

'There were some real characters there. It was a great way to get to know the place. As old Joe, who held up the bar most evenings, would say, "I wouldn't have missed it for quids, mate".'

Kathleen smiled, and as she looked around at the children she had a warm feeling inside. Life had not turned out as she had imagined it would, but at least now they had a chance to look forward to a future. Even though that future would not include Finn Malone, at least the O'Sullivans could try to do justice to the wonderful thing he had done for them in leaving them Eureka Park. Not to mention the twenty thousand pounds to put into it and tide them over until they started to make an income of their own. She had no illusions that it'd be an easy run. Still, as James had said, if they all knuckled down and got stuck into their new life, surely they would make a success of it, and Finn would be proud of them.

Chapter 19

When James got in touch with Brian Medlow, Finn's friend who had been looking after the horses, he was relieved to hear his friendly manner down the phone.

'Good to hear from you, mate,' he said in a slow Australian drawl. 'I've been away in New Zealand looking at a couple of mares, otherwise I would've come to Malone's funeral. He was a good bloke. I was more than happy to help him out with his horses, I've got more feed down here than I know what to do with. He'd sold most of his yearlings, so there's only fifteen horses all up down here, plus the stallion.' There was a pause down the line. 'So the bugger left you Eureka Park, eh.' James heard the chuckle in his voice. 'Have you any idea how to run a horse stud, mate?'

'I've had a lot to do with horses. Not so much with racehorses. Mostly hunters. I've got a young local fellow starting with me next week, recommended by one of the sheep farmers who's a regular at the Telegraph. He said the fellow has had plenty to do with horses and is a good worker. I spoke to him on the telephone and he seems keen enough. He's picking fruit down in Victoria at present. Said he'd be able to get up here next week.'

'Well, how about coming on down here for a couple of days before he arrives? You can see how we run the place. I might be able to give you a few hints. Then we can load up the horses and get them back up to Eureka. Malone left his float here. The stallion's a fine-looking beast. Believe he's sired a few good foals that are causing a bit of a stir around the place. And a couple of the mares are in foal. So you'll be kept busy.'

When James got off the phone and told her what Brian had said, Kathleen said he should take up his offer.

'It'll be a great way for you to learn the ropes. We'll be fine. Lillie will be here to help me.'

***

Two days later, when James had finally managed to crank Finn's truck into life, he drove down to the Medlow Stud. A group of whitewashed stables sat next to a two-storey brick building, presumably the house. Everything was set back from the road behind a thick row of poplars. Driving up the avenue James thought the land looked rich and fertile and he could see a sizeable racetrack running around the outside of the paddocks, which were enclosed by post-and-rail fences.

'G'day,' Brian Medlow said when James found him with a couple of strappers outside the stables. Over six feet tall, he was thickset with greying hair and a wide smile that revealed slightly crooked teeth. He was wearing what James now realised was more or less the uniform of men on the land in New South Wales: a wide-brimmed felt hat, checked shirt, V-neck jumper and moleskin trousers, though Brian's were more spattered with mud than most. He put down the shovel he was using to unblock a drain and held out a roughened hand. It was obvious he did his fair share of the hard work around the place.

'Come on inside,' Brian said, indicating a doorway at the side of the building. 'I've got a kettle in there. I'll make us a cuppa.'

As they sat at a Laminex table sipping tea from enamel mugs, Brian told James how he had bought four hundred acres twenty years before and set it up as a stud. He pointed out the window to the two-story white brick building set in a lush garden surrounded by tall trees. 'Built the family home with my own two hands and the help of a couple of local brickies.' He grinned. 'I managed to snaffle the land next door not long ago. That's why

205

I'm a bit under-stocked at present and was able to help Malone out.' He paused, crinkling his brow. 'You knew him a long time, eh?'

James nodded. 'Since we were at school in Dublin together.' He took out his pipe and fiddled with the bowl. 'You mind if I smoke?'

'Go for it, mate. I'm not a smoker myself. If I was I reckon it'd be the pipe. Now, come and I'll show you around. Maybe I can pass on a few tips. First let's go on down and have a look at Malone's horses. I got Joe, my head bloke, to put them all in the bottom paddock. Apart from the stallion, Caesar. I've got him held up in the yard out the back of here. Malone had a couple more stallions and he sold them off last spring. But this one's a bloke you wouldn't want to get rid of. In fact, why don't we start there? Then go on down to the others.'

James thought the stallion was indeed a fine-looking beast. As black as the ace of spades, he stood about 15.3 hands with a powerful shoulder and hip. And when he moved, James could see he had an impressive gait.

'Wouldn't mind that bloke myself,' Brian said. 'If you've no objection I might send a couple of my mares over to Eureka for him to service a bit later on when they come in season.'

James smiled. This sounded a good start to the O'Sullivan stud. 'I'd appreciate that very much.'

'Come on, I'll show you the rest.'

They walked through a wooden gate and crossed a paddock where a few of Brian's horses were grazing contentedly.

'They seem in good condition,' James said.

'It's been a bumper of a spring.' Brian pointed to a couple of mares over by a dam overhung with weeping willows in the bottom paddock. 'Those two mares of yours are the ones in foal. Should give you a good drop before too long.'

'They look close.'

'Within the next couple of months.' Brian took his hat off and scratched his head. 'Did Malone leave his papers in order? In regards to the stud?'

'Yes. I discovered them the second day I was there. The solicitor told me that although he'd let the house and garden go downhill, he was meticulous about his horses. By the look of his studbooks that would seem the case. In fact,' James added, 'I brought them with me. They're in the car. I thought if you had a moment we could go through them.'

'Not a problem, mate. Now, why don't you go grab your bag, or whatever you've brought, and I'll show you where Lorna's put you up for the few nights you're here. Then you can join me for a whisky before we light the barbeque.'

'Thank you,' James said. 'I must say again how kind it is of you and your wife, not only to put me up, but to share your knowledge with me.'

'No worries, mate. I reckon you'd do the same if the boot were on the other foot.'

***

Brian's wife Lorna was a petite redhead with skin freckled and creased by the sun. After the three of them had devoured the steaks Brian had cooked on the makeshift barbeque under an elm tree in the back garden, Lorna brought them coffees and they sat on the back verandah. To James, Lorna seemed a no-nonsense woman who called a spade a spade and didn't give a hoot what anyone thought of her. Including how much she swore.

'What the bloody hell got into your friend Finn to do something like that?' she said, stubbing out a cigarette in the ashtray balanced on the arm of her chair. 'Silly damn bloke. He should've spoken to someone about his problems. Men tend to

207

bottle them up inside. Us women, well… We like to share them around. Maybe that's why we're less likely to top ourselves.'

'He didn't look like the sort of bloke to give into desperation,' Brian said. 'Mind you, I never saw him tanked. He was always as sober as a judge. Or if he wasn't, he put on a damn good show.'

'I thought he had it beat,' James said. 'In fact I think he did. Then I believe something happened in London on his way back from Ireland that sent him off again.' As he said it, James felt the usual bitterness towards Jessica, even though he'd told himself a hundred and one times that Finn should have had the strength to resist the temptation. 'But you're right,' he said to Lorna, 'God knows what got into him to do such a thing.'

'Well,' she said, standing up and stretching her arms in the air. 'Who knows the working of the mind?' She stepped to the edge of the verandah and picked a leaf off the rhododendron bush overhanging the railing. 'He wasn't in debt, was he?' she asked, turning around. 'I mean a hell of a lot of farmers get into debt, mortgage their places to the goddamn hilt and don't know how to get out of the mess. That's when they do themselves in. Bloody tragic. I know of at least two blokes who've done that over the past decade. You reckon that could've been Malone's problem?'

James shook his head. 'No, Finn was well off financially as far as I know. In fact he left me quite a bit of money to work the stud with.'

'Ah… Then it probably was the grog that did him in. Bloody awful hold it gets on some poor bastards. In any case,' she added, eyeing her husband, 'I reckon I'll call it a night. Leave you two to chew the cud on your own.'

'Thank you again,' James said, standing up to say goodnight. 'I've had a grand evening.'

'Our pleasure.' She smiled. 'I'd love to meet the family sometime. Particularly your wife. Kathleen, isn't it?'

'Yes,' James said.

'She must be finding it all a bit of a strain. All that packing up and leaving Ireland, then finding out what happened to Malone and taking over Eureka Park. I'd heard it was in a bloody awful way.'

James nodded. 'We're managing to get it back in order.'

'Well, when you're settled in a bit more maybe I could drop by and see if there's anything I can do to help. Or,' she laughed, 'I could kidnap Kathleen and take her up to Tamworth to do a spot of shopping. Girlie things.'

'I'm sure Kathleen would like that very much. I worry she may get lonely out there on her own. Particularly when our daughter Lillie starts school up in Tamworth in the New Year.'

'I'll give her a holler and have a chat. I know how lonely it can get on the land. I was cut up when my kids started boarding school down in Sydney.'

'How many do you have?'

'A boy and a girl. They'll be back for the school holidays soon. Then,' she laughed, 'I'll be wishing they be off again. 'Gerald's okay. Maddie's a different kettle of fish, isn't she Brian? A real free spirit. Tests us both.' She grinned as she leant down to kiss Brian goodnight. 'I always thought a girl would be a piece of cake. How wrong I was.'

'How old is she?' James asked, wondering if she and Lillie might be the same age.

'Sixteen going on twenty.'

'Our Lillie's only fourteen.'

'Enjoy it while you can. Once they get a bit older they seem to change. Boys and all that. Drives us round the bend, eh, Brian.'

'Ah, she's not that bad.'

Lorna chuckled, patting Brian on the shoulder. 'Tell me that after she's been home for a week, bored stiff and wanting to head into town to party with all the wrong crowd.'

She left Brian and James to enjoy a port under a sky sprinkled with stars, which to James seemed even brighter than the stars that lit the sky above the Kerry Mountains. In their twinkling midst was the outline of a new moon, which reminded James of the shape of the boomerang Finn had brought Marcus last time he had come to Rathgarven. James wished that Finn was with them now. For surely that's how it should be: the three men sipping port and discussing the state of the nation and the prospects of their horses.

'I don't want to be worrying you,' Brian said, 'but I did hear a rumour doing the rounds that Malone owed a bit of money around the place. Fuel, vets, horse feed, farriers. Nothing huge. No doubt it all adds up. Anyone mention that to you?' He gave a shallow cough. 'He even owed me a bit. Not that I'm chasing that up now that the poor bloke's gone.'

'Oh,' James said with concern. 'I'm sorry to hear that.'

'Ah, nothing too much. Mainly vets' fees while his horses were here. And he'd agreed to pay me for agistment. As I said, I've had plenty of feed, so that's no great drama. Even so, I reckon if he owed me a few quid, he may well have owed others. Maybe, as Lorna suggested, it all got the better of him.' He raised his bushy eyebrows. 'Just a thought.'

'It's not something that crossed my mind,' James said, trying to control the alarm bells starting to ring loudly in his brain. 'You may well be right.' He took a deep breath to steady his voice. 'I'd best see the solicitor when I get back.'

'Not a bad idea, mate. Could put your mind at ease.'

When they had finished their ports, Brian turned to James. 'Reckon I'll call it a night as well. We start early round here. Undoubtedly Lorna will have breakfast ready for us after we come in from the track. What's say I see you round 5.30? I've got a couple of two year olds in training. You can see them have a run.'

'Sounds good,' James said.

That night James tossed and turned through the long hours. Had his friend left him with debts that would eat into the money he had bequeathed him? And which they didn't yet have. The solicitor had said it would take time to come through. Or were Brian and his wife jumping to conclusions? He hoped that they were; he couldn't imagine how he would tell Kathleen, who had earmarked that money for so many things, as had James. Apart from their everyday living expenses, there were school fees, school uniforms, and all the costs involved with the stud, which were bound to mount up before they could hope to reap any sort of an income. If Finn hadn't left them that twenty thousand pounds James felt sure he and Kathleen would have decided to sell Eureka Park and start over again somewhere else with something smaller, which would have given them a bit of spare change. If Brian's suspicions were right, they might have to do that anyway.

The thought of that made James sit up in bed, and he knew he would be unable to find sleep tonight, no matter how hard he tried. To have lost Rathgarven was one thing. To lose Eureka Park would put more strain on Kathleen than James could imagine — not to mention the rest of the family. He wondered where Finn had got the money to pay Jessica if he owed money. Or was it paying Jessica that had strained his finances? I never should have allowed him to do that, he thought. Was it possible that Jessica had insisted on even more money and Finn hadn't told him? That was how it had started for James. A little to begin with, but then as Jessica got older and her circumstances changed, her demands put more and more pressure on the finances of Rathgarven. Until that last time, which had pushed James to gamble and lose. When Finn said he would see to it that she never made any more demands on James, had he had to pay her more to do it? James was going to pay him

211

back as soon as he got on his feet here. Sadly he never had that chance.

Giving up on sleep, he stepped out onto the verandah and lit his pipe. When his watch showed 5.15, he was still there. He headed back inside and got dressed, grabbed his coat and tweed cap, and went to meet Brian down at the stables.

***

Over the next few days James tried to put his fears from his mind as he learnt how Brian ran Medlow Stud. It was going to be much harder than he had imagined. Although many hunters were thoroughbreds and in fact retired racehorses, running a racehorse stud was a lot different from owning a few hunters. The first thing Brian told him was that he'd need a realistic business plan. How much would he be able to invest in the stud? How much grain and hay would he need in a year? What would the insurance be? What were the workers going to cost? What would he need to put aside for vets and farriers? And the other bits and pieces that would constantly come up.

'The hands-on work in running a horse stud is unrelenting,' he said. 'But it's also immensely rewarding. You need to hire the sort of bloke that says "Wake me up for the foaling, even if it's in the middle of the night." And you'll need to reward him for hard work. Nothing huge. Enough to make him think he's appreciated. What you don't want is to have blokes upping and leaving all the time. Then you've got to train a new one. Bloody waste of time.'

Brian was a good teacher and by the time the weekend came round James felt he had picked up enough pointers to be able to welcome Finn's horses back to Eureka Park.

'The kid brother of one of my stable hands blew in a while back,' Brian told James the day before he was to leave. They were down in a room off the stables and Brian was going through the

212

Eureka Park stud books with James. 'I promised his mother I'd give him a run. Good young bloke. Has a knack with horses. Seems to have built up a bit of a rapport with your Caesar.' He paused. 'To be honest… With my daughter Maddie coming back I'd be glad if you'd give him a go. Last time she was home they seemed a bit close. Made Lorna uncomfortable. Why don't you give him a go. At least he'll see you out until your other fellow starts. If he's any good you can keep him on. It'd be doing me a favour if you gave him a run. I've actually paid him up for a couple of weeks ahead, but that doesn't matter. He's not here this week, he'll be back on Sunday. Jack's his name.' He looked out the window at Finn's Ford truck parked next to the stables. 'He can drive your ute up. Save you coming back down once you've got all the horses up there in the float.'

James was overcome at the kindness of this man. 'Thank you,' he said. 'I'll pay you back for his time. And rest assured I'll pay you what Finn owed you as well.'

'As I said before… That was a debt Malone owed me. It's not your debt, mate.'

Early on Saturday morning Brian helped him load the mares into Finn's horse float, which had been parked out the back of the stables. James could have waited until tomorrow when Jack came back, but he felt confident he could cope on his own on this first trip and Jack could come with him on the next, when they'd load up Caesar and the rest of the horses. Although he'd driven small horseboxes to hunt meets back in Kerry, James hadn't driven such a large float. Driving slowly and carefully on the dusty road, he went over and over in his mind what he could do if it turned out Finn owed all of the twenty thousand pounds. Or even most of it. Selling some of the horses would be one option. Then again, the horses were going to be their only source of income. As he drove through a cloud of dust left by an overtaking ute, he tried to convince himself that they would work it out one way or another. They had to.

In the meantime I'd best concentrate on getting this lot back to Eureka in one piece, he told himself as he swerved to avoid another pothole, which was met by a chorus of indignant snorting from the back.

Chapter 20

After James and the rest of the family had made sure the horses were happy in the front paddock, they sat around the table having the Irish stew that Kathleen had made for dinner in the pressure cooker she had found in the bottom cupboard.

'I feel I learnt a lot during the week at Medlow Stud,' James said, lifting the glass of beer Kathleen had poured him. 'And the Medlows are a lovely couple.' He looked at Ronan who had come home on the school bus that evening. 'You can come down with me tomorrow to fetch the rest of the horses. And Caesar, the stallion.'

'Can I come too?' Lillie asked.

'I'm afraid there won't be enough room.'

James told them how Brian Medlow had insisted on the brother of one of his stable hands coming to help out..

'He'll stay on here for the time being. Jack's his name. I haven't met him, but I gather he's worked up a good rapport with Caesar.'

As he looked around the table at the happy faces of his wife and children he hoped his concerns about Finn's finances were unfounded. He had thought of telling Kathleen what the Medlows had said, but when he saw the optimism in her eyes on seeing the mares arriving, he decided not to say anything until he had been to see Colin Towers. The lawyer would be able to put his mind at rest, and it would only be worrying Kathleen unnecessarily to tell her anything before he'd spoken to him.

Nonetheless, that night he tossed and turned, keeping Kathleen awake. Eventually she asked if he was okay.

'It must be all that time in the horse float... The jerky movement on that dirt road and trying to avoid all the potholes that's making me restless,' he said. 'I'll get up and read for a while.'

At three o'clock he crept back to bed and managed to grab a couple of hours sleep.

On the trip down to Medlow Stud later that morning Ronan turned to him. 'Are you nervous about having the horses back at Eureka?'

If Ronan were older James thought he would confide his worries about Finn. As it was, Ronan had enough on his plate settling into a new school. It wouldn't have been easy for him; he knew teenage boys could be the devils of bullies to a new student. Not that Ronan had said anything.

'Sure, I'm a bit nervous,' he said. 'But… with Jack, the young fellow coming to us from Medlow Stud and the other young bloke starting next week, I'm confident we'll cope.'

'Well, I'll be there on weekends to help.'

'Unless you're playing rugby,' James grinned. 'I daresay that's bound to take priority.'

Ronan smiled. 'I got a game in the First Fifteen on Wednesday.'

'Well done.' James shifted the gears and slowed down to avoid a rabbit scuttling across the road in front of them. 'You're settling in, then?'

'Yeah. It's okay.'

'And you're happy with living at the Thompsons?'

'It's fine, Dad. They're great.'

'And Dave?'

'We get on really well.'

'But you still miss your friends back in Cork?'

Ronan glanced out of the window at the landscape of open paddocks with the odd house scattered here and there. Turning back he smiled, 'It's okay, Dad. As I said, Dave's great and I've made another few good friends. So stop worrying.'

James put his hand on Ronan's knee. 'Of course I worry about you. But I'm proud of the way you're handling it all. And well done again on the rugby.'

'Thanks. I hope I get another game in the First.'

'I'm sure you will. Which,' James added with a chuckle, 'makes me doubly pleased I've got these young fellows to help me. For I'd bet you a pound that many of your Saturdays will be tied up on the rugby field.'

When they got closer to Medlow Stud, Ronan cleared his throat. 'One of the fellows at school said Uncle Finn owed his father money. He runs the menswear shop in the main street. Uncle Finn got a couple of suits from him before he went back to Ireland but he hadn't paid for them when he died.'

'And your friend told you that?'

'Yeah. It sorta came up. He was asking me how we were settling into Eureka Park. He said he'd heard his parents talking about how Uncle Finn was an alcoholic and owed money around. They wondered if that was why he killed himself.'

'So your friend knew he'd committed suicide.'

'Yeah. Everyone knows.' A long pause. 'So do we have to pay off Uncle Finn's debts?'

James turned to him. 'I'm going to see the solicitor on Monday. In the meantime please don't say anything to your mother. I don't want her worried unnecessarily.'

'Sure. But, gees, Dad, it could be a heap of money he owes.'

'Well, let's hope it's not too much. Now,' he said, looking at his watch, 'why don't you open that thermos of tea your mother packed. And that brown paper bag with the sandwiches. I'll pull over on the side of the road. We can have a bit of a break.'

As he manoeuvred the float up onto the verge, James tried to hide his concern from Ronan. How many more people did Finn owe money to?

Kathleen knew James well enough to work out he was worrying about something. As far as she could see he had slept hardly at all over the weekend. At first she thought it may have been simply that he was nervous about bringing the horses home to Eureka. But in the back of her mind she had a feeling it was something more than that.

Then on Sunday afternoon as they stood watching Jack, the Medlow's tall, good- looking stable hand, trying to calm Caesar, who was cavorting around in his stable, tail swishing theatrically, James told her he needed to go up to Tamworth in the morning to see the solicitor.

'He forgot to get me to sign a form that has to be lodged,' he said. 'Damn nuisance, but there you go. At least I'll be able to drop Ronan off at school instead of him catching the bus.'

'Couldn't he post it to you?'

'It needs to be lodged by the end of the week. I'll leave early and be back mid-afternoon.'

'Would you like me to come with you?'

'No. You stay here. Keep an eye on things. Jack might need a hand.'

'It's no bother for me to come. I'm sure Jack and Lillie can cope here.'

'No, you stay here. It's just a form to sign.'

Kathleen could hear an edge to his voice, but she decided to let the matter drop. She really didn't feel like driving up to Tamworth if it was only going to be a short visit to the lawyer. She would be going up next week anyway to sort out Lillie's uniforms. Although Lillie wouldn't be starting school until the end of January, Kathleen had heard there was a uniform pool where second-hand tunics and blazers could be had. She also wanted to get some more clothes for the younger boys, who were growing at such a rate that they seemed to be bursting the seams of their clothes day by day. When Finn's money came through she thought she would splurge on a Singer sewing machine. Then she could make the children's clothes herself.

James pulled out his pipe from his pocket and knocked it on the heel of his boot. Whether it was the late-afternoon sun shining on his face, somehow he looked drawn.

'You seem tired,' she said.

'I think I'm a bit worn out with all the driving. That's all.'

'And now more time in the car. When you're with the solicitor can you ask him what's the hold up on the money from Finn? I know these things take time, but even so it'd be great to have it on hand.'

'Yes,' James said, 'it would, wouldn't it? I know you've got it earmarked for quite a few things. So have I. Now,' he added, looking at his watch, 'before dinner I'll go and give Jack a hand with that stallion. He seems to be playing up a bit.'

'I've got a joint of lamb in the oven. Should be ready in half an hour or so. Come up when you can.'

Kathleen strolled up towards the house and watched the sun disappear behind the distant hills, looking for all the world like the red glow of a lantern being extinguished by a slow puff of air. How lucky they were that Finn had left them his property. She had only been here for a few weeks, but somehow it had a feeling of home, particularly now that the horses were back. Once the money came through, they'd be able to make it even more so. As she reached the garden gate Lillie came out of the front door, laden with bedding.

'Where are you off to?'

'Dad asked me to take some things to Jack. He's bunking down in that room in the stables. You know… the one next to that sort of lean-to kitchen.'

'But he's eating with us?'

'Yeah, I think so. He seems nice, doesn't he? Freddie follows him around like a shadow.'

'I know, poor Jack. It's great to see he's so good with the horses. Particularly with Caesar.'

'Yeah. He's got a real knack.'

Kathleen swore she could see Lillie blush. Maybe it's not just Freddie who's got a crush on Jack, she thought.

Inside, she went through to the kitchen to check on the lamb. The fuel stove was a bit tricky compared to the Aga at Rathgarven, and of course there Maisie had done most of the cooking. After she closed the oven door Kathleen stepped over to the sideboard and folded up the aerogram that had come from Alice this afternoon. Although she had been sad to hear of Finn's death when James had rung to tell her, Alice was also delighted the family had fallen on their feet and inherited Eureka Park. *I've little doubt you'll make a roaring success of it,* she wrote.

> *Despite it being one of the coldest snaps in history, I'm warm and cosy in my rooms. I must say I'm having great fun watching my new television. Bonanza's my favourite, but I hate to admit it, I'm also quite partial to that dreadful English soapie,* Coronation Street.

Kathleen smiled as she put the letter on the edge of the dresser for James to read when he came in. There was also an aerogram from Jessica. Kathleen had skimmed it earlier and put it aside to read properly later. She had been surprised to see that Jessica was still living in London.

> *I know I should go back to India. But I can't bear the thought of that ghastly heat any more. I must be getting old, my sweet. Mind you, I only have to look in the mirror to work that tragedy out. Such a cruel world, isn't it?*

Kathleen shook her head. She folded the letter away and went to the drawer of the pine dresser to take out the knives and forks and lay the table. It sounded as though Jessica was going to try and push poor Clara into a marriage of convenience. Not so much a convenience for Clara as a convenience for Jessica.

Oh, Clara, Kathleen thought, as she placed the cutlery around the table, don't let your mother rule your life.

***

'You've got to be joking,' James said as he sat in Colin Towers' office the next morning. 'It can't be so.'

'I'm afraid that's how it looks. As the executor of the will I received another outstanding bill yesterday. From the Australia Hotel, actually. Isn't that where Malone was to put you up?'

James took a deep breath. 'Yes, that's right. It appeared no booking had been made, so we ended up in a hostel.'

'Maybe the hotel didn't take Malone's booking in the first place as he owed them too much money.'

'Oh!' James sighed and reached for his pipe. 'It's hard to comprehend how Finn could run up debts like that. It seems so unlike him.'

'I'm not sure he was so much in debt as just slow paying his accounts. And, of course, that can all add up.'

Yet he'd obviously paid Jessica off, James thought angrily. Was Jessica now going to be responsible for the O'Sullivans losing Eureka Park as well?

'How much of the twenty thousand pounds do you think will be needed to clear the debts?'

'It's hard to say…'

'Are you telling me that it might be more than twenty thousand pounds? That we may need to sell Eureka Park in order to cover Finn's debts?'

'I wouldn't go that far.' Colin Towers pulled a handkerchief from his pocket and blew his nose. 'I've been made aware that a neighbour across Snake Gully Road, which adjoins your property along the western border, is interested in buying that ten-acre paddock abutting his place. Maybe you could consider selling that. Should cover a bit.'

'Oh!' James said. 'How much do you think that's worth?'

'Depends. If you were to put it on the open market, not a great deal. To him it's possibly worth a bit.' He paused. 'Maybe a thousand pounds.'

'By the sounds of things that wouldn't go far.'

'I should have a clearer picture in a week or so.'

'In the meantime you hold onto the money? Is that how it works?'

'As executor, yes.' He raised a brow. 'Have you any money at all to keep you going?'

'We have a small amount we managed to bring from Ireland. But that's being eaten into at a great rate.'

'I'm sorry,' the lawyer said. 'Rest assured I'll try and get it all sorted out as soon as possible. In the meantime, maybe you could go and see a bank. They may be able to tide you over. I gather the Bank of New South Wales is lending a bit at present.'

'And what collateral could I give them? I mean… if we might lose Eureka Park to Finn's debts?'

'I'm sure you won't lose all of it. Depending on how much you need to borrow, maybe the bank can take a first mortgage over part of the land.'

Here we go again, James thought. Just when I thought we had a clean start. Even if the bank were to lend them some money, how would they make the repayments? He stood and began to pace.

'What would you do if you were in my shoes?'

'I'd go to the bank,' the lawyer replied. 'See if they can help out. If they can, maybe you could sell the land to your neighbour to cover the repayments.'

James sighed. There seemed little option other than to get a loan. 'Do you know anyone at the bank who I should talk to?' he asked.

'The manager's not a bad bloke. If you like I can make an appointment with him for next week. In the meantime, as I said, I'll do all I can to get this mess sorted out as soon as possible. At least if you have a loan that can tide you over.'

James nodded. 'Thank you. I'd appreciate it if you could make an appointment.'

With that, he picked up his tobacco pouch and put it and his pipe in his pocket and made his farewells. Outside in the Holden he slumped down in the seat and sighed heavily. What I need is a strong whisky, he thought. He checked his watch. It was only 11.30. Too early for a drink. Instead, he put the key in the ignition and started the engine. For a moment he thought of not telling Kathleen anything until he'd been to see the Bank of New South

Wales. Then reason prevailed. She had a right to know. If Ronan had already heard rumours Finn owed money around the place, those rumours might easily reach her ears too. And if James admitted he'd known and hadn't told her, she'd have every right to be furious.

***

When James drove up to the homestead Kathleen was out in the garden tackling a flowerbed. She watched him park the Holden under the wattle tree next to the bare patch of dirt he was preparing for a vegetable patch where the new chickens and a couple of turkeys they'd bought from a friend of the Hogans were pecking happily. Once it started to get dark Freddie would chase them into their coop, a chore he relished, along with collecting the eggs.

'Hi there,' she said, lifting her head and giving James a bright smile. 'Glad you're back. You can help me pull out that dead oleander bush over there. It's got a trunk like an elephant and I can't budge it.'

'Of course,' James said. 'Then how about a cup of tea? There's something I need to tell you. Over a cup of tea would be best.'

Kathleen stood up and wiped her hands on a rag she had stuck in her belt. 'What do you mean?' she asked, taking her hat off and pushing a sodden piece of hair back from her forehead, 'I thought you were just going into Tamworth to sign some papers.' She moved a bobby pin to hold back her hair and looked to where he'd parked. She wondered if he'd had an accident on the way home.

'Good heavens, James! Don't tell me you crashed the Holden on the way back?'

'No,' James said. 'Nothing like that. Let's pull that bush out then I'll go put the kettle on.'

224

'The bush can wait,' Kathleen said, eyeing him worriedly. 'I'll get the tea. You sit down on the verandah. You look beat.'

And he certainly did. Kathleen wondered if he wasn't doing too much in this heat. It was getting hotter and hotter each day. Inside the homestead was not too bad if there was a breeze coming through the open windows and doors, but outside it was so hot it made doing anything seem much harder, including driving to Tamworth and back as James had just done. It wasn't as hot as Calcutta, nonetheless Kathleen thought come the height of summer it could get up there.

A short time later she came outside with the tea tray. After she poured them each a cup she looked long and hard at James. 'So…?'

James gave a nervous cough. 'I don't really know how to tell you this. However, it appears Finn owed quite a bit of money when he died.'

Kathleen's eyes widened. 'My God! Do you think that's why he killed himself?'

'It could well be so.'

'Oh. How awful. Poor Finn.' Then the ramifications sank in, 'And we've inherited those debts? Is that it?'

James nodded. 'I'm afraid so. Colin Towers is not quite sure how much he owed. Bills are still coming in.'

'Surely he couldn't have owed that much. You know what I mean. He was not long back from Ireland for God's sake. He flew. That would have cost money. And he stayed at the Shelbourne.'

'I know. Maybe that's why he was slow in paying his debts here.' James picked up his teacup and took a small sip. 'Evidently he might have owed money to the Australia Hotel. Maybe he owes money to the Shelbourne as well. And Qantas.'

'They'd hardly give him credit?'

'It appears people did. He was a persuasive sort of fellow. People trusted him. Without doubt he hoped to pay those debts off. Then… Well, we know what happened.'

'When his creditors saw the death notice they decided to act.'

'Something like that. They possibly would've held off till he got around to paying. Now that he's dead they wanted to get in line.'

Kathleen gazed out over the garden, saying nothing. A few minutes ago she had been feeling quite happy. She enjoyed gardening and seeing the results of her work was rewarding. Between the house and getting the garden back into some sort of order, she was feeling more and more confident that the family would be happy here. Now this. Finally she asked, 'So what do we do now? Will we need to sell up here?'

'I hope not. Colin Towers suggested we go and see the Bank of New South Wales. They're supposedly lending money. And we could sell off that paddock on the other side of Snake Gully Road to cover the repayments. Evidently our neighbour's after it.'

'And when that's all gone?'

'Maybe we could get something smaller. Cheaper.'

'No, James,' she said adamantly. 'We're not moving. Not unless they come with a bulldozer and doze us out. I could get a job,' she said, picking up her cup of tea and taking a long sip.

'You?'

'Yes, me. I'm not completely useless, James. I used to work in India, remember. And I did those translations for the Indian Embassy in Dublin.' She forced a smile. 'Without patting myself on the back, I can also take a decent photograph and I know how to work a Gestetner. It so happens I was reading the *Quirindi Advocate* when I was waiting for the boys' bus a few days ago and saw they're looking for an office dogsbody. Mornings only. It may not pay much. But at least it'd be a foot in the door if I got the job. It could cover some of our living costs… and hopefully a few other things.'

'Kathleen…'

'Beggars can't be choosers. One thing I know is that I don't want the children uprooted from here when we've just settled in. It doesn't have to be forever. It might get us through a sticky patch. That and selling the land on Snake Gully Road.'

'Why don't we wait and see how it all pans out?'

'And let our own debts mount up? No, James. You concentrate on getting the place going here. I'll go to Quirindi tomorrow and apply for that job. All that can happen is that they say no. And if they do, I'll look for something else. Maybe the Hogans have something at the hotel. As you know I can carry out a decent clean. And wait on tables.'

James went to her and put his arms around her. 'The *Quirindi Advocate*, perhaps. Cleaning… no.'

'Well, let's see what eventuates.' She put her hand on his. 'In the meantime, come and help me pull that oleander bush out.'

As James helped her heave the bush from the hard ground, Kathleen was more determined than ever that she wouldn't allow anyone to take this home from her. Even if she had to take two jobs.

Chapter 21

The next morning Kathleen put on her second-best dress and, leaving Lillie in charge of getting James's and Jack's lunches, she dropped Marcus and Freddie to the bus stop and drove across to Quirindi to see about the job at the *Advocate*. She had thought of ringing up first, but then decided it would be best if she went in person, as they were sure to ask her to come in anyway and she thought she would enjoy the drive through the countryside. She had soon realised that driving distances in Australia's vastness was the norm. She parked the car in George Street and found the place easily. When she told a young girl sitting behind a counter what she was there for, she told her to take a seat.

'I'll tell Mr Lyons, the editor, you're here.'

Kathleen looked around. She had never been into a newspaper office before. The floor was covered in green lino and the chairs were shabby and scratched. Next to her sat a steel ashtray on a black pedestal overflowing with butts. A few copies of the *Advocate* were strewn on a coffee table next to the wall. Some had been there so long they were going yellow around the edges. She touched the skirt of her linen dress and wished she'd worn something more appropriate. Maybe a pair of trousers, or at least a skirt and blouse.

'Mrs O'Sullivan… Mr Lyons will see you now,' the young girl said, coming around the counter.

'Thank you,' Kathleen said, and followed her down a long, dark hallway to an office at the end. Inside, a man wearing a white shirt and a pair of brown braces sat behind a desk. Although he was pleasant looking, his skin was pale, no doubt from endless days of sitting at this desk instead of being out in the sun. Even James had a good Australian tan already, as did the children. And

Kathleen had quite a bit of colour despite wearing a hat whenever she was outdoors.

Mr Lyons stood up when he saw her. 'Good morning, Mrs O'Sullivan,' he said, moving forward to greet her. 'Tim's my name.' He looked at the young girl. 'Madge tells me you're here about the office job.'

Kathleen nodded. 'I saw it advertised.'

'I'm afraid that position has been filled.' He motioned for her to sit down on the other side of his desk, which was covered by a large piece of blotting paper dotted with blotches and doodles and numerous notebooks, pens and pencils and an overflowing glass ashtray.

'Madge, maybe you could bring Mrs O'Sullivan a cup of tea,' he said as he lit up a cigar.

Kathleen shook her head. 'No, thank you. I haven't long had breakfast.'

If there was no job available she could see no reason to prolong the interview.

'I hear you've taken over Finn Malone's stud out at Eureka Park,' Tim Lyons said, ashing the cigar in the ashtray. 'Sorry to hear of his passing. Damn sad case. Too many Aussie farmers do themselves in.'

Kathleen gave a sad smile. 'So I believe.'

'Well, not much we can do about the poor sod now.' He paused, as if thinking something through. 'Maybe you could do me a column. You know what I mean… being Irish and settling into a new life here in Australia. Show how you and your kids, and your hubby, are adjusting to the Aussie bush.' He chuckled. 'Snakes, kangaroos, all of that. A human interest column. Can you take a decent photo?'

'I do like taking photos. In fact I've had some published in a couple of English magazines.'

'That's good. You can take some photos of the place. Drop in the negatives with your copy. Yeah. I reckon that sort of article could go down well.'

We may not be living at Eureka Park for long, Kathleen felt like saying. Not if Finn Malone's debts keep mounting up like they are.

'How much would you pay me?' she asked bravely.

'Depends how they go, love. Maybe three quid to begin with.'

'And how many could I do a week?'

'Steady on, love. Just the one. Friday. That's the day that would work best. Then they have it for the weekend.'

'Oh! I must admit I was hoping to earn a bit more than that.'

'Well, let's see how it works out. First of all I've got to see if you can write. Maybe you could send me a sample column.'

'Yes. Of course.'

'It's a start, love.'

'Thank you. I appreciate that.'

Tim Lyons stood up to indicate the meeting was over. As he saw her to the door he smiled. 'I look forward to receiving your first column.'

Later, when she told James what had happened, he laughed. 'You'll be a bit like mother with her column in Ireland.'

'It won't bring in nearly enough money to pay back the bank.'

'Every little bit will help.' He paused. 'When you were out I spoke to Brian Medlow and told him what I'd found out at the lawyers. He said two of his mares have come into season over the weekend. He wants to send them up for Caesar to service. He's insisting on paying me a good fee. He also said he'd mentioned Caesar to a couple of his friends and they, too, would like to send their mares up. What's more, he said he'd been mulling it over the weekend and he'd like to buy two of our yearlings. He'd been eying them off when they were with him. He didn't want to say anything when I was down there in case I thought he was rushing me. Now as things turn out, I think we should take up his very kind offer. As you know, a couple of our mares are not long off foaling, so we'll have others coming on line.'

'What have we done to deserve that man's generosity?'

'Once we get on our feet, I'll pay him back twofold. Rest assured I will. In the meantime, I think we should say yes to his offers. And with your three pounds an article I'm sure we'll muddle through.'

'The editor's got to see my first column. He may not like it.'

'I'm sure he will. And even if he doesn't, we'll still manage. Besides, now that he's given you that idea, I'm sure you'd be able to sell your photos and articles to other publications.'

'Like the *Women's Weekly* or *Home Journal*?'

'Yes. Why not?'

But the editor did like Kathleen's article and her negatives, which she also had black and white prints made of in a small camera shop in Quirindi. In fact Tim Lyons said he wanted to make it into a half-page column. Which meant she could include two photographs. Even though the three pounds a week wouldn't go far, it was a start. And together with Brian Medlow's offer, it'd surely allow the family to stay at Eureka Park. For the time being, anyway. Unless, of course, Finn's debts kept mounting up and even the bank loan and the remainder of the twenty thousand pounds wouldn't cover them.

This was something Kathleen refused to let herself think about.

***

Christmas 1963 was so unlike the Christmases the O'Sullivans had celebrated at Rathgarven that Lillie thought it was almost as though it was a different event altogether.

'Do you think Santa will find us here?' Freddie asked, concern etched on his face. The family was up in the bush behind Snake Gully Road cutting down a fir to have as their Christmas tree.

'You don't believe in Santa,' Marcus snorted. 'He only comes to those who believe.'

'I do believe,' Freddie snapped back. 'Well, I sorta do …'

'We'll have to wait and see if he comes,' Ma said. 'I did write and tell him where we are, so hopefully he'll find us.'

'I bet he comes on a kangaroo, rather than a reindeer,' Freddie declared.

Ma smiled. 'That sounds reasonable. A kangaroo would know the way much better.'

So on Christmas Eve Freddie left a glass of milk and a biscuit next to the fireplace in the living room and dutifully hung a stocking from the mantelpiece for Santa to fill.

'Yippee, yippee do!' he shouted, waking everyone up at crack of dawn on Christmas morning. His stocking was full of little gifts. 'Well done, Santa, you did find us after all.'

Before ten o'clock mass at the church on the hill in Gullumbindy, Dad handed the presents out from under the proudly decorated Christmas tree in the corner of the room. Lillie and her brothers had hung decorations made from different coloured crepe paper across the ceiling, and Lillie had strung the Christmas cards along the mantelpiece on a piece of string. They'd set up the crib in the empty fireplace. There was a card from Sheelagh, saying how much she was missing Lillie, and also one for the family from Clara, who said she and her mother were going to Dublin for Christmas, catching up with some distant relations. She was looking forward to seeing Alice at her hotel. Lillie wondered if

Ronan had got a separate card at the Thompsons. If he did, he didn't say. There were also cards from Grandma, Maisie and Paddy. Ma also showed Lillie the card Jessica had sent.

Lillie was excited to discover she had been given a transistor radio like Ronan's. With the money she'd saved from doing odd jobs down at the stables, for which her father paid her half a crown, she gave her mother an apron with yellow wattle on the front, and her father a new pipe. Ronan got a second-hand pair of RM Williams boots from his parents and Marcus was given a pellet gun. But the one who was most excited was Freddie, who got the bushman's hat he had longed for. Lillie's mother had tied shoe-laces with corks onto the brim, like the hat the sheep musterer was wearing.

At Rathgarven, Maisie and Kathleen would serve a huge roast turkey, ham and all the trimmings piping hot on Christmas Day. But here at Eureka Park, with the temperature hovering above 90 degrees Fahrenheit most days, Lillie helped Ma cook the turkey in the cool of the evening before. Jack and Ronan had killed the bird a couple of days earlier (much to Freddie's consternation; he said he'd have none to eat, seeing as the turkey was his friend). After mass they lay out a smorgasbord on a long trestle table under the maple tree in the back garden where they had invited the Hogans to join them. Lillie was pleased that Jack was also there. Lillie really liked him. He was good fun and made her feel special. Whereas Ronan often made her feel silly for asking questions, Jack took the time to answer her questions, no matter how stupid he may have thought they were. One of the things she had been

233

unable to work out was why snakes left their skins behind. For there was only one thing worse for Lillie than finding a snake, and that was finding its skin. It meant the snake was somewhere close by. Probably hiding.

'They shed their skin so they can grow more,' Jack had explained, picking a skin up with a stick and hanging it on the stable yard fence.

It was the way he said it that made Lillie feel grown up. He also spent ages teaching her how to crack a whip, and then taught Marcus and Freddie how to do it as well. Ronan, of course, learnt in one go. That was Ronan for you. Now, as she took a plate of ham out to the trestle table, she glanced at Jack sitting on a rock under the gum tree in the corner of the garden. Lillie had expected him to have Christmas at the Medlows' place, where his brother was, but although he went down for a few days, he'd come back up here to spend Christmas with the O'Sullivans. Normally he wore a pair of blue jeans and a checked shirt, maybe a windcheater if it was cold. Today he had on a pair of cream trousers and what looked like a newly ironed blue shirt. His hair also looked different. Sort of smoothed down with oil or something. Like on Ronan, she preferred it when it flopped over his eyes.

The new stable hand, Arthur, had started a while ago, on his return from fruit picking in Victoria (much to the delight of Marcus and Freddie, he turned out to be part Aboriginal). He had gone home to his family who lived on the other side of Tamworth. It seemed to Lillie that he fitted in well with Dad and Jack. And he had a real way with the horses. He showed Marcus and Freddie how to throw a boomerang so that it came back. But the best thing of all was when he showed Lillie and her brothers how to light a fire by rubbing two sticks together. He said his grandfather had showed him how to do it. Lillie couldn't believe it when the sparks started coming out of the wood.

'Arthur's a magician,' Freddie had cried out in excitement. 'He can do magic.'

'Come and help yourselves before the flies get in first,' Lillie called out to everyone, as she valiantly tried to keep the flies away from the meats and the salad she'd made from the lettuce, tomatoes and cucumbers she'd picked that morning from the veggie patch.

When they were all sitting around the table out of the hot sun beneath the maple tree — and after Dad had said grace — he raised his glass of beer. 'To our first Australian Christmas,' he said. 'And thank you to our new friends who have joined us.'

'Hear, hear,' reverberated around the table.

Later Lillie couldn't help noticing Freddie take a second helping of turkey and stuffing. When he saw her wink at Ronan, he said, 'He's dead now, so I might as well have some. Otherwise it'd be a waste, wouldn't it?'

For dessert was a pavlova Lillie had helped Ma make with their own eggs and dressed with blueberries and strawberries from the garden. Lillie glanced at her mother and thought how beautiful she looked, even if there was a slight sprinkling of grey in her hair. Her face was tanned from the sun and the blue and white dress she wore really suited her. Lillie smiled as she remembered how excited Ma had been when her first article, together with two photographs she'd taken — one of the horses down by the dam in the front paddock and one of Dingo playing with Marcus and Freddie by the river — had appeared in the *Quirindi Advocate*. Since that first article she'd had one in every week, which she told Lillie helped with finances around the place. Even so, Lillie knew that none of the twenty thousand pounds Uncle Finn had left them had yet come through, and she imagined her parents were worried sick as to where the next pound would come from.

Chapter 22

The gymkhana site was a paddock at the end of a dry, dusty road next to a community hall and a small creek. Lillie thought it was nothing like the shows in Kerry. No one was dressed up at all, even the competitors were just wearing jeans and bush hats, whereas at the Kenmare Show everyone dressed in jodhpurs and jackets and wore proper riding hats.

Deb had invited her to come along to this gymkhana at Werris Creek, and Kathleen was glad to see her daughter have a chance to get out. It was the second week of January, and still weeks from school starting.

'Mum will drop us off on her way to visit a friend near Currabubula, and pick us up on her way back,' Deb explained. 'A gymkhana is sort of like a show. Not as fancy. They have all sorts of things. Barrel races, egg and spoon races and even cross-country. I'm not competing because my horse is lame, but I thought it might be fun to go.'

A couple of judges stood in the centre of the ring, judging the riding and jumping competitions. Other officials were getting the next lot of competitors ready. But it had a very casual feel to it, particularly the flag and barrel races in an adjacent paddock. All around the outside of the ring were horse floats and horses tied up under the gum trees, some of them eating out of nosebags, others standing watching what was going on. A few had their eyes closed against the hot wind. Most of the horses had fly veils over their eyes to protect against the hordes of blowflies buzzing around their heads.

'It's all the horse manure,' Deb said, as they wandered around the ring looking for a spare spot to watch the competitions.

It turned out that Jack and his brother were competing in the jumping event on a couple of horses his brother had floated up from Medlow Stud. As Lillie watched Jack enter the ring she thought what a good rider he was. As he rode past she threw him a smile, but he didn't seem to notice. When he finished his round, knocking one pole down, the next competitor rode in on a big chestnut horse with a white star on his forehead.

Deb let out a low whistle. 'Wow. That's Brad Hickey. He's a real dish. He wins everything with that horse. I'll introduce you to him later. His father's a friend of my Dad's.'

Later, when Deb and Lillie were buying an icy pop from the ice cream caravan, Deb pointed to where Brad Hickey was standing talking to a pretty blonde girl wearing a white top and jeans. He had, of course, won the jumping competition.

'You want to meet him? That's his girlfriend. They've been going out for yonks.'

Lillie felt shy and was about to say she didn't want to be introduced, when Brad saw Deb and waved.

'G'day, Deb,' he said, wandering over with his arm around his girlfriend. 'How've you been?'

'Great,' Deb said. 'Congrats on your win.' She looked at Lillie. 'This is Lillie O'Sullivan. She lives out past Gullumbindy at Eureka Park.'

'Ah. The O'Sullivans, eh. My old man said you'd taken over out at Finn Malone's place.' He held out a hand. 'Brad Hickey.' He indicated the girl at his side, 'This is Sally.'

Lillie took hold of his hand and smiled at Sally. Brad Hickey had a mop of dark hair, eyes the colour of a broody sky and skin burnt brown by the sun. Lillie thought he was the best-looking fella she'd ever seen in her life.

After he'd moved on, holding Sally's hand, she turned to Deb. 'Gees... no wonder he's the local heart-throb.'

'Yeah. But he's also a bit up himself. And in any case, as you can see he's well and truly spoken for. Now,' she said, pointing to the other side of the ring, 'let's go and watch the barrel race. I always like that.'

As Lillie watched Brad Hickey and his girlfriend disappear into the throng, she wished she had a boyfriend to hold her hand. Lately she'd found herself thinking more and more about the opposite sex. Maybe it was because Sheelagh had skited in her last letter that she had a steady boyfriend. *Sheelagh Cassidy's head-over-heels in love*, she wrote. *And he's the best kisser in the whole of bloody Ireland.* Or was it because Lillie's breasts were starting to fill out, making her no longer feel like a child? Even though Jack had never hinted that he liked her in any way other than as a friend, she couldn't help fantasising about what it'd be like to kiss him. But maybe that was only because he was around all the time. Now she found herself wondering what it'd be like to kiss Brad Hickey. Gees you're warped, Lillie O'Sullivan, she told herself. Neither fella would give you a second thought.

***

When it came time for Lillie to start boarding at St Dominic's in late January, Ma drove her into Tamworth and bought her new underwear and two new nighties, which they took in and packed away in the tiny steel cupboard next to the bed she'd been given in the stark dormitory. There were no other students there, so Lillie and Kathleen had it to themselves.

'I've got even less space than I had at school in Cork,' Lillie complained, trying to squeeze her things in.

'Here, let me help,' Ma said, and grabbed Lillie's socks and knickers and put them in the cupboard. When she stood up Lillie realised she had tears in her eyes.

'Ma, what's the matter?'

Kathleen wiped her eyes and smiled. 'I'm being silly. It's just that I'll miss you when you're up here.'

Even though Lillie was excited to be starting a new school, she also felt tears threaten and tried hard to hold them back. 'Don't be sad,' she said. 'I reckon you and Dad will be glad to get rid of me. And in any case, I'll be home at weekends.'

'I know. I've got kind of used to you being around all the time, that's all.'

At Rathgarven Ma always had Alice or Maisie to talk to. Now there would be no other women around during the week. Even though she had Jack, Arthur and Dad there, and, of course, Marcus and Freddie when they weren't at school, it wasn't the same. She was bound to get lonely.

Before she had a chance to say anything, Ma put her arm around her and gave her a squeeze. 'You can't spend the rest of your life at Eureka without an education. So let's get this cupboard in order and then we can go and have "the last supper".'

They had dinner at the Central Hotel on the corner of Peel and Brisbane Streets, and stayed the night upstairs with the sound of the juke box downstairs vibrating through the floorboards. The next morning Ma dropped her off at the school gate. A week earlier Lillie had sat an exam and was pleased to be told she would be in Deb's class. But as she walked down the long corridor to her classroom, she felt even more nervous than on her first day at the convent in Cork. She was glad that at least she knew Deb, who knew all the other girls.

'Come and I'll introduce you to my friends,' she said to Lillie at the morning break. She pulled a yoyo out of her tunic pocket and wrapped the string around her finger. 'You'll love Sasha. She's a real hoot.'

And Sasha was. When Lillie was at school in Cork there was a girl in her class who was the class clown. Always mucking about, being silly and getting into trouble. That was Sasha.

It also turned out that the girl from the milk bar in Gullumbindy *was* a real bully, like Deb said. Her name was Sandra and her uniform was shorter than the others. Since Lillie had last seen her she had peroxided her hair a brassy blonde. For some reason she and a couple of her friends took a real dislike to Lillie. On her second afternoon, Sandra and her friends bailed Lillie up in the loo downstairs as she washed her hands in front of the mirror. Lillie was on her own.

'Where the hell did ya learn to talk like that?' Sandra sneered as the other girls looked on and sniggered. 'On another planet, eh! For sure as an emu egg it ain't this one.'

'Your accent's not that great either,' was all Lillie could think of to say. 'At least people can understand what I'm saying. Now… if you'll excuse me I'll leave you here to ogle your ugly face in that cracked mirror. You may even crack it a bit more if you keep looking.'

Sandra whipped around and poked her in the chest. 'Ah yeah,' she spat. 'I reckon you're the one who broke the mirror. With a face like that it's not hard to see why.' She looked Lillie up and down. 'And with a figure like that I don't reckon you starve at home.'

'Leave me alone,' Lillie said. 'Why are you so mean?'

'Yeah, leave her alone,' one of the other girls said, beckoning for Sandra to come with her. 'She's not worth worrying about.'

'I haven't finished yet,' Sandra snarled, pulling Lillie's ponytail so hard tears came to her eyes. 'Did you know that Finn Malone, the fancy man who left you everything, was a rotten drunk and used to bash up his wife? My Dad reckons that with that on his conscience, who could blame him for shooting himself.'

'Stop it,' Lillie shouted. 'Uncle Finn's wife came to his funeral. Why would she do that if he used to bash her up?'

'Oh, Uncle Finn is he now?'

'I hate you,' Lillie threw at her. 'You're the meanest girl I've ever met. And I've met some, believe me.'

With that she rushed out and ran as fast as she could up the stairs to the classroom, which thankfully was empty. She sat at her desk and let the hot, sticky tears trickle down her cheeks. Taking out a handkerchief she wiped them away before anyone could see.

A few minutes later Deb came in looking for her. 'You okay?' she asked. 'I saw you flee up here.'

'Yeah, I'm fine,' Lillie muttered, trying to stop from blubbering.

'You're *not* fine,' Deb said, giving her a worried look. 'Is it Sandra?'

Lillie nodded. 'Why does she hate me so much?'

'Probably because she doesn't like me and she knows you're my friend. She's nothing but an ugly bully.'

Lillie looked at Deb and the tears she was trying so hard to curb flooded down her cheeks. 'She said dreadful things about Uncle Finn,' she sobbed. 'That he was a drunk and used to bash up his wife. She said everyone's saying so.'

'They are not,' Deb said, coming over and putting an arm around her. 'She's jealous your family inherited Eureka Park, that's all. Her family live in a pretty ordinary place outside of Gullumbindy. Her father's an alcoholic. Rumour has it he beats her mother.' Deb stood up straight. 'Perhaps he beats Sandra as well… and…' She paused and Lillie thought she was about to say something more, but there was the clatter of feet running up the stairs and soon the rest of the girls would be pouring into the classroom.

Wiping her eyes with her sleeve, Lillie tried a smile. 'Thanks Deb. I'll be fine, truly I will.' She then picked up her pen and pretended to be writing in her exercise book.

It wasn't just Sandra who gave Lillie a hard time. Most of the nuns were great, except for one, Sister Bernadette, who seemed to dislike her intensely, making Lillie chew her fingernails whenever she was in her class. One morning, as Sandra and her friends sniggered in the background, she whacked Lillie over the knuckles with a feather duster and berated her for getting her algebra wrong: 'You dense Irish girl,' she shouted in front of the class. 'Why in the name of the Lord can't you work that simple problem out in that thick brain of yours? Coming from the land of saints and scholars. Who would believe it?'

The harder she hit, the more Lillie was determined not to show it hurt. That night she cried herself to sleep behind the white curtains of her cubicle in the dormitory. To stop herself being heard she put the pillow over her head. I hate this school, she thought. I'm never going to fit in. Even if Deb's nice to me, everyone else thinks I'm a freak. She couldn't wait to go home to Eureka Park on Friday, where she could go down to the stables and talk to Jack, who would be nice to her.

***

This weekend Deb was staying up in town with a cousin who lived in North Tamworth. Before Lillie got on the bus she came over and said goodbye.

'I'm sorry for what Sandra's doing to you,' she said. 'I told Sister Margaret about it. Maybe you should tell her as well.'

'And get bullied even more? No thanks.'

When she got on the bus she sat next to Ronan and told him what had happened with Sandra and showed him her bruised fingers from the feather duster.

'Good on you for not crying in front of the nun, li'l sis. Why give her the satisfaction of knowing she was hurting you?' Something in the way Ronan said this made Lillie wonder if his teachers hit him.

'Do you get hit?' she asked. 'By the brothers, I mean.'

Ronan shrugged. 'Everyone gets the strap now and then.'

'But you've never said.'

'Because that's just how it is.'

Lillie sighed. 'Anyway… What about the horrid things Sandra said about Uncle Finn?'

'She's making it up. And, as Deb told you, her father's an alcoholic. His mind's probably half shot.'

'Like Uncle Finn's was?'

'Something like that.'

When Lillie was sitting beside Ma in the car at Gullumbindy, waiting for Ronan to come back from the milk bar where he'd gone to get a cool drink, Ma asked her how it had gone.

Lillie looked out of the window to where a couple of dogs were scavenging through a rubbish bin, scattering litter all over the ground. 'It was fine,' she said, trying to sound cheerful. 'I liked it a lot.'

Kathleen eyed her. 'You don't sound as though you liked it a lot.'

'I'm tired, Ma. That's all. The bus was hot.'

'How was Deb? Did she introduce you around?'

'She was great. And yes, I met lots of other girls.'

'What about the nuns? Are they nice? And the girls in your dormitory?'

Lillie thought Ma had enough worries trying to keep the wolf from the door at Eureka Park without having to worry about Lillie as well.

'Ma, they were all great. I really liked it. And it was fun.'

Fortunately at that moment Ronan came back and Ma turned her attention to him.

When she got home Lillie took off her uniform and went outside, where she found Dingo lying under a wattle tree chewing on a bone. She sat beside him and stroked his head. She was so pleased to be home and not in that awful school. She wasn't sure how she was going to be able to go back up on the bus on Sunday night. All of a sudden she felt really homesick for Rathgarven. For Sheelagh. And Maisie and Paddy. Most of all she wished with all her heart that Grandma was here. Lillie mightn't be able to worry Ma with what had happened, but Grandma would have listened and given her good advice.

Ronan came and sat down beside her. 'You okay, li'l' sis?'

Lillie threw him a half smile. 'Yeah. I'm fine.'

'There's bullies everywhere,' he said. 'The best thing to do is try to steer clear of them. That's what I do.'

'You get bullied too?'

'Yeah. It happens. I guess it might be to do with the fact that we have inherited Eureka Park. People get jealous.' He grinned. 'Can't say I blame them.'

'We didn't *ask* to inherit it! Or for Uncle Finn to die! And we lost Rathgarven.'

'That's how the cookie crumbles.'

'It's not fair,' Lillie said. 'I've done nothing to that girl. And I did nothing to that nun. They're awful.' With that she burst into tears.

'Come on,' Ronan said, giving her his handkerchief. 'Let's go find Jack. We can have a whip-cracking competition.'

After a moment Lillie took his handkerchief, wiped her eyes and forced a smile. 'Oh yeah! And you win. As always.'

'Of course.'

As she walked towards the stables with Ronan her mood lifted. At least she had two whole days before she had to go back to school. And she was looking forward to seeing Jack. And the horses.

Chapter 23

The children love exploring the Australian bush, the excitement of finding a kangaroo in the paddock or discovering a discarded snakeskin. Ireland doesn't have snakes, as folklore tells us St Patrick put his crook into the ground and drove them all into the sea. Outside the window I can see two brilliantly coloured rosellas perched on the fence and our dog, Dingo, is happily chewing a bone under the wattle tree. In the oven is a batch of pumpkin scones and I even made some Anzac biscuits yesterday. I think I am fast becoming an Aussie bush wife...

Kathleen sat at her desk looking out the window at the cold winter's morning. It wasn't exactly the truth she was writing in her column. Despite her initial relief at having inherited Eureka Park, with Lillie and Ronan away at school all week she struggled with homesickness and the isolation. She missed the ruggedness of Kerry, the smell of salt and seaweed, and not having Alice and Maisie around. She missed the Fitzpatricks and her girlfriends in Kenmare and being able to pop into Burn's Butcher or Kelly's Bakery in Sneem to talk to the locals. Here at Eureka there was no one. She even found herself pining for her time at the Telegraph Hotel, where there were always people coming and going. Despite her daily chores, her photography, her column and the garden, she couldn't wait until it was time to collect Marcus and Freddie from the front gate. What's more she and James were snapping at each other as they struggled to make ends meet. Finally Finn's money had come through, however, rather than being twenty thousand pounds it was only seven thousand. And James and Kathleen had insisted that Dawn get her two thousand pounds first before any was given to them.

'I'm afraid the rest has been eaten up with debts,' Colin Towers told them.

Although they hadn't had to sell the land on the other side of Snake Gully Road, they had borrowed money from the bank, which was costing them in interest and repayments. So it wasn't long before that seven thousand pounds had a huge hole bored into it. Kathleen thought James was spending too much money on the stud, even though he had let Arthur go in order to cut costs. James thought Kathleen wasn't economising enough in the household, despite the veggie patch thriving and the chickens keeping them in eggs. James and Jack ran a few sheep in the far paddock and Jack slaughtered one every now and then to put in the freezer. But there were endless other necessities, like the boxes of groceries she got once a fortnight from Quirindi. Not to mention petrol and the children's expenses at school.

Now, as she typed, James came in to get the cheque book. Kathleen sighed. 'Another cheque! Who's it for this time?'

'The vet.'

'Does it need to be paid right now?'

'I said I'd put it in today's mail.'

'It's never-ending, isn't it? Whether it's Rathgarven or here. Too many bills. Not enough money.' She opened the drawer to get the chequebook out. 'I'm beginning to know how Finn felt. It probably was his money worries that sent him off the rails. We've got to be careful we don't go the same way.'

'Kathleen…'

'I don't mean suicide. We seem to be at each other's throats about money all the time. It could destroy us, James, if we're not careful.'

'Things are bound to improve once we can sell a few more yearlings and those mares drop…. and,' he smiled, 'I've got quite a few more assignations for Caesar. Brian Medlow has really put the word out. And that ad I placed in the *Leader* seems to be working.'

'I hope to God you're right.'

After he'd gone she returned to her writing but her heart wasn't in it. Instead, she went to the kitchen, made a cup of tea and took it outside. Perched on the edge of the verandah she listened to the sound of the crickets and watched a white cockatoo trying to peck a branch off the lemon tree. She stood and shooed it away. It hadn't taken long for Kathleen to realise the cockatoos were a darn pest, just as Finn had said. She thought of him again now. Was it really money worries that had sent him on the road to destruction? Or was it something else? Once Dawn had left, had he become so lonely out here on his own that he could see no future, despite the O'Sullivans coming? She wished she had been able to make contact with Dawn's friend Winifred Black to get a sense of the frame of mind he had been in when she last saw him. But it was obvious she didn't want to be friends, or even talk to Kathleen. The last time Kathleen had been in to see Martha Hogan she had asked her if she'd seen Winifred around.

'There's something odd about that one,' Martha said. 'When I saw her at the post office I asked her when she'd last seen Finn Malone. Without so much as a word she was off out the door.'

'I wonder why she doesn't want to talk about him.'

'Maybe it's not him. Could be something else that's eating her.'

Kathleen would have liked to ask Dawn if she'd heard from her, but Dawn had written to them wishing them luck with Eureka Park and saying she was going to use the two thousand pounds Finn had left her to go travelling overseas. Neither James or Kathleen had heard from her since.

The following afternoon, when she collected the mail from the letterbox at the front gate as she waited for the bus to bring Marcus and Freddie home from school, she opened a letter from the *Quirindi Advocate*. With horror she read that she'd been given the boot. Tim Lyons, the editor Kathleen had worked with, had moved on to the *Daily Telegraph* in Sydney and the new editor decided that although he liked her column, he was replacing it with a Dear Abby agony column.

She sighed angrily. Darn that new editor! How could he? Though she couldn't help wondering if he'd have kept her on if she'd told the truth, rather than making up a sort of fantasy of what life was like at Eureka Park. How could she tell James she'd been let go? She'd come to rely on the three pounds for housekeeping. Also the columns and photographs gave her a purpose each week and she enjoyed taking them in to the office, where she could talk to the staff. A couple of times she had had a cup of coffee with Tim Lyons, who made her feel special, telling her how much he liked her photographs.

'You've got a real talent for capturing the Australian bush as it is,' he said one day, looking at a photo Kathleen had taken of three kangaroos down near the dam. 'Makes me feel as though I'm part of the scene you're photographing.' He picked up a photo of a flock of pink and grey galahs perching in a gum tree with a few of the horses grazing underneath it. 'Your photos remind me a bit of Hans Heysen's paintings.'

Praise like that gave Kathleen a feeling of worth, something she used to have when she worked in Calcutta, but had seemed to lose when she became reliant on James to provide. To be told she had talent boosted her confidence no end. Now all of that was gone.

She was still thinking of how she would tell James when a cloud of dust heralded the school bus. What would the children think of their mother being replaced by a Dear Abby column? Even though she was furious, she couldn't help smiling. She might even write to the column herself.

Freddie burst from the bus and scrambled into the back seat. He leaned over the front seat and handed her a piece of butcher's paper. 'Ma… Look what I did. It's a painting for you to put on the fridge. See… it's Dingo riding on Caesar. Isn't he clever?'

'You're the one who's clever,' Kathleen said, giving him a kiss on top of his mop of unruly hair. 'I think it's a terrific painting.'

'Why would Dingo be riding Caesar?' Marcus asked sulkily.

'Because he's clever,' Freddie said.

'And because he and Caesar are good friends,' Kathleen added. 'Now, shut the door and we'll go on up and have a snack. Even I'm hungry. I made some chocolate crackles this morning. Jack loved them.'

Driving up through the paddocks with the horses grazing happily on either side, Kathleen felt her mood lift. Blow the stupid *Quirindi Advocate*. She would find something that paid much better.

Even so, by the time she had prepared dinner and put it on the table that night, her mood had deteriorated again. She thought of telling James before dinner that she had lost her job, but something held her back. He looked whacked after a day of ploughing the lucerne field. I'll tell him after dinner, she thought as she served him a piece of shepherd's pie. When I've put the boys to bed. By that stage, James had fallen asleep in the armchair in the living room with his book on his lap and she was loath to disturb him.

***

The next morning, after she had driven the boys down to the bus stop, Kathleen was hanging out the washing when with horror she saw a snake wriggle out from under the jasmine vine near the house. James and Jack were in the paddock on the other side of

Snake Gully Road doing some fencing so that they could move a couple of the older mares down there. Mesmerised, Kathleen stared in terror as the snake lay basking in the sun. I've left the back door open, she thought. If I try to scare it away by throwing something at it, it's sure to get inside and crawl under a cupboard, or a couch, or worse still one of the children's beds. She knew James kept a rifle in the woodshed. With her eyes still fixed on the snake, she sneaked over, went inside and found it. Then she looked for the bullets, which he kept on the high bench. Loading the gun, she crept outside and checked if the snake had moved. She shivered when she saw it was now nearer the back door and was about to slither inside. Lifting the gun, she took aim, grateful for the lessons she'd had in India during the war. The first shot blew its head off. But it still kept wriggling. Although she was sure it was dead, she shot again and this time she got it in the back.

Now it lay motionless.

Frightened that Dingo might come and start playing with its remains, she put the rifle back in the shed, got a spade and shovelled the mess to one side; she would take it down to the river and throw it in the water for the fish. She had read enough about snakes to work out it was a deadly red-bellied black, and shivered at the thought that it could have bitten one of the children if it had got inside. Once she'd got rid of its remains, she checked her watch. James and Jack would be coming in for lunch before too long. If it were just Kathleen and James they could settle for a sandwich. With Jack there, Kathleen felt she had to cook a hot lunch.

She had put a cauliflower cheese in the oven before she went to hang the washing out. It would now be well and truly overcooked. Scrambling back up the bank she made her way to the kitchen.

'I killed a snake,' she announced, standing back after serving lunch and trying to look smug. 'It was outside the door. I thought it would get in.'

'Jees, Mrs O'Sullivan,' Jack exclaimed, putting down his fork. 'How did you kill it?'

'I shot it with James's rifle from the shed.'

'Crikey,' Jack said. 'I thought I heard a shot, but reckoned it was along at the neighbour's place.' He shook his head. 'I'd no idea you knew how to use a rifle.'

'I learnt in India.' She was about to say who had shown her, then changed her mind with Jack there. 'I threw the remains in the river.'

James got up from his chair, put his arm around her and gave her a squeeze. 'I'm very proud of you.'

You wouldn't be if you knew I'd been fired from the *Advocate*, she thought. Whether it was the emotion of having shot the snake, or losing her job, Kathleen decided to leave them be and go to her room, feeling she might burst into tears. Shortly James came in and saw her sitting on the bed. It didn't take Einstein to work out she was upset.

'I can understand you being so emotional,' he said, sitting down beside her. 'You must've got a dreadful shock with the snake. You did so well to kill it before it got in the house.'

'It's not just the stupid snake,' Kathleen blurted. 'I didn't tell you before, but I lost my job at the newspaper.' She shook her head and fiddled with the edge of the eiderdown. 'They're replacing me with an agony column… Dear Abby. Can you believe it?'

James smiled. 'Well, it just shows the sort of readers their paper has if they've replaced you with that. Your column was way over their heads.'

'That's ridiculous, James. It's not a bad paper, as you know. They didn't think I was good enough. And, I must say, I can't say I blame them. Although it was all right to begin with, I was running out of ideas. They must've seen that as well. What I should have written is the truth. How Finn left us with debts. How you and I bicker a lot of the time. And I know I shouldn't feel sorry for myself, but I do feel lonely with the children at school. Maybe if I'd written that the readers might've had more empathy.'

James walked over to the window and looked out for a long moment before he turned back to her. 'I was only thinking the other day, now that Arthur's gone, why don't you get more involved with the horses? Melody, one of the mares who's not far off dropping her foal, seems to be in difficulties. It'd be great if you could sit with her for a while. Although the vet came out, she needs someone to calm her down. She seems to be in a lot of pain and quite disturbed.'

Kathleen joined him at the window and looked onto the garden, which was now a riot of colour. 'You're trying to make me feel useful.'

'No,' James said. 'I could genuinely do with your help. Come with me now and I'll show you where she is.'

Kathleen was silent, mulling over what James had asked. Since Arthur had left James and Jack were flat out keeping up with everything. If it were just the running of the stud, they would be well and truly on top of it. It was all the work that needed doing on top of that. Apart from the ploughing for planting lucerne, many of the paddocks seemed to be overrun with thistles, which needed to be chopped down or pulled out. And some of the fences in the far paddocks still needed upgrading. Although she often helped out with the feeding and filling the water troughs with the hose from the dam, she had thought before of asking James if he needed more help, then decided she might be getting in the way. Yet, she couldn't bear to think of a mare in pain. She remembered how painful her own childbirths had been. Besides, it sounded as though James could really do with the help.

Furnishing him with a small smile, she said, 'If you really think I'll be useful... well... give me a moment and I'll come on down and see what I can do.'

Fifteen minutes later James led her into the far stall where Melody was lying on the hay. When Kathleen saw the distressed look in her eyes, she knelt down next to her head and rubbed her behind the ears. As soon as the mare felt Kathleen's hand and heard her soothing voice she seemed to calm down.

'There,' James smiled. 'I told you you'd be a help to her.'

And that's where Kathleen remained, on and off between her duties at the homestead, until the cutest little black foal with a white star on his forehead arrived at three o'clock one morning. Kathleen was about to rush and get James and Jack to help with the birth, but then time ran out and it was just Kathleen there to catch the foal as it came out and tried to stand up on wobbly legs. The moment Kathleen saw him he reminded her of Joker, the horse she had often ridden at the Tollygunge Club in Calcutta. After much deliberation they decided to call him Shannon Boy after the Shannon River, which was so dear to James and Kathleen as they had spent their honeymoon at a private hotel on the shores of the Shannon in Tipperary. The foal now gave her a role she relished, and a whole new subject for her photography. She photographed him and his mother from every possible angle as he frolicked in the front paddock, scampered up and down the dam wall and scooted from one fence to the other. He really is the cutest thing, Kathleen thought as she developed one of his photos in the small darkroom she had set up next to the stables. And she couldn't help thinking that Finn would have loved him, too.

Chapter 24

'You want to come and stay at my place next weekend?' Deb asked Lillie. It was the Friday after Lillie's fifteenth birthday, and the girls were sitting up the back of the school bus on the way home from Tamworth.

'That sounds great,' Lillie said.

She and Deb were three seats behind Sandra. Lillie hadn't spoken to Sandra since their last altercation, when she had come up to her in the playground and asked if she still believed Finn Malone hadn't bashed up his wife. What Sandra didn't realise was that Deb was standing around the corner and overheard her, and Deb had raced around to give her a piece of her mind.

'If you say anything like that again,' Deb shouted, eyeballing her, 'I'm going to tell Mother Superior what you're doing. And, what's more, you tell your father if he spreads any more untrue gossip around the place, my Dad will get the police to sort him out.'

Deb had been so angry her cheeks looked as if they were going to explode right there and then, and Lillie thought she would hit Sandra in the face. Sandra must have thought so too, as, with much muttering, she shoved off. Since then, every time Sandra came near her, Lillie would quickly move away. And she made sure that she never went anywhere on her own where Sandra and her group might find her. If she wanted to go to the toilet in the playground Deb always came with her. Fortunately Sandra wasn't a boarder, as she lived with an aunt during the week, so Lillie didn't have to worry about her after school hours.

'We could camp out on Saturday night,' Deb was saying. 'To save the feed on our place we run some of the stock on the long paddock.'

Lillie raised an eyebrow. 'The long paddock?'

'The side of the road. A couple of our stockmen stay out with the sheep. Sometimes on the weekend I help out. It's kinda fun. We have a camp fire and bunk down in sleeping bags.'

'Don't you get scared? I mean… snakes, spiders and things.'

'If you zip up your sleeping bag they can't get in.'

'I've never slept outside at night. It'd be fun if you're sure nothing will get me.'

Deb glanced along to where Ronan was sitting with a couple of boys from his school, including the one Deb had told Lillie she fancied. 'You reckon your brother would like to come?'

Lillie smiled. 'Oh yeah? And if he comes, he might ask Dennis. Is that the idea?'

'No. I've gone off Dennis.'

The penny dropped. 'Ah! So you fancy Ronan? Is that it?'

'Well, he's not a bad sort.'

'You think so?' Lillie giggled, eyeing her brother as he laughed with his friends. 'I've never really thought of him in that way. Still, I suppose he's not bad looking.'

'You reckon he has a girlfriend?'

'Not that I know of. He sort of likes a girl back in England. We've known her since we were little. Her mother's a good friend of my mother's.'

'What about in Tamworth? I heard he's really good at rugby. And the team and a few girls sometimes hang out at Fitzroy's milk bar after a game.'

'He hasn't hinted he's got a girlfriend. Mind you, I'm probably the last person he'd tell.' Lillie glanced at Ronan again. 'Why don't you ask him yourself if he'd like to come camping?'

'He'd probably reckon I'm chasing him or something.'

Lillie laughed. 'Isn't that exactly what you *are* doing?'

'Please, Lillie.'

Lillie sighed. 'All right then. I'll ask him over the weekend. But he often plays rugby on a Saturday. Sometimes he doesn't come home at all on the weekend. Other times my parents go up and get him after the match.'

'Ask him anyway.' Deb reached into her school bag and pulled out a packet of Twisties and offered some to Lillie. 'What's the girl in England like?'

'Clara? Pretty. Blonde. Wears gorgeous clothes.'

'Oh!'

'As I said, she's more like a cousin to us really. So I wouldn't worry too much about her.'

Which wasn't exactly true, but she wasn't going to tell Deb that. If she did and Ronan found out he would kill her for telling Deb his business.

'What about you?' Deb asked. 'You fancy anyone? Like that fellow, Jack? The bloke you said's working for your Dad? You reckoned he's really nice.'

'He's a lot older than me. Still, he's so easy to talk to. And knows so much about horses. You should see him crack a whip. He taught us all.'

As the bus was about to pull into Gullumbindy, Deb scrunched the packet of Twisties into a ball and squeezed it into the pocket of her tunic. 'Well, see if your parents will let you come. And make sure you ask Ronan. It could be a heap of fun.'

Lillie stood up and grabbed her school bag from the rack above their heads. She saw Ronan also getting his bag and made her way towards him.

'Sure. I'll ring you tomorrow,' she called to Deb, who was getting off at the next stop. 'Let you know.'

'Let you know what?' Ronan asked, stepping down from the bus beside her.

'Deb's asked me to stay at her place next weekend and to go camping with the stockmen.' She grinned. 'She asked you as well.'

'Really!'

'Yeah. For some absurd reason she fancies you. She wanted to know if you had a girlfriend.'

They walked across the road to the large stringybark where they usually waited to be picked up by one of their parents. Sitting down on a log under the tree, Lillie pulled out a set of Freddie's jacks from her school bag and started to play, throwing the knucklebones up in the air and catching them on the back of her hand. She knew she was far too old to play such games, but she didn't care, Freddie loved playing them with her.

'So have you?'

'Got a girlfriend?'

'Yeah.'

'None of your business, li'l' sis. But as a matter of fact… no I don't.'

'Still pining for Clara, are you?'

'Lillie! Because I don't have a girlfriend doesn't mean I'm pining for someone else. And, in any case, I've got a game of rugby next weekend. Thank Deb all the same. She's a really nice girl. But I'm not looking for a girlfriend if that's what she's after.'

Now their mother pulled into the side of the road and Lillie put Freddie's jacks back in her school bag.

'Hi there,' Ma called out, winding down the window. 'Hop in. I've got to go to the corner store. How about an ice cream?'

Lillie slumped into the back seat behind Ronan and her mother and wondered how she'd break it to Deb that Ronan wasn't interested in going camping — or in Deb. She also wondered if Ronan still kept in touch with Clara. Lillie hadn't heard from her since that Christmas card, but she had no idea whether Ronan got letters from her at the Thompsons. If she asked him he'd just tell her to mind her own business, as usual.

***

The next Saturday night, Lillie lay by the campfire with Deb. She couldn't get over how many stars there were in the sky. She had never really lain outside looking up like this at night before. It was as if the whole sky was alight with twinkles and sparkles. Earlier on she and Deb had cooked tinned sausages on a grill over the stones and gobbled them up wrapped in bread smothered in tomato sauce. Before she came to Australia Lillie had never eaten sausages this way. Now that's the way she loved to have them, although she preferred the fresh sausages her mother got from the butcher at Gullumbindy, rather than the ones in tins.

Because Lillie had come out to the long paddock with Deb, the two stockmen had gone into town for a few beers, leaving the girls to mind the sheep. Lillie had been given Buster, Deb's mother's piebald horse, to ride and Deb had her own grey mare, Madge. Both horses were hobbled on a stake close by. This was another thing Lillie had never seen before. At first she thought how cruel it was, then Deb assured her it wasn't and the horses were used to it.

'It's better than waking up in the morning and finding the horses have taken off,' she pointed out, doing up the buckle on the leather strap around Buster's leg earlier on.

'I suppose you're right.'

When she had done up the buckle on Madge's leg, she turned to Lillie. 'A pity Ronan didn't come. He could've ridden Dad's horse.'

'I know. But he seems really set on rugby.'

'You reckon if it wasn't for rugby he would've come?'

'Not sure. He didn't really say.'

258

Lillie had chickened out and not told Deb Ronan wasn't interested in her as a girlfriend. She hoped Deb would take the hint and let it drop. And to give her her due, she hadn't mentioned it again.

'I love this time of night,' Deb murmured as they sat by the fire. 'When the fire goes out it'll get quite cold. Now it's perfect, isn't it?'

'It seems so different to Ireland. Ma says it's the smells. Eucalypt and dust. And the sheep of course.'

'Your Mum's really nice. How long have she and your Dad been married?'

Lillie thought for a moment. She'd seen a couple of wedding photos of her parents, but had never really asked when they were taken. As far as Lillie was concerned they'd been married a lifetime.

'Gees, I don't know. Before Ronan was born. He's seventeen. So probably eighteen years. What about yours?'

'They're not married.'

'Really?'

'Yeah. Mum was married before. She had an affair with my Dad. Then she fell pregnant with me and told her husband I wasn't his, and he kicked her out. Seeing as Mum's a Catholic she couldn't get a divorce. She got a separation or whatever they call it, but she can't get married again in the Catholic Church. Dad's a Catholic as well. Mum said that seeing as the Catholic Church wouldn't let them get married within the church, there was little point in getting married at all.'

'Wow. So your mother was pregnant with you when she was married to someone else?'

'Yeah. They weren't going to tell me. Guess who spilt the beans?'

Lillie shook her head. 'Who?'

'Sandra.'

Lillie's eyes opened wide. 'Sandra! My God.'

'Spot on. As soon as I started at St Dominic's. When I asked Mum if it was true, she told me what had happened.'

'Jeepers! But who was your Mum's first husband?'

Deb waited a while before answering. During the silence Lillie heard the crackling of embers within the fire and the high-pitched chirp of crickets in the bush. It was as if they were one heck of a squeaky choir.

'Sandra's Dad,' Deb said finally.

Lillie sat bolt upright. 'You're joking, surely?'

'Nope. That's him all right. They reckon that's why he turned into an alcoholic. Why he's pissed out of his mind most of the time. He used to be a miner but I don't reckon he does much now. Sandra's probably so mean to you because you're my friend. If the rumours hurt you, they'd hurt me. And also my mother, who her father loathes so much for what she did to him.'

Lillie thought for a moment. 'When was Sandra born? I mean… It must've been soon after your mother left him, cause she's our sort of our age, isn't she?'

'Yep. As soon as her father kicked Mum out he took up with Sandra's mum, Winifred.'

'Winifred?'

'There's only one Winifred around here that I know of. You met her? She used to help out in the corner store in Gullumbindy, but she doesn't do that anymore. Not since she got sick a while back.'

'Oh. I sort of met her outside the church once,' Lillie said. 'But she had to rush off. Mum said she was a friend of Finn Malone's wife, Dawn. Evidently Dawn told Ma and Dad that she had asked Winifred to look in on him at Eureka now and then after she took off to Sydney. Ma thought she might have gone out not long before he died, seen what sort of state he was in. But Ma didn't get a chance to ask. She sort of took off like a rocket when we were introduced.'

'I wonder why? Mum says she's a lovely person, so she can't understand how she ended up with Sandra's dad. But there you go… Interesting story, eh?'

Now that Lillie knew about Deb's parents, she thought back to when she had met them earlier on. They didn't look like a couple that would have had a passionate affair. Even though Deb's mother was really nice and was probably much the same age as Ma, she was a bit scrawny and her skin was marked by the sun and deeply wrinkled. And Deb's father was no oil painting, with sandy freckles and sunspots all over his face, and wispy ginger hair. Lillie wondered what they had both looked like when they had fallen in love. Were they ever in love? Or did Deb's mother fall pregnant and they'd been forced to get together? Though if that was the case, maybe Deb's mother would have stayed with Sandra's father and pretended Deb was his. Whichever way it was, it made Lillie's family seem so ordinary. Still, it did make her wonder what her own parents had been like when they had fallen in love. She couldn't imagine them being young and courting. She wondered if they'd been each other's first love. Or, like Deb's parents, had they been with someone else before they got together?

'How about a Milo?' Deb asked, bringing her thoughts back to where they sat by the campfire. 'I've got some powdered milk. I'll put some water on to heat in the billy before the fire goes out.'

'That sounds great,' Lillie said.

When they were sitting with steaming mugs in their hands, Deb said, 'I'm surprised you didn't know about my parents. I reckoned everyone round here knew.'

'Well, I certainly didn't. And I don't think my parents do either. In any case, who cares? Or if they do care, they're not worth worrying about.'

'I'm glad you think like that. And,' Deb added, sipping from her enamel mug, 'I'm glad I've got you for a friend.'

Later, as the girls lay in their sleeping bags, which they'd carried rolled up beside their bulging leather saddlebags, Lillie too, was chuffed she had Deb as a friend. It also made some sort of sense of why Sandra was so awful to her. Lillie had been flummoxed as to why she had taken such a dislike to her when she didn't know her at all. She also wondered if in some strange way that was why Sister Bernadette had been awful to her as well. Mind you, since Lillie had refused to let the nun see she had upset her, and had also made a bit of a mark by practising for hours to get in the hockey and softball teams, Sister Bernadette had let up on her somewhat.

Nestling down in her sleeping bag after Deb had gone out like a light in her own bag beside her, Lillie listened to the eerie sounds of the night. Hearing something rustling in the undergrowth, she was terrified it was a snake. She pulled the sleeping bag tight around her face just in case. Again she thought of Deb's parents. I must look at them more closely tomorrow, she thought. Should she tell her parents they weren't married and that Deb's mother had fallen pregnant to Deb's father when she was married to someone else? Maybe they'd be horrified and would refuse to let Lillie come out to their place again. Before she fell asleep she decided to keep it a secret from them. But she might tell Ronan.

***

'So what do you think?' Dave asked Ronan. It was Saturday afternoon in Fitzroy's milk bar; Chuck Berry was rocking out on the jukebox and they were celebrating their rugby win that afternoon. Dave was with Jude, a girl he'd been dating for a few months. He'd asked Ronan to come on a double date, as Jude's friend Meg was also coming. The girls had gone to powder their noses and the boys were sitting in a booth.

'She's really nice,' Ronan said, fiddling with the straw in his milkshake.

'So?'

'So what?'

'You reckon you might like to take her to the movies next week?'

Ronan shook his head. 'I promised I'd head home next weekend.'

Ronan hadn't committed to going home. Even so, he didn't want to commit to going to the movies with Meg either. Although she was a great girl and very pretty, with lovely brown eyes, Ronan wasn't really interested. The whole time he had been sitting here talking to her he was thinking of Clara. What she was up to? Was she on a date as well? With one of those boys Jessica had picked out for her?

'Well, another weekend, then?'

'I'll think about it,' Ronan said.

'Think about what?' Jude asked, as the girls came back to the booth.

Ronan and Dave stood up to let them slide in next to the wall.

'Whether we want another milkshake,' Ronan said. He looked at Meg. 'What do you think?'

At that moment Maria, who ran the milk bar with her husband Leonidas, waddled over to clear the table. Maria's Greek accent was so thick it was sometimes hard to understand, but she always made a great fuss of the young ones when they came in, which was one of the reasons her milk bar was so popular.

Meg patted her stomach. 'After that doughnut I don't think I could have another thing.'

'Ah, get ons with you,' Maria laughed, patting her own rounded stomach. 'The milkshakes theys be good for you.'

'Come on, Meg,' Jude said. 'Let's have another one. Then Dave and Ronan might dance with us. There's some room up the back near the jukebox.'

Dave winked at Ronan. 'Now that sounds like an offer too good to refuse.'

Ronan smiled. 'Why wait?' He stood up and held a hand out to Meg. 'Let's have a dance now while Maria gets our order.'

And, as he walked to the back of the milk bar with Meg, Ronan decided to try and put Clara out of his mind. Going over to the juke box he chose 'Come A Little Bit Closer', a song by the Delltones. He was soon mouthing the words and with a smile he pulled Meg close to him. But as he did, he wished with all his heart that the girl in his arms was Clara, which was unfair to Meg. So as soon as the song ended he took her back to their booth. When they'd finished their drinks the two girls caught a bus going in one direction and Ronan and Dave caught a bus going in the other, back to the Thompsons' house. As soon as he got to his room, Ronan sat down and picked up his guitar. When they first moved into Eureka Park he had found a guitar leaning against the wall in the living room, which he assumed must have been Uncle Finn's. Although it was totally different to the harp, he soon found that he could strum a tune. And before long the family would sometimes sit in the living room after dinner and Ronan would play and they would sing along. His father had a good voice so Ronan would let him lead. But every time Ronan played he would think of Clara and how she would sing along when he played the harp back at Rathgarven. At first this made him sad, but as time went on he was comforted by the music he played. The only song he couldn't bring himself to play was 'Molly Malone', for that was Clara's song. He looked at the card she had sent him last Christmas here at the Thompsons. On the front were two deer standing side by side in the snow under a fir tree on the edge of a frozen river. Inside she had written:

> *I wish we were those two deer, side by side in the snow by that river. Instead I'm here in London. And you are on the other side of the world. When Mummy and I go to Dublin and go down to the Fitzpatricks I can't believe I'll be in Kerry by the Kenmare River and you won't be there.*

Since that Christmas card he'd heard nothing, despite having written to her. Shifting his eyes from the card to the strings on his guitar, he tried to concentrate on what he was playing, but soon found he had no feeling for it. He put the guitar down and picked up a copy of *To Kill a Mockingbird*, one of the books his class had been given to read for English literature. Turning the pages slowly he forced himself to put Clara out of his mind and become immersed in the racial injustice of the American Deep South in the 1930s.

Chapter 25

When Lorna Medlow drove her jeep up to Eureka's homestead one Wednesday afternoon and greeted Kathleen with a warm hug, Kathleen felt as though she had known Lorna all her life. She loved her down to earth, easy-going attitude. When she'd phoned, she explained she would have been in touch earlier except she'd been back and forth to Sydney for treatment for skin cancer — treatment that, happily, had been successful.

Kathleen made them a pot of tea and they took it out onto the verandah, where they sat and chatted for over an hour, and Kathleen felt she'd found the friendship she had been missing so much. Lorna confided the problems she was having with her daughter, Maddie, who seemed to have gone off the rails, and Kathleen found herself confiding how she and James were often bickering about money.

'Ah, Brian and I were always at each other's throats about that. Nothing surer to try a marriage like money worries. Fortunately we're a bit better off these days, so it's not money we argue so much about. It's more likely to be Maddie.' She scrunched up her nose. 'Brian reckons I'm too hard on the kid. Believe me, if I wasn't strict, I reckon she'd be in real trouble by now. In fact, that's something I wanted to bring up with you. It's Jack, the young brother of one of our stable hands, who I know's up here working with you. Nice young man. But not the sort of bloke I want Maddie to end up with. That's why I suggested to Brian he get Jack to come up here. Blow me down didn't I find him back at our place the other day. What's more he and Maddie were smooching down behind the stables when I came across them. I soon gave him short bloody shift and told him to get going. I'd be grateful if you could keep an eye on him. Try and tether him here as much as you can. I reckon it's only a passing fad on Maddie's part.' Lorna grinned. 'She's fallen in and out of love more times than you could count on your blessed toes since she was the ripe old age of thirteen. Still, I wouldn't be surprised if Jack isn't taking it more seriously.'

'Oh,' Kathleen said. 'I'd no idea. I knew he goes down there a bit. I presumed it was to see his brother.'

'Ah, he sees his brother all right. He also sees Maddie when she's home.'

'Do you want me to talk to Jack?'

'No. Just see if you can keep him busy here. If you talk to him he's sure to leak it to Maddie. Then all hell will break loose.'

Later on the two women went down to the front paddock and Kathleen showed her Shannon Boy and his mother, Melody. When he saw them, Shannon Boy neighed and galloped towards them, tail frisking.

'Damn good-looking horse,' Lorna said. 'Wouldn't be surprised if he wins a few. I'll tell you what I'll do. Tommy Brown, the Sydney trainer, dropped in to our place the other day. He and Brian have known each other forever and a day. He's always on the lookout for a promising young horse he can train up. What's say I tell him to pop in here next time he's up this way? He can have a look.'

'Thank you,' Kathleen said. 'That'd be great.'

***

When Tommy Brown drove up in his big black car ten days later, tilting his wide-brimmed hat to Kathleen, she took to him straight away. He had a wonderful smile and honest eyes. He'd rung a few days earlier to say he was coming up to Tamworth and could drop in to look at Shannon Boy. Now here he was, watching Shannon Boy galloping around the paddock. Kathleen got Jack to put him

267

through his paces on the lunging rope, and Tommy poked and prodded and ran his hands all over him. He was more than impressed.

'Bring him on down to me next year,' he said, patting Shannon Boy on the rump. 'I know a lot of other trainers like to get them training earlier on but I prefer to wait until they're at least eighteen months.'

After he'd gone, Kathleen was so excited she rushed in to ring Lorna.

'He doesn't take many on,' Lorna said. 'So he must think he's got a real chance.'

It was Lorna who suggested that, as Maddie had grown out of her dappled-grey pony Muffin, they pass her on to Lillie, who was so happy to have her own pony again. There was no way that they could have afforded to buy her one.

Chapter 26

Lillie took Muffin for a long ride along the river, letting the pony splash in the water. As she rode, her thoughts were fixed on next week's dance. It was a fundraiser for the rural fire brigade, to be held in Gullumbindy's community hall. Everyone was talking about it, and people were coming from all around the district. A bus was even bringing people from Tamworth, and another bus from Quirindi.

'I think I'll wear my red skirt and a white t-shirt,' she'd said to Deb as they made plans for the big night.

'Mum said I could buy that dress in Marcus Clark's,' Deb gushed excitedly. 'You know… the one we saw in the window last week.'

'Gosh,' Lillie had said, trying to hide her envy at the thought of that yummy yellow dress. 'You'll look gorgeous.'

As she brought Muffin back to the stables, she thought again how she would love to have something new to wear. But she didn't want to ask her parents, as she knew finances were still tight. Her mother hadn't had a new dress since they got here, so for Lillie to ask if she could get something new would send her into one of those talks about being grateful for what she had and 'making do'. And, unlike Ronan, Marcus and Freddie, she hadn't grown much, so the clothes she already had still fitted her. Even so, she couldn't help thinking of Deb's new yellow dress. For some reason she thought of Clara, and how she would have something spectacular to wear if she happened to be here. Even Sheelagh would have concocted something special. Thinking of Sheelagh made her wonder about that fella, Seamus Flaherty, and she wondered if he was liking Canada.

'G'day, Lillie,' Jack said, disturbing her thoughts as he sauntered out of the feed shed.

'Are you going to the dance?' Lillie asked. 'You know… the one the Farmers and Graziers' Association is putting on to raise money for the fire brigade.'

'Yeah, I know. But I won't be here. I'm heading to Sydney. Your Dad's given me a few days off.'

'Oh. So what's down in Sydney to take you away from a dance? Or should I say, *who's* down in Sydney? I bet it's a girl.'

'Mind your own business, Lillie O'Sullivan,' Jack laughed.

'That's what Ronan always says.'

'Well… I reckon he's on the right track.'

But as she put Muffin back in the paddock, she knew she'd hit the nail on the head. Though how he would have met a girl that far away she had no idea. Maybe he'd known her from before he came here? Was that why he showed no interest in Lillie? She tried not to be jealous, for at times she still fantasised about kissing him. If she was being really honest she sometimes had what Father Fogarty would describe in the confessional as 'bad thoughts', imagining Jack fondling her breasts and even touching her a bit more, which made her quiver all over. But any passion she felt for him was obviously wasted, as he already had a girlfriend. And seeing as the other fella she fancied, Brad Hickey, also had a girlfriend, she wondered if she'd ever fall for anyone who was unattached. She knew one of the boys on the bus fancied her, because Deb told her so, but she didn't fancy him. Maybe at the dance she would meet someone. Which made her look forward to it even more.

Despite this, when the night of the dance arrived, she was a bit nervous as she and her family drove up to the community hall. Kero lamps hung from the rafters inside and gave out a welcoming glow, and hay bales were spread around to sit on. Just outside the side door there were a number of old oil drums with onions and sausages sizzling on the top. Lillie had seen them used before at Deb's place when her mother was cooking for the shearers. They worked like a sort of barbeque with a wood fire inside. In a corner a band was playing and there was a makeshift bar where glasses of beer were being handed out to the men from a large keg.

Lillie was carrying a sponge cake, which she and Ma had made that afternoon, as everyone had been asked to bring a plate with something for pudding.

'Talk about taking coals to Newcastle,' Ma laughed, pointing to a table already overflowing with cakes, pavlovas and tarts. 'But better take ours over, Lillie.'

Lillie placed the cake down with the others and saw Marcus and Freddie race over to their friends in the far corner. She went back to join her parents and Ronan, and Deb came over in her new yellow dress and greeted everyone.

'Lucky you,' Lillie gushed, touching the fabric. 'It's gorgeous.'

'You like it?'

'It's beautiful,' Ma said.

Deb looked at Lillie in her red skirt and white top. 'And you look great.'

Again Lillie tried not to be jealous of Deb's dress. But it made her feel drab. Even so, she was pleased for Deb, as she knew how much she'd coveted that dress, which was unusual for her. Deb normally only wore jeans. Lillie looked at Ronan and wondered if the dress was to impress him.

'Mum and Dad are over there,' Deb said, pointing to a group of adults. 'I'm sure they'd love to talk to you, Mr and Mrs O'Sullivan.'

Lillie went over with Dad, Ma and Ronan to talk to Deb's parents and was glad she hadn't told them about Deb's mother's first marriage and how she and Deb's father got together. It could have been awkward if she had. Thankfully it didn't seem as though

Sandra and her parents were there — that would be even more awkward. Particularly as she knew Ma wanted to suss out whether Winifred, Sandra's mum, had seen Uncle Finn before he died, and would be bound to approach her.

Leaving their parents to talk between themselves, Deb and Lillie went to join a group of girls from school and Ronan sauntered over to a few of his friends on the far side of the hall. Now a fellow who caught the school bus came over and asked Deb to dance. And then Lillie's heart gave a flip. Brad Hickey was sauntering across the floor, looking as handsome as ever. The closer he got the more she realised he was coming towards her.

'Hi Lillie,' he said with a lopsided grin. 'Like a dance?'

Lillie's heart flip turned a massive somersault. And she just knew her face was as red as that shiny fire engine parked outside the door. Even so, she said confidently, 'Sure, why not?' and stood up to take his hand. As she did she saw Deb wink at her over her partner's shoulder. She had never really danced with a boy before, although at school the girls often danced with each other to music from the transistor radio. She wished that she could have practised with another boy before dancing with Brad Hickey. But when he led her to the dance floor and put his arm around her as the band played a Frank Ifield ballad, she soon found she was moving to the music easily. She was sure she was the envy of most of the other girls, many far prettier than she was. Why Brad had asked her to dance she was at a loss to know.

'Where's your girlfriend?' she asked, looking up at him.

'Away up north. Tenterfield. Her sister lives there. So,' he added, glancing over at Ma and Dad, 'your parents took over Finn Malone's place. He and my Dad were mates.'

'Oh. Really?'

'He was a great bloke. Let me exercise a couple of his racehorses out at Eureka a few times. It's a mighty great place, being on the river like that.' He cleared his throat. 'I wonder why he committed suicide? He didn't seem the sort to do that.'

'That's what everyone says.' She raised an eyebrow. 'You knew he was an alcoholic?'

'I knew he liked his grog. Then so does my old man. When he's in his slops he gets all maudlin and reckons there's no way Finn Malone would've killed himself.'

'Really!' Lillie stepped back and looked up at him. 'Why's that?'

'Because he reckons he was a happy drunk whenever he was with him. And if he was going to kill himself he would've done it when his wife left, he was so cut up about it.'

'I only met his wife once, but she seemed nice.'

'My mum was sad when she took off. They went to school together. Anyway,' he grinned, 'how're you liking living in our part of the world?'

Lillie felt like saying that right this minute she could think of no better place to be than in the arms of Brad Hickey, whether in Australia or anywhere else in the world. Instead she said, 'It's a lot different to Ireland, but I really like it.'

'Yeah, it's not a bad place, though I'd like to travel one day. Wouldn't mind heading to Ireland. I've always wanted to go hunting. They reckon Ireland's the place to do that.' Lillie told him how her parents went hunting in Kerry and before she knew it she was telling him about Merlin and how much she missed him, even though she now had Muffin. Then the music speeded up and they pulled apart to twist and jive to the beat. She was really enjoying herself when the band stopped for a break and he saw her back to her seat. 'Thanks for that,' he said. 'No doubt I'll see you around some time.'

'Yeah,' Lillie said. 'And thanks a lot. It was great.'

'Wow,' Deb said, sitting down beside her. 'Lucky you. You really fancy him, don't you?'

'Fine lot of good it'll do me. It's just that his girlfriend's away.'

Deb laughed. 'Well, at least you got to dance with him. And maybe he'll ask you again.'

Much to Lillie's regret that was the last she saw of him that night as he left shortly afterwards. When Deb got up to go to the loo she wandered over and sat down beside her parents.

'I saw you dancing with that young man,' Ma said. 'You made a lovely couple.'

'Ma! He probably felt sorry for me. That's why he asked me.'

'Nonsense. You look very pretty tonight, darling.'

'He said his father used to be a friend of Uncle Finn's and he can't believe he killed himself. Do you still think he did?'

Ma nodded. 'There's no other possible explanation. People don't like to think of people doing something like that. It's much easier to imagine a different scenario.'

'Like what?'

'Oh… I don't know. That it was an accident or something.'

'How could it have been an accident? You said he had the gun right next to him. And that there were whisky bottles everywhere.'

'That's what I mean. Maybe he got drunk and started to play with his gun. Then it happened.'

Lillie shrugged. 'Down that mine in the middle of nowhere? Ma, that's not very likely.'

'You're probably right.'

Lillie looked outside to the sausage sizzle. 'You want me to get you a sausage in bread?' she asked. 'They've got lots of onions cooked as well.'

Her mother nodded. 'Thank you, darling. That'd be great.'

As Lillie went over to where they were handing out the sausages, she wondered again about what Brad Hickey had said.

And how many other people in this hall didn't think Uncle Finn had killed himself on purpose.

***

On the night of the end-of-year prize-giving at Christian Brothers, Ronan was excited to receive an award for best and fairest in rugby. Although he passed all his exams, he didn't win any academic prizes, but his results were good enough to get him into the degree in agriculture he wanted to do at the university in Armidale. Tea and biscuits and cocktail frankfurts and sausage rolls with tomato sauce were served after the ceremony in the school hall. Some of the talk turned to Prime Minister Robert Menzies' introduction of national service the year before. A few of Ronan's mates wondered if they'd be conscripted. Some even wondered if they'd be sent to Vietnam, as the war seemed to be escalating.

'You'll be right, mate,' Dave said to him. 'You're not an Aussie citizen.'

Later he asked his father what he thought. 'You reckon we should become Aussie citizens?'

'We certainly plan to,' James said. 'It's something your mother and I've talked about quite a bit. What do you think?'

Ronan was about to tell his father he was still aiming to go home to Ireland when he had saved up enough money, so it wouldn't really affect him. Then he decided to play along, rather than upset his father at this stage.

'Yeah,' he said. 'I reckon it's a good idea to become citizens.'

'You might get conscripted if we do.'

Ronan thought through the ramifications. If he was conscripted, it might put an end to his plans of returning to Ireland. Or would it? In the Army he should be able to save more money

275

than if he was at uni and working part-time. If he saved enough maybe he would get back sooner and be able to see Clara. Ronan still hadn't heard from her since that Christmas card before she went down to Kerry; she owed him at least two letters. He wondered if she had met someone else. He'd tried to take his mind off her by asking a couple of girls out on dates, including Meg, who he had taken to the movies and then back to Fitzroy's one afternoon. But he'd backed away when he realised she was taking it more seriously than he was. Hovering always in his mind was Clara.

'If I get conscripted,' he said to his father, 'I suppose I'll have to take it on the chin.'

'Well, let's see what pans out. We won't rush to become naturalised yet. The next thing you've got to do is get your driver's licence. And find somewhere to live in Armidale while you're doing your agricultural course up there.'

Ronan looked across to where Dave was talking to another friend of his. 'Pete and Dave are going up there too. It'd be great if we could board together. Pete's looking out for some digs.'

'That sounds good,' his father said, picking up a sausage roll and dipping it in tomato sauce. 'And Ronan, your mother and I are very proud of what you've achieved. I know it wasn't easy coming to Australia at your age and having to leave your friends behind. What you've done is to be admired.'

'Thanks,' Ronan said. He laughed. 'And you and Ma haven't done too badly either.'

As he went over to join his friends, Ronan realised he was looking forward to the future. The only cloud on the horizon was Clara. If he at least got a letter from her he would feel so much better.

But when New Year 1965 came and he still hadn't heard from her, despite sending another letter and a Christmas card, he decided she really had met someone else and didn't want to tell him. Jessica had said in her card to the family that they were going to Ireland again for Christmas, which made him wonder if it wasn't someone in Ireland who had captured her. In any case he decided to try and put her out of his mind and spent the break before uni started working hard on the stud with Jack and his father, and going out to Dave's uncle's place, where he helped with the cattle branding and drenching and even learnt how to crutch a sheep. A few nights a week he worked at the Telegraph Hotel helping Barney behind the bar. He'd got his driver's licence, so his father let him borrow the ute to drive in and out.

'Make sure you drive safely,' Ma said, the first night he went in. 'I won't sleep a wink until you get back.'

He enjoyed working with Barney and talking to the locals. Many of them had farmed the land for generations.

'One thing you've gotta know if you're going to make a living from the land,' one farmer told him when he heard Ronan was going to do an agriculture course, 'is that you don't own the land, mate. The land owns you.'

The only patron he didn't like was a hefty bloke who he soon worked out was the father of the girl who had bullied Lillie at school. He was a big talker with an ugly mouth and smoked constantly, ashing his cigarettes messily on the bar and wiping the ashes onto the floor where Ronan had to sweep them up.

'Over here, mate,' he'd shout at Ronan, knocking his empty glass on the bar. 'What's a bloke got to do to get another goddamn drink around here?'

Barney had told Ronan to try and slow down his drinks. 'He's a fricken ugly drunk. Got into more brawls than a prize fighter.'

'So how's the lucky O'Sullivan family doing out at Malone's place?' he asked Ronan one night when he was the only patron in the bar and Barney was out the back fetching a new keg.

'You lucky buggers landed on your feet all right, didn't you? Just as well the bastard topped himself, eh?'

Ronan was about to tell him to get lost when two farmers came in and he went to serve them. Then the bar filled up and Ronan made sure he steered clear of him, apart from pouring him another beer when he looked like creating merry hell if he didn't. At the end of his shift when Ronan went outside to get in the ute, the man was there, leaning against the back of the ute.

'Yeah,' he said, coming forward and poking Ronan in the chest. 'Bloody lucky Malone did what he did.'

'If you'll excuse me,' Ronan said, moving to the driver's door. 'I need to get on home now.'

The man staggered towards him and Ronan pushed him away, but not before he threw a punch and got Ronan on the nose. With blood pouring down his chin, Ronan gave him another push and the man reeled back, then rallied and staggered forward again, raising his hand. Ronan was just managing to fend him off when he heard a car drive into the yard and a woman called out.

'Leave him alone, Jim. Come over here. I'll take you home.'

The man shouted, his voice slurred, 'Don't you bloody well tell me what to do, Winifred.'

'I think you should go,' Ronan said calmly, wiping his nose and trying to ignore the shooting pain, 'before you do something you might regret.'

He opened the door of the ute and got in. As he drove out of the yard he saw the man stagger over to the car where the woman called Winifred was waiting. What was all that about? When he'd put a bit of distance between himself and the pub he pulled over and got out a handkerchief to wipe his face He felt his nose. It didn't seem broken, but it sure did hurt. Was the man just an ugly drunk, as Barney said? Or did he have something else on his mind?

The next day he told Lillie what had happened.

'Sounds like he's a real bully,' Lillie said, getting up to inspect his nose. 'Just like his daughter. You be careful of him.'

Lillie told him how Deb's mother had once been married to him, and how she had ended up with Deb's father.

When Ronan got over the shock, he said, 'Well, that explains a lot. He and his daughter obviously hate us because you're Deb's friend.'

'Yeah… but don't go telling Ma and Dad what I told you. Makes it awkward for Deb and her parents.'

'But everyone must know.'

'I didn't. And you didn't until now. It's his wife, Winifred, I feel sorry for. It was probably her who came to pick him up. Deb says she's really nice.'

'Yeah… it was a Winifred he called out to.'

'Poor woman.'

From then on Ronan tried to ensure that Barney was the one who served Sandra's father his beer. He also took to parking the ute near the back door under the light from the window. Even so, as he finished his shift each night Ronan always looked around in case he was ready to jump him.

When it came time for him to start at the New England University in Armidale, his parents drove him to the station in Tamworth to catch the train up with his mates Dave and Pete.

'Good luck,' James said, shaking his hand.

'Thanks Dad,' he said. 'I'll try and make you proud.' He went over to his mother and gave her a kiss. 'I'll write and let you know how it goes, Ma.'

As he walked to the train with Dave and Pete he looked back and swore he could see tears in Ma's eyes. Although he would still be coming home to Eureka often, he supposed she thought this was one more step he was taking to a life away from her.

A few minutes later he leant out the window and held her eyes. 'Take care,' he called out. 'And make sure the others do as well.'

That night the boys checked into the rambling weatherboard house they were sharing around the corner from the university. Even though the rooms were tiny, they each had one of their own and there was a kitchen and bathroom and a second toilet off the back verandah.

In Ronan's first week he managed to find a job at night in a local pub, and before too long he'd saved up enough money to buy himself a second-hand Mini, which he drove back and forth to Eureka. He really liked uni and living in Armidale, particularly as he managed to get into the uni rugby team and played a few games. He also enjoyed the night life, going to a few dances. There was even a disco he, Dave and Pete would go to, along with the drive-in theatre, which showed some damn good films.

'You still going back to Ireland by the time you're twenty-one?' Lillie asked him one long weekend when he'd driven home and they were down by the river. Ronan had a fishing line in the water and Lillie was holding a piece of meat on a string, hoping to snare a yabby.

'Of course.' He raised an eyebrow. 'You gonna come with me? Remember I promised to take you.'

'I remember.' Now she raised an eyebrow. 'So it's only Grandma you want to see?'

'What do you mean?'

'Nothing. I just wonder why you haven't got a serious girlfriend here, that's all. And Ma said Clara seems to be spending a lot of time in Ireland lately.'

'So?'

'Forget it. As sure as anything Clara's forgotten about all of us. I haven't had a letter for so long I can't remember. We didn't even get a Christmas card this year. At least Sheelagh sent me a card.'

At that moment Ronan's line jumped with a fish on the end. By the time he'd hauled it in and put it in the bucket along with the ones he'd caught earlier, he had enough to feed the whole family. He'd light the fire he'd made out of river stones in the back garden and cook them on the grate over the flames. As he climbed the embankment to the homestead beside Lillie, he thought she was probably right. He should forget Clara and get serious with someone over here. There was one girl at uni he'd been eying off. Perhaps he should ask her out?

Chapter 27

That winter of 1965 was unusually cold with a heavy frost lying on the ground for many hours some days. When the nights closed in, Kathleen would draw the curtains and light the fire in the living room, where the family would gather at weekends, playing cards, reading, singing along as Ronan played the guitar or watching television on a second-hand TV set the Hogans had kindly given them when they won a new set in a raffle. Although it was warm and cosy in the house, it was often freezing when they were exercising the horses early in the mornings. So when spring arrived and the elm tree in the front garden suddenly sprouted shiny new leaves, the prunus burst into bloom by the front gate, the daffodils Kathleen had planted beside the garden path waved gleefully in the warmer weather and the foals ran around in wide-eyed wonder, tails swishing, legs going in all directions, everyone's hearts lifted. Shannon Boy, who was turning into a fine specimen, brought Kathleen such joy as he gambolled in the paddock with the other foals. Although they'd sold off a number of yearlings over the past twelve months, there was no way Kathleen wanted to part with Shannon Boy, though the time was soon arriving when he'd have to be broken in if he was going to be the great racehorse she envisaged. In the meantime she wanted him to enjoy his carefree childhood for as long as he could before he went to Tommy Brown.

She and Lorna were seeing a bit of each other, as Lorna was up and down to her dentist in Tamworth. Sometimes she would ring Kathleen and they would meet for lunch at the Telegraph Hotel in Gullumbindy. Last time they met she told Kathleen that Maddie was enjoying being at university down in Sydney.

'She's planning on being a teacher,' she said proudly.

Kathleen was pleased for Lorna and Brian that Maddie had settled down.

But then one afternoon, when James was away in Brisbane with Brian looking at a new stallion, Kathleen went along to the manager's cottage where Jack was now living. She had made an apple pie, Jack's favourite, and saved him a large piece. She also wanted to check how Jack was keeping the place, as she hadn't been down for quite a while. When she knocked on the door Jack came outside. As he did, Kathleen couldn't help notice that there was a girl inside.

'I didn't know you had anyone else living here,' Kathleen said.

'Maddie caught the bus up a few days ago,' Jack said. 'I picked her up in the ute from Gullumbindy.'

'Maddie?' Kathleen exclaimed. 'Maddie Medlow?'

All Kathleen could think of was Lorna asking her to try to keep Jack at Eureka Park and away from Maddie, and how proud she and Brian were that she was at uni, studying to be a teacher.

'And you didn't tell us she was coming here?'

He looked sheepish. 'No. I sort of snuck her in. I was going to tell you when Mr O'Sullivan came back.'

'So her parents think she's still down in Sydney?' Kathleen knew she sounded cross.

'Yeah. Reckon so.'

Kathleen sighed. 'Honestly, Jack. How could you?'

'Would you like to meet her, Mrs O'Sullivan?'

Kathleen thought of saying no, but then decided it was best she did at least meet the girl. Then she could report back to Lorna.

She nodded. 'I suppose so.'

'Maddie,' Jack called out. 'Come meet Mrs O'Sullivan.'

When Maddie appeared at the door Kathleen's heart missed a beat and she found it hard to swallow. There was little doubt that the tall, dark-haired girl standing in front of her was not only very pretty but also wearing a wedding ring.

'You're married?' Kathleen exclaimed.

'We eloped,' Maddie said, giggling. 'We got married at a registry office in Sydney.'

'But you're far too young!'

'I'm eighteen. And dressed up I look much older, don't you agree?' Maddie smiled.

Kathleen shook her head. 'Jack, Maddie's parents will kill you.'

'Don't be cross, Mrs O'Sullivan,' Maddie said. 'Jack says we'll live here if that's okay.'

Over the last two days the phone lines had been down due to the gale-force winds and torrential downpour they'd had. Even the crossing on the road into Gullumbindy had flooded and they were more or less stranded at Eureka Park. Freddie couldn't get to school and Lillie and Marcus, who was now also living with the Thompsons and going to the Christian Brothers, might not get home on the weekend. So, much as she wished to reach for the telephone at the moment, Kathleen couldn't ring Lorna.

'I've absolutely no idea if it's okay or not,' she finally stammered. 'But one thing I do know is that as soon as the phones are working I'll need to let your mother know you're here.'

She then almost threw the piece of apple pie at Jack and stomped back to the homestead. She'd been cruel to the young couple, but Jack had taken advantage of the trust they'd shown in him by giving him the house and allowing him time off to go down to Sydney. And Maddie had let her parents down in the worst possible way. She wondered how she would react if it was Lillie who had eloped. In a way Kathleen thought she would cope better if it were Lillie. It was just that Lorna had asked her to keep an eye on Jack. And she had let her down.

The next morning the phones were back on and Kathleen braced herself to ring Lorna. 'I don't know how to tell you this,' she began, 'but I'm afraid Maddie's up here.'

'Bloody hell,' Lorna exclaimed. 'What in God's name is she doing there?'

'She came up on the train. She's in the manager's cottage with Jack.'

'But I only spoke to her a few days ago…'

'Lorna, I think you'd best come up as soon as you can. With all the rain the crossing has been closed, but when the electricity man rang to say they'd fixed the telegraph pole that was down, he also said the crossing's now open again.'

'Trust Brian to be away at a time like this. And James.'

'Yes,' Kathleen said. 'I wish he was here too.'

'I'll get in the car and come up right now. And woe betide that girl when I see her.'

But by the time Lorna arrived that afternoon and Kathleen took her down to the cottage, Jack and Maddie had disappeared. The house was empty of clothes and the ute, which Jack normally parked near the back door, was gone.

'Didn't you hear them go?' Lorna asked accusingly.

'No. As soon as I heard the crossing had opened I drove Freddie in to school. That's obviously when they took off. Then I was busy doing bookwork, so didn't notice that Jack wasn't here. In any case I didn't want to confront them again until you were here.'

'I asked you to keep an eye on him,' Lorna said. 'Hold him up here.'

'I'm sorry. I didn't click that he was going to Sydney to see her.' She paused. 'And there is another thing.'

'What?'

'They're married.'

'Married? How the hell could they be married?'

'A registry office in Sydney apparently.'

Kathleen wondered if this would be the end of their friendship as Lorna paced furiously, running a hand through her messy hair.

'Brian will kill him,' she said. 'I know he will.'

'I think they're very much in love.'

'That won't stop Brian.' She sighed. 'I thought if he was up here Maddie would be safe.'

'Jack's a grown man, Lorna. I couldn't watch him twenty-four hours a day, every day of the week. He was entitled to time off. Away from here.'

'I'm sorry,' Lorna said, trying a small smile. 'I shouldn't be blaming you. I should've seen it coming. I wondered why Maddie didn't come home for her birthday. And when I suggested that Brian and I go down to Sydney, she said she was going out with her friends.' She sighed. 'And this has left you high and dry without anyone to look after the horses while James is away with Brian.'

Kathleen nodded. 'I can't believe Jack would leave us in a pickle like this. He doesn't seem the type to do that.'

She had no sooner said that than she saw Jack drive back in in his ute. But there was no sign of Maddie. She watched as he made his way over to her and Lorna.

'Maddie didn't want to see you, Mrs Medlow,' he said. 'When she heard Mrs O'Sullivan was ringing you she wanted to get out of here. I've taken her to a friend's place. She'll wait for me there until Mr O'Sullivan comes back tomorrow to look after the horses. Then I'll go join her and we'll head up north.'

'Where is she?' Lorna demanded.

'She doesn't want you to know.' Jack looked her straight in the eye. 'But I'll look after her, Mrs Medlow. Don't you worry about that.'

'She can't just disappear like that.'

'I tried to get her to wait for you. But as you know, Maddie's not one to be bossed about. This is what she wanted. She reckons you'd try to talk her out of marrying me…'

'Brian will have your bloody guts for garters, young man,' Lorna said. 'Make no mistake about that.'

Kathleen put her hand on Lorna's arm to try and calm her down. 'Lorna, come up to the house and I'll put the kettle on. In the meantime, Jack, you go see to the horses. I appreciate that you've at least come back to do that.'

'We'll let you know where we end up, Mrs Medlow,' Jack said. 'I promise you that.'

Lorna shook her head and looked from Jack to Kathleen. 'Apart from getting the police out I don't suppose there's much we can do?'

'And you wouldn't want to do that, would you? Mrs Medlow, Maddie's old enough to look out for herself.'

As Kathleen walked back to the house with a furious Lorna, she thought how right Jack was. Maddie was indeed old enough to decide what she wanted to do. She recalled when she was not much older, all alone in India during the war after her parents had died. She had been able to make her own decisions then. As she had later on.

Chapter 28

It was a wet Friday night and Lillie was lounging in a chair in front of the TV watching Billy Thorpe performing on *Bandstand*, her favourite program, and wishing she hadn't got her hair cut into a bob, when her mother rushed into the room waving an aerogram.

'Would you believe Clara's got engaged to Charles Fitzpatrick?' she said. 'I've only just opened Jessica's letter, which came this afternoon.'

'Charles Fitzpatrick?'

'Yes. Hugh's older brother. You probably can't remember him. He wasn't at Drominderry House much. He lived in Malaya with his parents for years.'

'And Clara's engaged to him? How incredible.'

'Here, read what Jessica's got to say. I must admit it all sounds very romantic.'

Lillie put her bottle of Coke down, took the aerogram from Ma and started to read. Clara was doing an Arts degree in London and it appeared Jessica and Clara had gone over to Ireland again for a month during the university break. They'd taken a flat in Dublin for the week of the acclaimed Dublin Horse Show and stayed on. From there they'd driven down to County Kerry and popped in to Drominderry House. It was while they were there that Clara had met Charles, who'd recently come back from Malaya after Lord Fitzpatrick died from lung cancer. As Charles's own father had been killed in a shooting accident in Malaya, Charles was now the inheritor of Drominderry House. And the title. His mother had chosen to live in England, but Charles was living with his grandmother in the family home, where Hugh still spent his holidays. Jessica described how the romance unfolded:

From the first moment Charles set eyes on Clara, he fell head-over-heels in love. For the month we were in Dublin he drove up once a week. He's doing a part-time course at Trinity and stays with a friend who has a flat in Merrion Square next door to where Oscar Wilde used to live. Each night he took Clara out for dinner, or sometimes they'd go for a drive into the countryside for a day. When we returned to London, Charles wrote to Clara often. Ultimately he came over to London to continue the courtship. And, my darling, Kate, guess what? He asked her to marry him. At first she was hesitant. Needless to say I soon put her straight. I know she's very young. But heavens above, a proposal like that is not to be sniffed at. Anyway, my sweet, thank God she finally agreed, so long as she could go travelling first. I think she's bonkers to dilly dally, but there you go, that's daughters for you. He's such a lovely man. I know he'll make Clara very happy. Not to mention the fact she'll become Lady Fitzpatrick and mistress of that magnificent estate. It's such a pity you're not all still close by at Rathgarven, particularly as I'm bound to spend a lot of time at Drominderry.

Lillie handed the letter back to her mother. 'Jees… it sounds as though Charles Fitzpatrick's besotted. So must Clara be, to accept his proposal. Despite Jessica seeming to think she wasn't so sure to begin with.'

'She does seem young to take on so much responsibility,' Kathleen said, folding up the aerogram. 'But I'm sure she'll do a great job.'

'What do you think Ronan will make of it?'

'I'm sure he'll be delighted for her. As we all should be. And delighted for the Fitzpatrick family. It'll make up for their sadness with the passing of dear Lord Fitzpatrick. And Charles's father.'

'You don't think Ronan will be upset?'

'Why for heaven's sake would he be upset? He and Clara were friends when they were more or less children. I can't imagine he's given her a second's thought lately.'

'I suppose you're right.'

Even so, after Ma left to tell Dad, who had come up from the stables, Lillie wondered if she should ring Ronan and see what he made of it. Apart from anything else he was bound to be flabbergasted that Clara was going to marry a lord. Particularly Charles Fitzpatrick. But as he was away on a sheep station up north for a few weeks, putting his study into practice, she couldn't contact him anyway. She wished Jack were here so she could gossip with him about it. She really missed him. She had got such a shock when she rang home one night and Ma told her what had happened with him and Maddie Medlow.

'Wow… So that's the girl he was going down to Sydney to see,' she'd said to Ma.

'I promised Lorna I'd keep an eye on him. And what did he do? Run off and marry Maddie.'

'Gosh, Ma, you couldn't help that.'

'No, I suppose not.'

'But what will Dad do without him?'

'Arthur's coming back. He rang your father a few weeks ago to see if there was any work. He was always good with the horses and it was only that we couldn't really afford to keep him on.'

Then last weekend Ma had told her that Lorna Medlow had rung and said that Jack and Maddie were living on a cattle farm up in the Mapleton area in the hinterland behind the Sunshine Coast. Jack was working on the farm and Maddie was now pregnant.

'I think Lorna's more or less come to terms with it now,' she told Lillie. 'She even said she promised to go up and help out when the baby's due.'

Lillie had been pleased that they'd worked it out. She really liked Mrs Medlow. With her swearing and knockabout way of dressing, she was different to Ma in many ways, but she and Ma got on really well and she always made time to talk to Lillie when she popped in to Eureka.

Now she thought of Clara living at Drominderry House. She didn't really remember the place that well, but Ma had always said how magnificent it was. Lillie tried not to be jealous that Clara would be living there on the Kenmare River with Maisie and Paddy. But she was.

What would Ronan think? He was sure to be a bit upset, even if was a long time since he'd seen Clara.

Two weeks later when Lillie rang home, Ma told her she had had a letter from Clara, asking if she could come and stay at Eureka Park. She was going to India first, then Hong Kong and finally to Australia.

'Won't it be lovely to have her?' Ma was thrilled. 'I hope you don't mind if she shares with you, darling.'

'No, of course not.'

Inwardly Lillie thought: I bet she'll come with all the best clothes and make me feel dull and fat again. Even so, she was looking forward to hearing what she thought of marrying Charles Fitzpatrick and going to live at Drominderry House. In a way it was a bit like a fairytale.

***

That weekend Ronan was back and Lillie had her chance to ask him about Clara when the two of them were down in the stables feeding the horses.

'So, what you think of Clara marrying Charles Fitzpatrick and going to live at Drominderry House? She's certainly taking a step up in the world, eh?'

'I'm sure she'll be very happy.'

'And what about her coming here?'

'It will be good to see her again,' he said, stepping over to the hessian bag of chaff in the corner and filling up a steel bucket.

'You're not jealous she's marrying Charles Fitzpatrick?'

'No. Why should I? We were childhood friends, Lillie. And, as everyone knows, you grow out of childhood.' He took the bucket over to the stable of a grey mare that was about to foal. 'Besides,' he said, turning around, 'I've met a really nice girl at uni. I've been taking her out for a while now. So why would I be jealous of Clara marrying Charles Fitzpatrick? I'm actually very happy for her.'

'I didn't know you were dating someone.'

'Did you expect me to put it in the newspaper? The dashing Ronan O'Sullivan's dating a girl?'

'Ha ha. Sarcasm is the lowest form of wit. Anyway, what's she like?'

'She's good fun. And what's more she likes watching me play rugby. More than I can say for you, li'l sis.'

'I would watch you, but I'd have to catch the bus up.'

'I know. Only joking.'

Lillie wondered if Ronan had sex with his girlfriend. It wasn't something she could come straight out and ask. All the same she was curious.

'Imagine Maddie Medlow getting pregnant so quickly after getting married.'

'If they hadn't wanted to they could have used something.'

'Oh! Like what?'

'A condom or something.'

'Do you use one?'

Ronan shook his head. 'Gees, Lillie. How many times do I have to tell you to mind your own goddamn business?'

So he probably does have sex. Maybe I'm the only girl in the whole of New South Wales who hasn't had sex. Apart from Deb, that is. Lillie was pretty sure Deb hadn't had sex either, or she was bound to have told her.

That night after dinner Ma got up from the kitchen table to answer the phone. When she came back she was smiling. 'That was Clara. She'll be with us in the New Year, in six weeks' time. Isn't that exciting?'

'Goodness. That's not far off at all,' Lillie said. 'I can't wait.'

Ronan, who was taking his turn to dry the dishes, looked around. 'No, it's not far off at all.' He put the tea towel down and walked towards the door. 'Reckon I'll call it a night. I've got an assignment due in on Monday.'

'Of course, darling,' Kathleen said.

Despite the fact Ronan was dating, and most likely having sex with the girl up in Armidale, Lillie still wondered how he'd feel when he saw Clara again.

***

When she wasn't at school Lillie found that, although she really missed Jack, she came to know Arthur quite well, as she was spending more and more time down at the stables helping out. Often when they were mucking out the stalls together he would tell her stories about the bush and how his grandparents lived a few miles off the road out to Bourke, where he sometimes went to visit. He told her his mother, who was white, taught at the mission school and had fallen in love with his father when she was working in the area and he was a stockman on a nearby cattle station.

'When she got up the duff with me they came to town to live,' he told her. 'Since they broke up m'old man spends most of the time back in the bush with m'Pop.'

'What about your mother? What's she doing now?'

'She met a white fella. They've got three kids.'

'So do you see them much?'

'Now and then. It's better being with m'old man.'

'Do you eat witchetty grubs when you're out in the bush?'

Arthur chuckled. 'Yeah. They're not bad.'

'Really? What do they taste like?'

'When you cook 'em the outside's a bit like a crispy chicken. Inside's like an egg.'

'Not sure if I like the sound of that.'

The next afternoon, as they were washing the stables out, Lillie and Arthur saw Dingo sniffing the ground down next to the water trough. Lillie thought it might have been a bone, and Arthur wandered over to see what he was on about. He crouched down on his haunches and fossicked in the dirt. Picking up a handful he put it close to his face. When he stood up, he held a used cartridge in his hand.

'I reckon someone's shot a rabbit or something round there,' he said. 'There's traces of blood in the dirt. And this cartridge.'

'Gosh, how could you work out there's blood there?'

Arthur grinned. 'I'm not part blackfella for nothun.'

'It must be from a gun Uncle Finn had,' she said. 'Don't think Dad or Ronan have shot anything down here, although Ronan's shot a few rabbits and snakes in the paddocks and Mum shot a snake up near the house. Best put it somewhere away from Dingo. He might swallow it.'

Arthur pointed to the ledge above where the saddles were kept. 'I'll put it up there and throw it out later.'

Once again Lillie felt really sad about what Uncle Finn had done. She shivered, and wondered if the cartridge was from the gun he had shot himself with. Nonetheless, she put it out of her mind as she got ready to go into Tamworth with Deb to see *Dr Strangelove* at the movies. Deb's mother was going to pick her up from Gullumbindy where Ma would drop her off. When they arrived at the theatre there were a couple of fellas Deb knew who joined them sitting up the back, eating Jaffas and giggling. When the boy sitting next to Lillie took her hand she wasn't quite sure what to do, but in the end she let him hold it right through the movie. Afterwards when they went down to Fitzroy's for a milkshake and ice cream he put his arm around her. At that moment Brad Hickey came in with a group of friends and sat down at the next table. He smiled at her and she got goose bumps all over and moved the boy's arm away.

When Brad got up to leave with his friends, he came over. 'G'day Deb. How you been?' he said, running a hand through his hair and standing there looking gorgeous.

'Great,' Deb said.

Then he looked at Lillie and asked how she was

'Fine, thank you,' she smiled.

'You look great,' he said.

'Thanks,' she said, hoping no one, particularly Brad Hickey, noticed that she was blushing bright red.

But Deb had; she knew how much Lillie fancied him. When he left she looked at Lillie and said, 'Yeah, it's real hot in here, isn't it,' and laughed. 'That's why you're the colour of the strawberry on my ice cream.'

Lillie wondered if the way she felt about Brad Hickey was how Clara felt about Charles Fitzpatrick. Even though Ronan had a girlfriend, would he get goose bumps like this when he saw Clara again? For the fancy-sounding Lord Charles Fitzpatrick's sake, she hoped not.

Later, as they waited for Deb's mother to pick them up, they looked at the Christmas decorations in the shop windows. Lillie couldn't believe the year had gone so quickly. Soon it would be the New Year and Clara would be arriving.

Part Four

Eureka Park
1966 to 1968

Chapter 29

Ronan looked anxiously down the railway line to see if the train from Sydney was in sight. He and his mother and Lillie were all at Tamworth station this Sunday afternoon waiting for Clara to arrive. It was hard to believe that it was nearly two and half years since he had last seen her. He wondered how much she had changed. Since he'd started dating Trish he'd tried hard to put Clara out of his mind, and at times he'd succeeded. But when he'd heard she was to marry Charles Fitzpatrick, she slipped her way back into his thoughts more and more. It wasn't long before he realised he was extremely jealous of Charles Fitzpatrick.

The moment Clara stepped down onto the platform, he could see that, although she was even more beautiful than he remembered, her sweep of blonde hair hanging loosely on her shoulders, she was still the same Clara. She wore a pair of blue jeans and a white t-shirt that clung to her full breasts and accentuated her slim waist. She'd also grown a good two inches and was taller than Ma, who rushed forward to take her in her arms.

'Aunt Kathleen,' Clara said excitedly, shoving her sunglasses high on her forehead above her vibrant blue eyes. 'How gorgeous you look! I swear to God you haven't aged a minute since I last saw you.'

Then it was Lillie's turn to greet her warmly with a kiss on the cheek.

'And Lillie… I love your bob,' Clara said. 'I nearly got mine cut like Cilla Black has hers, but Mummy talked me out of it.'

Now she looked over and saw Ronan. For a moment both of them stood staring at each other, before Clara's face broke into a radiant smile.

'Oh Ronan,' she cried, coming over to him. 'I can't believe it's you. Last time I saw you we were children. Now you're a man.' She looked up at him. 'You must be over six foot.'

'Hi Clara,' he said, returning her smile. 'It's great to see you again. And I believe congratulations are in order. You're to become Lady Charles Fitzpatrick.'

'Yes, I am.'

Ronan could see she wasn't sure what to do next and he wasn't, either. So to relieve the awkwardness he stepped forward and gave her a warm hug and kissed her lightly on the cheek. 'You look beautiful. Even more than I remember.'

'Ah, get on with you, Ronan,' she laughed, stepping back. 'I might've grown, but I look just the same.' She glanced across at Ma and Lillie, who were watching them. 'Imagine me being here in Australia. It's so different to England and Ireland. I couldn't believe it on the train up. All so sparse and brown. And,' she added, wiping her forehead, 'so much hotter. I can't wait to get to Eureka Park and have a swim in that river you told me about, Ronan.'

'Well,' Ma said, beckoning Ronan, 'you get Clara's luggage and we'll head back there right now. Marcus and Freddie are bursting with jealousy that we've got to see you first. And James is keen to see you as well.'

'And I can't wait to see them too,' Clara said. She moved over and put an arm around Lillie. 'I'm glad I had that night in the hotel in Sydney. I don't feel tired at all despite that long flight.'

Ronan stowed Clara's luggage and got behind the wheel. Ma sat beside him, with Clara and Lillie in the back seat.

'Do show us your ring,' Ma said, turning to Clara.

Clara held up her hand with a large diamond in a gold setting. 'I wanted something simple.'

'It's beautiful,' both Kathleen and Lillie said at once.

'Show Ronan,' Lillie said.

Clara leaned over and showed Ronan.

'That's some diamond,' he said, taking his eyes off the road for a second. It must have cost a small fortune, he thought, but then to the Fitzpatricks, it was probably a drop in the ocean.

Clara looked a bit embarrassed. 'I actually wanted something smaller, but Mummy said I should have this one.'

'She helped you chose it?' Ma asked.

'Sort of. Charles and I picked out a few and then Mummy came in and helped me make the final choice.'

And I bet it didn't take her long to choose the largest, Ronan thought, chiding himself for being such a bad sport.

'Now tell us about Drominderry House,' Kathleen said. 'How's Lady Fitzpatrick? And how are dear Maisie and Paddy?'

'They're great. I think they were very excited when they heard Mummy and I would be coming there to live. Well, Lady Fitzpatrick said they were, anyway.'

'I'm sure they will be, darling.' Kathleen smiled. 'And you've seen darling Alice as well. How is she?'

'Last time I saw her she was fine. Missing you all, of course. But she looked good. And I think she's happy in Dublin. I haven't seen her since I knew I was coming over here. Otherwise I'm sure she'd have loaded my suitcase with pressies for you all.' She grinned. 'I wish I had a grandmother like her.'

Ronan knew Clara's paternal grandparents had died years ago in India. And Jessica's mother had died about fifteen years ago, having returned to England from India after her husband died in Calcutta after the war.

'We do miss her,' Ma said. 'But we ring up from time to time and write often.'

Clara looked at Ronan in the rear-vision mirror. 'How's uni, Ronan? And,' she laughed, 'have you met the love of your life?'

Ronan smiled. 'I've got a nice girlfriend. I'm sure you'll like her.'

'Well, you'll have to introduce me.' She looked at Lillie. 'And how about you? Are you madly in love?'

Lillie laughed. 'I wish I was. But no, I haven't met anyone I really like who likes me.'

'Lillie's far too young to be thinking of things like that,' Ma jumped in. 'She's got to get her Leaving Certificate first.'

Clara grinned. 'She's only a few years younger than me and I'm getting married. I wanted to leave it a bit later to get engaged, but Mummy said I should accept now or Charles might change his mind.'

'Well, I think it's a great idea you decided to do a bit of travelling first.'

'Thank you, Aunt Kathleen. I wish Mummy thought the same. She was a bit annoyed with me. But dear Charles understood totally.'

'Have you got lots of photos of him?' Ma asked.

'In my suitcase. I'll show you when I get to Eureka Park if you like.'

'That would be lovely, darling.' Ma turned to Ronan with a bright smile. 'Won't it Ronan?'

Ronan nodded. The last thing he wanted to do was to gush over copious photos of Lord Charles Fitzpatrick with his huge estate and pots of money to go with it, which was making Clara's mother more than happy. When he'd first heard Clara was marrying Charles the first thing he had thought was how Jessica would be beside herself with joy. She'd achieved what she had set out to do: marry her daughter off to a wealthy and titled husband.

'Sure,' he now said, trying to sound enthusiastic. 'I'd like to see some photos of the dashing prospective groom.'

His mother turned back to Clara. 'Jessica sounds so delighted that you're marrying Charles. She'll love being able to visit you now and then.'

'Oh, she'll be doing more than that. Charles said she can have the flat at the side of the house as her own. It's got a lovely view of the Kenmare River. And buckets of sun.'

'Oh, how lovely. Jessica will adore that.' Ma paused. 'So she's definitely not going back to Calcutta?'

'Heavens no, Aunt Kathleen. She and Phillip are getting a divorce. I think she sees her future as spending more time in Ireland with us. It'll be great to have her with me when I'm settling in. Even though Lady Fitzpatrick will be there, there'll be so much to learn.'

It was only a couple of years since Clara had told Rory that Jessica gave her the heebie-jeebies. How things change, he thought.

'Your mother will keep her place in London?' Ma asked.

'I'm not sure about that. She may give it up.'

'And live with you full-time,' Ronan said. As the words left his mouth he thought he could see a slight cloud pass over Clara's eyes.

'That's more or less the idea. She and Charles get on so well. And of course she adores Lady Fitzpatrick. And with dear Maisie and Paddy there it's sure to be fun.'

As he drove Ronan wondered if Clara really meant that. Starting life in a new house with a new husband would be difficult enough without having to contend with her mother being there all the time. Even when they were children, Ronan could remember Clara complaining about how controlling Jessica was. Hearing now how she'd more or less bullied Clara into accepting Charles Fitzpatrick's proposal straightaway only confirmed it. There was no doubt that Jessica was delighted with the turn of events. *Lord* Charles Fitzpatrick would undoubtedly shower the mother of his bride with loads of money and gifts, and keep her in the lap of luxury.

You are a cynic, he chided himself. When he glanced again at Clara in the rear-vision mirror he had to admit that she looked more than happy with the situation. And why shouldn't she be?

***

All Lillie's insecurities came back in a rush. Clara was even more beautiful than she remembered and even though she was only wearing a white t-shirt and blue jeans, there was something about the cut of the jeans and the way the t-shirt clung to her slim waist. She tried to work out what Ronan was thinking, but he gave nothing away.

When they arrived back at the homestead she saw Marcus and Freddie rush out to greet Clara as she got out of the car.

'Golly gosh, look at you,' she said to Freddie, picking him up and giving him a twirl. Freddie grinned so widely it was as if someone had given him ten shillings to spend on lollies at the Gullumbindy corner store. 'And, my oh my, what about you!' Clara laughed, turning to Marcus, who had Brylcreemed his hair especially for the occasion. 'Quite the teenager now, aren't we?'

When she saw Lillie's father she rushed over and gave him a warm kiss on the cheek. 'Uncle James, you haven't changed one tiny bit.'

'Don't know about that,' he smiled. 'It's always terrific to see you, Clara.'

'Mummy said to say a special hi to you.'

'Did she now? Well that was kind of her.'

A flicker of something Lillie couldn't read passed across Dad's eyes, but then it disappeared and she wondered if she'd imagined it. As Clara stood back with a huge grin from ear to ear, exclaiming how wonderful Eureka Park looked, it was obvious to Lillie that, like her mother, she had the ability to charm the birds from the trees. Surely Ronan couldn't be unaware of how beautiful Clara was. It really wasn't fair that someone should look like that — and be such a nice person.

They made their way inside to the kitchen, where Lillie got a bottle of lemonade out of the fridge and Ma made a pot of tea. From the pantry cupboard she brought out the chocolate cake she'd made especially for Clara's arrival.

'How delicious,' Clara enthused. 'Do you have a cook? Like the wonderful Maisie?'

Kathleen shook her head. 'No. We make do with what I manage to scrape together.'

'And she does a great job,' James added.

'I do my best. With Lillie's help.' She smiled at Clara. 'Now tell me, where are the photos of your Charles? It seems like centuries since I've seen him. And even then he didn't come to Drominderry House that often.' She turned to Ronan. 'You met him a couple of times when you were much younger.'

'Really? Can't say I can remember him.'

Clara went to her suitcase and pulled out two photos.

'Quite the young lord, isn't he?' Ma said, as she and Lillie studied a picture of Charles in cricket whites with a green cap on his head. The other snap was taken down by the Kenmare River in front of Drominderry House, and showed Charles with his arm around Clara. Lillie thought how happy they looked.

'When's the wedding?' she asked, peering at Charles's face. Although one wouldn't describe him as madly handsome, he had a certain air. But he did look a lot older and more sedate than Clara.

'August,' Clara said. 'In Christchurch Cathedral in Dublin.'

'Gosh,' Lillie exclaimed. 'It's going to be some wedding.'

'We're having the reception at the Shelbourne.'

'My oh my,' Ma exclaimed. 'It should be spectacular.'

Clara looked around the family. 'I wish you could all be there.' She settled her eyes on Ronan. 'It'd be such fun if you could be.'

'Ah,' Ronan laughed, 'you'll have so many guests you won't miss us one bit.'

'I will so,' Clara said. 'In any case I'll send lots of photos.'

When tea was finished and the kitchen tidied up, Lillie took Clara to their bedroom where she quickly unpacked a few things before they all went down to the river for a swim. Deep shadows were forming across the water and on the far bank Lillie could see that the neighbour's cattle had come down for their usual drink with a gaggle of wild geese paddling happily next to them.

'How divine is this!' Clara exclaimed, scrambling down the bank. 'Your very own swimming hole right at your back door. It's nearly as good as the Kenmare River.' She dragged a sandal off and placed her toe in the water. 'Gee whiz! It's so warm.' She pulled her toe out and looked closely. 'I've heard of leeches. Are there any in here?'

'Not that we've seen. They may well be waiting to leap onto the skin of a tasty English girl,' Ronan laughed. 'Probably far juicier than us Irish.'

'Get on with you,' Kathleen said. 'Don't you take any notice of him, Clara. There are no leeches.'

'What about crocodiles?'

'They're up in the Northern Territory or far north Queensland,' Lillie said. 'The most you have to look out for are snakes.'

'Ronan killed one last week,' Freddie piped up with great excitement. 'Right there where you're standing.'

Clara looked down at the ground and playfully expressed fear and trembling. 'My goodness… surely you're joking?'

'No, I'm not. It was a whopper.' Freddie held up his arms to show the length. 'Ronan shot it with a gun. He shoots lots of snakes. They're everywhere. One even came up to the back door and Ma shot it right through the head. It was a red-bellied black one. They kill you in a second.'

'Enough of that,' James said. 'Poor Clara will be on the next plane home.'

'Well, it's true,' Freddie protested. 'You better not leave your bedroom door open… or the bathroom. They like water.'

'Freddie,' Kathleen exclaimed, wagging a finger at him. 'You're teasing poor Clara.'

Clara laughed. 'Don't worry. I can take it. But, young man,' she said, ruffling
Freddie's hair, 'you watch out… I'll soon find a way to get back at you. Make no mistake about that.'

Dingo was first in for a swim, paddling across to a small sandbank in the middle of the river where he scrambled ashore, rolled in the sand, and shook himself thoroughly. Then everyone placed their towels down on the pebbly beach and started to get undressed. Clara removed her jeans and top and stood there, looking magnificent in a white bikini. Even though she had come straight from an English winter, Lillie noticed how her skin was a soft caramel against the white of her bikini and looked to see Ronan's reaction, but he was already wading in. He dived below the surface and came up downstream, where he shook his hair out of his eyes, before swimming to the other side and back. Soon everyone was in the river, shouting and splashing water over Clara, who gave as good as she got.

Later, as they clambered up the bank, Lillie thought that, despite how frumpy Clara made her feel, it was fun to have her here.

***

306

Lillie was fascinated to see how Clara fitted in with the family just as she did at Rathgarven. Marcus and Freddie adored having her around. So did Dad and most of all Ma, who now had another woman to keep her company when Lillie and her brothers weren't there. She was also a great help with the horses and got on really well with Arthur, who taught her all sorts of things about the bush.

'He said he'd try and find me a witchetty grub,' she laughed. 'Not sure it'd be to my taste.'

On Saturday afternoon Lillie and Clara were down in the bottom paddock watching Ma put Shannon Boy through his paces. He was due to go down to Tommy Brown's stables, Burra Lodge, in a couple of weeks. Lillie knew Ma would miss him dreadfully when he went. Over the last few months Lillie had watched his progress as Ma and Arthur gently broke him in. Now he was quite used to the saddle, after objecting furiously to begin with and throwing Arthur off a number of times when he first mounted him.

'I'm dreading the day he leaves,' Ma now said, doing up the girth. 'I know it's in the best interests of the stud, and if Tommy manages to make him a Group One winner, Eureka Park will become famous.' She gave Shannon Boy a kiss on his star. 'And my initial premonition that he was destined for greatness will be proved right.'

Later, as Clara and Lillie leant on the fence watching Arthur gallop Shannon Boy around the track with Ma eyeing him closely from the middle, Clara said, 'I thought Ronan would have come home for the weekend. Does he stay up in Armidale often?'

'Depends. If he has a rugby match on,' Lillie said, 'or a party or something. Not sure what's on up there this weekend. Maybe he's taking his girlfriend out.'

'Have you met her?'

'No, not yet.'

'You think it's serious?'

'Sounds like it.'

'Oh, really?'

Even though she was engaged to Lord Charles Fitzpatrick, was she jealous that Ronan had a girlfriend? It made Lillie think.

'Your friend Deb sounds fun,' Clara said, changing the subject. 'I'd love to meet her.'

'I'm sure you will. They've been flat out shearing sheep. Deb helps in the sheds at weekends so I haven't seen much of her except at school. But she's having a birthday party in a few weeks at her place. Ronan and I are going. I'll ask her if you can come too.'

'That would be fun. I'd love to see an Australian sheep farm. Is she your best friend?'

'Yes. Though there are some other girls at school I like as well. One's a day boarder and I sometimes stay the weekend with her if I've got a hockey or softball match on.'

'Do you like school?'

'I hated it at first. Now I quite like it.'

Lillie kicked the grass. She did like school now and was doing okay in her studies. She loved English literature and thought she might try to get into a course at uni when she left school. She wouldn't mind teaching, but would prefer to go to a university, like Maddie Medlow had until she ran off with Jack, rather than a teacher's college. Would Clara miss not having a career? Mind you, being married to a lord with a huge estate was probably a career in itself.

'Will you finish your degree?' she asked.

'I want to. Maybe I can do it by correspondence or something.'

'What sort of wedding dress are you going to have?'

'I saw a divine one in *Vogue*. Lace with a nipped-in waist and a high collar. I'm getting it copied.'

Lillie smiled. 'You seem very happy.'

'I'm a bit nervous. It's a huge step. But Charles is a dear. And it'll be fun to get married. And, as I said, Mummy's over the moon. The patter of little feet and all that. Not to mention when Lady Fitzpatrick passes on, she'll be sort of matriarch of that huge estate when she comes to live with us. It'll add to her prestige enormously. She'll probably find an Irish lord herself before too long.'

Lillie wanted to ask whether she wasn't marrying Charles Fitzpatrick because her mother wanted her to. Instead she said, 'Won't you find Drominderry House daunting? I mean…It's a bit like a castle.'

Clara laughed. 'I know. It terrifies the life out of me sometimes. But don't forget Mummy will be there, and of course the wonderful Maisie.'

Lillie felt a dreadful pang of jealousy. She didn't mind the thought of Maisie looking after Clara. But the thought of her being at Jessica's beck and call upset her more.

Even so, she gave Clara a bright smile. 'I'm sure you'll cope fine. And if Charles is as nice as you say he is, it'll be great fun.'

'I hope I manage okay. If I don't Mummy will kill me.'

'Why would she do that?'

Clara laughed. 'Only joking. She just wants the best for me.'

And, Lillie thought, that's exactly what's she's got: a rich and titled husband for her daughter, and a wonderful estate on the glorious Kenmare River to go with it. A place where Jessica can also stay.

Chapter 30

It was a hot weekend in February with a strong northerly blowing and the sun beating down on the parched countryside. It had been ages since they'd had any decent rain and although Eureka was very dry, out Deb's way it was even drier. Deb said they were having to hand feed the sheep with the hay stored for the winter. Marcus and Freddie were on a school camp and Ronan, Clara and Lillie had driven up to Tamworth to drop Ma off at the station — she and Lorna Medlow were catching the train to Brisbane. Lorna's sister lived at Hamilton and Lorna had asked Ma to accompany her on a visit there. Now that Clara was here to help, Ma was looking forward to getting away from Eureka for a few days. Ronan had put off coming home the last few weeks. He had been frightened by the strong feelings he still had for Clara when he saw her again. Knowing she was about to marry Charles Fitzpatrick, he was sure those feelings could only cause him trouble. If he stayed away he thought he might forget that she was at Eureka Park. But hard as he tried, he couldn't shift her image from his mind. A few times he thought of going down to see her, then changed his mind and instead took Trish out to a couple of parties and to the movies. He really liked Trish and he suspected she was falling in love with him. But he knew he wasn't in love with her. If he was in love with her he would have been able to cope with seeing Clara again. In the end he decided it was best that he stayed up in Armidale.

But then Ma had rung and said he was being rude not coming home to see their family friend. 'Even if it's just for a few days,' she said. 'I'd hate for Clara to go back to Ireland for her wedding and think we all hadn't been glad to see her.' And so he had come home.

Now, as they neared Gullumbindy on the way home, he could see grass fires burning along the side of the road. The volunteer fire brigade was out in force, dousing the flames with hoses from their trucks. A fireman waved their car to a halt.

'Where you headed to, mate?' he asked.

'Eureka Park,' Ronan told him. 'Out past Gullumbindy.'

'Don't know if you'll be allowed through, mate. There's one hell of a bloody monster burning out along that road.'

'We've got to get through,' he said, anxiously, knowing it was just Arthur and his father out there with the horses.

'Yes,' Lillie piped up from the back. 'We must.'

Beside him Clara sighed: 'But if it's that bad it might be too dangerous.'

The fire fighter peered off into the distance towards Gullumbindy. 'All you can do is try, mate. If there's a chance of any danger, though, they won't let you through.'

Ronan nodded. 'I understand.'

The smoke was so thick it was difficult to see where they were going. When they got to Gullumbindy it seemed to clear a bit, so he pulled over and rushed into the Hogans' house and tried to ring Eureka Park. There was no answer, which was not surprising as his father was probably down at the stables.

He came out and shook his head at the girls. 'No answer. Mrs Hogan said Bill's out fighting the fires our way. The flames have jumped the road at the Farrells' place up the road from Eureka. The Farrells rang the Hogans looking for extra help.' He held his hand against the wind. 'If this easterly keeps up, the fires will be heading straight for Eureka Park. But we might have a chance of getting through before they get there.'

From the colour of the sky as they sped along Wattle Creek Road towards Eureka Park it appeared that the fire was still some distance away. Nonetheless, all it would take was a slight change in the wind direction to turn it around. As the smoke got thicker and thicker, he drove on in trepidation.

At the entrance to Eureka Park, they saw flames only a little way off.

Clara gasped, 'Oh my God!'

Lillie leapt out and opened the gates.

'Where do you think the horses are?' Clara asked, looking around at the empty paddocks.

'I reckon Dad and Arthur have taken them down to the river,' Ronan said. 'We've practised that before.'

'They might be in the stables,' Lillie said.

'No, I reckon the river,' Ronan said. 'The stables could go up if this fire gets any closer.'

They screeched to a halt by the homestead. Ronan told Lillie to check the river while he went to the stables, where he could hear horses whinnying in distress. The smoke was so thick he couldn't see far in front of him. He looked at Clara and saw how terrified she was. Grabbing her by the hand, he told her to come with him. At least with her by his side he could be sure she was safe. Despite the fear running through his veins he couldn't help notice how soft and warm her hand felt in his and his heart beat hard against his chest.

'Ronan, look,' she shouted, pointing back towards the front gate.

Not only could he hear the crackling, now he could see the flames rising high into the air.

Lillie rushed back up to them. 'Dad and Arthur have got most of the horses down there with Dingo. Dad said they took them down there when he heard on the radio that the fire was near. But Shannon Boy and Melody are still in the stables.'

'You go back and help Dad,' Ronan shouted. 'We'll try and get those two out.'

Ronan told Clara to wait outside the stables as he went in. As he moved forward he spoke to Shannon Boy, who was pounding the floor with his hoof. 'Come on, young man,' he coaxed, looking anxiously at the thickening smoke visible outside the far door. Rearing up on his hind legs the young horse lashed out, missing Ronan's face by an inch.

'Ronan, be careful,' Clara shouted from the doorway when Shannon Boy lashed out again. 'He's really freaked out and could do anything.' She looked to the next stable where Melody was also pawing the ground.

'I'll try getting Melody to come out first. Then he might follow,' she shouted to Ronan. 'If we don't get them out soon we'll have to leave them or we'll be burnt alive.'

Just as Clara got to Melody and tried to take hold of her halter, the mare reared up, snorting and thrashing wildly. She caught her hoof in the halter rope, which snapped in two, letting her break free. With horror Ronan watched her bolt out the door, turn left and gallop down the driveway towards the flames near Wattle Creek Road.

'Oh my God. She'll get burnt,' Clara cried out in anguish. 'I'll go after her.'

'No!' Ronan yelled.

As he struggled with Shannon Boy's halter, the colt reared up and careered forward, dragging Ronan with him. Eventually, after much coaxing, he calmed down enough for Ronan to get him out and away from the stables. Together he and Clara cajoled him down to the river, where the other horses were stamping and snorting wildly.

'Lillie, you stay with Arthur and the horses down here,' James shouted. 'Clara and Ronan, come with me. We'll need to get some water onto the stables and the homestead.'

As he climbed up the bank, Ronan could see flames leaping higher and higher and the smell of burning was thick in the air. It wouldn't be long before the fire was upon them.

'We need to get the pump going,' his father hollered. 'I'll spray the stables. Ronan, Clara grab the garden hose and start on the homestead. We've got to make sure everything's soaked.'

As they raced through the garden gate to the homestead, they could hear the sound of gum trees exploding and the sky simmered and glowed menacingly. Please, please God make the wind change direction, Ronan prayed.

'Pump's going,' his father called out. 'Should have water through your hoses now.'

Ronan rushed to the tap and turned it on, handing Clara the hose.

'See if you can reach the gutters. We cleaned them out not long ago. But there's been some strong winds. I'll get the hose out the back going.'

'Is it coming closer?' Clara bellowed, her eyes wide with fear.

Before he had a chance to answer, he heard a truck roaring up the driveway. Four firemen jumped out, dragging hoses with them, which they sprayed around the perimeter of the garden and nearby grass before one brought a hose inside the garden and dragged it out the back.

''Good work, love,' he said to Clara as he pushed past. 'We've got it pretty much under control. It's stray embers that's the worry now.'

Ronan took hold of Clara's hose and continued spraying the roof. She stood back and ran a hand through her sodden, smoky hair.

'Oh Ronan, thank God for those firemen. I couldn't bear it if you lost everything. First to lose Rathgarven because of the Irish economy… and now this fire here at Eureka. It would be too awful.'

He was astounded that her thoughts had been for the O'Sullivans and not herself.

'Are the stables okay?' he called out to his father who was now walking through the garden gate, running a handkerchief over his sodden forehead.

'I managed to put out the stray cinders before they took hold. The firemen said the main damage is in the bottom paddock down by Wattle Creek Road, where the sheep are.'

'That's where Melody was heading,' Clara said. 'We should go and look for her in case she's in danger.'

'Yes, you do that,' James said. 'I'll go help Lillie and Arthur with the horses down by the river.'

It took Ronan and Clara half an hour of driving around in the ute to find Melody. It seemed that in her terror she had tried to jump the barbed-wire fence dividing Eureka Park from Wattle Creek Road. In doing so, the broken rope of her halter had caught on the wire. In her frenzy to get free, the barbed wire had tangled around her leg. That was where the fire had found her, half burning her alive. The only part of her body that remained unscathed was her head. Seeing the pain and terror in the mare's eyes, Ronan wished with all his heart that her head had been burnt to cinders too, and then she might have died, putting her out of her agony.

'Oh my God,' Clara cried, pacing around in a circle, one minute looking at the horror of the mare, the next minute unable to look.

Ronan's heart was beating like an eggbeater and the nauseous reek of charred flesh mixed with the smell of burnt grass made him feel like throwing up.

'The poor, poor thing,' Clara sobbed. 'She must be in agony.'

Ronan nodded. 'How horrible.'

He watched Clara step ever so slowly over to Melody, who had now gone into a sort of trance, her eyes staring straight ahead, almost as if she had lost consciousness. A mercy really, Ronan thought. Clara gently patted her on the head, her tears dropping onto her face.

Watching Clara, Ronan felt such tenderness as he had never felt before. 'I'll need to put her out of her agony,' he said. 'You stay with her and I'll get my rifle.'

'To shoot her!' Clara gasped.

'It's the only humane thing to do.'

'But shouldn't your father or Arthur do that?'

'No,' Ronan said. 'I'll do it. They've enough on their plate with the other horses. I'll be back as quickly as I can.'

As he drove up to the homestead to get his gun Ronan tried to control his emotions. It was one thing to shoot a rabbit or a snake. What he was about to do was worse than he could imagine, but he had no alternative. And there was no way he was going to ask Dad to do something he wasn't prepared to do himself. Or Arthur for that matter. He was staggered at how Clara was coping. Over the many years she had been coming to Rathgarven they had often got into scrapes together, but he had no idea that she was made of such grit. With a pang he thought once again what a lucky man Lord Charles Fitzpatrick was.

Ten minutes later he was back at the gruesome scene and Clara was still consoling Melody.

'You go over there behind the ute,' he said to her, not wanting her to have to watch what he was going to do.

'No,' she said. 'I'll move away a bit, but I'll talk to her while you do it.'

'Are you sure?'

'Yes. I'm sure.'

So, as Clara spoke softly to Melody, he lifted the gun and shot the mare through the skull, all the time shaking so much that he was surprised he was able to hit his target. With relief he saw Melody's body collapse lifeless to the ground.

'Oh Ronan,' Clara cried, rushing over to him. 'She must have been in so much pain. And to think it took all that time to find her. The poor, poor mite.'

'Yes,' Ronan said, putting his arm around her.

Clara wiped tears away from her eyes. 'Shannon Boy will wonder where she's gone. Fret for her.'

Ronan held her tightly. 'He'll be okay. After all, he's got Ma to look after him.'

He looked around at the devastation the fire had caused down here in the bottom paddock. Normally this was where the sheep grazed. As far as he could see it was black ash.

Now Clara wiped soot from his cheek with her hand. 'Oh Ronan,' she said, looking at him with tears still streaming down her face. 'Oh Ronan. That must have taken so much courage.'

He thought of the times he had kissed her back at Rathgarven. Under the mulberry tree. On the island. All he wanted to do now was hold her in his arms and kiss her passionately. But he couldn't. She belonged to another man. Instead, he took her hand and brought it to his lips.

'Thank you, Clara, for being here with me while I did this.'

'I'm glad I was,' she said, wiping her tears with her other hand.

'Now,' he added hurriedly, afraid he would be unable to control the urge to kiss her, 'we best head back up and see how the others are getting on.'

She held his eyes as she slowly took her hand away. 'Yes,' she said, moving away. 'You're right... we'd best go find the others.'

'You get in the truck. I'll deal with those poor burnt sheep in the corner over there. Relieve them from their agony.'

'I'll come with you,' she said. 'It's not something you should do on your own.'

'Clara, I'm fine. Truly I am.'

She shook her head. 'No. I want to be with you.'

Ronan nodded. Together they walked over to the huddle of distressed sheep. As Ronan lifted his gun once again and fired time after time, he felt tears threaten. But whether they were tears for the desperate animals he was putting out of their misery, or tears of frustration that Clara was going home to Ireland to marry Lord Charles Fitzpatrick of Drominderry House, he wasn't so sure.

Chapter 31

Kathleen saw the horse float coming up the driveway. The time had come: Shannon Boy was off to his new home. It wasn't until Lorna had dropped her off on her way back to Medlow Stud from the train station the week before that Kathleen realised how close they had come to losing Eureka Park in the bushfire. But her relief was soon tempered when she discovered what had happened to Melody.

Clara was with Ronan when he told her. 'I'm so sorry,' Clara said. 'Maybe if we'd found her sooner…'

'No point in thinking that,' Kathleen cut in. Despite her dreadful anguish, she didn't want to add her own distress to Clara's and Ronan's. 'I'm just grateful that you found her when you did and were able to end her agony.' She put an arm around Ronan. 'And those poor, poor sheep. That must have been so awful too. I'm very proud of you, darling. What you did couldn't have been easy.'

Ronan looked at Clara. 'I don't think I could have shot Melody if Clara hadn't been there to comfort her.'

'Well, I'm immensely proud of you both.'

And she really was. Not just of Ronan and Clara, but also James, Arthur and Lillie for how they had coped. She was also very relieved that no one had been hurt and that the property had got off relatively unscathed apart from a number of fences needing replacing and quite a bit of burnt pasture. But fences could be rebuilt. Grass would grow back. Lives wouldn't. Dreadfully sad as it was to lose Melody, Shannon Boy hadn't seemed to fret too much after the first day or so. Nonetheless, the mare's loss was also a blow financially. What she and James hadn't told the rest of the family, as it would cause even more distress, was that she was once again in foal.

Kathleen refused to let herself dwell on what had happened. Australia was a land of extremes: floods, droughts and bushfires. They weren't the first people on the land to be hit by a fire, and wouldn't be the last. All they could do was get on with it and remember Melody for the fine mare that she was. And that she had given them Shannon Boy.

Now Tommy Brown's horse float had arrived and she went to direct the driver where to park down by the stables. She had Shannon Boy in there ready to go. Yesterday she had taken a heap of photos of him. By himself and then with the children. Clara had wanted a special one of her with him to take back home.

'When I'm at Drominderry House and hear he's won the Melbourne Cup I'll be famous,' she'd laughed.

Lorna had told Kathleen she'd find it hard to let Shannon Boy go, and she was right.

'Just remember you're doing the best thing possible,' she'd said on the phone last night. 'We had a young foal I adored. When he went down to Tommy I lost my heart. Then he did so well I was really pleased I'd sent him.'

Although they'd practised putting Shannon Boy in their own float here at Eureka, he wasn't too keen on this one. So it took James, Kathleen and Arthur quite a while to coax him up as he snorted and pranced about. When he was finally aboard, Kathleen tied him to the railing at the front of the box and kissed him on the forehead.

'This is a great opportunity, young man,' she said. 'Now you make the best of it.'

She stepped down from the float and stood beside James. 'He'll be just fine,' he said, placing an arm around her waist.

'I know,' she said. 'But I'll miss him.'

'You'll be able to go down and see him when he's settled in, Mrs O'Sullivan,' Arthur said.

'Yes, you're quite right, Arthur,' Kathleen said. 'It'll be good to see how he comes on.'

Kathleen wiped a tear from her eye as the horse float disappeared down the driveway towards the front gate, and smiled at James.

'Silly me. You'd think it was a child I was seeing off. Not a horse. Now come and I'll make you both a cup of tea. Then I've got to go and get Lillie and Clara.' The two girls had stayed the night in Tamworth with a school friend, and Kathleen hoped Lillie would find a dress she liked for Deb's birthday party as Kathleen had saved up some of her housekeeping money to give her as a surprise, knowing she was envious of Clara's beautiful clothes.

***

When Kathleen picked the girls up in front of Marcus Clark's, Lillie was gushing about the dress she'd found.

'You'll love it, Ma. It's sort of like a shift in a lovely floaty material… quite short.'

'Not too short I hope.'

'Minis are all the rage, Aunt Kathleen,' Clara said. 'And Lillie looks super in this one.'

Kathleen smiled. 'I'm sure she does.'

'It'll be such fun to see a real Aussie wool shed,' Clara said. 'I'm thrilled Deb is having her party in one.'

'A bit different to Drominderry House,' Kathleen laughed.

'I was telling Lillie how much Mummy's looking forward to visiting me there. She can't wait to help me have my first dinner party. And have the first hunt meet there. I think she's got a list already of who she's going to invite.'

'Won't Charles and his mother have a say?' Kathleen asked. 'I mean… it's not as though Jessica will own the place.'

'Ah, I think that's the point. She may not have to worry about the upkeep and all that, but she can still invite her friends. Charles assured her she can regard it as her own place as much as she likes.'

'What about his mother?'

'Poor Lady Fitzpatrick isn't well at all. She hardly leaves her room now.'

'Oh. How sad. She's always been such a vibrant woman. I hate to think of her being unwell.'

'She *is* getting on.'

'She's not that old!'

'Oh, I know that. She seems old, that's all.'

'That's because she's not well. I'm sure when she's better she'll be back to her old self.'

'You're probably quite right, Aunt Kathleen. How awful of me to have her with one foot in the grave already. I'm really very fond of her. And so is Charles.'

'Anyway,' Kathleen added, 'undoubtedly Jessica will be a great asset to the place. As will you, my darling.'

'Do you think so? I must admit I'd rather Charles wasn't a lord with a huge estate. It is rather daunting.'

'Darling, I know you'll be brilliant.'

Having said that, Kathleen thought back to when she had arrived at Rathgarven as a young bride after returning from India all those years ago. How nervous she had been, wondering how she'd cope with having James's mother in the same house. At least Kathleen hadn't had to contend with her own mother living there as well. But her own mother would be a much easier woman to live with than Jessica would ever be. There was no way in the world Jessica would be able to stop herself making suggestions as to how the place was run. In a way I wouldn't mind being a fly on the wall to see how it all pans out, Kathleen thought. The person who would have to compromise the most was Clara.

***

'My God,' Deb exclaimed to Lillie as they sat on one of the hay bales scattered about the woolshed. 'You didn't tell me she looks like that. I may not have asked her if I'd known. All the fellas will be lining up to dance with her. You and I won't have a chance in hell.' She eyed Clara and Ronan as they talked to the daughter of one of her parents' friends. The party was in full swing.

'Oh, you don't have to worry about Clara. As I've told you, she's engaged to an Irish lord. And having a huge wedding in Dublin.'

'True. Still… she is gorgeous, isn't she? And she has that great accent.'

'Yeah, I suppose she does.'

Ronan came and joined them, leaving Clara talking to the girl, who was waving her hands around animatedly.

'Fun, isn't it?' he said, sitting down next to Deb and looking around. 'Your parents have put on a great do.'

'The band's great, isn't it?' Deb glanced over to where her parents were serving out soft drinks to the young ones. 'Mum said they'll play till eleven.'

Clara walked over and sat down. 'That girl was really interesting, Deb,' she said. 'She told me she went to London for a year after she left school. She loved it.'

'I may not be able to take you overseas, but would the birthday girl like a dance?' Ronan asked, standing in front of Deb. 'What's say we show this lot how it's done?'

Lillie felt like kissing her brother, for she knew how much that would mean to Deb, who was looking gorgeous in a red spotted mini dress, not unlike the one Lillie was wearing, except

323

Lillie's was blue. Clara was wearing a short white skirt and a pink halter-neck top, which showed off the great tan she had got being at Eureka. Across the room Lillie saw a boy she quite liked dancing with one of the girls who also caught the school bus. When the song ended she saw him escort the girl back to her seat, then start across the floor. For a moment she thought he was going to ask her for a dance. To her mortification, she saw it was Clara he was aiming for.

'Heavens no,' Clara said when he asked her for a dance, flashing her ring. 'I'm an engaged woman. Lillie's the one you should be dancing with.'

Lillie felt like a complete idiot. 'I'm sorry,' she stammered. 'I've gotta go see someone.' With that she rushed out to the loo, which was up near the stockyards. She thought of spending all night outside, rather than being a wallflower. Then she decided that was silly. In any case, Deb, or even Clara or Ronan, would probably come to look for her. So in the end she fiddled with her hair in the cracked mirror above the grimy sink and went back inside. Deb and Ronan were still dancing and Clara was still speaking to the fellow from the bus. No one seemed to have noticed she had gone outside at all, which made her feel even worse.

Ronan saw Deb back to her seat, and asked Lillie for a dance. She was feeling so down she refused.

'Have it as you will,' he said. 'Don't say I didn't try to get you up.'

He asked Clara if she'd like a dance and she said yes.

'Well… Ronan's almost family,' she laughed, winking at Lillie. 'And I didn't go much on that other fellow anyway.'

A boy Lillie had met at the gymkhana came over and asked her to dance, which made her feel much better. Even though she didn't like him in a romantic sort of way, at least she wasn't left standing on the edge of the dance floor looking like a complete nerd.

'You're a great dancer, Lillie,' he said when he saw her back to her seat. 'Maybe we can have another dance later?'

'Yeah. That'd be great,' she said, wondering why it couldn't be someone she really fancied who had taken a shine to her. Like Brad Hickey.

'Sorry,' Deb had said when Lillie asked hopefully if he was coming. 'He's gone to a showjumping event in Brisbane. But he would've brought his girlfriend anyway. So you wouldn't have had a hope.'

As Lillie sat there, she noticed Ronan was still dancing with Clara. Deb had gone over to talk to a group of their school friends, and Lillie went over to join them. When the band finished playing, she saw Ronan and Clara head outside. She thought of going to join them, but they seemed so engrossed in conversation she felt she might be intruding. After the band started up once more they came back onto the dance floor. This time the band played a slow ballad. As Ronan held Clara close to him, he had a look on his face Lillie had never seen before. It was a look she'd have loved someone like Brad Hickey to have on his face when he danced with her. Oh, Ronan! she thought. If Charles Fitzpatrick could see you dancing with Clara like that, he'd be furious.

Don't go there, Ronan. Please... just don't.

Chapter 32

Kathleen was sad when April came around and it was time for Clara to leave and get organised for her wedding to Charles Fitzpatrick in August.

'But why can't you stay longer?' Freddie asked.

'Because I have to get my wedding dress organised. And Mummy needs me to help chose her outfit as well. And we have to send the invitations out. There's so much to do.'

'Well, I don't think it's fair,' Freddie protested as Clara said goodbye to him and Marcus as they left for school the day she was to leave. 'I think that lord or whoever he is should come here to live. Then you could stay.'

Lillie laughed. 'I can't see Lord Fitzpatrick wanting to live here, Freddie.' She looked at Ronan. 'Can you?'

Ronan, who was about to drive back to Armidale, dropping Lillie off at school on the way, smiled. 'No, I can't.'

Kathleen watched Clara kiss Lillie goodbye, and then Ronan.

'Goodbye, Clara,' he said. 'And good luck.'

Kathleen saw Clara and her son hold each other's eyes for just a second. But in that second Kathleen felt something familiar about that look. It was a look she had given her squadron leader all those years ago when they had first met. Maybe it's time Clara did go back to her lord, she thought. Although she didn't suspect anything had gone on between Clara and Ronan, maybe too much time away from her fiancé was not good.

Ronan abruptly jumped in the car and he and Lillie drove off, with Lillie waving out of the window. And straightaway, without saying anything, Clara turned around and went inside to pack.

Later in the day Clara sought James out to say a final goodbye before Kathleen drove her to the train. 'Take care, Uncle James,' she said, giving him a huge kiss.

'You look after yourself, Clara. And do tell your mother how we're looking after Finn's place for him. Undoubtedly she'll be sad to know he'd started drinking again, causing him to do what he did.'

To Kathleen it was as if James wanted Clara to tell Jessica again how Finn had succumbed to the drink and that's what had killed him. Why was James rubbing it in?

'Anyway,' he added, walking them to the car, 'we loved having you, Clara. And good luck with the wedding. Make sure you send lots of photos.'

'I promise I'll send heaps.' After saying goodbye to Arthur and then kneeling down to kiss Dingo, she got in the car next to Kathleen and they drove off. 'I'm going to miss Eureka and everyone so much,' she said, waving out the window.

'Ah,' Kathleen said, placing a hand on her knee. 'As soon as you see your Charles you'll forget all about us.'

'That's not true.'

Despite her misgivings earlier on, Kathleen thought it probably was true. With the excitement of the wedding, then the honeymoon and moving to Drominderry House, the O'Sullivans, including Ronan, were bound to fade into the distance. Later, as she drove home, Kathleen felt quite low. The house would be so quiet without her.

***

That night poor Freddie, who Clara often collected from the bus stop after school, walked around with such a maudlin look on his face that Kathleen felt awfully sorry for him.

327

'Why does she have to marry that silly lord? he asked, when Kathleen tucked him into bed. 'Couldn't she find someone here to marry?'

'She's in love with him.' Kathleen smiled. 'One day you might find someone to love like that.'

'But I love Clara.'

'And I'm sure she loves you, darling. It's just that you're a little too young for her.'

'Ronan's not. Why can't she marry him?'

'Because she's marrying Charles Fitzpatrick. And, in any case, Ronan has a girlfriend, Trish up in Armidale.'

'He never brings her here.'

'Maybe he'll bring her here one day soon.'

'I bet she's not as pretty as Clara.'

'Well, we'll have to wait and see, won't we?'

As she said that Kathleen hoped Ronan *would* bring Trish down to meet the family. From what he had said, she sounded lovely.

'He'll bring her down to meet us in his own time,' James said when Kathleen raised the subject. 'Don't pressure him.'

'I'm not pressuring him,' Kathleen had answered, testily. 'I'd like to meet her, that's all.'

All that Kathleen wanted was that Ronan would be happy. And if Trish was making him happy, she knew she would like her very much.

***

As time went on Kathleen felt a huge void without Clara, and she missed Shannon Boy, though she often rang up Tommy Brown to see how the colt was getting on.

'He's settling in quite well,' Tommy said. 'So don't worry about him.'

Kathleen was concerned about him being confined in a stable most of the time instead of roaming the wide-open paddocks of Eureka Park, but she had to put her trust in Tommy. Now that she had more time on her hands, she put extra effort into her photography, often spending hours up in the bush taking photos of the wildlife. One day she even managed to photograph a kangaroo with a joey peeping out of her pouch, and a koala nestled in a gum tree. Getting up early she captured some spectacular sunrises and at the end of the day, beautiful sunsets. Lorna was her greatest fan, so Kathleen made up a small album to give her for her birthday.

Two days later Lorna rang. 'I showed that album you gave me to a friend. She loved them. She reckons there's a cousin of hers in Tamworth who owns a gallery. He might give you a chance to sell a few. You need to get them out there. They're too good to be hiding in boxes at your place.'

So Kathleen mounted a few of her photographs, which she'd enlarged from the negatives, and took them in to the gallery. Much to her delight the proprietor, Roger Mann, said he would give her some wall space to display them.

'I'll take thirty per cent of the takings and you get the rest.'

'Thank you,' Kathleen said, chuffed that he was taking her efforts seriously.

A week later he rang up and told her he'd sold three photos: the one of the kangaroo with her joey, one of Shannon Boy resting his head on the post-and-rail fence, and one of the wattle trees in full bloom near the dam in the bottom paddock. Kathleen was delighted, especially when he told her that he might let her have her own exhibition if they sold many more.

'I've made ten pounds,' she said excitedly to James when she got off the phone. 'How about that?'

'Well done,' James said. 'Spend it on yourself. Buy a new dress or something nice.'

This annoyed Kathleen, who hoped the income from her photographs might become more than something to spend on treats like a new dress. She wanted to make a real business out of it. For although things were less tight at Eureka now that they had sold quite a few yearlings and Caesar and the other stallion they had purchased were more than earning their keep, every little bit helped. To that end she decided to take a series of photographs that she could group together. People might even buy the whole series if she did have her own exhibition; instead of selling just one photograph, she might be able to sell five or six. She was going through some photos to see what could be suitable when Lorna Medlow called in on her way home from spending the weekend with an old school friend in Gunnedah.

'What a great idea,' she said when Kathleen told her what she was doing. 'I can see people having a whole row of those photos on a wall. You can give them names. Like *The Thoroughbred Series*, *The Wildflower and Wildlife Series*, *The River Series* and heaps more.' She picked up a photo and held it in her hands. 'Do you know what? I think I might even put an order in myself. For Jack and Maddie. I know Jack would love to have a reminder of his time here. Yes… Can you do me a Eureka Park series? With the homestead, stables, horses and anything else you can think of?'

'Oh Lorna, are you sure?'

'But I am. They've moved into a new house on the place Jack's working at. I gather it's run-down and neglected. These will be just perfect to cheer it up a bit. And maybe you could do me some for the nursery.'

'It's lovely that they've now got baby Margo.'

Lorna opened her bag and showed Kathleen a photo of a round and jolly baby with a mass of dark curls. 'I'm headed up there again in a couple of weeks. Could you have my photos ready by then? I can pick them up on the way through.'

'Of course. And, Lorna, I'm so glad it's all worked out okay with Maddie.'

Lorna smiled. 'Maybe not quite like I'd imagined, but that's life, isn't it?'

As Lorna drove off after they'd had another cup of tea, Kathleen was happy for her friend — and for Jack and Maddie and little Margo. She was excited, too, that she had her first order for her 'series' photographs. She would need to get cracking to have them ready in a couple of weeks.

Chapter 33

It was a cold and wet afternoon in July when Tommy Brown rang Kathleen.

'I've given him a few runs against the other horses here,' he told her. 'I know he's got potential, but he's not performing as I'd imagined.'

Kathleen's heart sank. Was he going to ask her to bring him home?

'I'll keep him on for a while longer, however we'll need to have another look in a few weeks. No point in taking your money if he's not going to make it.'

'Yes, of course,' Kathleen said. 'I quite understand.'

Should she tell James? Maybe it was better to leave it for a few weeks and see if Shannon Boy improved. Kathleen was paying some of the trainer's fees out of the money she was making from her photographs, so it wasn't all falling onto the stud. Not only had Lorna paid for her order for Jack and Maddie, Kathleen was also managing to sell quite a few of the 'series' at the gallery and was getting ready for an exhibition. Even so, Shannon Boy's fees were a drain on their finances — something James had brought up more than once.

Now the phone rang again and she picked it up. She hoped it might be Lorna and she could chew over what Tommy had said. But it wasn't Lorna. It was the telephone exchange to say there was a call from England. On the line was Jessica, and she sounded in a dreadful state.

'Oh Kate,' she spluttered, 'you won't believe what's happened.'

'What do you mean? Are you ill?'

'Nothing like that.' Kathleen heard her sobbing down the phone. 'But it's just so awful I can hardly bear to tell you. Clara's called off her engagement to Charles Fitzpatrick.'

'Oh my goodness,' Kathleen exclaimed. 'Why would she do that? She seemed so happy about it when she was here.'

'She tells me she's decided she's too young. And she doesn't want all that responsibility. The humiliation for poor Charles! Not to mention his family. And imagine it — all those engagement presents that have to go back.'

'Oh, Jessica, I'm so sorry,' Kathleen said, trying to soothe her. She realised how devastated Jessica must be; not only was there the humiliation for the Fitzpatrick family, Jessica would also be humiliated.

'What's Clara going to do?' Kathleen shouted down the line, which was now fading in and out. 'I mean… Where is she? She must be beside herself.'

'She told me she was going overseas again. She took off yesterday for Paris.'

'Goodness! Does she know anyone in Paris?'

'Yes, she has an old school friend there.'

'Do you know where she's going to after France?'

'Lord alone knows. Maybe she'll come back over to you. She told me she was so happy with you there at Eureka Park. I've been stewing over that for ages. I'm wondering if something happened when she was there. Did you notice anything? I mean… do you think she met someone there who may have made her change her mind about marrying Charles?'

'Not that I know of.'

'Are you sure?'

'Jessica, I wasn't with her twenty-four hours a day. As far as I know she met no one else while she was here with us. Anyway, this must be costing you a fortune.'

'Never mind. What about that dance in a barn she told me she went to?'

'It was for Lillie's friend Deb's birthday. She went with Lillie and Ronan.' Kathleen was starting to get really angry. It seemed as if Jessica somehow wanted to blame her for Clara's behaviour. 'Jessica,' she said, trying to control her voice, 'if you think she met someone else over here, why don't you ask her yourself?'

'I did. She denied anything.'

'Well... I think you'll find she's telling the truth. Why don't you believe what she told you? She thinks she's too young to take on that responsibility. And... quite frankly, Jessica I must say I think I agree with her. When she got home she probably realised what she was letting herself in for. Even if she does love Charles, she possibly felt she had more living to do before she settled down.'

'It was all organised,' Jessica bemoaned. 'I was going to live with them at Drominderry House. Well... not all the time. But certainly part of the time.'

Kathleen shook her head. The truth was starting to come out. Jessica was definitely more upset for herself than for Clara and Charles Fitzpatrick. Kathleen had put up with Jessica's selfishness for as long as she'd known her. Now it was really starting to irritate her.

'Are you sure you're not more upset for yourself than you are for Clara and Charles?'

'My sweet... what a dreadful thing to say. Of course I'm not. I'm trying to work out what went wrong. When she left here she seemed perfectly happy with the prospect of marrying Charles. When she came back she seemed different somehow. And then this.'

'I'm sorry,' Kathleen said. 'I wish I could help you, Jessica... but honestly I'm as much in the dark as you are.'

'She'll need to make it up to me,' Jessica said.

'Jessica… it was her decision to make. Not yours.'

'You're taking her side, aren't you?'

'I'm not taking anyone's side.'

'I thought you were my friend. That I could rely on you to let me know what was going on. Quite frankly, Kate, I'm disappointed in you.'

This is going nowhere, Kathleen thought, and it's costing Jessica an arm and a leg. The exchange had already given two extensions of time. I refuse to be made responsible for Clara's decision and Jessica's unhappiness.

'Jessica, I must go,' she lied. 'James is waiting for me down at the stables. The vet's coming and I need to be there.'

'Really! Well, don't you worry about me,' she said, sounding put out. 'Do what you have to do. Go, my sweet. Go.'

Kathleen heard the line go dead. For some time she stood in shock. She'd never heard Jessica speak like that before. It was the tone of her voice that confounded Kathleen. It was more than embarrassment or disappointment that the wedding had been cancelled. It was real resentment. Kathleen worried for Clara. It was obvious Jessica was going to be of little consolation to her. It wasn't a decision to be made lightly. Having made it, Clara would undoubtedly be riddled with remorse for having hurt Charles. The one thing she would want more than anything else at a time like this was a mother's shoulder to cry on. Not a mother infuriated by her decision. For a moment she thought of the looks she had seen pass between Ronan and Clara when they were saying goodbye. But she soon pushed that right out of her mind. Clara was too young and had realised it. That was enough reason for pulling out of the marriage.

When she had calmed down she went and found James in the stables to tell him what had happened. And how Jessica seemed more concerned for herself than for Clara.

James was cleaning the hoof of a new stallion they had just bought at a William Inglis sale along with three more brood mares. Putting down the hoof, he sighed. 'I feel for Clara. It must've been a huge decision to make. But I've no sympathy for Jessica at all. She's a…'

He stopped himself and turned away.

There was something in his voice that gave Kathleen a start. 'She's a what?' she asked.

'Oh, nothing,' James said, picking up the stallion's hoof again. 'She's very selfish, that's all… Only interested in what's good for Jessica. I've always known that. Maybe you're starting to find out.'

As Kathleen went back up to the house she thought he was probably right. Jessica always had, and always would have, Jessica as her number one priority. But seeing the angry look in James's eyes when he said he had no sympathy for her made Kathleen wonder if Jessica had ever done anything to James to make him dislike her so much. Something Kathleen knew nothing about.

Maybe I'm imagining it, she thought. He's probably worried for Clara, who he's always loved dearly. The same as I'm worried for her. She was glad she'd decided not to tell him about Tommy Brown's phone call. It would only add to his bad mood.

***

'How dreadful for everyone,' Lillie exclaimed when she got home from school that Friday evening and Ma told her what had happened. She imagined the turmoil the Fitzpatricks must be in, let alone Jessica. And of course Clara must be shattered as well.

'Do you think anything happened here to change her mind?' Ma asked. 'I mean… Jessica seems to think she might have met someone else while she was here. I told her that was

336

ridiculous. Surely you or Ronan would've told me if you thought she had.'

A vision of Ronan and Clara dancing together flashed before Lillie's eyes, but she wasn't going to blurt out her suspicions to Ma. It would just make it awkward all around. And in any case, Lillie was probably imagining the whole thing. Why couldn't everyone believe what Clara had said? That she was too young? It's what everyone thought, anyway. Even so, Lillie couldn't help thinking that she mustn't have been really in love. If she were, surely her age would make no difference. Maybe when she went back and saw Charles again she decided he wasn't the one for her. They say absence makes the heart grow fonder. In this case it might have done the opposite.

'One fella asked her to dance at Deb's party,' she said to Ma. 'But she gave him short shrift.'

'Well, it's beyond me,' Ma said. 'Jessica seemed to think she might want to come back here after staying with her friend in France.'

'Here? Why would she want to do that?'

'She told Jessica she was really happy here with us all.' She smiled. 'Freddie will be beside himself if she does decide to come back.'

'There's nothing for her here, Ma. Surely she'd want to go somewhere more exciting? Like other parts of Europe.'

'When you're upset, as she undoubtedly is, she might want to be with people she knows.'

She obviously knows her friend in France, Lillie thought, but said nothing.

In the end, no one heard from Clara, so they had no idea what her plans were. Even Ronan didn't hear a thing.

'No, why should I?' he replied when Lillie asked. 'If she contacts anyone it would probably be Ma.'

'Just wondering, that's all.'

'Well, you'll have to keep wondering until we hear something.'

But as Christmas came and went no one did.

Chapter 34

Two days after the family welcomed in 1967 with a New Year's Day lunch at the Telegraph Hotel as guests of the Hogans, Ma received a phone call. Clara was in Hong Kong and wanted to visit Eureka Park. And so come a muggy Saturday afternoon in February, Lillie found it hard to believe that here was Clara sitting at the kitchen table with her and Ma.

'I wasn't able to do it,' she said. 'I realised I didn't love him. I couldn't tell him that. So I said I thought I was too young. Mummy, of course, was furious. I've never seen her so cross. You'd think I'd tried to murder the Queen, not called off an engagement.'

'I daresay she was upset for the Fitzpatricks,' Ma said. 'It must've been a dreadful blow for them all. Not just Charles.'

Lillie wanted to say it'd be the gossip that Jessica would have got herself in a stew about. Gossip in Ireland spreads faster than a fox fleeing a pack of hounds. And with Charles a lord, it wouldn't be long before that gossip spread to England as well. Possibly even India.

Ma put her hand on Clara's knee. 'So what do you think you might do in the long term, darling?'

Clara sighed. 'I needed time to think. That's why those months with Dominque in France were so good. I'll stay here for a while, if you'll have me. Then go back to England, I suppose. Enrol at uni.' She looked around the kitchen. Through the window they could see Dingo lolling in the shade of the maple tree with a couple of chickens pecking in the dirt nearby. 'I do love it here,' Clara said.

Ma smiled at her. 'Of course you can stay here, darling. As long as you like.'

'Thank you, Aunt Kathleen.'

'But who paid for your fare?' Ma asked, getting up to put the kettle on to make a cup of tea.

Clara paused before answering. 'Charles did.' She sounded embarrassed. 'I think he thought if I got rid of the travel bug totally, I'd come back to him. But there's no way I can go back.' She paused again. 'Is that awful? To take his money when I don't love him?'

Ma shook her head. 'It was his money to give. Maybe one day you can repay him.'

Clara nodded. 'He's an awfully good man. I'm sure he'll find someone to love. Someone who loves him as well.'

Poor Charles Fitzpatrick, Lillie thought, even though she couldn't remember ever having met the man. Apart from feeling so humiliated, he must be broken-hearted. And annoyed at having to fork out that cash on the off-chance his bride might come running back to him. She wondered how Lady Fitzpatrick and Hugh, not to mention, Maisie and Paddy, had taken it all. Drominderry House must be in total shock.

'You'll have to ring your mother and tell her where you are,' Ma said to Clara.

Clara nodded. 'I suppose you're right. I'll ring her after dinner.'

Inside her head Lillie kept seeing Ronan dancing with Clara at Deb's birthday party.

'Does Ronan know you're back here?' she asked.

Clara shook her head. 'Not unless you told him.'

'So you didn't write to him from France?'

'No. As I said, I just needed time on my own to think. I didn't write to anyone.' She looked at Ma. 'I thought of writing to you. But then I just couldn't. It took me those months to be sure in my own mind that I had done the right thing.'

***

That night as they prepared for bed, Clara told Lillie she'd spoken to her mother who was furious that she'd come back here.

'Why?' Lillie asked. 'I mean… surely she's pleased you're with us. And not off somewhere by yourself.'

'That's what I would've thought… but that's Mummy for you. She still thinks I should go back and get on with the wedding as though nothing has happened. I think she's living in a dream world.'

'It must've been traumatic calling the whole thing off.'

'It was. Though Charles was so understanding. He really is a dear.'

'Was it just that you felt you were too young? Or did you decide you didn't love him after all?'

Clara pulled her nightie over her head and went to the dressing table to brush her hair. 'A bit of both, I suppose.'

'So there's no one else, then.'

Clara turned around abruptly. 'What makes you think that?'

'I dunno. Just curious. Anyway,' she added, getting in under the covers, 'I think you were very brave. I'm not sure if I'd have had the courage to do what you did.'

'Better than going through with a sham marriage. That would've been so unkind to Charles.'

'Yeah,' Lillie said, snuggling down. 'You're probably right.'

***

When Ronan walked into the kitchen the next day after driving down from Armidale, Lillie watched him go over to Clara and give her a kiss on the cheek.

'Ma told me what happened,' he said.

Clara smiled. 'Yeah. Just one of those things.'

341

Lillie tried to see if she could read anything in their expressions. There was nothing.

'How's Trish?' she asked her brother.

There was a beat of silence, and Lillie was sure he glanced at Clara. 'We broke it off.'

'I'm sorry to hear that,' Ma said. 'I was looking forward to meeting her.'

Ronan threw her a bright smile. 'We're still good friends, so you might well meet her one day.'

'Why did you break it off?' Lillie asked, knowing she was pushing her luck. When he didn't answer, she laughed. 'Yeah, yeah, I know… mind your own business, Lillie.'

Ronan grinned. 'You're learning, li'l sis.'

As she moved over to put the kettle on, Lillie was suspicious. Clara breaks it off with Charles Fitzpatrick and Ronan breaks it off with Trish. Again she remembered the look she had seen on Ronan's face when he was dancing with Clara at Deb's birthday party.

She wondered if her suspicions would be proved right.

***

One evening a few weeks later, when Deb was staying over at Eureka Park and sleeping on a camp stretcher between Clara's and Lillie's beds, they all went trekking into the hills. They pitched their tents by a waterfall and built a fireplace out of stones. Ronan got the fishing lines out and soon landed a large Murray cod which Lillie wrapped in alfoil to cook on the stones. Clara had made a potato salad that she had carried in her saddlebag in a Tupperware container. Ronan had packed a couple of cans of beer, which he kept cold by standing them in the creek. Around them was the light swish of a soft breeze in the gum trees and the hum of birdsong.

As Lillie looked around, she thought how lucky they were to be up here in the hills, seemingly without a care in the world. She looked across at Deb and gave her a bright smile. 'How good is this?'

When they'd finished eating and had washed the dishes in the creek, they laid their sleeping bags by the fire and sat around singing along as Ronan played the guitar. He had carried it slung across the front of his saddle. Lillie loved it when he played for the family after dinner in the living room at the homestead. On one of those occasions Lillie realised he also had a good singing voice. Often he would leave the singing up to Dad, but now Lillie suspected that was because he didn't want to show Dad up.

As Ronan played the guitar and sang the Bob Dylan song 'Mr Tambourine Man', she could see Clara's and Deb's eyes glued to his face.

When he stopped singing and took a sip of his beer, Freddie cried, 'Go on, Ronan. Please, please.' So Ronan played 'Molly Malone' and Clara sang the words. Lillie already knew that she had a lovely voice, for she remembered how she had stopped outside the library door at Rathgarven and heard her sing when Ronan was playing the harp; later Ronan had played 'Molly Malone' for the family and Clara had sung. And Clara often sang along to the latest hits on the transistor radio they both listened to in their bedroom. But Lillie had forgotten how haunting 'Molly Malone' was.

As Ronan and Clara sang together, they locked eyes across the fire. It was then that Lillie knew without a doubt why Clara had called off her wedding to Charles Fitzpatrick, and she felt incredibly sorry for him. She also wondered how Clara's mother would react if she knew that Ronan was the reason her daughter had thrown away the opportunity of marrying a lord, and all that came with it.

One way or another, she was bound to be furious with the O'Sullivans.

Chapter 35

Six weeks after the camping trip, Clara announced she was moving to Armidale. Marcus and Freddie were out camping in the hills with Arthur, and Ronan was in Armidale as he had a rugby game on the following day. So it was just Kathleen, Lillie and James with Clara in the kitchen that Saturday night.

'I'd like to get a job in Armidale,' she said, startling Kathleen, who was checking on a chicken casserole in the oven. 'Much as I love being with you all, I've got to earn some money of my own. My working visa will run out before I know it and I want to save up so I can visit the Greek islands on the way home to England. Everyone raves about them. Besides, I can't live with you forever. You've all been terribly kind and I'll always remember my time with you.'

'Why Armidale?' James asked. 'Wouldn't you be better to go to Sydney? I would've thought there'd be more opportunities there.'

Clara fiddled with her place mat. 'Ronan said I could rent one of the rooms at his digs.'

'Oh!' Kathleen stopped stirring the casserole and placed it back in the oven to cook for a few minutes more. 'Really!'

She put the oven glove down on the edge of the sink and considered Clara's pretty face. Over the past few weeks Kathleen had noticed Clara and Ronan spending more time together when he was home for the weekend. A few times they had gone riding into the hills by themselves, Ronan on the mare Kathleen normally rode and Clara on Lillie's Muffin. At first Kathleen thought they were consoling each other on their breakups. But she began to suspect there might be more to it. Was that why Clara had called off her marriage? And why Ronan had split with Trish? She wasn't sure how she felt about this. She loved Clara, but if Jessica were to get a hint that Ronan was the cause of Clara's broken engagement, all hell would break loose. There would be no way in the world Jessica would believe Kathleen hadn't known what was going on.

Perhaps I should have seen it happening, she thought. If I had, maybe I could have put an end to it. And Clara would be back in Ireland and married to Charles Fitzpatrick. Then again, I of all people know what it's like to be totally blinded by love. No matter what anyone said, it would make no difference to how Clara and Ronan felt.

Kathleen went to the oven once more and took out the Pyrex casserole dish and carried it to the table, where a dish of mashed potatoes and beans she'd picked earlier in the day from the veggie patch were already waiting.

'One of his flatmates is leaving,' Clara said. 'There's a spare room, so it seems a practical thing to do, rather than trying to find somewhere to rent. And Ronan said the dentist he went to wants an assistant. I can also get a job in the evenings in one of the hotels. I really do want to save. So, all in all, it seems like a good idea.'

'What about your mother?' Kathleen asked. 'Won't she expect you to come home sooner?'

Clara picked up her glass of water and took a sip. 'Now that I'm not going to be Lady Fitzpatrick with a huge estate in County Kerry for her to visit, I don't think Mummy would give a toss what I did.'

Kathleen sat down and served out the casserole and the vegetables and handed the laden plates around. 'Oh, I'm sure that's not true,' she said. Though, remembering the last conversation she'd had with Jessica, she wasn't so sure. 'Even if you think that,' she said to Clara, 'we'd best let her in on your plans. Despite how you feel about her, I'm sure she'd want to know what you're up to.'

'Yes,' Clara said, finishing a mouthful of beans, 'you're probably right.'

'So when are you thinking of moving?'

'On Monday, if that's okay.'

'Golly,' Lillie said. 'That soon.'

'Well… the room's available now, so I thought I might as well go up straightaway.'

'We'll miss you,' Kathleen said. She looked at James. 'Won't we, darling?'

'Oh, don't worry,' Clara laughed. 'I'll be down often. I'll make sure I hitch a ride with Ronan.'

Kathleen studied her face, but Clara gave little away. Maybe it is best that she goes to Armidale, she thought. If there is something going on between her and Ronan, up there they can sort it out away from the family's prying eyes.

'That's great, darling. We'll look forward to that. Now,' she added, 'you and Lillie can do the washing up and James and I will retire to the living room.' She smiled. 'Maybe you could bring us a cup of tea.'

***

On the school bus on Monday Lillie told Deb how Clara was going to Armidale to share digs with Ronan.

'It sounds as if she really fancies him,' Deb said. 'And he fancies her as well.'

Sheelagh said more or less the same thing after Lillie wrote to tell her that Clara had broken off her engagement. Lillie's old friend had dropped out of school and was living in a flat with a couple of other girls in Dublin, where she had a job as a waitress around the corner from Trinity College.

And guess who came in for a cup of tea the other day? None other than that fella, Seamus Flaherty. He's back

Lillie grimaced. Poor Charles Fitzpatrick. The gossip had even spread to Dublin. And imagine Seamus Flaherty being back in Ireland. And winning a scholarship to Trinity, where he could live out his fantasy of becoming the next Brendan Behan.

The Saturday morning after Lillie received Sheelagh's letter, she and Ma went out riding, and Lillie told her what Sheelagh had said about the gossip of Clara's broken engagement spreading to Dublin.

'Well, let's not spread it around the whole of Australia as well,' Kathleen said, as they trotted together. 'Hopefully Charles will find a new girl shortly and will forget all about Clara.'

'Do you think Clara broke off her engagement to Charles Fitzpatrick because of Ronan?' Lillie asked.

'Possibly. However, it's really none of our business, darling. Ronan's a grown up. So is Clara. You shouldn't worry about them so much. What will be will be. In any case, he could do a lot worse than Clara. And she would be darn lucky to get our Ronan.'

Later, as Lillie sat at her desk to do her homework, hard as she tried she couldn't concentrate. All she could think of was Ronan and Clara up in Armidale. What were they doing? Were they sleeping together? Somehow, when she'd found out Ronan was probably sleeping with Trish, it hadn't worried her all that much. Imagining him with Clara was different. Why, she wasn't sure. Maybe it was just because she had always imagined Clara as part of the family.

Chapter 36

To Ronan it was as if the time since the family had arrived at Eureka Park had gone as fast as the rocket the Russians had launched to Mars a number of years before. Now it was the spring of 1967. Harold Holt was Prime Minister of Australia and sentiment against the Vietnam War was escalating. It was just over a year since the Battle of Long Tan, when eighteen Australian soldiers had been killed and twenty-four wounded, and just recently Australian casualties had once again been heavy in the Battle of Suoi Chau Pha, with six dead and nineteen wounded. Although he and the rest of the family were now Australian citizens, as yet he hadn't been conscripted to fight in Vietnam, although a few of his friends at uni had. If his number came up he was prepared to go and fight with his fellow countrymen. Despite being deeply in love with Clara.

The day of the bushfire he realised beyond doubt that he was not in love with Trish. He was still in love with Clara. Deb's birthday party had confirmed it. That night, as they sat outside on a hay bale between dances, Ronan had asked her why she hadn't written to tell him she was engaged to Charles Fitzpatrick. The silence had stretched between them.

'I tried a few times… then… well…'

'Are you in love with him?'

She fiddled with a piece of string on the hay bale. 'I thought so,' she said finally. 'Now I'm not so sure.'

'Why's that?' he asked.

Her beautiful blue eyes held his. 'Because…'

'Because what?'

'Now that I've seen you again… Well… That's made me unsure.'

Ronan took her hand. What he wanted to say was: *I love you, Clara. Break off your engagement.* But he was too much of gentleman to say that.

'He has a lot to offer you, Clara.' He forced himself to get the words out. 'A lot more than I can ever offer you.'

'If you're talking material things, well… I suppose he does. And Mummy would be furious if I broke it off.'

'It's not your mother you should be worrying about. It's you, Clara. You alone.'

'I know. Even so, I can't help feeling sorry for her. If I marry Charles it'll make her life so much easier.'

Ronan had put his arm around her shoulders and squeezed her hard against his body. 'That's not a good enough reason to marry someone.'

'I thought I did love him, Ronan. Truly I did. He's such a good man. He loves me dearly. And I know he'll do anything for me. It'd break his heart if I broke off the engagement at this stage.'

Ronan had looked out over the sheep yards; he could hear the lambs bleating. 'Why don't you go back to Ireland, see how you feel? If you discover you do still love him, much as you must know it would break my heart, go ahead and marry him.'

They sat in silence. Eventually Clara nodded. 'Yes. I think that's what I'll do. I'll go back and see him. Try and work out how I feel.' She stood up and looked down at Ronan. 'But I've never forgotten that kiss we shared under the mulberry tree. And the ones on the island.' She reached out and touched his face. 'Never.'

'Nor have I,' Ronan said.

'Will you kiss me now?' Clara asked.

All Ronan had wanted to do was take her in his arms and kiss her. But if he did, there'd be no going back for either of them. If he could have offered Clara what Charles Fitzpatrick was offering her, he wouldn't have hesitated. But he couldn't.

He shook his head. 'Not now, Clara. If you are prepared to give up everything Charles has to offer you, then I'll kiss you for the rest of my life. To kiss you now would be unfair. To you. To me. To Charles.'

Clara gazed at him steadily. 'Yes. You're probably right. I'm being a silly romantic. You're the practical one.' She looked towards the door of the barn. 'Let's go inside and have another dance. And I'll go back to Charles and sort myself out.'

Ronan stood up and looked at her longingly. 'If you decide to come back here, I'll be waiting for you. You can be sure of that. I promise.'

A week later Clara had left for Ireland. And Ronan didn't hear from her, which made him so anxious he found it difficult to concentrate on his studies. In the meantime he decided to break it off with Trish. It wasn't fair to her, feeling as he did about Clara. His heart leapt when his mother rang and told him Clara had broken off her engagement. But even then he didn't hear from her. The months that followed were agony; all he knew was that she was staying with a friend in Paris. Finally Kathleen had rung to say Clara was coming back to Eureka Park. And when he came down from Armidale and she looked into his anxious eyes, he knew without a doubt that she'd broken off her engagement so that she could be with him.

On her first night back at Eureka Park, he had waited until Marcus and Freddie had gone to bed, his parents had retired to watch TV and Lillie was doing her homework, before he asked Clara to come for a walk with him. Together they'd strolled down to the river. They sat on the sand and Clara told him that when she went back to Ireland she realised she no longer loved Charles.

'It's you I love,' she said, putting a hand to his face. 'You I've always loved.'

At that Ronan took her in his arms and kissed her passionately. They broke apart and marvelled at each other.

'I spent that time in France coming to grips with what I'd done,' Clara said, running a hand through his hair, 'but in the end I knew it was the right thing.'

Since that night they had spent every spare moment together. It was Ronan's suggestion that she come up to Armidale, take over the spare room in his digs and work for the dentist he'd gone to.

On Clara's second night in Armidale they'd gone to the drive-in theatre to see *The Graduate*. Afterwards they drove up to the lookout and watched the twinkling lights below. Seeing a grassy patch under a wattle tree a little further away, Ronan got out of the car and carried the rug they had used to keep them warm during the movie and spread it on the ground. He took Clara's hand and together they fell to the ground, kissing and fondling each other.

'Undress me,' Clara whispered, placing Ronan's hand on the buttons of her dress. 'Please, Ronan, undress me.'

'Are you sure?' he asked.

She squeezed his hand. 'I've never been so sure in my life.'

Slowly Ronan undid the buttons. She wasn't wearing a bra, so he could clearly see her beautiful breasts. Lowering his head, he kissed her warm skin and caressed her nipples between his lips. At the same time his hand moved up under the soft fabric and inside her silk panties where his fingers felt her moistness. As if he'd opened a door to a hidden treasure, Clara wriggled out of her dress and panties. Now she was naked. Above them the moon peeked out from behind the clouds and the stars were so bright it was as if an angel above had switched them on especially. With her glistening body lying beside him on the rug, Ronan had never seen anything as perfect. 'You're so beautiful,' he whispered, his fingers exploring the satiny smoothness of her thigh.

'And now it's your turn,' Clara whispered in his ear, and undid the buttons on his shirt and the zipper of his jeans.

For some time they lay there naked together, playing pleasurably with each other. To Ronan it was as if he'd known Clara's body intimately all his life. Following the curve of her breasts with his hand, he caressed her flat belly.

'I worship you, Clara,' he whispered, moving his hand between her legs, causing her to gasp for breath.

'I love you, Ronan,' she whispered. 'More than you'll ever know.'

Later, after he'd entered her and she had called out in ecstasy, arching her back and begging him to never stop, they lay in each other's arms.

'Oh, Ronan,' she said. 'What if I'd never known love like this?'

It was early morning before they folded up the blanket and returned to Ronan's digs, where they made love again in Ronan's bed. After that Clara slept with him every night; each time he was careful to use a condom.

***

James and Kathleen decided to throw a party at Eureka Park for Ronan's twenty-first birthday.

'We won't need plates or knives or forks. We can eat the snags and steaks wrapped in bread with tomato sauce,' Ronan had said to Kathleen, trying to persuade her not to go overboard with preparations.

'We *will* need plates,' she said firmly. 'And knives and forks. It'll be done properly or not at all.' She smiled the smile Ronan loved so much. 'It's not every day our eldest son turns twenty-one.'

The day of the party, Ronan and Clara drove down from Armidale. In addition to Ronan's friends, his parents had invited the Hogans and a few of their neighbours in for the afternoon as well. Lorna and Brian Medlow were also coming and were spending the night in Gullumbindy at the Telegraph. Even Father Fogarty had accepted an invitation.

Lillie told Ronan she'd invited Deb, however she was loath to leave the family property, as a pack of rogue dogs had got in and attacked a heap of their prized merinos. Her father had to shoot the injured sheep.

Now, as Ronan watched Clara coming down the bank to where he was preparing a fire to cook on by the river, he felt his heartbeat speed up. She looked so beautiful, wearing a pair of blue jeans and a white shirt. Somehow that simple outfit looked more glamorous than if she was dressed in the fanciest of ball gowns.

All in all, there were about thirty guests. Dingo, egged on by the family yelling at the top of their voices, 'Go, Dingo, go!', won the dog race Ronan had organised, with Bill Hogan's Ned coming second. A few of Ronan's friends had brought kayaks on roof racks, so there was a kayak race on the river as well. Even Arthur had a go and came second to one of Ronan's mates. When they were all sitting around by the river, James stood up and made a toast to his son. Although feeling embarrassed in front of everyone, inwardly Ronan was very moved by his father's speech.

Many of the revellers had pitched tents along the river and that night, after Ronan's parents and the older guests had gone, the younger ones gathered around the campfire. Ronan played the guitar and Clara led the singing. As he gazed across at Clara, Ronan had a huge urge to make love to her. As if sensing his thoughts, Clara held his eyes and he knew she was thinking the same thing. Although he hadn't pitched his own tent down here, Ronan decided then and there that as it was such a lovely night, he and Clara would sleep by the river. He'd go back up to the house and get a couple of blankets.

When Lillie and his brothers had gone up to bed and the rest of the revellers were in their tents, he and Clara placed the blankets down on the grass. They made long, lingering love, then lay under the stars, listening to the chirp of crickets and the gentle lap of the water running over the stones in the river below.

Ronan leant over and fondled Clara's breasts, cupping them in his hand and taking her nipples within his fingers.

'Will you marry me, Clara?' he asked.

Clara pulled back a little and looked at him.

'Perhaps not straightaway,' he added. 'I'll need to finish uni first and get a real job. I haven't had a chance to tell you, but Dalgety's rang this morning and said they'll take me on in their farm management division when I finish up at the end of the year.'

It was that phone call that had prompted Ronan's proposal. He'd thought long and hard about what he wanted to do and the experience he'd get at Dalgety's should set him up for life if he ever got a chance to own his own place. He belonged on the land. Here in Australia. Or back in Ireland.

'So I'll be able to support you,' he said. 'We'll just have a small wedding with Father Fogarty presiding.' He chuckled, rolling her on top of him. 'With the church at Gullumbindy full of flowers and you walking down the aisle with orange blossom in your hair.'

Clara laughed. 'And where would you get orange blossom in Gullumbindy?'

'True. Maybe blossom from a jacaranda tree.' He touched her hair. 'The purple will suit you beautifully. And afterwards we could have a celebration at the Telegraph Hotel. The Hogans would love that. And we could get our own piece of land with lots of animals. Young Fred would be tickled pink. And,' his eyes twinkled, 'we'll have a whole rugby team of kids.'

'Honestly, Ronan, you're crazy. A rugby team, no. But yes,' she said, her eyes gleaming with happiness, 'yes, of course I'll marry you. Nothing would give me more happiness. And our wedding should be just like you said. I think that would be perfect.' She paused and Ronan could see mixed emotions in her eyes. 'On the other hand, you don't suppose it's a bit soon after I broke off with Charles to announce anything? What would people think?'

'Who gives a damn what people think? We love each other. That's what matters.'

Clara leant forward and kissed his forehead. 'Still… maybe we should leave it for a little while before we tell anyone. Especially Mummy. She'll be furious with me.'

'I thought she liked the O'Sullivans?'

'Of course she does. Even so… well… You know what I mean.'

Ronan touched her lips with his fingers. 'I think I can keep it a secret. Mind you… only for so long.'

'Oh, Ronan. I do love you. So very much.' She paused. 'But if I marry you I'll have to pay Charles back the money he spent on my fare. Otherwise I'd feel dreadful.'

Ronan smiled. 'I think that is a must.'

Now they made love again, even more passionately than before. As long as he lived, Ronan knew he'd always remember the moment Clara had agreed to marry him.

Chapter 37

With Arthur's help, during the summer school holidays Lillie had trained Muffin to show jump, practising in the bottom paddock where she and Arthur had set up some jumps. On the morning of the Quirindi Show, Arthur drove her and Muffin across in the horse float.

It turned out Brad Hickey was competing on his large bay horse in the same showjumping event she was in. After a clear round he cantered past Lillie and Muffin, who stood waiting their turn. Raising his hat, he did a mock bow as he recognised her. As usual when Lillie saw him, her heart missed a beat. The next competitor knocked four poles down. After that it was an older man, who had one refusal and then knocked two poles flying. Now it was Lillie's turn.

She leaned down and patted Muffin on the neck. 'Go, girl,' she coaxed. 'Let's kick the butt off the rest of these horses.'

Muffin cleared the first ten jumps beautifully and when they got to the triple-bar, the last jump, Lillie could see a jump-off coming up. Just as she thought: *Yes! We did it!* Muffin nicked the last pole. 'Oh no,' Lillie wailed as she looked back and saw it hit the ground. Nevertheless, she patted Muffin gently on the neck to tell her she'd done a great job.

Half an hour later, when the other competitors had finished their rounds, Lillie realised they'd got third place to Brad Hickey's first. As they stood in line for the presentation of the rosettes, he leant over and held out his hand.

'You two did really well,' he said in his deep voice. 'You were unlucky with the last jump.'

'Thanks,' Lillie said, taking his firm hand in her sweaty palm. Much to her horror, she felt the colour rising in her cheeks and she had to look away and pretend to fiddle with her stirrup.

Later he came up to her when she was eating a hot dog and watching the flag race.

'How's Deb?' he asked.

'She's great,' Lillie said, wiping the tomato sauce from her lips.

'Can I call you some time?' he asked.

Lillie looked at him, not quite believing what she was hearing. 'What about your girlfriend?'

'We've broken up.'

Lillie grinned. 'Well… In that case, yeah, why not?'

Driving home with Arthur that evening, she wondered, much as she fancied him, if she shouldn't have played harder to get. But if she'd refused he'd probably have gone and asked someone else.

A few days later he rang. 'G'day, Lillie,' he drawled down the phone. 'How're you doing?'

'Good thanks. What about you?'

'All the better after hearing your voice.'

Lillie was glad he couldn't see her blushing.

'Do you want to go and see the Seekers?' he asked. 'They're on in Tamworth next week. There's a Sunday afternoon show. Maybe you could catch an early bus back to school?'

Lillie waited a moment before answering, trying not to sound too enthusiastic.

'Yeah. Why not?' she said. 'I've heard them on the radio… They're really good. I'll see what I can organise. My brother has a few days off uni but I know he's got to be back in Armidale for rugby practice at three-thirty on Sunday, so he might drop me off on the way through.'

'That'd be great. What's say I meet you at Fitzroy's at one? We can walk along.'

When she put the phone down she hurried to her bedroom and tried to work out what to wear. Finally she settled on a pair of three-quarter length blue jeans and a red and white striped top, which would go with her red loafers. She then rushed out excitedly to tell Ma and ask if she could go.

'Yes. If Ronan drops you off. But don't go building it up too much,' Kathleen warned. 'Then it might be a disappointment.'

'He's really nice,' Lillie said. 'All the girls like him.'

'Yes, I saw him at the dance, remember? Be careful, that's all I'm saying.'

After getting such a lukewarm reaction from Ma, she hurried off to ring Deb, who was much more enthusiastic.

'Oooh!' she exclaimed. 'I knew he'd get rid of that girlfriend. Lucky you.'

On the drive up with Ronan on Sunday her stomach was churning terribly from nervousness and excitement.

'You sound like a washing machine,' he chuckled. He looked at her intently. 'You sure this bloke's okay? I've heard he's got a bit of a reputation.'

'He's perfectly okay, thank you very much.' As she got out of the car, she leant over and gave him a kiss on the cheek. 'I'll be fine. Truly I will. And give my love to Clara. Sorry she couldn't get down.'

He smiled. 'She was pissed off she had to work. Once a month the dentist does a Saturday morning.'

It turned out to be a fun, starry couple of hours. The crowd tapped their feet to the music and Brad held her hand. Lillie's heart thrilled. They even met Judith Durham outside the venue when the show finished. After they had a milkshake back at Fitzroy's, Brad dropped her a little way from school so that no one would see.

Before she got out of the car, he gave her a long, lingering kiss, which made her body tingle all over.

'Can I ring you during the week?'

'We're not allowed to take phone calls unless it's family. But what about Friday night when I'm home?'

'Sure, I'll ring then. Maybe I could come down on Saturday and we could go for a ride?'

'You could ride Sadie, the mare Dad rides now. She's never got in foal but he keeps her because she's fun to ride.'

'Sounds great.'

For days afterwards she walked around in a cloud of euphoria. Deb asked if she was on some sort of medication.

'Or are you just in love?'

'Well… I'm not taking any medication...'

'Lucky you,' Deb said. 'You'll be the envy of every girl in the district.'

Lillie thought Deb was probably right. She couldn't wait until next Friday night when Brad would ring her and they'd arrange for him to come down on Saturday.

***

He rang at seven on Friday as promised and said he would drive down in his ute in the morning. Lillie told him she would pack a picnic and they would ride to her favourite spot further along the river.

'When you go out riding with Brad, make sure you take Arthur with you,' her mother said before she, Dad and her brothers left the next morning to join Clara and watch Ronan play rugby in Tamworth, where his uni team were playing against the local Tamworth team.

'Ma! I'm nearly eighteen. I think I can look after myself.'

'I hope so,' Kathleen said. 'In any case, we'll be back late afternoon.'

After they left she made some sandwiches and filled a thermos, all the time shaking with nervousness. What if he didn't like her when he saw her again? But when he drove up at twelve and she went out to greet him, he pulled her to him and kissed her deeply.

'You look great,' he said, winking. 'I love those tight jeans.' He patted her on the bottom. 'They show off your bum to perfection.'

Lillie blushed. She'd agonised as to what to wear. These jeans *were* tight, but she really liked them.

Brad looked around and down to the river. 'Finn Malone did a good job to find this place. Such pity the bloke did himself in.'

'So you think he did commit suicide now? You weren't so sure before.'

'Reckon he did. There doesn't seem much else to go on.'

'No, there doesn't. When were you last out here exercising the horses for him?'

'About a month before he was found. But God knows when the bloke actually did the deed.'

'And he seemed okay then?'

'Yeah. He told me about you lot coming. Seemed to be looking forward to it.'

'And he wasn't drinking?'

'He seemed sober enough.'

Her parents had told Lillie how Uncle Finn had gone to Brisbane to dry out. Brad must have seen him after he came back. But then he must have started drinking again when he killed himself. It was all so sad.

'Anyway,' she said to Brad, 'I've saddled Sadie. And I've got lunch packed. So if you're right we can head off.'

'Sure am.'

An hour or so later they lay on a rug beside the river. They'd finished their sandwiches and half the bottle of wine Brad had brought and insisted Lillie help him drink. Brad rolled over and kissed her hard on the mouth, all the time fondling her breasts. The combination of the wine and the hot sun made Lillie quite tipsy. As if in a blur she felt Brad remove her top and undo her bra, releasing her breasts. Taking off his own shirt, he ran his hand across her waist and undid her jeans. Through her fuddled, aroused brain, Lillie realised she was about to lose her virginity. Despite fantasising about such a moment, this frightened the life out of her.

'Brad… No…'

'Trust me, it'll be okay,' he whispered, pulling on what Lillie supposed was a condom. 'I promise.'

Now he was on top of her, his mouth pressed on hers. Lillie wriggled but there was no way she could free herself from his grasp. He roughly pulled her jeans down and urgently spread her legs wide apart. She felt him enter her and an agonising pain shot up inside of her. She wanted to cry out, but Brad's tongue was so far inside her mouth she could make no sound at all. Each excruciating thrust felt as though it was tearing her apart. Finally he let out a primal cry of satisfaction before moving off her to grab a cigarette. For some time Lillie lay in stunned silence. She had read about the act of making love in novels, and Sheelagh had told her about it in a letter.

My God, Lillie. Wait till you try it. If you strike the right fella it's like taking off into space. You never want it to end.

What had just happened bore little resemblance to what Sheelagh described. It seemed more like rape than the tender moment Lillie had imagined it would be. Yet there was no way she could accuse him of forcing himself on her. After all, here she was, alone with him, having consumed enough wine to fuddle her brain. By lying on this blanket with him she had more or less given her consent, even though she had asked him to stop. Eventually she sat up and looked at the rug they'd been lying on. Ma's tartan rug. With horror she saw it was covered in blood. Her blood. She felt so embarrassed that she scrambled up.

'Can you move?' she asked Brad. 'I need to wash the blanket.'

He looked at the blood and then at Lillie. 'I'm sorry,' he said. 'I didn't realise you hadn't done it before.'

Oh yeah! Lillie wanted to shout. *It's something I do every day of the week!*

'That's okay,' she said. 'You weren't to know.' She paused. 'But I did ask you to stop.'

'Did you? I didn't hear. I thought you were enjoying it. In any case, there's no way I would've been able to stop. You should've said you didn't want to do it before we started.'

'Yeah,' she said, forcing a smile. 'You're probably right. It was my fault. I should've said.'

Stepping down to the river she placed the rug on the ground before she waded into the water. As she stood there, with the cool current splashing against her bare legs and washing away her blood, a dreadful guilt engulfed her. What would her parents think? While she wasn't overly religious, what she had allowed to happen was a mortal sin. If she had enjoyed it, this wouldn't seem so bad. You're an idiot, Lillie O'Sullivan she rebuked herself, trying hard to stop the tears threatening to spill down her cheeks.

After a moment Brad came down to the water's edge, picked up the rug and waded in, washing the blood off.

'I'm sorry,' he said again.

'It's all right,' Lillie said. 'But I'd like to go home now if you don't mind.'

Out of the water they got dressed in awkward silence, packed up the picnic things and stuffed them and the rug into their saddlebags. They rode back to the homestead and put the horses back in their paddock.

'You sure you're okay?' Brad asked again as Lillie walked him to his ute.

'I'm fine. Truly I am.'

'I'll give you a holla,' he said, getting behind the wheel, 'in a day or so.'

As she watched him drive away, the tears that had been threatening started to flood down Lillie's cheeks and she wiped them away with her sleeve. At that moment Arthur wandered out from the stables. She wished now that she had asked him to come with them.

'You all right? he asked, lifting his stockman's hat and looking at her with concerned black eyes. 'Why are you crying?'

'I'm not crying,' she said. 'I got something in my eyes riding back from the river.'

'Ah. That's it. Anyway, you have a good picnic?' He looked at her wet hair. 'And a swim?'

'Yeah. It was great.'

Arthur helped her unpack the saddlebags. When he pulled out Ma's wet rug she smiled.

'I dropped it in the water when I was shaking the crumbs off.'

'Ah. Easy to do.'

The way he said it, Lillie was sure he knew exactly what had happened.

Grabbing the remains of the picnic and the rug, she took them across to the homestead, where she hung the rug on the clothesline to dry. She would tell Ma the same story she told Arthur. Once she got inside the house she ran a hot bath and lay in it for some time, trying to relieve the pain between her legs.

Today she'd lost something she could never recapture. And there was no way she could tell anyone what had happened. How she had tried to stop Brad. If she did blurt that out, even to Deb, all anyone would say was that she had brought it on herself. She thought of Clara and Ronan. She couldn't imagine Ronan hurting Clara the way Brad had hurt her. Surely all sex couldn't be like what she had just experienced, otherwise no one would do it willingly.

Four days later Brad rang her up and said he was back on with Sally. 'I really like you, Lillie,' he said. 'It's just that Sally and I have some unfinished business.'

Thanks, Lillie wanted to shout down the line. Thanks a lot! You could've told me that before you stole my virginity.

But instead she said, 'Thanks for letting me know. I hope you're both very happy,' and rang off. Shaking with hurt and fury, she rushed to her bedroom, flung herself on the bed and cried herself to sleep.

A few weeks later when her mother asked her why she wasn't seeing Brad any more, she lied. 'He's gone away.'

And she said much the same to Ronan when he asked. But he was so involved with Clara that Lillie didn't think he cared much about what his sister was doing anyway. It was only Deb she couldn't fool.

'He broke it off and he's gone back to Sally,' Lillie said when Deb asked her how it was going.

Deb shook her head. 'If he's like that, you're better off without him.'

Lillie thought that Deb was probably right. But that didn't stop it hurting. The sad thing was that when she looked back to when she lost her virginity, it would always be something she'd rather forget, rather than remember fondly. But then again, she supposed she wasn't the first girl to be in that situation.

Chapter 38

Kathleen stood back and appraised the photographs she'd hung. She was pleased with the selection she'd chosen for this, her first exhibition. Not only was there a good representation of the Australian bush, she had also developed a few negatives from her Calcutta days.

'I think you've chosen well,' Roger Mann said, coming to stand beside her. Over the time she had been selling her photographs in his gallery she had got to like Roger very much. 'And you've chosen the frames beautifully,' he said. 'They really show the photographs off.'

Normally Kathleen only mounted her photographs. For this exhibition she had them framed in a shop in Tamworth and was delighted with the result, although she'd had to add a bit to the price to cover the cost. She hoped that wouldn't put people off.

'Thank you, Roger,' she said. 'How many people do you think will come?'

'Hard to say. We've had fifty acceptances, nonetheless at times some just turn up. And, of course, others who say they are coming sometimes don't.'

Kathleen tried not to feel nervous. 'If we have fifty I'll be more than pleased.'

He walked over to where Kathleen had placed one of her series. These photos depicted scenes along Wattle Creek Road on the drive from Eureka Park into Gullumbindy. There was one of the ruins of a timber outbuilding with weeds and a gum tree sprouting through the roof; the remains of a farmhouse burnt by the bushfires; a copse of trees around a dam and a huddle of sheep sheltering from the sun under a weeping willow. 'I think these are my favourites,' he said. 'They're so typical of the Australian bush.'

He looked towards the far wall. 'But I do like your Indian ones as well.'

Lillie was putting up a large photograph of the river in front of Eureka Park. Kathleen had taken it on dusk and the colours reminded her of the Hooghly River in Calcutta — all mustards and browns, with the overhanging trees reflected. She was pleased to see Lillie smiling. Although she had told her that boy, Brad Hickey, had gone away, Kathleen suspected he hadn't and that he had dropped Lillie, causing her great sadness. But Kathleen didn't want to pry. If Lillie wanted to tell her she would. The same as Ronan would tell her when he was ready what was happening with Clara.

'Who's that gorgeous boy?' Lillie asked, pointing to one of Kathleen's Calcutta photographs that featured a little boy sitting on an Indian Chief motorbike and laughing, his luminous dark eyes gleaming in the sun. 'He looks as though he's having such fun.'

Kathleen smiled. 'His name was Sanjay. He lived in the native town on the outskirts of the city.'

'He's looking at someone off to the side. Who was that?'

Kathleen waited a moment before answering. 'Oh, I don't know… probably some other children.'

But it wasn't other children he was looking at. Kathleen remembered so well when that photo had been taken. They had gone to the native town on the Indian. When Sanjay saw them he had rushed over, demanding to be allowed to sit on the bike. Kathleen remembered wondering whose eyes were the happiest. Sanjay's or her squadron leader's as he gently placed the little boy up on the seat.

'Who owned the bike?' Lillie asked.

Kathleen smiled. 'Oh, just a friend of mine and Jessica's. But come,' she beckoned, pointing to a small pile of photos still needing to be hung, 'let's finish getting these up. Before we know it, it'll be six and people will start arriving and we won't be ready.'

The last photo she hung was the one she'd taken of Shannon Boy and Clara before Clara went back to Ireland to marry Charles Fitzpatrick. It was such a lovely photograph she had asked Clara if she could use it in the exhibition.

'Of course, Aunt Kathleen. I just wish I could come down for your big night, but I can't get time off from my job. It's only the dentist and me. If I'm not there he'd have to shut up shop. And it's such a pity Ronan's away on work experience on that property out west. He's devastated he's going to miss it.'

Kathleen smiled as she looked at the photograph. Having blotted his copybook when he first went down to Tommy Brown, Shannon Boy had now more than earned his keep. In fact he had won his last two races. He'd even won a Group One race at Rosehill, and the whole family and Clara, who had come down for the weekend with Ronan, had yelled and screamed at the television set to urge him on, celebrating afterwards with flutes of champagne. Soon after that win Tommy Brown had rung up with an offer from another of his owners to buy him. For days Kathleen and James agonised. Finally they decided to let him go. In a way Kathleen had said goodbye to him when he went down to Burra Lodge, knowing he was unlikely to come back to Eureka Park. If they took the offer they could watch his progress from a distance and still feel very proud of having produced him. And know that the money they got for him could be put back into Eureka Park in order to produce more great foals. Much as she missed Shannon Boy, Kathleen had a feeling that Finn would have agreed they had made the right decision.

She smiled as she imagined him laughing and saying, 'You can't get too attached. If you do you'll stuff up all my work. Yours too.'

Straightening the photograph, she looked at her watch. She stepped over to where she had left her handbag, picked it up and went to the bathroom to freshen up her lipstick and run a comb through her hair before the guests arrived. Looking in the mirror Kathleen could see there was certainly a lot more grey in her hair now, but she didn't mind. In fact she quite liked it. She wasn't so sure about the deep wrinkles around her eyes, despite James telling her they were smile lines. And with Shannon Boy's contribution to the stud, and now with her first exhibition about to begin, she had been smiling a lot more lately. With one last look in the mirror she left the bathroom and went to greet James, Marcus and Freddie who she could hear arriving. Then she saw Lorna and Brian Medlow. And Father Fogarty. And the Hogans. How lucky she was to have such good friends, who had made the trip up to Tamworth for this.

By eight o'clock it was finished and the fifty-odd guests had left in a merry throng. In the corners of twenty-five of Kathleen's photographs there were little red sold stickers.

'Well done, darling,' James said, handing her a glass of champagne. 'You were a roaring success.'

'It went much better than I thought,' she laughed. 'I was awake most of last night imagining I wouldn't sell any.'

'Did you see that woman talking to Lorna and me earlier?' James asked as they stood before a beaming Sanjay sitting on the motorbike. Even it had a red sold sticker.

'Yes,' Kathleen said. 'She's that friend of Dawn's. Winifred Black. I was surprised to see her here. I would have come over but she was gone before I could.'

'She didn't stay for long. As soon as I went up to talk to Lorna she made as if to leave. But before she did she stopped and beckoned as though she wanted to say something to me privately. Then she seemed to change her mind. Just said that Finn had talked to her about his days in India. And that he had known you when you were there.'

'So she knew you were a friend of his. And had taken over Eureka Park.'

'Evidently.'

'She didn't say anything else? I mean about seeing him before he died?'

'No, nothing.'

'All very strange,' Kathleen said.

'Yes,' James said. 'It is a bit.' He put his arm around her and smiled as he looked at the motorbike in the photo. 'That was certainly some bike. I don't think I've ever seen another Indian.'

Kathleen shook her head. 'Neither have I.'

As she said that, she wondered what had happened to it. Was it still in India? She also wondered about Winifred Black. Why had she come all this way to Kathleen's exhibition if she didn't want to talk to her or to James, knowing they had taken over Eureka Park after Finn's death? After all, Dawn had asked her to look out for him.

***

It was an unseasonably cold December night when James glanced around the table at his family and thought how blessed he was. It was now over four years since the family had arrived at Eureka Park. Lillie had completed her Leaving Certificate and, although she wouldn't get her results until the New Year, she thought she had done quite well, particularly in English literature. Marcus had always been their difficult child, but the Christian Brothers seemed to be settling him down. And Freddie was just Freddie, growing at a rapid rate, but still the fun-loving boy he always was. He looked at Ronan who had grown into such a fine young man; and he had finished university and would officially graduate early next year, was playing rugby for the local team and had already started work at Dalgety's in Armidale, where he was still living in digs with Dave, Clara and two other students. He was enjoying travelling to a number of different properties in the area to give advice on stock and machinery.

'He's a bloody good bloke you've got there,' the manager had told James last time he went in to see him about a new tractor. 'Works damn hard and gets on well with the locals. Would think he was a local himself.' He'd then laughed. 'Well… I suppose you lot *are* regarded as locals, eh!'

This evening James noticed Ronan fidgeting nervously at the table. Then his son stood up.

'Ladies and gentlemen, quiet, please,' he declared in a mock announcer's voice. 'Order!'

Everyone stopped talking and stared at him.

'We've waited a long time to make this announcement.'

'What announcement?' Freddie asked excitedly.

Ronan smiled, gazing down at Clara. 'I'd like to introduce you to my future wife. The most beautiful girl a man could ever hope for. I think I've loved her from the moment I first set eyes on her when we were five years old and she used to steal my chalk in the nursery at Rathgarven.'

James tried not to show his shock. Although he had a fair idea that Ronan and Clara were an item, he'd had no inkling it was this serious. His first thought was of Jessica. How would she cope? How would James cope with her response?

'Wow! That's fantastic,' Freddie exclaimed with joy, pushing his seat back and rushing over to them. 'I knew you should marry Clara.' He looked at Clara's finger. 'Where's the ring?

'We're choosing it tomorrow,' Ronan said.

Even Marcus, who was normally laidback, grinned as he sauntered over to give Ronan a pat on the back and Clara a warm embrace. 'Gees, you two! That's awesome.'

'Gosh, how exciting,' Lillie said, going around to congratulate them both. 'I'm really happy for you.'

Now Kathleen smiled at James before she went over and embraced Ronan and Clara heartily. 'Darlings that's wonderful.'

Finally James stood and moved around the table to shake Ronan's hand. 'Congratulations to you both. And welcome to the family, dear Clara,' he added, giving her a kiss on the cheek.

'Thank you, Uncle James,' she beamed. 'I'm so happy to be part of you all. And so will Mummy.'

I'm not so sure about that, James thought. He had a strong suspicion Jessica would be furious Clara had given up a life at Drominderry House and all it entailed, particularly for Jessica herself, to marry Ronan. After Clara had phoned her mother to let her know she was back at Eureka Park, Jessica had written to Kathleen to say how disappointed she was they hadn't sent her straight home to undo the damage she'd done by flitting off and letting Charles Fitzpatrick down.

'Honestly,' Kathleen had said when she read the letter to James, 'she really is the pits at times. How does she think we can send Clara home?'

Now James looked at Kathleen's happy face. Although she'd been annoyed with Jessica for only thinking of herself when Clara had broken off her engagement, she was sure to be pleased to have her friend as part of their family. Now more than ever James would have to keep Jessica's threats a secret.

'Have you told your mother yet?' he asked Clara.

'Well, no,' she said. 'We were planning on making a trunk call tonight if that's okay. After we'd let you all in on the secret.' She looked at her watch. 'We'd best wait another hour or so or we'll wake her up too early. As we all know, Mummy's not an early morning person.'

Ronan looked at Clara lovingly. 'Clara's agreed to marry me in the autumn. After the wedding, if we save enough money, we'll go to England for our honeymoon, so Clara can see her mother. And we'll go to Dublin to see Grandma.'

'How wonderful,' Kathleen clapped her hands. 'We'll have to start planning straightaway.'

'We want to have our wedding at the church in Gullumbindy,' Ronan said. 'With Father Fogarty doing the honours.'

'How lovely,' Kathleen said. And now,' she added, 'I feel a glass of champagne's in order. I just happen to have a bottle in the fridge. Then you can ring Jessica.'

When everyone had been poured a flute, including a mouthful for Freddie and an inch for Marcus, James proposed a toast: 'To Ronan and Clara.'

'To Ronan and Clara,' reverberated around the room.

James gazed at his smiling family. The only glitch on the horizon was Jessica. How would she cope with this news? The small church in Gullumbindy would be a bit different to Christchurch Cathedral in Dublin where Jessica would have been in her element had Clara married Charles Fitzpatrick. True to her word she hadn't tried to make contact with James for any more money since they had been in Australia. So he wondered if she would be able to afford the fare to Australia for the wedding — unless she had found another source of funds. Would she even want to come?

Chapter 39

While Clara went to the phone to ask the overseas telephone exchange to get her mother on the line, Ronan stood with his back to the fire and looked around the room. Marcus and Freddie had gone to bed, but Lillie, Ma and Dad were still here in the living room discussing wedding plans. Ronan felt as happy as a pig in mud. Clara was already so much part of his family's life that he could see how thrilled they were to welcome her formally into the fold. The only one who had seemed slightly hesitant was his father. Maybe he was worried they were too young to make such a commitment. Then again, Clara had been even younger when she had become engaged to Charles Fitzpatrick, and his father had seemed okay with that.

In the background he could hear Clara talking to her mother. All of a sudden she raised her voice and he moved to the door.

'What do you mean I can't marry him?' she shouted down the phone. 'You've always adored him. And Aunt Kathleen's your best friend.'

Feeling anger rise up inside him, Ronan rushed to join her.

'She wants to speak to Aunt Kathleen,' Clara said, putting her hand over the mouthpiece.

'Why?'

'God alone knows. Can you get her?'

Mystified, Kathleen went to the phone. When she came back into the living room, it was as if every last drop of blood had been drained from her body. Ronan watched her move to the drinks cabinet and pour herself a stiff glass of whisky. He had never seen her drink whisky before.

'What was all that about? he asked her.

'Perhaps Mummy had too many gin and tonics last night. Or she's lost her marbles,' Clara muttered in disbelief. 'She sounded really odd on the phone. She wouldn't talk to me. She wanted you, Aunt Kathleen.'

'She hadn't had too much to drink,' Ma said.

'Well then, tell us what she said?'

Ma shook her head. 'I'm afraid I can't do that. Not yet. I need some time.'

'Time for what, Ma?' Ronan demanded. 'What could you need time for? Obviously Clara's mother doesn't think I'm good enough for her daughter. Did she say why?'

Ma looked at him. Tears started rolling down her cheeks. 'I'm afraid I have to go and lie down now. Could we talk about this in the morning?' She stared forlornly at his father. 'I need to discuss what Jessica told me with James.'

'This is ridiculous,' Clara exclaimed. 'I mean… What's Mummy going on about? She sounded so adamant that I should come home right now and not get married to Ronan. I think she definitely must have gone quite batty or —'

'Oh Clara, I'm so sorry …' Ma said. She looked to Ronan. 'So very sorry…'

A silence prevailed as never before. Normally this room was full of chatter, laughter and music. Now it seemed as if it was in mourning.

'Maybe she thinks it's too soon after breaking off with Charles Fitzpatrick,' James suggested helpfully.

'No. It's not that,' Ma said, moving towards the door. 'Nothing to do with that at all. It's my fault. Totally my fault.' She looked at James imploringly. 'Please… can you come with me?'

After they both disappeared through the door Ronan was so confused he found it difficult to think. One minute he'd been on top of the world and now that world had come crashing down like a rugby scrum. How dare Jessica spoil his and Clara's happiness! He looked at Clara, whose eyes were wet with tears.

'I don't get it... How can it be Aunt Kathleen's fault?' she sobbed.

'I honestly don't know,' Ronan said, and went and put his arms around her, trying to calm her.

'I want to ring Mummy back,' she cried.

Ronan felt Ma was trying to shield Clara from Jessica. Why, he had no idea. But he felt the best thing to do would be to get Clara out of here. Away from the phone.

'Come for a walk with me down to the river,' he said, giving her a squeeze. 'In the morning we can see if we can work it out.'

Clara glanced at Lillie, who was looking totally bewildered.

'Do what Ronan says,' Lillie said. 'Although it's cold, it's a lovely night with the moon out. I'm sure it'll all be okay in the morning. There must've have been a misunderstanding, that's all.'

'Yes,' Clara said, solemnly. 'I suppose you're right.'

Outside on the verandah, Ronan took Clara's hand. 'No matter what that was all about, it won't make any difference to us,' he said. 'I promise you.'

Clara started sobbing. 'She's always been like that. I bet it's because she wanted me to marry Charles so she could go and live at Drominderry House. That must be it. I can't think of anything else. Sometimes she behaves like a spoilt brat.'

Although Ronan was completely bewildered by what had happened, he tried to sound upbeat. 'Well, she's not going to spoil our happiness.' He led her down to the riverbank and he pulled her down beside him. 'Nothing can spoil that.'

He kissed her tenderly and wiped her tears away. Soon a small smile appeared on her face. 'Yes,' she said, 'you're quite right. Nothing can spoil that, can it?'

***

The next morning Ronan and Lillie were in the kitchen washing up the champagne flutes when his father came out about eight o'clock. Ronan thought he looked as if he hadn't had a wink of sleep. His hair seemed greyer and his shoulders stooped. Marcus and Freddie were off rabbit trapping with Arthur and Clara was still asleep.

'I'll take your mother a cup of tea,' James said, glancing at the kettle on the stove.

Lillie jumped up. 'I'll get it, Dad. And I'll make some toast. You sit down.'

She put some bread in the toaster, lifted the kettle from the stove and filled the china teapot. Covering it with a floral cosy she put it on the painted wooden tray, together with a piece of toast with butter and what Ronan knew was Ma's favourite ginger marmalade.

'Is Ma okay?' she asked, worry etched in her grey eyes as she handed her father the tray.

Ronan thought Dad seemed sadder and crosser than he had ever seen him. Then he seemed to pull himself together and gave them both a forced smile.

'I'm afraid she's had a dreadful shock. And so have I.' What he said next sent a chill through Ronan. 'I'm not sure if she'll ever get over it. Or if I will, either.' He looked out the window at the softly falling rain. 'If any of us will.'

Ronan felt sick inside. What had Jessica said that was causing this sort of reaction?

'I want to see her,' he demanded.

'No, Ronan,' James said. 'Not now.'

He picked up the tray and walked out of the kitchen, leaving Ronan and Lillie standing in shock.

378

Ronan made to follow him. 'I'm going in to see her,' he said to Lillie. 'This is bloody ridiculous.'

'Please don't, Ronan. It'll only make matters worse if Dad said not to. Why don't you go and see if Clara's awake? You can take her a cup of tea.' She came over and put a hand on his shoulder. 'Give them time to sort out whatever the problem is.'

***

Much to Ronan's consternation, Ma stayed in bed all morning. At one o'clock he was surprised to see Father Fogarty arrive and go with Dad into the bedroom. As he left the priest seemed quite disturbed. Ronan asked him what was going on, but he just shook his head.

'I'm afraid I'd be breaking your mother's confidence to tell you that, Ronan. She will explain it all in her own good time.' He looked out the window to where Marcus and Freddie were playing with their kite. Dingo was running around in a state trying to catch it. 'In the meantime, I thought I'd take those two larrikins in to the Hogans for the night,' the priest said. 'They're expecting me for dinner. In the morning they can drop Marcus at the bus for Tamworth and Freddie at school.'

'But why?' Ronan asked. 'I mean…. What's the matter?'

'I'll get their things ready,' Lillie said, throwing Ronan a look that made it very clear that she was more than happy her little brothers were getting away from whatever was happening here.

Half an hour later they were gone and James came out to where Ronan was sitting on the back verandah with Clara and Lillie.

'Can I go and see her now?' Ronan asked, jumping up.

'No, son. She's writing you a letter. Father Fogarty suggested it. I'm afraid she's not up to seeing you right now. But she wants you to know. In her own words.'

379

'Gees, Dad! Wants me to know what?'

James sighed deeply. Reaching for his pipe he knocked it on his shoe before pulling out his leather pouch and filling the bowl. Holding his silver lighter to the bowl he took a long, deep draw. All the while, Clara, Ronan and Lillie continued to stare at him in confusion.

'I'm afraid it's up to your mother to tell you what happened, Ronan. It's not up to me.'

'I don't give a damn,' Ronan said, trying to push past him. 'I'm going in to see her.'

His father held up his hand to stop him. 'No, Ronan, please! Don't do that. Let her try and come to terms with this in her own way.'

'Come to terms with bloody what...?'

'Swearing won't help matters,' James said. 'Try to be patient.' He looked at Lillie. 'Maybe you could take your mother a cup of tea, Lillie.'

***

When Lillie knocked on the door of her parents' bedroom there was no answer.

She knocked again. 'Ma, it's Lillie. I've brought you a cup of tea.'

'Come in,' her mother said.

Once inside she got a dreadful shock. Ma was on the bed, sitting propped up by cushions, a pad of notepaper and a pen in her hand. She looked as though she had aged twenty years in the space of a day. Her eyes were red from crying and her beautiful face was all blotchy.

'Oh Ma,' she said, going over and placing the teacup on the bedside table. 'What's happened?'

380

Kathleen put the pen down and wiped her nose with a handkerchief. She took a deep breath. 'Lillie, dear Lillie… What have I done? I've ruined Ronan's life. Clara's too.'

Lillie's heart gave dreadful lurch. 'What do you mean, Ma? How could you have done that?'

Ma looked towards the window and then back again to Lillie. 'What's happened is just too awful. But I can't tell you now. I must tell Ronan first.' She started crying and Lillie put her hand out to comfort her. 'I'm writing him a letter,' Kathleen sobbed, picking up the pen again. 'Father Fogarty suggested it.'

'Why would you write him a letter? He's in the kitchen. I can get him and you can tell him now.'

Kathleen tried to curtail her sobs. 'No. Don't send him in. I wouldn't be able to tell him. It's best I write it in a letter.'

It was such a strange thing to do, to write a letter to someone who was in the same house. Lillie wondered if Ma hadn't had a stroke or something. Or was she having a nervous breakdown?

'But what's so bad you have to put it in a letter?' she asked.

'Darling, please leave me now. I can't explain. Not until Ronan knows.'

Lillie looked at her mother forlornly. 'But…'

'Go, Lillie. Please. Leave me be.' She picked up the notepad. 'Leave me to finish this letter.'

Lillie shook her head. 'Okay, I'll go. But Ronan and Clara are so confused. And upset. We all are. Dad looks dreadful.'

'I know, darling. But there's nothing I can do to make things better. All I can do is try and explain to Ronan in this letter.'

Lillie felt she had no option other than to let Ma be. 'Well at least drink that cup of tea,' she said, pointing to the teacup. 'And I've put a shortbread biscuit on the saucer.'

Kathleen tried a smile. 'Thank you, darling.'

Lillie gave her a small smile and went back to the kitchen.

'What did she say?' Ronan asked as soon as he saw her. 'Did she explain what's going on?'

'No,' Lillie said. 'She didn't.'

'I'm going to try Mummy again,' Clara interrupted. 'Whatever she said to Aunt Kathleen has upset her dreadfully. She shouldn't have done that.'

'Clara, there's little point in ringing your mother,' James said. 'I don't think she'll tell you anything. Not until Kathleen does.'

'My God! This is all so ridiculous.' Clara was almost screaming now and Lillie thought she was going to lose it completely. She looked at Ronan. 'She's your mother, Ronan. Do something. Please!'

'There appears to be nothing I *can* do. I'm so sorry, darling.'

James went over and put his arm around her. 'Ronan's right, Clara. There's nothing he, or anyone else for that matter, can do. Except be patient.'

Lillie felt so distressed and confused that she wanted to burst out crying. But that would only make matters worse. As Dad said, all she and the rest of them could do was be patient.

Chapter 40

Just as Ronan was contemplating going in and confronting his mother no matter what, his father brought out a letter from her. Clara had decided to go for a ride on her own to try and calm herself down, so there was only Lillie with Ronan.

'I think you should go off somewhere quiet and read this,' James told him. 'Ma said that if you can ever forgive her, she'd like to see you when you've read it.'

'Jesus bloody Christ!' Ronan no longer cared that he was swearing in front of his father. 'Forgive her for what, Dad?'

'Read the letter.'

'What about Clara?'

'When you've digested what Ma has told you, you should then tell Clara.'

Ronan held the piece of paper in his hand as if it were a grenade about to go off. 'What does it say?'

James shook his head. 'I'm afraid you'll have to read it yourself. Quite frankly, I haven't read it. It's between you and your mother.'

'Why the hell can't she tell me what's happening, rather than all this carry-on?'

'Please read the letter, Ronan,' James said. 'In the meantime I'll take Dingo down to the river. I'll be there if you want to talk to me.'

After he had gone Ronan stood with the letter in his hand, shaking his head.

'I think you should read it,' Lillie said. 'Go into the living room. On your own.'

Ronan sighed. In the living room he chose the chair by the window. A sprinkling of sunshine fell on its fading Sanderson print. Slumping down among the soft cushions he started to read.

My darling Ronan,
I know I'm taking the easy way out by writing you this letter. But I don't know if I could tell you the whole of what I'm about to disclose without breaking down. To watch your face would be too much for me to bear. And, in any case, I don't know that you'd let me tell you the whole story without flying off the handle. This, I feel, is the best way.

My darling, I can't think of any other way to tell you this. Although a better father, and a father who loves you more, would be hard to find, James is not your true father. Your father, dear Ronan, is his brother Dermot, who, as you know, won the DFC for his bravery during the Burma campaign and later died during a dangerous-low flying mission in Vietnam.

Ronan looked in horror at the paper in his hand. This must be some sort of sick joke. He knew Dermot O'Sullivan, whose portrait had hung in the hallway at Rathgarven, had been a squadron Leader with the RAF and was killed in action as part of a British–Indian and French taskforce during Operation Masterdom in Vietnam just after the Second World War had ended. During the Burma campaign his feat of shooting down three Japanese aircraft in a day was unmatched and he was awarded a DFC for his skilled leadership and enormous courage.

But Ronan had had no idea he had known his mother.

Jessica introduced us at the Tollygunge Club in Calcutta. At the time Dermot was seconded to headquarters from flying combat missions into South Burma. Over that period we fell very deeply in love. During the months he was on Operation Masterdom in Vietnam he still managed to get back to Calcutta to see me. The day I learnt of his death was the saddest day of my life. A week later I found out I was expecting you. Although I was overcome with such fear for our future I thought it might kill me, I was never in any doubt that I wanted to keep you, my darling.

Dermot and I hadn't married because he felt his missions into Burma were so dangerous that he didn't want to leave me a widow. But when the war ended we decided to go to Ireland and get married at Holy Cross church in Kenmare so that his family, who meant so much to him, could be there. And my beloved Aunt Mildred, who lived further along the river from Rathgarven. This is where I first met James. Dermot was keen to have the reception at Rathgarven where he had had such a happy childhood. But then he was seconded to Operation Masterdom and we had to put it off. Tragically his death put an end to our plans.

Fortunately, Finn was in Calcutta at the time I found out I was expecting you. As you are aware, he'd known the O'Sullivans since he was a boy. When I told him I was pregnant, he thought I should go back to Ireland. So I decided to go to my Aunt Mildred, although I didn't tell her I was pregnant. Being the great friend he has always been, Finn somehow found me a flight and helped me with the fare. He told me he would wire James and tell him what had happened.

After I arrived at Aunt Mildred's, James came to see me. Despite the fact he knew I'd been so in love with Dermot, he asked me to marry him. At first I refused, thinking he was only doing it out of duty. But he was very persuasive. Before I knew it we were married in Dublin. I *went back to Dublin when I was 'six months' pregnant. That's where you were born at the Rotunda, my darling. Three weeks overdue. No one ever queried the dates. With Lillie I was a month early and at that time a due date was harder to pinpoint than it is now.*

We agonised whether to tell you that James was not your real father. Alice was adamant we shouldn't. She felt that if we did, it was bound to come out somehow and cause a scandal. In those days to have a child out of wedlock, particularly in Ireland, was a huge dishonour to bring upon a family, particularly a family like the O'Sullivans. Besides, Alice and James both felt it was a fitting way to honour Dermot's memory that you should be the custodian of Rathgarven. For if James, as the eldest surviving son, had a son with another woman, that son would automatically inherit. And you, my darling, would be illegitimate. At the time I felt it was very noble of James and his mother to go to such measures to protect Dermot, myself and you, our child.

Dermot was a wonderful man, Ronan. A man you would be so proud to have as a father. I only wish with all my heart that he could have lived to be part of your life. And mine. I have the letters he wrote to me. You'll see from them, my darling, that he truly loved me. And I truly loved him. He had a wonderful motorbike, Ronan. It was an Indian Chief. It was his passion. The night I first met him he took me for a ride on it. I think I knew then I would fall in love with him. Do you know, Ronan, we thought the sun was ours. That it shone on us alone, no matter where we might be. He took me to all sorts of places, including the native towns, picnics by the Hooghly River and horseriding in the hills. But I mustn't go on. I just want you to realise you're the product of a great love. Every time I look at you,

I see Dermot. In some ways you don't look like him at all. He had blue eyes and you are taller. But in manner and speech, you are the image.

Ronan knew what Ma was telling him was no joke. He felt a huge wave of sadness flood through him. How could his parents have kept this from him? He thought of the man he'd always known as Dad down by the river with Dingo; Ma in her bedroom. His hands were now covered in sweat as he held the pages and he could feel perspiration running down his forehead. Soon the perspiration was mixed with angry tears. For a moment he thought of screwing up the letter into a tiny ball and throwing it into the wastepaper basket. But like a magnet, his eyes were drawn back to his mother's writing.

If I hadn't married James, I may have married someone else and James and your grandmother might never have got to know you as they have. I know Alice is eternally grateful that you are so much part of her life. Every time she looked at you, she told me she could see Dermot. When we said we were coming to Australia, I think it was you she knew she would pine for the most, even though she adores your brothers and sisters.

Now, my darling Ronan, I wish with all my heart that we hadn't kept the identity of your real father hidden. We should have told you. You've every right to be furious with us all. In fact you may never forgive us, and I wouldn't blame you. Not that I think what we concealed would have made a difference in the long run in regards to the next thing I'm going to have tell you.

Ronan swallowed hard. How could there possibly be more?

Ronan felt a huge wave of nausea sweep over him. He put his hand to his mouth and swallowed hard. When he tried to read his mother's words again, they blurred before his eyes. Blinking hard, he finally managed to focus. There was no doubt what Ma meant. He had thought finding out James was not his father was the worst moment. But no, the worst moment was here right now. Waiting for him.

would have tarnished your father's memory. But, Ronan, it was wartime then. We were all living each day as it came, never knowing if there would be another. And in Dermot's case, sadly there wasn't. Yet the gift he left me was a gift beyond anyone's wildest dreams. And you, my darling, darling boy, have been the son that I know he would have dearly wished for. As you have been the son that James always wished for, as well.

Even though Dermot won a DFC, to me the greatest deed he ever did was to leave me you.

Ronan stood and began to pace, his heart pounding. He felt such anger as he'd never felt before. Clenching his fist he punched the wall with force, not caring who could hear. Shaking with fury he went back to the letter.

Poor, poor Clara. She should have married Charles Fitzpatrick. That's why Jessica was so adamant. But then again I know how much you love her. How much she worships you. Please understand James's role, too. His only crime was to protect you and me and go along with his mother's wishes. For James loves his mother dearly. And she had already lost her husband. Then she lost her youngest son. To let her have her way was a small price to pay. Or so we thought.

Had we told you who your real father was, I don't know if this story would have had a different ending. You might have found out more about Dermot. Followed a trail that led you to his affair with Jessica. Although I doubt she'd have told you the truth unless she'd discovered you and Clara wanted to get married. But others may have known. Even then, would either of us have guessed that

Clara was a result of that? Or would I? I always knew Guy Preston wasn't Clara's father. That thought is bound to haunt me forever.

And you, my darling, you never had the chance to find out the truth.

Chapter 41

The nausea Ronan felt before came back more strongly now. His whole life had been a sham. What words could he possibly find to tell Clara she'd been sleeping with her brother? That they had committed incest? How in God's name could he flick a switch and think of her as his sister? Their life was in ruins.

He looked out the window to see if Clara had returned from her ride. But there was no sign of her. For a second he mulled over leaving Eureka right now and just disappearing from her life without a trace. Surely that would be preferable to having to tell her that the love they shared was incestuous. He could envisage the shock and horror in her eyes when he told her. He thought of taking off without seeing his mother. But he wanted to make sure what he'd read was not some sick joke. So instead, he went to the bedroom door. Without knocking he threw it open and marched inside. She was lying on the bed, her face wet with tears.

'Is it true?' he asked. 'Tell me.'

Kathleen sat up and looked at him. 'I'm so very sorry,' she said, her body wracked by sobs. 'I wish I could say it's not… but yes, I'm afraid it is true.'

'Thanks,' he said. 'I just wanted to make sure.'

Turning his back on his mother he stomped out of the room and slammed the door shut behind him. When he got outside he leant over the flowerbed and threw up. He knew the man he had thought of as his father was waiting for him down by the river. He didn't care. As long as he lived he never wanted to see his family again.

Down at the stables he found Clara putting the saddle and bridle away. 'We're leaving,' he said.

'Now?'

'Yes, right now.'

'Why?'

'I'll tell you when we get going.'

'Can't I get my things?'

'I'll get them. You finish up here.'

Five minutes later Ronan had thrown some of his belongings into a duffle bag and asked a bewildered Lillie (who he'd hurled his mother's letter at, telling her to read it as it would explain all) to get Clara's things from her bedroom, and he and Clara were in the car, speeding down the driveway, tyres screeching, dust flying up behind them.

When he pulled over on Wattle Creek Road and told her what he had found out, she stared at him in utter horror.

'Is this some sort of sick joke?'

'No. I'm afraid it's not.'

She leapt out of the car. 'I don't believe it,' she shouted. 'It can't be true. How can it be?'

'It was during the war,' Ronan said, going after her. 'All sorts of weird things happened.'

'I bet my mother made it up.'

'No, Clara. She might be a bitch, but there's no way she'd make something like this up. She wouldn't destroy your life like that. It's why she was so keen for you to marry Charles Fitzpatrick. Maybe she guessed you were in love with me after your last visit to Rathgarven.'

'I was. But oh my God, Ronan! What if I'd got pregnant?'

Ronan knew his next words would be the hardest he'd ever had to utter. 'We probably shouldn't see each other for a while.' He picked up a twig and clamped it between his teeth. 'I don't think I could trust myself if we do.'

Clara scrambled up the bank of grass and paced around. When she reached the barbed-wire fence she kicked the wooden post angrily. After she'd kicked it for the fifth time, Ronan went to her. She turned around, placed her head on his shoulder and sobbed. As Ronan stroked her hair he could see his own tears falling between the strands.

'You can take me to Armidale to get my things,' she said, lifting her head. 'I'll stay the night at the St Kilda Hotel. Then I'll go down to Sydney. Decide what to do. Maybe I'll go back to England.' Her body heaved with more sobs. 'Perhaps I'll marry Charles Fitzpatrick after all.'

Ronan forgave her for that, he was sure she didn't know what she was saying. Then again, after what had happened, who was he to tell her what she should do?

Eventually he said, 'Is that fair to the man?'

'Do you think what's happened to us is fair?'

'No, it's not fair at all.' Ronan tried to think of what he could say that might make her feel any better. Or make either of them feel any better. 'Maybe after some time apart we can see each other again. As brother and sister.'

'No, Ronan. Once I'm gone, that's it. I never want to see you or your family again.'

'Clara please…' He went to touch her, but she shoved him away and stomped back to the car. She got in and slumped down on the seat, slamming the door. Ronan got in behind the wheel.

'Take me to Armidale, Ronan,' she said without looking at him. 'And when I've got my things, let me go. Every time I think of us sleeping together I feel sick to the core.' She paused. 'How can something that was so beautiful become so hideous?'

Ronan sighed. 'We didn't know. It wasn't our fault.'

Clara started crying again. All Ronan wanted to do was reach out and comfort her. But this was not the time. All the way to Armidale whenever he began to speak she told him to stop. It was as if she was too upset to listen. Or talk. All she did was stare blankly out of the window. Ronan thought it was the longest trip of his life.

On arriving at their place, Clara turned to him. 'I don't care what time it is over there or how much it'll cost, I'm going to ring Mummy. I want to hear it from her own mouth.'

Ronan nodded. 'If you think it will help, do. You can use the phone in the hallway.'

'Will you wait?'

'Yes.'

With that she jumped out of the car and headed to their digs. While she was gone Ronan held on to the faint hope that when she came out she would say it was all some ghastly mistake. Yet Ma was so sure it wasn't. And in his heart Ronan knew it wasn't either.

Ten minutes later she got back in the car with her bags. 'It's true,' she cried. 'Oh God, how I hate her. Why didn't she tell me? Why did she have to keep it a secret?' She sobbed and sobbed. 'It all adds up. I never looked anything like my father, like Guy Preston. Now I know why.'

Ronan put his hand out to touch her, but she flinched and moved away.

'Take me to the St Kilda,' she said, her voice quivering. 'Please, Ronan. Now.'

At the hotel he got out to take her bags inside and check there was a room. When she got the key they stood looking at each other, neither knowing what to say. When he moved forward she put her hands up.

'Don't touch me, Ronan. Please. I'll write and let you know where I am.'

She then turned and walked away.

Trying to control his emotions, Ronan went back down the steps to his car. Through tears he started the ignition and drove up to the lookout where he had first made love to Clara. He turned the engine off and sat staring down at the lights of the town below, then he put his face in his hands and wept. It was as if a dyke had burst and there was no way of controlling the flow. As far as Ronan was concerned his life was finished. Without Clara, how could he go on? He had loved her virtually all his life. To discover that that love was incestuous was more than he could bear. He flung himself out of the car, walked around, knelt and touched the ground. The ground where he and Clara had made love.

'Oh, Clara!' he cried. 'Clara!'

It was some time later when he stood up and wiped his eyes. He looked around. If he stayed in Armidale, every moment of every day there'd be something to remind him of Clara. And there was no way he could go back to the room they had shared. He would spend the night here, where they had been so happy. But when it was 4 a.m. and he was still there, he got in his car and drove around town. He stopped in front of the St Kilda Hotel. Which room was Clara's? A light was on in a window at the far end of the building. Was she still awake, like he was?

After some time he drove on. When it was 8.30 and he knew Dalgetys would be open, he went into the manager's office and resigned. The university could post his graduation certificate to him.

Chapter 42

Kathleen thought every car that drove up to the homestead might be Ronan. Every time the phone rang she hoped it would be him. As the days went by and she realised he wasn't going to come back or ring, she got more and more depressed and found it difficult to leave the bedroom. She berated herself for not telling Ronan whose son he was. And for not guessing that Jessica may have had an affair with Dermot before she introduced him to Kathleen. Was I so blinded by love that I didn't see the obvious? Why didn't I see Dermot in Clara? Because not for one minute did I think of looking. She thought of Finn. Did he know? He flitted in and out of Calcutta and saw Dermot. And Jessica. Surely if he had an inkling he would have said something? Was it a secret he took to the grave, never imagining the consequences of his silence? If he were alive and living here at Eureka Park, and saw how close Clara and Ronan were becoming, surely he would have somehow stopped it happening. Why oh why did he have to go kill himself like that? But blaming a deceased Finn was fruitless. As was blaming anyone other than herself. She was a complete idiot for not having guessed.

It wasn't only Ronan she had alienated. It was also Lillie, who came storming into the bedroom after Ronan and Clara had taken off, brandishing the letter Kathleen had written.

'Ma, how the billyo could you keep a secret like that about Ronan's father?'

Kathleen eyed her sadly. 'Because we thought it for the best.'

'Well you've ruined his life that's for sure. And here's me thinking he was my brother and…'

'He's still your brother, Lillie. Nothing's changed.'

'Oh yeah, Ma. Try telling that to Ronan and Clara.' She stomped off leaving Kathleen bereft.

One night Kathleen rang Jessica and gave her a blast down the phone. 'What was the point of keeping your affair with Dermot from me?'

'Pride, my sweet. I didn't want you to think Dermot preferred you to me.'

'But look what's happened. Ronan's taken off to God knows where. And poor, poor Clara…'

'If she and Ronan hadn't got together no one would've needed to know she was Dermot's daughter. And she'd be happily married to Charles Fitzpatrick.'

'Well, you should have thought of the consequences before you let her come to Rathgarven.'

'How was I to know they'd fall in love?'

Kathleen sighed. 'Have you any idea where she is?'

'Unfortunately no.' A long pause. 'I haven't heard from her.'

'Aren't you worried about her?'

'Of course I am… but what can I do? When she comes to her senses hopefully she'll come back here and contact me.'

'If she does, can you please tell her we're very concerned for her.'

When she hung up Kathleen collapsed into tears once more.

One afternoon as she was sitting in the chair by the bedroom window feeling miserable, Lorna Medlow arrived.

'I rang and got James,' she said, coming into the room after knocking. 'He's very worried about you.'

Kathleen wrapped her dressing gown around her body and looked forlornly at her friend. 'Did he tell you what's gone on?'

'He said it was best I come up and talk to you. Do you want to tell me about it?'

Kathleen nodded. 'Oh Lorna… You won't believe the awfulness of what's happened.'

'Try me.'

After a moment Kathleen pointed to a chair nearby. 'Sit down and I'll tell you.'

Having let her talk for close to ten minutes without interrupting, Lorna stood up and placed an arm around her. 'You poor, poor thing,' she said, stroking her hair. 'I can quite understand why you're hurting so dreadfully.'

Kathleen sniffed. 'What makes it even worse is that I wouldn't be surprised if Ronan and Clara had been sleeping together. That alone would turn their minds. For Lord alone it's turning mine.'

Lorna sighed. 'At least she didn't get pregnant.'

'Yes, I suppose that's something.'

'I thought I had problems with Maddie… My God, that's nothing compared to what you've been through.' She gave her a hug. 'Dermot O'Sullivan sounds like a bloody good sort. I can quite imagine why you fell for the bugger. But why the hell would that Jessica woman hold onto a secret like that for so damn long?'

'Apart from what I've told you, I really don't know.'

'You reckon she's got a screw loose?'

'No.'

'What if she made the whole thing up?'

'I know in my heart she hasn't made it up. When I think back it all falls into place. The timing. Everything. Now that I think back to the first time Jessica introduced me to Dermot, it was obvious she was besotted by him. She couldn't take her eyes off him. She even told him to contact her, that he knew where to find her. And when I started going out with him, she sort of changed her attitude to me. What she told me is definitely true. There's no doubt about it. And that, Lorna, is why I've destroyed Ronan's life. And Clara's.'

Lorna got up and went to the window and gazed out. When she turned back to Kathleen she said, 'And what are you doing now, eh? Destroying your own life. And the lives of the rest of the family while you're at it. Ronan and Clara are young. They'll get over it in time. It's you I'm more worried about. And James. Lillie and the younger boys, too. For their sakes you've got to pull yourself together.' She sighed heavily and turned back to the window. 'Look at those dancing daffodils and the wattle in full bloom. Spring is out there. Don't be a bloody idiot and keep it waiting.' She glanced towards the door. 'I'm going out to the kitchen to make a cup of tea and a plate of sandwiches. When I come back we'll talk some more. Then I want you up, showered and damn well dressed. After that we're going for a walk down to the horses.' Without waiting for Kathleen to answer she began to move. 'I mean it, my friend. Up and dressed.'

Kathleen wiped her eyes. Lorna was right. She could hide in this room for the rest of her life or she could get on with it. Although she didn't agree with Lorna that Ronan and Clara would get over what had happened, she had to admit that time was a great healer. In a way it had healed her over the years.

What had happened with Ronan and Clara couldn't be erased. But it could be made worse by Kathleen behaving as she was. Besides, she wasn't the only one hurting. James was finding it hard to focus on running the stud and Lillie was still furious and hadn't been in to see her since that initial outburst. As yet they hadn't told Marcus and Freddie what had happened. To them Ronan and Clara had just gone back to Armidale as they normally would.

She stood, stepped over to her wardrobe and pulled out a pair of jeans and a white shirt. She went into the hallway and called out to Lorna, who she could hear rattling cups and plates in the kitchen. 'I won't be long in the shower.'

'Good on you,' Lorna called back. 'Tea will be ready when you've finished.'

As Kathleen stood under the scalding water a few minutes later, she was grateful for the true friend Lorna had proved to be. It took someone like her to point out how she was damaging the rest of the family by wallowing in self-pity.

***

When James picked up the mail at the front gate the following week, he recognised Ronan's handwriting straightaway. He ripped the envelope open and started to read.

Thought I'd let you know I've decided to join the Army and go to Vietnam, he wrote. James felt his eyes water as he read on.

> *Apart from wanting to lose myself in oblivion— and I couldn't give a damn whether I get shot to smithereens — I feel it's a war that needs to be fought. Besides, as my father was such a hero in Vietnam I best go there and prove myself as well. Keep up the family tradition.*

He blamed everyone for what had happened: James, his grandmother and Finn Malone for keeping the secret of his birth from him. Most of all he blamed Dermot O'Sullivan, his mother and Jessica. He said that when he told Clara she was so freaked out that she'd taken off. And he'd no idea where she'd gone.

> *You can all have that on your conscience as well. And Ma, I'm glad you had such a riotous time in Calcutta with James's brother! Pity it had such tragic repercussions.*

What hurt James was that Ronan refused to refer to him as Dad. For some time he sat with the letter in his hand, working himself into a stew. No wonder Ronan said Clara was freaked out. Apart

400

from anything else, James suspected she and Ronan had been sleeping together. To discover they were brother and sister would have traumatised them both. As it had traumatised James. He was still trying to come to terms with that on top of discovering Dermot was Clara's father. Now to know his son was going to Vietnam. The same country that had claimed his father. Clara's father. James's brother. When he was really worked up he started the engine and drove back up to the homestead. Inside, he went to find Kathleen who was in the kitchen preparing dinner. While he'd tried to curtail his anger so far, Ronan's letter had proved his breaking point. He almost threw the letter at Kathleen, even though it would probably set her back again when she had seemed to pull herself together after Lorna's visit. Although they'd gone over and over what had happened in Calcutta, he was too angry to care.

'Your son seems to think Calcutta was one huge brothel during the war,' he seethed. 'Again, I ask… How in God's name were you so blind not to see that Jessica was playing around with Dermot before you? She was supposed to be your best friend, after all.'

'And he was your brother.'

'I wasn't there, was I? You were.'

And so it went on until James stormed out, got in the car and drove into Gullumbindy where he went to bar of the Telegraph and ordered a strong whisky. He was glad the Hogans were nowhere to be seen. If Dermot hadn't been killed in action, James felt he'd happily have killed him now. Surely he should have realised what the repercussions of his actions might be. James knew only too well that Kathleen had married him to give his brother's son the O'Sullivan name and the right to his ancestral home, even though he was not the son of the heir. That was Marcus.

It was Father Fogarty who suggested that James and Kathleen tell Marcus and Freddie separately what had happened with Ronan and Clara.

After getting over the shock, Freddie's main concern was that he mightn't see Clara again, and he was worried about Ronan.

'Even if he's not your son, Dad, you do love him, don't you?'

'Of course I do. As much as I love the rest of you.'

'He must be really sad about Clara.'

'Yes, he is,' James said.

'Will he come home soon?' he asked Kathleen.

'I hope so, darling,' she said, putting her arm around him and kissing the top of his head. 'I hope so.'

When they told Marcus, he shook his head. 'You're telling me I'm actually your oldest son, Dad. I should've inherited Rathgarven if we still owned it?'

'I'll hear no more talk of that,' James said. 'As far as your mother and I and anyone else is concerned, Ronan's still the eldest son.'

'Oh, really.'

'Yes. And now, young man,' James sounded even crosser, 'you can head down to the stables and help Arthur muck out the stalls.'

As he sat on at the Telegraph, James was so angry he wondered if he shouldn't tell Kathleen about Jessica blackmailing him. After another sip of whisky he decided no. Although he was angry with her, she had enough to contend with right now. Knowing, apart from everything else, that her son was going to fight in Vietnam. He regretted being so hard on her. Was it because it brought the whole matter of Dermot up again? And James was jealous. Jealous of the love his wife had shared with his brother; a love so strong that it would always imprison a part of Kathleen's heart. In some ways it would be easier for James if Dermot were alive. It would be more of a fair fight. To Kathleen, Dermot would always be a dashing young hero. How could one fight the memory of a love like that?

Knowing if he had one more drink he'd be unable to drive home, he made his way to his car. As he drove, he realised that despite knowing her passion for him was unlike the passion she'd had for Dermot, he was bloody lucky to have Kathleen by his side. Somehow they'd have to work out how to get through what had happened with Ronan together. If they didn't, the whole family would be destroyed.

***

Lillie was still furious with her parents and had hardly spoken to Ma. She and Dad had barely spoken either, apart from him saying she shouldn't be too hard on Ma.

'It wasn't really her fault that Jessica kept Clara's father a secret.'

Lillie was about to abuse him for the secret he, Ma and Grandma had kept for so long, but decided to shut up. The only one she felt she could talk to about what had happened was Deb. After all, she had her own family skeletons.

'I don't know how I can forgive my parents for keeping it all a secret,' Lillie said to her. Deb now had her licence, so Lillie had asked her to meet her at the picnic ground by the creek at Gullumbindy. There she told her the whole sorry story — and how freaked out she was by the thought of Clara and Ronan sleeping together when they were brother and sister.

'If Ma and Dad had told Ronan who his father was, none of this might have happened.'

'Not necessarily. Not if Clara's mother didn't tell anyone who Clara's father was. Anyway… your poor Mum's probably hurting a lot. If you keep giving her the cold shoulder it'll only make matters worse for her. When I found out from Sandra about Mum and Dad I thought of giving them heaps. Then I asked myself what good would it do? It was all so long ago. The same with your parents. It's just a pity Clara and Ronan had to fall in love like that.'

'If only Clara had gone ahead and married Charles Fitzpatrick.'

'Obviously her mother thought that as well. She was probably worried she'd fallen hook line and sinker for Ronan.'

'Maybe you're right.'

'Anyway… I reckon you should ease up on your Mum. She's a really nice person, Lillie.'

Deb was right. It must have been such an awful time for her in India, more or less on her own. No wonder she was happy to marry Dad and be able to go to Rathgarven to live. That night Lillie lay awake for hours imagining Calcutta during the war when this awful saga had started. She remembered the picture of her mother in the sapphire-blue ball gown that used to hang in the hallway in Rathgarven, and tried to envisage her mother so in love that she had been oblivious to what might have happened with Clara's mother and Uncle Dermot.

The next day she decided to do what Deb said and be nice, not only to Ma, but Dad too. He must be hurting heaps as well, particularly the thought of Ronan going to Vietnam. That scared the living daylights out of Lillie, so she could imagine how her parents felt.

When she found her mother out in the garden weeding she plopped down on the grass beside her. 'Tell me more about Calcutta, Ma. Where was that photo of you hanging in Rathgarven taken? The one of you in that sapphire-blue ball gown with the white orchid pinned over your breast. Where your hair's pulled up in a sort of chignon. You're standing next to a clematis vine in a lovely garden. Were you living with my grandparents?'

'Oh, that one,' Kathleen said, putting down her trowel and smiling. 'No… it was quite a while after my parents were killed. It was taken in the gardens of the Maharani of Cooch Behar's beautiful home in Calcutta, which she used when she visited from the palace in West Bengal. Before the war I used to work for her and had a small apartment in the grounds. I still lived there during the war.'

Lillie gave her a warm smile. 'You must've been so sad when your parents were killed.'

Kathleen nodded. 'They were in the wrong place at the wrong time.' She paused. 'I was up in Darjeeling with Garrison Headquarters and only found out two days after it happened.' She smiled. 'Jessica was working in the same branch. I have to say, no matter what's happened since… she was marvellous to me then. As was the colonel in charge of Garrison Headquarters. A nice man, who we both found good to work for.'

'Was it Uncle Dermot you were going out with that night in the photograph?'

Kathleen's eyes misted over. 'We were going to a ball for servicemen at Government House. He'd come back from a combat mission into South Burma.'

'I always thought it was a beautiful photo.'

'When you think of the chaos going on outside those stone walls, it was so serene where it was taken in those glorious gardens.'

'Surely you must've had some photos of Uncle Dermot?'

Kathleen shook her head. 'I didn't need any photographs, apart from the one that hung at Rathgarven. I've always had his face etched so clearly in my mind.'

'You still miss him very much, don't you?'

'Yes,' Kathleen said. 'I do. But then again, it was all so long ago.'

'Was it Uncle Dermot who the little Indian boy was laughing at in the photo in your exhibition?'

Kathleen nodded. 'Yes. He told me Sanjay had saved his life when he'd had an accident on his motorbike and a cobra had nearly bitten him. Sanjay had chased it away with a rock. That's why they had such a special bond.' She looked away. 'I wonder what's happened to Sanjay now.'

'Maybe you and I should go to Calcutta one day. We might be able to find out.'

Kathleen shook her head. 'No. The past's best left in the past.'

'Tell me what he was like,' Lillie probed. 'Uncle Dermot, I mean. To me he was just Dad's brother who'd been killed in combat and won a DFC.'

Kathleen smiled. 'He was a lot like Clara. Tall, blondish, with startling blue eyes. In fact, you'd never guess Ronan was his son. In looks Ronan's taken after my side of the family. Yet he pushes his hair back on his forehead as Dermot did. He walks like him. Even sounds like him. When Ronan's voice first broke, if he was in another room I'd swear it was Dermot come back from the dead who was talking. It gave me such a jolt. Even now his voice does that to me.' Kathleen paused. 'Well, it did... before he took off like that.' She drew a deep breath and let it out again.

'Dermot could play the guitar like Ronan does. When we went on picnics in India, he'd sing to me while he played. Although he was one of the best pilots in the RAF, he was incredibly gentle. He hated all that dreadful slaughter. Particularly dropping bombs when he thought they might kill civilians. We often talked about that. It was something that distressed him enormously.'

Lillie smiled. 'Gees, Ma he sounds almost too good to be true. Didn't he have any faults at all?'

'Oh yes,' Kathleen laughed. 'He was a typical Irishman. Full of fun but also political angst. Even though he fought for the British, he never forgave them for what they'd done to Ireland over the years. And of course he was there as a small boy, like your father, when Rathgarven burnt down. He also drank and smoked far too much. Perhaps if he hadn't died so young, it might've caught up with him. He was also quite reckless. On his motorbike. And in the air. But we were so young that all seemed rather glamorous.'

Lillie lifted her hand to shoo a fly away. 'Have you told Grandma about Clara? After all… she now has a new grandchild.'

'Your father rang her a few days after we found out. I was worried the stress of it might kill her. But your father said we'd hidden enough secrets. No more.'

'What did she say?'

'She was worried for Ronan. Not only for his heartbreak, but also that he and Clara might have got married and had children. And, of course, she was furious with Jessica for not telling anyone. She was also annoyed with Dermot.'

Lillie nodded. 'But Ma… What about you and Dad?'

Kathleen smiled. 'It's taking a bit of time to come to terms with what's happened, that's all.'

Lillie reached for her mother's hand, and as she clasped it, she felt tears fall onto her skin. She desperately hoped that Ronan would write home or ring soon. She hated to see her parents hurting, and she was really worried for him as well.

Chapter 43

It was a lonely Christmas and New Year without Ronan at Eureka Park. In the New Year Lillie received her Leaving Certificate results in the mail. She didn't break any records, except in English literature, for which she got a distinction.

'I can get into Sydney Uni on those marks,' she told her parents as they all sat on the verandah in the late-afternoon light. 'But first I want to go back to Ireland to see Grandma. So I'd like to head to Sydney and get a couple of jobs to pay for my fare.'

She felt bad to be leaving them when they'd been through so much. But she really did want to go to Ireland. Somehow after all that had happened she was missing it more than ever. And Grandma.

'We'll miss you incredibly, however I think that's a great idea,' Ma said.

Lillie could see she was trying hard to be cheerful.

'Yes,' Dad said. 'You've got to go spread your wings. I agree with Ma.'

Lillie got up and gave each of them a kiss.

'I'll miss you both heaps, but at least you'll have Marcus and Freddie about.'

What she didn't say was that she hoped she might be able to see Ronan when she was in Sydney. She had rung Dave, who was living at the same digs in Armidale, doing a post-graduate course, to ask if he'd heard from him, and he'd told her Ronan had written to say he was down at Kapooka near Wagga Wagga, where all the new recruits went. From there he would go to Holsworthy in Sydney for his infantry corps training. By the time Lillie got to Sydney, Ronan should be there too.

Before she left she met up with Deb in Gullumbindy for a coffee at the milk bar. She had now got her driver's licence so was able to drive herself in.

'Would you believe what Mum told me last night?' Deb said, when they took their seats by the window.

'No. What?'

'Sandra's mum, Winifred, killed her dad.'

'Oh my God! How?'

'She took to him with a carving knife in the kitchen.'

'Jees… Why would she do that?'

'Lord knows. Mum heard about it when she went to a CWA meeting yesterday. It'll probably be in the papers tomorrow. Mum said he was always a bully. Maybe he bullied her once too often. Sandra wasn't there. She's gone to Brisbane to live.'

Despite Lillie never having forgiven Sandra for those first days at school and the awful things she'd said about Uncle Finn, she didn't deserve this.

'So where's her mum?'

'Jail, I suppose. Maybe she can get off on self-defence if he was bullying her. Who'd know?'

Lillie took a sip of her coffee. 'Your mum said she's really nice, so I hope she's okay.'

'Yeah… Let's hope so. Anyway,' Deb added, 'fancy us, eh. You off to Sydney and me off to uni in Armidale. I'm going to miss you so much.' She paused and fiddled with her coffee spoon. 'Have you heard from Ronan?'

'No. But that's one of the reasons I want to go down there — to see him if I can. By the time I get there Dave told me he should be at Holsworthy Barracks on the outskirts of the city. I didn't tell Ma and Dad in case he won't see me.'

Lillie wondered if Ronan would see her. Or would she bring back too many memories of what had happened?

***

In Sydney Lillie found a flat to share with two other girls in Manly and started working two jobs. During the day she sorted books in a library. Four nights a week she waitressed in a coffee lounge on the esplanade at Manly. She wrote home often and missed them all heaps. Whenever she opened a letter from Freddie she could hardly read it without tears dropping onto his squiggly writing. Once Ma enclosed a cutting about Sandra's mother, Winifred, who was charged with murder and awaiting trial. Although Lillie hadn't told her parents the whole story, she had told them that Deb's mother had once been married to Sandra's dad. And as Winifred used to be a friend of Uncle Finn's ex-wife Dawn, they were taking an interest in the case.

The first thing she had done when she got to Sydney was to ring Holsworthy Barracks. At first they were loath to give her too much information about where Ronan was, but in the end she got out of them that he would be back from an exercise in the bush the next day. She left a message for him to ring her. The next night she waited anxiously for his call, but it didn't come. Two days later she left another message. When the weekend came around and she still hadn't heard, she rang again.

'I'm sure your messages have been passed on,' the switchboard operator said. 'Who did you say you are again?'

'His sister.'

'Yes, of course.'

The way she said it made Lillie think there might be lots of girls who rang up saying they were a soldier's sister, when in actual fact they were girls in pursuit of a boyfriend.

'Please,' Lillie said. 'Can you tell him it's urgent?'

She didn't mind saying that, for as far as Lillie was concerned it *was* urgent.

410

The next day he rang. As he had the next day off he reluctantly agreed to meet her at the Oaks Hotel in Neutral Bay the following afternoon. Lillie fidgeted nervously as she sat at a table under the plane tree in the beer garden waiting for him to arrive. When he walked in she got a dreadful shock to see how much weight he had lost, and that his lovely thick hair was now a crew cut.

'Good to see you, li'l sis,' he said with a languid Ronan smile and leant down to give her a kiss on the cheek.

'Ronan, when are you going to stop calling me li'l sis?' she said, holding on to his arm as if she never wanted to let go. 'When I'm sixty?'

'Ah,' Ronan grinned, 'I might think about it then.'

Lillie studied his face. To a casual observer there was little change, apart from being thinner. However, to Lillie his eyes weren't as brilliant as they used to be. It was as if something had died in them. And the set of his mouth was slightly harder than she'd seen before. Even the sound of his laughter wasn't quite as unreserved as it once was.

After they got their drinks Ronan asked her how their parents were. And Marcus and Freddie.

'They sound okay on the phone,' Lillie said. 'Missing you, Ronan.'

'I'm sorry for that.'

'As you can imagine it's taken Ma a while to get over what Jessica did in keeping that secret and you taking off like that. But she's putting a heap of photos together to do another exhibition at the gallery. And there are a couple of new foals. That's keeping her busy.' She took a sip of wine and held his eyes. 'But Ronan, what about you? How are you liking the Army?'

'Not so bad. I've made some good mates. And,' he said, patting his flat stomach, 'the regime keeps me fit.'

'I can see that.'

There was an awkward pause as they both sipped their drinks.

'I'm so sorry about what happened,' Lillie said, placing her hand on his. 'The whole thing's just so awful.'

'You're right there.'

'Have you heard how Clara is?'

'I've only had one letter from her. She said she was okay and living in a flat in London with an old school friend. She's decided to go to university.'

'Did you write back?'

'She didn't give me the address. She just wanted me to know she was all right.' He smiled dejectedly. 'Before she left she said she might marry Charles Fitzpatrick after all.'

Lillie touched his hand again. 'I bet she said that in anger. In any case I'm sure we would've heard if she had. Sheelagh would've told me. Or Grandma. It would've been in the Irish papers.'

'I suppose you're right.'

'She'll write to you, Ronan. Give her time.'

'Not sure what the point of writing would be. There's little that can be done about the situation.'

'You could still be friends.'

'We could. Nonetheless it's best we don't see each other.'

'Why?'

'Because I'd find it too difficult.'

There was a pause before Lillie asked the question she'd been throwing around in her mind ever since she'd arranged this meeting.

'Why don't you come back with me to Eureka when I go next? The longer you leave it the harder it'll be for everyone.'

Ronan fiddled with the Toohey's coaster on the table. 'I'm not sure if I could face them.' He picked up his beer and took a sip. 'It wasn't pleasant last time I was there.'

'I know. But they're really hurting, Ronan. And Freddie's missing you heaps.'

'Yeah… I miss him too.' He kicked the ground with his heel. 'So when are you heading up there?'

'The weekend after next. Please think about coming. I know it'd mean a lot to Ma and Dad.'

He took another sip of beer and put the glass back down. 'As a matter of fact I do have that weekend off…'

'It's settled then. You can pick me up. We'll drive up together.'

He pulled out a cigarette. Ronan was never much of a smoker. This was the third one he'd smoked. 'Well, if you think they'd like to see me… What's say I pick you up at nine on Saturday week?'

Lillie threw him a grateful smile. 'Thanks, Ronan. Everyone will be so pleased.'

'Can I drop you back to your flat?' he asked.

'No. I want to do some shopping. There's a great little boutique around the corner. I'll catch the bus later.'

What she didn't tell him was that she'd been going out on few dates lately and tonight she was going to a dance at the Manly Surf Club. But she felt if she told him she was dating, it would make him sad about Clara.

As she waved him off in his Mini, she was happy she'd persevered in finding him. When she got back to her flat at Manly she'd ring Ma and Dad and tell them he was coming up. She could imagine the smile on Ma's face when she heard the news. Dad's too. And Freddie would be over the moon.

Chapter 44

Ronan was nervous as he pulled up outside Lillie's flat. How would he cope with being back at Eureka Park? The place where he had found out the man he'd called Dad wasn't his father. Where he'd discovered Clara was his sister. Where he'd been awful to Ma.

As he got out of the car he heard Lillie call out from the window above. 'Won't be a sec!'

Moments later she bounded out of the front door and onto the path. She looked lovely with her newly washed hair gleaming in the sunshine and a large smile on her face. At times Lillie drove him mad with her constant interrogations but he was very fond of her. Although he was nervous about what lay ahead, he was glad she had sussed him out and insisted he come to Eureka Park with her today.

'You look snazzy in that get up,' she said and planted a kiss on his cheek.

Ronan had come straight from a dawn parade and was still in uniform. They set off and six and a half hours later, after stopping to get a hamburger in Muswellbrook, they were driving along Wattle Creek Road. A sick feeling churned Ronan's stomach as they passed the spot where Clara had jumped out of the car in horror.

He turned to Lillie. 'This is more or less the spot where I told Clara she was my sister.'

Lillie put her hand on his arm. 'It must have been awful for you.'

'It wasn't nice, that's for sure.'

'I do wish she'd contact us.'

Every day Ronan waited for another letter from Clara. None came. All he wanted to know was whether she was coping okay.

'Yes,' he said to Lillie. 'So do I.'

Driving up through Eureka Park's paddocks, Ronan saw the horses grazing happily. How different it all looked to when the O'Sullivans first arrived and there were no horses. He tried to swallow the lump in his throat as he remembered driving up here with Clara in the back of the car when she first came to Eureka. How she had been talking about her marriage to Lord Charles Fitzpatrick and showed them all her ring. He remembered how he had tried not to become jealous. If only she had gone home and married Charles. How different their lives would be now.

At the homestead he parked the car and he and Lillie got out. When he first saw Ma walk down the garden path, then stop, he held back. It was as if they were two statues glued to the ground, unable to move because of the huge burden of love and regret filling every inch of them.

It was Freddie who broke the ice. Rushing forward, he gave Ronan an appraising look up and down. 'You look kinda sharp in that uniform. I wouldn't mind one of those myself. Reckon I should join the Army as well.'

Ronan tugged Freddie's ear. 'You might have to wait a few years, young Fred. But I reckon you'd make one heck of a soldier.'

Ronan moved across to give his mother a kiss and a warm hug. She held on to him like she'd never let go and he smelt the familiar shampoo in her hair, which was greyer than when he last saw her.

'It's good to see you, Ma,' he said, stroking her hair and trying to hide his shock at how much she had aged. He suspected he was the cause of most of it.

After Ma finally let him go, he turned to his father. 'And Dad, you look fit.'

Ronan saw how happy James was that he'd called him Dad.

'Welcome home, Ronan,' James said, holding out his arms to embrace him. 'Welcome home.'

Now Marcus came up and shook his hand. 'So what's it like being a soldier?'

Ronan told them how the first thing that had happened after he'd arrived in the bus with the other recruits at Kapooka was that they'd been herded into the Army barber, who cut off all his hair. Next he had to have a medical check before being issued with his uniform.

'That one? 'Freddie asked, as they all moved inside for the lavish afternoon tea Ma had prepared.

'I've got a few. For different occasions.'

He told them how he slept in the barracks, which were noisy and it was hard to get to sleep. How the fearsome sergeant major yelled and shouted if they weren't performing as he thought they should. How Ronan had to turn up for a parade every morning and watch out if anyone was late or marched out of step. He told them about the dining hall where the food was fairly ordinary.

'Nothing like yours at all, Ma,' he said, reaching for another slice of his mother's chocolate cake as they all sat around the kitchen table. 'But seeing there's nothing else to eat I soon got used to it. And,' he laughed, 'as Lillie said, I've lost weight, which isn't a bad thing.'

'What about the other soldiers?' Freddie asked.

'They're not a bad bunch. Some better than others, but that's anywhere for you.'

Ma poured another round of tea for them all as he told them how fit he was from all the cross-country and obstacle courses he had to do. How they had been dropped into the bush miles and miles away and told to find their way back with just a compass.

'So did you get back?' Freddie asked.

'He wouldn't be here now if he didn't,' Marcus scoffed.

Ronan smiled. Things never changed with Marcus and Freddie.

'So what's it like at Holsworthy where you are now?' Marcus asked.

'Not bad.' He laughed. 'At least the food's a bit better and the sergeant major's not so fearsome.'

What he didn't tell them was how desperate he'd felt on the long bus trip to Kapooka, wondering if he'd done the right thing joining up. How after the first week he thought he'd see if he could get out of it. But by then it was too late. He'd taken the oath and there was no escape. He had to make the best of it.

Now Ma insisted on taking a photo of him in his uniform before he got changed. Firstly he stood by himself under the willow tree outside the front fence, and then with Lillie, Marcus, and Freddie. Afterwards Lillie took one of him with the rest of the family. As he stood there under the willow tree with the family he loved so much, Ronan was pleased he'd taken Lillie's advice and come home. He hadn't realised how much he'd missed them.

✳✳✳

Ronan might have said he was fit but when Kathleen first saw him standing by the car she had a dreadful shock. Not only had he lost weight, he had also lost something else. At first she wasn't sure what that was, then she realised. He had lost his youth. He was no longer the Ronan she had known all his life. This man before her looked as though he had already been to war and suffered dreadfully. His face was drawn and his beautiful brown eyes had lost their sparkle. He would have seen a change in her as well, but she doubted it was as dramatic as the change in him. It took all of her self-control not to burst into tears, so she was pleased when Freddie had rushed forward to break the ice before Ronan could see the shock in her face.

After they'd had afternoon tea and he'd changed his clothes, she took him for a walk along the riverbank. Kathleen put her arm around her son, and felt her heart would fragment into tiny ripples, much like the ones cascading over the rocks in the river below. 'I'm so sorry,' she said, wiping tears from her eyes. 'So sorry, my darling.'

'It's all right,' Ronan said, giving her a hug. 'You weren't to know. No one was to know. Except Jessica. She really should have said something.'

Kathleen placed her hand on his. 'Have you heard from Clara?'

'One letter to say she was back in London and was okay. As you can imagine it'll take her a while to get over it.'

'I can quite understand.' She gave a small smile. 'Maybe… Well… Maybe one day she'll want to see her father's family again.'

'Not sure about that.'

'You must miss her so much,' Kathleen said.

Ronan nodded. 'It hasn't been easy.'

'I really miss her too. We all miss her. Poor Freddie's devastated.'

'Yeah, I bet he is.'

They were silent for a moment before Ronan said: 'Tell me more about my father. I'm afraid I didn't take much notice of what was in that letter once I discovered he was my father and… Clara's. What was he really like?'

Kathleen sat down on a rock and beckoned him to sit beside her. 'Where should I start?'

'At the beginning. When you first met him.'

It was an hour later, when the sun had disappeared over the far hills, that Kathleen finished talking.

'I'm sad I didn't meet him,' Ronan said. 'He sounds a really nice man.'

'Yes, he was,' Kathleen said. 'I suppose in hindsight I should have asked him about Jessica. After all, she was the one who introduced us. But then again, I was so much in love I didn't really mind who he'd taken out before me. And, in fairness, he never asked me who I'd gone out with before either. We were having too much fun to think about such things.'

'I'm surprised Jessica didn't say something when you and he got together.'

'Jessica has enormous pride. To think he preferred me to her would've devastated her. They probably met and got together when Dermot first started flying out of Calcutta and I was posted to Darjeeling with Garrison Headquarters as a Hindi interpreter. I was sent there from time to time.' She paused. 'If I think back to when Dermot died, Jessica was nearly as upset as I was. Maybe I should have guessed. Of course I didn't. And then when I found out about you, she was the only one I told, apart from Finn. I swore her to secrecy. She was brilliant and has never told a soul as far as I know. In all fairness, I don't suppose she'd have let on about Clara if you and she hadn't fallen in love. Although we all thought she wanted Clara to marry Charles Fitzpatrick because of his wealth and position, perhaps it was also because she'd guessed Clara was in love with you. Maybe that's why she was so adamant.' She sighed. 'All we can hope now is that Clara somehow gets over it all. And, you, my darling, can get on with your life without her as your wife. And that the Vietnam War is over before you have to go.' She caressed his face with her hand. 'It's enough that Dermot died there.'

'I doubt the war will end that soon. I leave in a couple of months.'

'Oh. That soon?'

'Yes.'

'It's such a horrid war. I hate watching the news.'

'Don't go worrying yourself, Ma. I'll be fine.'

'I pray to God so.' Kathleen looked towards the homestead. 'Now, let's head back to the house. I've got the steaks out for you to put on the barbeque. I've asked Arthur to join us. He's missed you while you've been gone. James thought it might lighten the mood with an outsider there.'

'He's still living in the manager's house?'

'Oh yes. He keeps it beautifully. And the garden's a showpiece. He often gives us vegetables. In fact we're eating some of his sweet corn tonight.'

'Yum, that sounds great.'

Together they walked back to the homestead. For the first time in a very long time Kathleen thought the family might get over the dreadful bombshell Jessica had dropped. The main cloud on the horizon now was Ronan going off to Vietnam. And she also worried for Clara. If only they knew where she was.

***

It was two months later when the family came to pick Lillie up from her flat to head out to Holsworthy Barracks for a farewell picnic before Ronan went off to Shoalwater Bay in far north Queensland. His battalion was to carry out a training exercise there before leaving for Vietnam.

The atmosphere in the car had been subdued on the way out to Holsworthy, but picked up once Ronan got in and Marcus and Freddie began to pepper him with questions about army life. They'd decided on a spot on the Georges River for their picnic, and when they arrived at the swimming hole, Dingo, Marcus and Freddie rushed down to the water and bounded in. Lillie and Ma set out the food on a rug under a Casuarina tree. Ma had made sandwiches and Ronan's favourite chocolate cake as well as plenty of Anzac biscuits he could take back to the barracks with him. Although the food all looked delicious, Lillie was too upset with the thought of it being the last time she would see Ronan before he left to eat much. After she and her mother cleared up, Dad and her brothers played cricket in the sand.

At one point Marcus caused a bit of a stir by saying: 'I don't reckon Australia should be in Vietnam. It's not right.'

'Thanks, mate,' Ronan said. 'Good to see I've got your backing.'

'Well,' Marcus said, 'I understand you wanting to go. But I don't see why Australia's there in the first place. Only because America's there. You know what I mean: all the way with LBJ —'

'Everyone's entitled to their opinion,' James said. 'Ronan's made a decision and we should back him.'

Marcus nodded. 'Yes, I know, but …' He saw Lillie glare at him, and decided not to take it any further. Although she didn't agree with the Vietnam War either, Lillie felt this was not the time to be saying so.

'Who's LBJ?' Freddie asked.

'President Johnston of America,' Ronan said. 'He's asked Australia to contribute to the forces in Vietnam.'

'And he shouldn't have done that,' Marcus said, throwing a stone into the river angrily.

'Marcus!' Kathleen exclaimed. 'Drop it. Okay?'

Lillie wondered if this wasn't an argument going on all over Australia. Vietnam was causing almost as much division and conflict within families as the Irish Civil War had done. But at least in Australia they weren't killing each other, even if at times they felt like it.

Finally the moment Lillie had been dreading arrived. There was a sombre mood as they packed up and prepared to take Ronan back to the barracks. Lillie sat between her parents in the front seat, her brothers were in the back with Dingo at their feet. As they drove Lillie tried to keep up a jolly banter, pointing out things they drove past. Ronan was also trying his hardest to lift everyone's mood.

'Hey, young Fred,' he chuckled. 'Look at that crane over there. Looks like it could move a mountain, eh.'

When they arrived at the barracks and they all got out to say a final goodbye, Lillie thought Ma's heart would break. Dad's and her own, too. Freddie was inconsolable.

Lillie went over to Ronan and gave him a monstrous hug. 'Good luck. And take care.'

Too upset to say anything more, she turned away and got back in the car. Out of the window she watched her parents say their final goodbyes.

When Ma got back in the car she turned around to Lillie in the back seat and gave her a small smile. 'We've all got to be brave. That's what Ronan would want.'

Now that Ronan was actually off to fight in those awful jungles crawling with Viet Cong, Lillie was terrified for him. Even so she wiped her eyes and tried to pull herself together.

'It's not fair,' Freddie sobbed into Dingo's fur, who sat on the floor with his head on Freddie's lap. 'It's not fair at all.'

Although Dad was stoic, it was obvious he was struggling to keep his composure as he walked to the car.

I know I shouldn't blame you, Clara, Lillie thought with a stab of anger, but if only you'd married Charles Fitzpatrick and hadn't come to Australia none of this would be happening. She tried to stop the tears running down her cheeks, but hard as she tried she couldn't. It was too much. She opened the door of the car and flew out to Ronan.

'Please, please look after yourself,' she said, looking up at him. 'And write whenever you can.'

'I'll be fine, li'l sis,' he said, smiling bravely at her. 'And of course I'll write.'

She then gave him another huge hug and a kiss and fled back into the car. As they drove off she saw him standing and waving after them. Lillie had never been so distressed in all her life. Not even when Ronan had taken off like that from Eureka Park. She wasn't given much to prayer, but now she prayed like she had never prayed before. *Please, please, God, look after him. Please.* She took Freddie's hand and squeezed it so hard she knew he was hurting.

But Freddie said nothing. He just let his own tears flow down his blotched cheeks onto Dingo's fur.

Part Five

Dublin, Kenmare River
Eureka Park
1968 to 1970

Chapter 45

Lillie had mixed emotions as she glimpsed the emerald fields below and her Aer Lingus flight came in towards Dublin airport. On one hand she was so excited that, at nineteen, here she was back in Ireland after five years, and the thought of seeing Grandma again made her feel her heart would split into a million pieces and scatter happily onto the patchwork fields below. On the other hand, Ronan, who'd promised to come home to Ireland before he was twenty-one, wasn't with her. He was ensconced at the Australian Task Force Base in Nui Dat in Vietnam and he would celebrate his twenty-second birthday there, without the family. Lillie had received a couple of letters from him, however it was hard to make out what he was really feeling, although he did say that it was incredibly hot. He couldn't tell her what sort of missions he was going on, but she had hoped he'd tell her more. Neither of them mentioned Clara. As far as Lillie knew Ronan hadn't heard from her since that first letter.

Lillie gazed out from the back of the taxi as it negotiated the ring road past St Stephen's Green on the way to Grandma's hotel. Everything seemed a little smaller than when she was a fourteen year old. Other than that, Dublin was as she remembered it. Screaming traffic, people everywhere, and the familiar green buses pulling into the kerbs. The rain pelted down in buckets, making the River Liffey and the stone buildings look grey and drab. She was so pleased to be back in Ireland she forgave them for that.

When she arrived at the hotel, she found Grandma waiting anxiously in the front parlour. When the family left for Australia, Grandma's immaculately styled hair had been grey; now it was white. Her skin had developed a papery texture, and the veins on her hands stood out like tangled vines. But her caring eyes were the same, even if they were now circled with deep lines.

'Oh Lillie,' she exclaimed, putting down her knitting and holding out her arms. 'My darling, darling Lillie. Look at you. You've got so grown-up. And even prettier. Do come here and give your old Grandma a kiss.' There were tears in her eyes. 'My, how I've missed you!'

As Lillie leaned down to give her a kiss, Alice stroked her hair and touched her lips to her forehead.

'I've missed you so much as well, Grandma.' Lillie straightened and her grandmother beckoned for her to sit next to her.

'You must be exhausted. And hungry. I'll order some sandwiches for you with my afternoon tea. And your luggage? Where is that?'

'The porter took it up to my room. Thank you so much for organising a room here.' She looked around at the warm and cosy drawing room with a fire burning in the grate. 'It all looks lovely.'

'Yes, I'm very happy here.' She rang a bell and soon a waitress appeared and took an order for sandwiches and another cup for Lillie's tea.

'Now, tell me all about the family,' Grandma said, when she had gone. 'Your mama, your father, Ronan and the little ones.' She paused. 'Do you think Ronan's all right in Vietnam?'

'I think so. He looks dashing in his uniform. Here,' she said, pulling out the photo she carried everywhere: the one of Ronan under the willow tree with the rest of the family.

Alice gazed at the photograph. 'He does look handsome in his uniform, doesn't he? So did his father. Dermot, I mean.'

Lillie nodded. 'He looked very dashing in the photo at Rathgarven.'

'He did indeed. It was taken not long before he died. Before that fateful flight over Vietnam. I never thought that photograph did him justice. Being black and white, you can't see his colouring.' She sighed. 'Now to think Ronan's in Vietnam too.' She let her eyes rest on Lillie's face again. 'But enough of all that. I can't believe you're here, darling.'

'Neither can I, Grandma.'

'Now tell me. Have you heard from Clara? I thought she'd have written to me when she found out about her father.'

'Ronan had one letter that I know of. To say she was in London. I'm sure when she settles down she'll get in touch with us.'

'No doubt you're right, darling.' Alice paused and fiddled with her knitting needles. 'As you say, it's best to leave it up to her.'

The waitress brought in a silver tea tray, and Lillie poured Grandma a cup of tea and handed her a curried egg sandwich on a small plate. She poured a cup of tea for herself and took a sandwich. Although lunch had been served on the plane, she was quite hungry.

When she finished eating she sat back and smiled. 'Oh Grandma… I've dreamt of this moment for so long.'

'And so have I, darling.'

They sipped their tea and the years fell away.

'Lady Margaret Fitzpatrick has asked us both down to Drominderry House for a visit,' Alice said, smoothing her tweed skirt.

'Goodness, has she?' Lillie paused. 'Do you think they've heard from Clara? Ronan said she might marry Charles after all. I know she hasn't or we would've heard. But do you think she's been in contact with them?'

'Margaret said they haven't heard a word from her. I didn't tell her whose daughter Clara turned out to be. It's really up to Clara to tell people if she wants to do so.'

'Yes, that's how Ma and Dad feel. Though we did wonder if Jessica would've told anyone.'

'Not that I'm aware of. And let's hope that's how it remains until Clara's happy with disclosing it.' She paused. 'Although dear Margaret's got Charles and Hugh at Drominderry House, she insisted she'd like my company. I do hate staying with people for long periods, but she sounded so adamant we stay a few weeks I could hardly refuse. Besides, Bette, my companion, has broken her leg and is staying in a convalescent place for a few more weeks. So it's a good opportunity. Margaret was thrilled when I told her you were here. She said we could have the small flat on the side of the house. No one's using it. I think it might cheer her up after what happened with Charles and Clara.'

Lillie wondered how she'd get on staying in the same house as Charles Fitzpatrick after what had gone on with Clara and Ronan. Even if Charles didn't know, it would be awkward to say the least. It could also be awkward with his mother. Even Hugh.

'Are you sure Lady Fitzpatrick and Charles want me to stay?' she asked. 'I mean…'

'Margaret was adamant you come. And if you remember Margaret, she's not one to take no for an answer. Don't you want to see Hugh? Not to mention Maisie? And Paddy? They'd be horrified if you didn't come.'

Put like that, Lillie couldn't say no. Besides, she was excited to be seeing Maisie and Paddy again. Although she couldn't remember meeting Charles Fitzpatrick before, she was curious to see what he was like. And she would be able to see how Hugh was looking after Merlin. Plus Drominderry House was on her beloved Kenmare River.

***

428

Under a bright blue sky, perfect summer weather for the long drive to Killarney, Lillie folded up Grandma's wheelchair and placed it in the boot of the small Fiat she'd hired. Grandmother and granddaughter chatted companionably as the little car sped along, and they took a break for lunch in Limerick on the way.

'It's so wonderful to be back,' Lillie said as they wound their way down the familiar road past Lough Leane and Moll's Gap. 'I missed these mountains so much.' She glanced across to the high peaks of Macgillycuddy's Reeks where black and white sheep grazed among the rocks on the slopes. 'And,' she laughed, 'I remember Freddie could never say Macgillycuddy's Reeks.'

'It is a funny sounding name,' her grandmother said. 'But the Macgillycuddys were a branch of the O'Sullivans in the olden days.'

'Really!'

'Irish history goes back a long, long way. So different to the European settlement of Australia.'

Lillie smiled. 'The difference between here and there is amazing, Grandma. You'd find it fascinating. The paddocks seem to go on forever. And rather than hedgerows there's barbed-wire fences. And they call waterholes dams. We have quite a few at Eureka and then of course there's the river. It's beautiful.'

'It does look lovely. I adored the photos of Ronan's twenty-first down there.'

What would her family be doing now? Lillie looked at her watch. Sleeping.

'Do you want to go first to see if we can spy anything of Rathgarven, Grandma? I know the gates will probably be closed. But we might be able to see something.'

'No,' Alice said. 'The memories would be too painful. Maybe Margaret will know how Donoghue's looking after the dear place. I don't think I could bear to ever go back while he's there.'

Lillie nodded. 'I think I feel the same.' As she drove she saw a donkey trying to snaffle something juicy among the foxglove over the fence, wagging his tail in frustration because he couldn't get to it. 'All the same, I wouldn't mind having a peek one day. To refresh my happy memories.'

'Ah, that's what happy memories are all about. Keep them as that. Don't go destroying them.'

Grandma's probably right, Lillie thought. I should remember Rathgarven as it was when I was fourteen years old. Not now with another family's stamp on it.

As they got closer to Drominderry House they passed a number of the larger estates hidden behind ivy-covered stonewalls, although Drominderry House's wall was the longest and highest. Huge iron gates stood between ornate stone pillars at the entrance.

They drove through and Lillie gasped when they came to the end of the tree-lined avenue. She had forgotten what a magnificent building it was. Built of splendid brownstone, its four turreted towers made it look more of a castle than a house. Extensive gardens surrounded it, with box hedges and green lawns dotted with bushes of azaleas, camellias, rhododendrons and fuchsias; down near the river stood huge shiny palms.

'It takes a better advantage of the Gulf Stream from Mexico than Rathgarven,' her grandmother said. 'Hence all those palms and exotic plants.'

Whereas Rathgarven was burnt down during the Civil War of the 1920s, Lillie remembered Grandma telling her Drominderry House had survived. She could understand why Clara's mother had wanted her to be mistress of such a glorious stately home. And Jessica would have been in her element.

'It's an incredible building, isn't it?' she said to her grandmother.

'The original home was built in the seventeenth century during a time known as the Plantations, when lands were confiscated from their Irish owners and granted to settlers from England.'

'Truly!'

'Yes. It's stayed in the Fitzpatrick family ever since.'

Lillie didn't envy Charles inheriting the enormous responsibility of an estate like this. Little wonder he wanted a wife to share it with. Heavens, Clara, she mused, perhaps you should've pretended you loved the man and gone ahead with that lavish wedding at Christchurch Cathedral in order to get your hands on this. And then, she thought sadly, Ronan might be with me now, rather than fighting in that awful war in Vietnam.

'Oh look,' Alice exclaimed. 'I do believe that's Paddy by that wooden gate over there.'

And sure enough it *was* Paddy. Despite the warmth, he wore his familiar tweed cap and Wellington boots. He held a pair of garden clippers in one hand, a shovel in the other.

Lillie stopped the car and leapt out to embrace him.

'Paddy! How wonderful to see you.'

Like her Dad, he was now a bit stooped. And when he removed his cap, she could see that his hair had thinned to just a couple of strands across the top of his head.

'Sure now,' he said with a beam from ear to ear. 'It does an old man's eyes good to be seeing a girl such as you.' He stood back. 'My, oh my! What a fine lass you've grown into!'

'Don't know about that, Paddy.'

'And they tell me young Ronan's gone and joined the Army?'

'Yes, he's in Vietnam.'

'Ah, is he now? And how about young Marcus? And that terror of a lad, Freddie? How would they be doing?'

'They're fine, Paddy. Still the nuisance younger brothers and fighting all the time. I've got some photos in the car. Come, Grandma's there.'

Alice was delighted to see Paddy, and rolled down the window and held out her hand.

'Ah, 'tis a grand day to be seeing you, Mrs O'Sullivan,' he said, raising his hat and taking her hand. 'And don't you be looking on top of the world.'

'And you look wonderful, Paddy,' Alice said. 'You haven't aged one bit.'

Which of course was a lie, but it made Paddy grin. Lillie reached into the car for her handbag and showed him the photo of Ronan and the rest of the family.

'My oh my. Haven't they all grown? And doesn't your mother look in fine fettle? And your father? I believe he's quite the Australian farmer now.'

'Yes, he is, Paddy. And so's my mother. It was a bit hard at first to make ends meet, and we had a dreadful bushfire and lost one of our lovely mares.'

'Ah, what a shame that be. And Marcus,' he said, handing the photo back to Lillie, 'he looks quite the young man. And you be telling young Freddie I still have that tortoise of his. It be eating me out of house and home.'

Lillie laughed. 'He'll be so pleased to know you've still got Mandrake.'

'Now,' Paddy said, looking towards the house. 'Lord Charles, young Hugh and his mother be expecting you. And Maisie be getting all things spic and span for you as well. She be in the kitchen fiddling with the Aga and fussing about. You drive your Grandma to the front entrance. Charles and young Hugh will be out to help with the wheelchair. I be catching you both later. There be a horse down in the front meadow that's gone and got itself all caught up in the brambles. I be on my way to untangle the unfortunate fella.'

'How awful. I hope he's okay.'

'Ah, he will as soon as I take these clippers to the brambles.'

Lillie drove on and as she pulled up on the gravel driveway in front of the pillared porch, the front door opened and Hugh came rushing out. He had grown, of course, but Lillie would have recognised him anywhere. She jumped out to greet him and they embraced, then Hugh stood back and looked her up and down. 'Gees, Lillie… you're so grown up.'

'Well, so I should be,' she laughed. 'I'm a good two years older than you. Anyway, it's wonderful to see you. Come say hello to Grandma.'

He greeted Alice warmly, then turned back to Lillie.

'Now tell me,' she said, 'how are you looking after my Merlin?'

'He's grand,' Hugh said. 'I've outgrown him, but I kept him as I knew you'd kill me if I didn't.'

'You're quite right there. I would have.'

Now a tall, angular sort of fellow with closely cropped, mousy hair joined them. If Lillie had ever met Charles Fitzpatrick, she certainly couldn't remember him. Although he had a nice face, he wasn't madly handsome. Nevertheless, as she'd thought when she looked at the photo Clara had shown her, he had a certain air. The well-cut tweed jacket, worn over an immaculate ironed-by-Maisie cream shirt with a stiff collar, toned well with his green club tie, and Lillie thought he probably would indeed make a good lord. Even so, he didn't look Clara's type. And he was certainly nowhere near as good-looking as Ronan. He came forward and introduced himself to Lillie and Grandma, then helped Lillie get the wheelchair out of the boot.

Another man emerged from the front door. He was slightly smaller than Charles and had a smiling open face boasting a sprinkling of freckles beneath a mass of gingery brown hair. He wore an Aran pullover over an open-necked shirt and beige corduroy trousers. As he walked towards them, a huge lopsided grin spread over his face. Lillie immediately thought he looked good fun. Then she did a double-take. There was no mistaking those sea-green eyes and those huge cow lashes.

'Sorry,' Charles said, seeing Lillie's dumbfounded expression. 'How remiss of me. Seamus Flaherty. He went to Trinity College with me in Dublin.'

Lillie burst out laughing. 'Well I never. Imagine seeing you here. The budding Brendan Behan.' She took a stab. 'Do you remember me?'

Seamus smiled. 'Indeed I do. I told Charles I remember you from when we caught the school bus together.'

Lillie couldn't believe he was here standing in front of her after all this time. The years had been kind to him. He was a really good-looking man. Stupidly she found herself blushing, wondering if he'd any inkling of how she'd fancied him.

He joined them at the front passenger door to assist Grandma out of the car, and Lillie heard her give a gasp. She looked so startled Lillie didn't know what had happened.

'You, young man,' Grandma said, peering closely at Seamus, 'have an uncanny resemblance to someone I once knew. I've never seen anything like it.'

'I'm told I look very much like my father.'

'And he is?'

'Kevin Byrne.'

Alice shook her head in disbelief. 'Goodness, gracious me. How amazing.' She looked at Lillie, who was standing next to Charles. 'This young man is the son of the soldier who saved the chalice in the fire that burnt Rathgarven down. You might remember I told you the story.'

As far as Lillie knew Seamus's father was a Flaherty. To hear his father was Kevin Byrne who had more or less saved

Grandma, her father and Uncle Dermot in that fire was beyond belief.

'And his dear grandmother, Moira, used to work with us at Rathgarven,' Alice went on. 'Well, I'll be damned. What a small world it is!' She turned back to Seamus. 'And what about your father?'

'He was killed by a German sniper during the war in France. After he died my mother married Donal Flaherty. I took his name.'

So that explains it, Lillie thought.

'How very sad that your father died,' Alice said. 'He was a good man. You should be extremely proud of him, as no doubt you are.'

'Indeed I am, Mrs O'Sullivan.'

'Did he become an officer?'

'Yes, he did. He was a brigadier when he died.'

'Ah!' Alice said. 'I would have thought as much.'

Seamus gave her a sad smile. 'I heard your son was killed as well. After the war, during Operation Masterdom in Vietnam.'

'Yes, he was,' Alice said, returning his smile. 'But enough about that.' She turned to Charles. 'How are you, young man. Or should I say, young lord?'

'I'm grand, Mrs O'Sullivan. And what a coincidence with Seamus. You'll have to talk about his father with him some more. But come,' he said, holding his hand out to help her into the wheelchair, 'my mother's waiting. I'll tell you how I am on the way to see her.'

'And Maisie?' Lillie asked Hugh. 'Where's she?'

'I'll show you. She mustn't have heard the car.'

Lillie looked to Charles. 'Go,' he said. 'I'll tell my grandmother you'll see her in a minute. She's on the other side of the house sitting under the chestnut tree. She was going to come around, except her legs are letting her down somewhat.'

Lillie went with Hugh to the back of the house and they found Maisie in the kitchen icing a cake.

'Oh my goodness me!' Maisie exclaimed, putting the knife on the bench and wiping her hands on her apron. 'Look at you, young lady.'

Lillie laughed and ran to her. 'Oh, Maisie. You haven't changed one bit.'

The laugh lines around her eyes were a little deeper, and the folds around her mouth didn't leap back into place quite as quickly as they once did, but aside from that Lillie didn't think Maisie *had* changed much at all. She was still the same Maisie Lillie had missed so much, and when they embraced Lillie smelt the familiar scent of her Blue Grass perfume, mingled with the aroma of cake and icing.

'Now tell me about your lovely mother. And your father,' Maisie said, standing back. 'And those boys. Particularly Ronan, who I'm told has joined the Army and is off fighting in that dreadful war in Vietnam.'

Lillie pulled out the photo and showed it to Maisie.

'Well I never,' Maisie said, studying the photo. 'Aren't they a grand lot. Look at Ronan in that uniform. And Marcus and young Freddie. How they've grown. And doesn't your mother look beautiful beside your Dad. What about your lovely Grandma? Is she well? I can't wait to be seeing her.'

'She's not bad at all. Older and frailer of course. She's gone around the side of the house to see Lady Fitzpatrick.'

'Won't they be having a lot to catch up on. You give me a hand with this tea tray and let's go around and join them.'

As Lillie helped Maisie load the tray she almost felt as though she was a fourteen year old again, helping her in the kitchen at Rathgarven.

At the side of the house Grandma sat under the chestnut tree talking animatedly to Lady Margaret Fitzpatrick. Charles,

Hugh and Seamus sat nearby. Lillie looked at Seamus. After Sheelagh's letter, perhaps I should have guessed he might visit Charles here at times.

Maisie rushed forward to greet Grandma, and took her outstretched hand. 'Ah, it's grand to be seeing you, Mrs O'Sullivan. Thanks be to God you be looking the picture of good health.'

Lillie placed the tea tray on the table. She didn't think Lady Fitzpatrick looked well at all, even though the fun and vigour that Lillie remembered was still there. She was pale and had lost a lot of weight. Lillie always remembered her as roly-poly, with a thick mass of steel-wool hair. But her hair had thinned out considerably. Old age, the death of her husband, and the aftermath of Clara's runaway bride act no doubt all contributed to her decline.

'I can't believe you're not shrivelled up like a roasted almond,' she said to Lillie. 'All that Australian sun must be so bad for the complexion. But tell me, my dear, how is your family? Do fill me in on all the gossip. I believe Ronan's joined the army and is off to fight the communist hordes in that ghastly war in Vietnam. Very noble of him, I must say.'

'Yes,' Lillie said. 'It is, isn't it?'

Seamus now stood to fill Grandma's and Lady Fitzpatrick's teacups. She remembered Sheelagh saying how all the waitresses at the café she worked at in Grafton Street fancied him, and how he had a girlfriend he would take there. She wondered if he was still taking out that same girl.

'Vietnam needs all the soldiers it can get,' he said to Lady Fitzpatrick, pouring from the teapot. 'War is a dreadful thing. You've only got to look at Ireland with us all at each other's throats.'

'Ireland will never be at peace,' Charles proclaimed. 'We'll always be fighting each other. Even if we're not involved in someone else's war.'

Seamus laughed. 'You're right there, Charles. And apart from the religion bit, to think the IRA and the business in the North could all be done and dusted if the British would give us back what's rightfully ours.'

Lillie imagined Seamus and Charles had many conversations like this, and that Seamus might add playfully, 'Including handing us Irish back Drominderry House, old chap.'

But Grandma could get very heated when politics came up.

'Has anyone heard any news of Rathgarven?' she asked, changing the subject. 'Are the Donoghues still living there?'

'They are,' Lady Fitzpatrick said. 'Regrettably I believe the place has been let go. The gossip is he might be placing it on the market soon.'

'Oh,' Lillie said. 'How sad if it's been let go like that. All the same, I bet he'd want an arm and a leg for it.'

'Prices have certainly improved since your dear parents sold to him. So no doubt it would be worth a bit now. Probably some ghastly rock star from England will snap it up.'

'How awful,' Lillie said, feeling quite sick thinking what might happen to her childhood home. She wished she was older and had made millions so she could buy it back herself. She wondered if her parents would be interested. But their life was in Australia now. Even so, she would let them know.

'Come on, Hugh,' she said, looking over at him, 'why don't you take me down to see Merlin? Maybe it's a furphy that you've still got him. I must see for myself.' She turned to Seamus. 'What's say you come as well? I'll show you the best little horse on earth.' Then she thought of Muffin at Eureka Park. 'Well, the best in Ireland.'

'I've already met your Merlin,' Seamus chuckled. 'Nevertheless I could do with a walk, so I'd be more than happy to come and have a chat with the old fella.'

As they walked across the meadow with Hugh to see Merlin, Seamus told Lillie how he found Drominderry House to be the perfect retreat for writing. He pointed out the boathouse on the edge of the cove and grinned.

'As Charles is always keen to have my congenial company, he loaned me the boathouse for the summer.'

Seamus said he had set up his typewriter so that he could look out over the rocks to the river. If he were experiencing writer's block, he would sometimes take himself out fishing in the Fitzpatrick's small wooden rowboat. Or he'd sit on the jetty dangling his feet in the water while he tried to think up scenarios for his novel.

'Failing all that,' he said with a twinkle in his eye, 'young Hugh here will tell you that I go on up to the house and annoy Charles. If it's that time of day, we'll share a bottle of red. Amazingly the words run easily then. It's only the next morning I realise the wine was doing all the talking.'

Lillie laughed. 'I thought Hemingway and Fitzgerald were always three sheets to the wind when they wrote. Brendan Behan certainly was.'

'They may well have been. What I write is supposedly historical. A lot of fact has to appear in there one way or another. After a few wines, fact becomes fiction.' He gave a hearty chortle. 'Or maybe fiction becomes fact. Either way it can be dangerous.'

When they came across Merlin, Lillie rushed forward and gave him a huge hug. She smiled at Hugh. 'Thank you for looking after him.' She stood back. 'Apart from being a bit greyer around the eyes he's just the same.'

'Ah, it was my pleasure. Now,' he said, looking across the meadow, 'I'll leave you two here with Merlin. I can see Paddy over there and I promised I'd help him hang that gate.'

After he'd gone Lillie continued to pat Merlin and run her fingers through his mane as she looked out to the river where a few sailing boats were tacking in the breeze. 'Isn't this the most glorious spot?' she said to Seamus.

'It is to be sure.'

'But tell me… What was Canada like?'

'Canada's not bad at all,' he said, rubbing Merlin on the rump. 'But Ireland's my home. As soon as I was of age, I came back.'

'And your mother and stepfather? And the other children?'

'They've made a grand life for themselves over there in Toronto. They ended up buying a hardware business. My stepfather said he used every bit of hardware available when trying to keep the machinery afloat in the dairy. So he thought a hardware store was a good fit.'

They said goodbye to Merlin and wandered back through the meadow. As they chatted Lillie realised that she still found Seamus immensely attractive. When he put his hand out to help her over the style dividing the meadow from the front garden, and held her hand for just that little bit longer, she felt a tingle run up her arm.

'It's lovely to see you again,' he said, holding her eyes with his. 'I did wonder how you were getting on in Australia.'

'You knew we went there?'

'Not until Charles told me. It was after that when I wondered about you.'

'Really,' Lillie said. 'I wouldn't have thought you'd remember me at all.'

'Ah, but I did.'

Inwardly, Lillie smiled. Maybe staying at Drominderry House will be more exciting than she'd imagined.

***

Lillie would remember that long hot summer in Ireland as one of the happiest in her life. While her grandmother and Lady Fitzpatrick spent their time chatting, knitting, playing cards and relishing Maisie's cooking, Lillie, Charles (who never once mentioned Clara), Seamus (who didn't seem to be dating anyone) and Hugh did everything together — that is, when Charles and Seamus weren't working. For Charles had plenty to do trying to keep Drominderry House afloat. And Seamus was now a writer of historical novels. He'd had one published in England to great acclaim and was trying to recreate that success with a story set during the Crimean War.

The four of them sailed in weekend competitions on the Kenmare River and went horseriding along the narrow laneways to different coves and swam at Derrynane Beach in front of the home of Daniel O'Connell, the renowned liberator, which had been recently opened to the public. Although Lillie rode one of the Fitzpatricks' horses, she spent ages sitting with Merlin in the field and grooming him. Maisie was in her element with so many young ones around. When Charles was caught up on estate matters, Seamus and Lillie would sometimes sit by the water or go out in the wooden rowboat like Lillie and Ronan used to do.

'You sure you're taking this seriously?' Seamus chided her once as they sat in the boat fishing and Lillie was reading a book. 'You can't expect the fish to bite if they think you're not interested.'

What he didn't realise was that Lillie was not reading her book. In fact, what she was doing was trying to control her emotions. For she realised Seamus was getting under her skin. Once again. It was those incredibly sexy eyes; the way he always seemed to be about to break into a happy laugh. But above all it was his love of literature, and how he talked to her as though she was the most important person he had ever met.

I'm falling in love, she thought. It's not puppy love like when I was fourteen. This is something totally different.

Chapter 46

Lillie couldn't help herself. Despite telling Grandma she wouldn't, one afternoon she drove across to Rathgarven to see if she could spy anything. As she suspected, the gates were locked. All she could see was the driveway, which looked neglected and overgrown. She felt a dreadful pang of anger towards that man, Donoghue. The least he could have done was keep it all looking loved. To her right was the public path that snaked down to the cove. She walked along it and sat on the bank. Picking up a stone, she threw it into the water and watched the ripples swirl and twist. Ronan had loved this cove so much. Was he frightened in Vietnam? She'd written to him a few times since she'd arrived in Ireland, but hadn't heard back. Surely he would be jealous of her being here right now. Or would he be sad that Rathgarven was no longer going to be his?

After ten minutes or so, she stood up and went back to her car and sat for some time. She thought of scaling the fence and seeing Rathgarven's house. But, being a well-known bookie, she was sure Donoghue would have guard dogs. So she started the engine and drove back to Drominderry House, where another happy reminder of her childhood at Rathgarven was waiting. At the thought of Seamus her heart lifted.

It was cold and wet the next afternoon when Seamus brought his manuscript to the flat Lillie was sharing with Grandma. Alice was out playing bridge with Lady Fitzpatrick and another couple. Lillie asked him to read it out to her. She thought he wrote beautifully and with great soul and told him so.

'While you were off gallivanting yesterday,' he said, 'I stopped to chat to your Grandma when she was sitting down by the water. I was carrying my manuscript and she insisted I read it to her. She's a much harsher critic than you. But she gave me some great ideas.'

'She used to write articles for English magazines, so she knows what she's talking about.'

Lillie showed him a photo of the gold chalice his father had saved from the ashes when Rathgarven burnt down in the uprising. Grandma always carried it with her, saying it was her good luck charm. Last night she and Lillie had been looking at it together.

Seamus held the photo up to the light. 'I'm mighty glad my father played a part in saving your father and his brothers. Otherwise you wouldn't be here.'

Lillie smiled shyly. 'That's a lovely thing to say.' She took the photo from him. 'Maybe one day you could write the story of this chalice. How it came to be at Rathgarven in the first place and how your father saved it.'

'I have indeed thought of writing about those tragic times. Maybe I will. And Rathgarven could play a role.'

Lillie felt so comfortable with Seamus, she ended up telling him how her father had gambled on a horse race and Donoghue had literally snaffled Rathgarven as payment of his debt. How much she loved the place and how heartbroken she had been to leave. How it had nearly killed Ma. Dad, too. And how Ronan had been distraught.

'That's where I was yesterday. Trying to have a look.'

'Did you succeed?'

'No, it was all locked up. Marcus and Freddie were too young to worry too much when we left. But I think Ronan lost a bit of himself when we drove out that last time. As did I. Even though I love Eureka Park, there was something about Rathgarven that got under my skin.' She looked towards the water. 'And now that I'm back by Kenmare River, I realise how much I miss it too.'

'Well, if the weather's okay let me take you out for a row tomorrow.'

Lillie smiled. 'That would be lovely.'

The next morning dawned bright and sunny, so in the afternoon they set off in the rowboat. Out in the cove Seamus stopped rowing and leant over and took Lillie's hand. For some time they sat there with the sound of the water lapping against the side of the boat.

'Is this not heaven,' he said, gently rolling his thumb over her skin.

Lillie sighed. 'It's beautiful.'

Now he lifted her chin and kissed her on the lips. Yielding her body to his, she felt a warm shiver of desire run up her spine and down to her groin. But when he lifted her blouse and put his hand on her breast, she moved away. Even though she was sure it would be different with Seamus, she still had depressing memories of that day with Brad Hickey by the river at Eureka Park. And how soon afterwards he had broken up with her. She didn't want what she had with Seamus to be spoilt. Although many girls of her age in Australia were on the Pill, Lillie wasn't. Not only was it proclaimed a mortal sin by the Catholic Church — one would burn in hell for daring to take it — Lillie was also too embarrassed to go to a doctor to ask. In any case, in Ireland it was illegal.

'It's okay,' Seamus said, when she pulled back. 'I understand.'

He ran his hand through her glossy hair. 'I don't think you realise how beautiful you are,' he said, kissing her on the forehead. 'I thought that the first time I sat next to you on the bus from Cork.'

'Did you now? Well, I didn't think you were that hot,' she lied, laughing.

'So why did you blush to the bottom of your shiny black shoes when I asked if you were going to that dance at Kingdom Hall in Sneem?'

'I did not,' Lillie exclaimed.

'Ah. But you did.'

Lillie was blissfully happy. Seamus made her feel so special. She may not be tall and slim like Clara, but Seamus seemed to like her just as she was, curves and all.

***

Now it was starting to get quite cold in Kerry with the nights closing in and Alice thought it was time she went back up to her hotel in Dublin.

'Why don't you stay on down here?' she asked Lillie one afternoon as they sat by the water, rugged up against the stiff breeze. 'You could stay for Christmas. Margaret told me how much she loves having you here. She says Charles has perked up no end with you and Seamus around to do things with.'

'That does sound tempting,' Lillie answered. 'I have an open ticket so I may think about doing just that.'

Grandma was no fool. Lillie was sure she knew exactly what was going on with Seamus and herself. She was torn. Christmas without Ronan at Eureka Park would be sad as it was, but if she wasn't there it might be dismal, particularly for Freddie. And she wanted to enrol at Sydney University. But she was desperately in love with Seamus and should a day go by without her seeing him, she missed him. Of course she could apply to a university here in Ireland, but she wasn't sure if they would take someone from Australia. Maybe if she went back home, they could both see how it panned out. If they couldn't live without each other, either Lillie would come back to Ireland, or Seamus might come to Australia. In the meantime they could write and there was always the telephone. This, she told herself, was a grown-up decision.

'I know. And I'll miss him, too,' she said to Grandma. 'But I promised Ma and Dad, and myself, that I'd go to university. And

Seamus will probably go back to Dublin after Christmas. In any case I promise I'll try to come back next Christmas.'

However, when Lillie told Seamus she was leaving, and had promised Grandma she would try and come back next year, he persuaded her to stay on a little longer.

'I can't see how another few weeks would hurt,' he said, kissing her tenderly. 'Then when you callously leave me to flit across the world, it'll only be a year till you're scurrying back to your handsome Irish lover for next Christmas.' He ran his finger across her top lip. 'I think I might survive that long. Any longer and I'll have to be going on a hunger strike.' He patted his stomach. 'Mind you, I could probably do with that.' They were lying in front of the fire in the boathouse, toasting marshmallows. Seamus leant down and kissed her again. 'Surely you could grant a poor sod a few more weeks of happiness?'

It was during this conversation that Lillie told Seamus about Ronan and Clara. She'd thought of telling him before but had put it off, as she wasn't sure how he would take it. After all, he was Charles Fitzpatrick's friend, and it wasn't your everyday family story. When Lillie explained everything that had happened, beginning with Ma falling in love with Dermot O'Sullivan and ending with Ronan having signed on with the Australian Army to go to Vietnam, Seamus stood up and went to the small fridge in the corner of the room to fetch a bottle of wine.

'Well, I'd better not tell Charles that,' he said, pouring Lillie a glass of wine. 'Though it's some story — a writer could make a good tale of it.' He handed the glass to Lillie. 'I must say Charles did seem besotted with Clara.'

'Did you ever meet her?'

'No. She was gone before I got there.'

'If she hadn't come to Australia, none of this would've happened. She'd be married to Charles, and Ronan wouldn't be in Vietnam.'

'Ah!' Seamus said, wrinkling his forehead and giving her a lopsided grin. 'Do you not think that brother of yours was there for the taking? It takes two to tango, my sweet. And no doubt your darling Ronan was easily got. But I can understand why you need to get back to your family. It's been a traumatic year by the sounds of it.'

A week later, Grandma's carer, Bette caught the train down from Dublin, and now that her leg had healed, drove her back to her hotel in the car Lillie had rented. Seamus assured her he would drive Lillie to Shannon airport when it was time to go. She would then fly to Dublin where she would board the connection for her return flight to Sydney. Saying goodbye to Grandma this time wasn't nearly as traumatic as it was when Lillie was a fourteen year old. This time she was sure she would see her again next year. Even so, she held her tightly before she got in the car.

'Take care, Grandma.'

'And you take care,' Alice said, brushing a tear away with her hand. She looked at Seamus. 'You make sure you hold her to her promise to come back next year.'

'Ah, that I will, Mrs O'Sullivan.'

As they watched the car head down the driveway and away from Drominderry House, Seamus put his arm around Lillie and she rested her head on his shoulder. Much as she wanted to be with him, she felt guilty that she hadn't gone back with Grandma.

***

The weekend before she left Drominderry House, Lillie suggested to Seamus that they take a picnic to a small hidden cove that she had once gone to on a primary school excursion. Charles had bought a new outboard motor for the rowboat, so after Seamus had dragged it out from the workshop at the rear of the boathouse and put it on the back of the boat, Lillie got in with the picnic basket.

They rowed out through the rocks and when they were in the open water, Seamus got the motor going. It was a beautiful autumn day with hardly a cloud in the pale blue sky. A formation of wild geese flew overhead and all around the boat fish jumped and dived. Across the water were the ever-changing colours of the Kerry Mountains, and as she looked at Seamus with the tiller in his hand, Lillie felt a huge rush of exhilaration.

Seamus tilted his tweed cap and gave her a broad smile. 'On a beautiful day like today on Kenmare River, and with a gorgeous lady by my side, what more could a poor sod ask for?'

When they reached the hidden cove, they dragged the boat up on the shore. Lillie laid out their picnic on a mohair rug under a tree. Seamus opened a bottle of champagne and handed her a glass.

'*Sláinte*,' he said with a wink.

'*Sláinte*,' Lillie said, taking a sip. She licked her lips. 'Yum.'

She gave Seamus a plate from the set in the wicker picnic basket that Lady Fitzpatrick had owned since she was first married. She then handed him the sandwiches she'd made earlier. When they'd finished the sandwiches, Lillie took out a bunch of grapes and some cheese. Soon Seamus was feeding Lillie one grape after another, and she was doing the same to him. When the grapes had all gone, Seamus leant over and put his head on her lap. Dappled light chased over the rug where they lay, and Lillie could hear the gentle sound of a soft breeze in the leaves and the water lapping against the speckled rocks.

Just when she thought Seamus had fallen asleep, he surprised her by raising a hand to softly caress her cheek. Then pulled her face to his and kissed her with such passion that she thought she would lose her breath. He tenderly undid the buttons on her shirt and exposed her left breast, gently placing her nipple between his lips. Fondling her other breast, he let his hand wander across her belly, sending such an exhilarating current through her being that, despite her best intentions, Lillie was lost. Unlike her experience with Brad Hickey, this moment was beautiful and joyous and had been waiting since the day she was born. When Seamus finally slid inside of her, thrusting gently at first and then more urgently, she experienced so much pleasure she cried out in ecstasy, never wanting it to stop. Now she knew that Sheelagh, and all the books she'd read, had not exaggerated the bliss of making love.

As they lay together afterwards, Seamus stroked her hair. 'I'm sorry,' he said, kissing her gently on the forehead. 'I promised not to do that.'

Lillie caressed his hand and smiled. 'It was beautiful. I'm sure one time can't hurt.' She felt such happiness as she had never felt before.

***

All too soon it was her last night at Drominderry House. With her things packed Seamus took her out to dinner at a new cosy restaurant in Kenmare.

'To the most beautiful colleen in all of Ireland,' he said, raising a glass of champagne and pushing a small green box across the table to her. When Lillie opened it she found a silver Claddagh ring nestled in the plush cushioning. 'So you won't be going and forgetting me,' he said, placing the ring on the fourth finger of her right hand. 'Now,' he continued with a gleam, 'the important bit. You've got to be sure you wear it with the heart pointing inwards to tell the world you've got a jealous lover waiting back here in Ireland.'

'You're daft,' she laughed, 'but thank you.' She leant across the table to give him a kiss. 'It's a beautiful ring. I'll treasure it always.'

The next afternoon Seamus drove her to the airport, dropping her at the front of the terminal. She had told him not to come inside, as she thought it would be too horrible waiting around in the airport, knowing that the inevitable would happen. And Lillie felt sure she'd burst into tears in front of everyone, which would probably embarrass Seamus terribly, not to mention herself.

After Seamus carried her suitcase to the kerb, he took her in his arms and gave her a long passionate kiss. Standing back he smiled that lopsided grin she'd grown to love so well.

'Don't you be going off and falling in love with someone else. If you did that, I'd have to shoot the poor bastard.'

For a moment they clung to each other. Then Lillie dragged herself away with tears running down her cheeks.

'I love you, Lillie O'Sullivan,' Seamus called out when she was near the terminal door, making a nearby group turn around to see who the lucky Lillie O'Sullivan was.

I'm stark, raving mad, she thought as she lifted her hand for a final wave. How could I leave a man I love like this?

Chapter 47

Kathleen turned over the letter from Ronan. It was the third time she'd read it.

All's good, he wrote. *I've been back in base camp at Nui Dat for over a week now. Food's not too bad and I have the odd game of poker. Won a bit last night.*

Kathleen knew he couldn't write much about the actual fighting, as it would be confidential and his letters would be censored. But she did wish that he was allowed to disclose more. To say how dangerous it was. Or whether he was in an area where there weren't too many Viet Cong. Were there mines in the area he patrolled?

> *I had a letter from Lillie yesterday. Imagine her meeting up with Seamus Flaherty again. Sounds as though the poor girl has fallen badly for him. Good luck to her.*

This made Kathleen feel dreadful all over again for what had happened to Ronan. Had he heard from Clara while he was in Vietnam? Would she even know that he was there?

Give Marcus and young Fred my love, Ronan wrote. *Dad too. And lots of love to you, Ma. I really miss you all.*

Kathleen smiled at the young Fred bit. Ronan had always called him that. They had such a special bond and she knew Freddie was missing him, and worried for him. Freddie was now up in Tamworth at school with the Christian Brothers, sharing a room with Marcus at the Thompsons. That poor Thompson family was all she could say. If the brothers fought up there the way they did here they must find it very tiresome. But to give the Thompsons their due, they never once let on that they did. Kathleen and James had become very friendly with them both over the years, and as far as Kathleen could see, they loved having the boys billeting there and often took them on outings and would go and watch their rugby games if Kathleen and James couldn't get up to see them. Sometimes the four of them would be there sitting on the sidelines drinking coffee out of a thermos, the men throwing advice to the players and the wives gossiping. She missed the boys so much when they weren't here and looked forward to Friday nights when she would pick them up from the bus and they would talk over each other to tell her about the week.

It was interesting to see how Freddie was growing into himself. He no longer gave in to Marcus like he used to. This, of course, caused more disagreements than ever. Nevertheless every now and then she would find them down by the river fishing companionably — until one caught a fish and the other didn't.

'You stupid dill… you moved and scared my fish away.'

And so it would go on.

To give Marcus his due, he had never brought up the business of being James's eldest son again. And when he was here on weekends he spent so much time helping Arthur, James, and the extra couple of stable hands they had taken on a while back, that Kathleen felt it might well be him who ended up taking over Eureka Park if Ronan decided to make the Army his full-time career. Although Freddie loved the horses, his great interest was the wild animals and birds around the place.

'I think I'd like to be a vet,' he told her one afternoon as they were trying to feed a baby bird that had fallen out of its nest. 'A vet that works in a zoo.'

Kathleen folded up Ronan's letter and put it on the sideboard for James to read later. She checked the steak and kidney pie she had going in a low oven for James and Arthur's lunch, then went outside and put on her riding boots and grabbed her Akubra hat. It was time to take Cosmo, sired by one of their new stallions, for a run. Although there were many other foals frisking by their mothers' sides, Kathleen had fallen in love with this chestnut one nearly as much as she had with Shannon Boy. Every time she did her rounds of the paddocks to check all was well he would rush over and nuzzle his nose into her face. She had worked out a good routine, which gave them both some exercise. She would saddle up Cosmo's mother, put her camera into the saddlebag, raise herself into the saddle and Arthur would then hand her Cosmo's lead rope. With a wave to Arthur they would set off. Not once had Cosmo tried to break free. It was as if he looked forward to this game and there was no way he was going to spoil it. Today they twisted their way through the bush towards the hill near Snake Gully Road, where she coaxed the mare into a canter and the three of them raced up the track. At the top of the hill Kathleen dismounted and tied Cosmo and his mother to a tree to graze. Getting out her camera she wandered through the bush to see what she could find. There was a kookaburra sitting on a tree stump that would make a great photograph. On her favourite rock she sat down and gazed over Eureka Park towards the river she had grown to love so much.

She thought of Lillie at Drominderry House on the beautiful Kenmare River. Although Kathleen missed Rathgarven at times, she didn't pine for it any more. Eureka Park was her home now. Despite what had happened with Ronan and Clara, and Ronan being in Vietnam, Kathleen and James had grown closer over the last few months. At times she still thought of Dermot, however it was as if she was a different person back then in Calcutta. Now it was James who she thought of most. James, who had made possible a life for all of them here in Australia, and on the whole it had been a good life. As each day went by she loved him more.

This afternoon she was looking forward to Lorna picking her up for their excursion to Chaffey Dam, where Kathleen could take photos of the water birds, pelicans, plovers, ibis and wild ducks that had made the dam their haven. Next month she had an exhibition of bird photographs scheduled for Roger Mann's gallery in Tamworth.

She stood and clambered back down to the horses, where she sat on the grass at Cosmo's head and let him nuzzle his nose against her knee. She was so grateful this little horse had come along when he did. With him she could try to forget about Ronan being in Vietnam.

***

James was doing bookwork in his office above the stables on Saturday afternoon when he heard a car drive up. Through the window he saw a policeman in a uniform that seemed too small for his burly frame, get out of a police car. James put down his pen and went down to greet him.

'Sorry to bother you, mate,' the policeman said, lifting his hat and pushing his greying hair back on his sweaty forehead. 'I wonder if I could have a moment of your time?'

He paused and looked around. There were a couple of stable hands washing out the stalls, Marcus was tinkering with the tractor nearby and Freddie was carrying a bucket of feed for one of the mares.

'Is it about my son in Vietnam?' James asked, fear rising in his throat.

If anything happened to Ronan, would it be a phone call? Or would it be a policeman arriving like this?

'No mate. Nothing like that. Might be better if we went somewhere private, though. What I'm about to tell you isn't general knowledge. Nevertheless, the powers that be reckoned we should let you know before it gets in the papers.'

James sighed in relief. 'Come,' he said, and beckoned for the man to follow him back upstairs to his office, where he showed him to a chair in front of his cluttered desk.

455

The policeman sat down and placed his hat on his lap. 'You're aware of the murder case about to start in town?' he asked. 'A woman killed her husband a while back.'

James had read about it in the papers and was amazed to see it was Dawn's friend, Winifred Black, who had murdered her husband. He and Kathleen had wondered what on earth had happened. Then Lillie told them Winifred had been married to Deb's mother's first husband. Lillie hadn't gone into much detail, and the three of them had discussed why Winifred might have done such a thing, given she seemed so timid. Lillie said the husband was supposed to be a bit of a bully and his daughter was as well.

'I knew there'd been an arrest. And the trial was coming up. But what's that got to do with me?'

'It's to do with your friend. The bloke you found down that mine.'

'Finn Malone?'

'Yeah, that's him. It was believed he committed suicide.'

'Believed? Are they now saying he didn't?'

'So it might appear, mate.'

'My God!' James exclaimed, finding it difficult to control the tremor in his voice. 'So how did he end up down that mine?'

''Supposedly Winifred Black's old man put him down there after murdering him.'

James gasped. 'You're joking.'

'No mate, I'm not. Winifred made a statement. Somehow it got leaked. That's why I'm here, as it affects you, being such a good friend of Malone's and taking over this place. We didn't want you to hear it from another source. Plus they may need to come out here to collect evidence.' He took out a pack of Camel and offered James one. Shaking his head James picked up his pipe. The policeman knocked a cigarette out of the packet and lit it.

'But why?' James stammered. 'I mean how?'

456

'It turns out Winifred was a good friend of Malone's wife,' he said.

James's nodded, lighting his pipe. 'Yes I was aware of that. Dawn told us she'd asked her to keep an eye on Finn after she left. Martha Hogan said Winifred used to help out in the corner store. I know my wife, Kathleen tried to make contact with her when we arrived, but she shied away. And she came to Kathleen's photographic exhibition in Tamworth a while back.' He paused, taking a deep draw of his pipe. 'I think she wanted to tell me something, but she took off.'

'Yes, she mentioned that, trying to get it off her chest. Lost her nerve. Anyway, she reckons what happened was that her old man followed her out here the morning of Malone's death. She'd promised Malone that when he came back from Brisbane after drying out, she'd help get the place in order for when you lot arrived. Her old man confronted her and Malone and accused them of having an affair. That's when the bugger took to her, hitting her hard and trying to drag her off. Malone grabbed his gun and told him to leave her alone and get the hell off his property. Rather than leaving, the bastard went to his ute, grabbed his own gun and shot Malone dead before he had time to react.'

James put down his pipe and placed his hand to his heart to stop it pounding. 'You're saying Winifred's husband killed Finn right here. At Eureka?'

'That's what she's saying. The bugger threatened to shoot her as well, and forced her to help him drag Malone's body to his truck, then drove across country to that mine where you found him. She said the old man used to work there when it was a going concern. She reckoned he planted Malone's gun and some empty whisky bottles he'd found back here to make it look like Malone was so drunk he'd taken himself off and topped himself.'

James shook his head. It was difficult to believe what he was hearing. He had always found it odd that Finn had killed himself. But to be shot like that.

'I wonder if Finn had been drinking when he was shot? I mean…'

'Nah… Winifred reckoned he was as sober as a judge. She'd been knocked to the ground and he was trying to help her up when the bugger got him in the head. Didn't have a bloody chance.'

'He shot him in cold blood?'

'Reckon so.'

'What a coward!'

'What's more, Winifred said Malone had been really looking forward to you lot coming. That alone could point to murder rather than suicide.'

'But Finn owed a lot of money…'

'So Winifred said when the question was put to her. He was a slow payer, but would've got round to it… then that happened.'

'He'd let the place go so much…'

'Winifred said he'd lost interest after his wife left. As I said, she was supposed to come out here to help him get it in order before you got here.'

James shook his head again, trying to fathom the dreadful scenario. 'So why didn't Winifred dob her husband in for the murder?'

'Blackmail. He threatened to tell the police that she was having an affair with Malone and that when he rejected her, she went out there and shot him in revenge. A woman scorned.'

'But surely she could have managed to tell her friend Dawn what had happened? After all Dawn used to be married to Finn.'

'Evidently they lost contact when Mrs Malone moved to Sydney. Perhaps when Dawn had come up for the funeral, if Winifred had known she was here, it might've been different.'

James thought back to Finn's funeral. Dawn had told them she was going to visit her friend Winifred, but the husband wouldn't let her in as she was in bed with a bad case of influenza. Obviously he hadn't told her that Dawn had come by.

'Once the daughter went up north, that's when she couldn't take it any longer,' the policeman said. 'She was supposedly threatening to go to the police, when, drunk as a skunk, he started slapping her around and took to her in the kitchen. That's when she picked up the carving knife and… well… we all know what happened next.'

James lifted his pipe from the desk and lit it again as he sat looking at the policeman. The laughing face of his friend flashed before his eyes. James wasn't sure whether to be pleased that he hadn't killed himself, or distraught that he'd been murdered in cold blood.

'Will Winifred Black get off?' he asked.

'If it can be proved the bullet that killed Malone came from her old man's rifle and not Malone's, then she's got a damn good chance of getting a fair hearing.'

James remembered seeing an empty cartridge on the ledge in the stables. At the time he'd wondered how it had got there. He had it in his hand when Arthur came up and told him how he and Lillie had found Dingo playing with it. They'd put it there so that Dingo couldn't get at it again. At the time James had thought it must have come from another of Finn's guns, rather than his John Rigby, as the cartridge was smaller than the .416 of the John Rigby. He was going to throw it in the rubbish, but somehow it had made its way from the pocket of his trousers and into his top drawer, which was full of bits and pieces. As far as James knew it was still there.

'Do you know if they recovered the bullet from Finn's skull?' he asked.

'That's not my field, mate. Though it appeared to be such a clear case of suicide they may not have bothered.'

James opened his drawer and rustled around. 'Our dog was playing with this one day,' he said and handed the cartridge to the policeman. 'I know it's a long shot, but it might help if it can be proved it came out of Black's gun. At least it might prove he was here at some stage with that gun.'

The policeman took the cartridge. 'Looks like it could come from a Winchester.'

'What sort of gun did he have?'

The policeman gave a small smile. 'I'm told the one they're holding as evidence is a Winchester. They found it in the back shed of the Blacks' home.' He stood up. 'I'll take the cartridge with me if you don't mind. I know there's probably lots of Winchesters round. Nonetheless it might help her case.'

'But how would they prove it wasn't Winifred who shot Finn?'

'She reckons she doesn't know how to use a gun. But that's up to the courts to decide.'

'Yes, of course,' James said.

'Anyway, I best be off,' the policeman said, heading for the door. 'We'll keep you posted, mate. Rest assured of that.'

After he left, James stood thinking for some time. Sad as he was for Finn's death, he now knew he was vindicated for doubting his friend had committed suicide. The scenario the policeman had painted was far more likely than a scenario of Finn taking himself off to a disused mine and shooting his brains out. He looked across to the home paddock where he could see Kathleen leading Cosmo on a lunging rope. He began to make his way towards her. What would she think when she discovered their friend had been murdered at Eureka? That he hadn't killed himself down that mine? Although she would be relieved to know Finn hadn't taken his own life, he hoped knowing the murder had taken place here wouldn't distress her too much. At least it wasn't near the house. He glanced across at the paddocks dotted with horses grazing contentedly; from the river came the sound of the water lapping over the stones.

The knowledge that Finn was murdered, rather than having committed suicide, made James want to honour his legacy here at Eureka Park more than ever. Rathgarven and Ireland would always hold a special place in his heart, but Eureka Park was his home now. He'd enjoyed building the business, and it was doing well, with four stallions servicing not only Eureka Park's mares, but many others. And there was a bumper crop of foals frolicking in the paddocks. Much to Kathleen's delight, Shannon Boy had gone on to win a place in the Cox Plate for his new owners, and some of the yearlings they had sold over the years had also had a number of wins, including quite a few at country, town and city meets; even a couple of Group One races at Randwick in Sydney.

The new owners of one of their mares, Kenmare Lass, had asked James and Kathleen to be their guests at Randwick on one occasion. James had been so proud of Kathleen in a tailored white suit and black hat as she mingled with the glamorous crowd. And they both marvelled at the razzamatazz of it all. With pride they watched Kenmare Lass win by a head as they stood under the ornate arches of the 1886 members' stand, which Kathleen said reminded her of colonial architecture in India. Yet, as he stood beside Kathleen that day, James couldn't help thinking back to how he had stood by the racetrack at Killarney and watched the horse he had bet on lose. And how that moment had changed their lives forever. As he had watched Kenmare Lass win that race at Randwick — and standing here now — he wished more than ever that Finn was by his side. Eureka Park stud was becoming so well-known there was now a waiting list for the services of its stallions. Finn had given him that opportunity and James would always be grateful to him for that. He knew what he had to do: he would ask

Father Fogarty to give Finn a full requiem mass, and he would build a small grotto by the river to commemorate his friend.

'What did the policeman want?' Marcus asked, sauntering down to the gate where he stood.

'Go and get Freddie,' James said. 'We'll walk down to Ma and I'll tell you all together.'

As he waited for them to join him, he looked up at the sky and had a strong feeling that Finn was smiling down from above. *Of course I wouldn't have done something so damn silly as to kill myself, dear friend. Not when you lot were coming.*

I should never have doubted you, James thought. Never.

Chapter 48

The first night she was back in Sydney, Lillie rang Eureka Park to speak to everyone. Luckily she'd been able to get her old room back in the Manly flat and had gone straight there from the airport. When Ma told her the whole story of how Uncle Finn had been murdered, she got a huge shock.

'Oh my God! Poor Uncle Finn! Sounds as though he didn't have a chance.'

'No,' Ma said. 'Tragically he didn't.'

'But do you mind living at Eureka, knowing he was murdered there?'

'It makes me feel all the more that we need to make a success of the place. The same as it does your father.'

As soon as she put the phone down, Lillie rang Deb in Armidale.

'Mum said that man was a brute,' Deb told her, 'and he'd often threatened her. Particularly after she left him. So she won't be surprised to know that he might have murdered Finn Malone. Dad was damn lucky he didn't do him in as well when he found out he'd got Mum pregnant.'

Lillie thought back to the day she'd found that empty cartridge with Arthur. Little did she know its significance.

The next week she was on her way home to Eureka Park for Christmas. When the train rattled into Tamworth she was excited to see Ma and Freddie waiting at the station. Ma looked so much better and Freddie seemed to have grown a heap.

'Dad and Marcus have a problem with a mare,' Ma said, giving her a huge kiss. 'So Freddie and I are the welcoming party.'

Lillie gave Freddie a hug. 'You've certainly grown,' she said, pulling his ear and laughing.

'You haven't,' Freddie said.

'You don't have to rub it in.'

'I'll show you the spot where Uncle Finn was murdered,' he said, excitedly. 'Down near the stables.'

'I was the one who found the cartridge case, remember.'

'Now tell me all about Ireland,' Ma said as they walked to the car. 'How is Alice? What it was like down at Drominderry House? And...' she smiled, opening the driver's door and sliding behind the wheel, 'tell me about your Seamus.'

By the time Lillie filled her in on everything they had arrived at the front gate at Eureka. Although Lillie missed Ireland already, particularly Seamus, she was excited to be back home. But how would she feel about Eureka now that she knew it was the scene of a murder? Yet when they got to the homestead and she rushed down to see Dad, Marcus and Arthur, and later when she stood on the spot where she had found the cartridge case, although she felt a great sadness for Uncle Finn, she found it didn't change her feelings about Eureka Park.

The next day she joined Ma, Dad, Marcus and Freddie as Father Fogarty said a full requiem mass for Uncle Finn at the church at Gullumbindy and followed it with a small ceremony at Eureka down by the river in front of the beautiful grotto her father had built for him. Set into the rocks and encased in glass was a lovely, laughing photo of him that had been taken in front of Eureka's homestead.

'And may the Good Lord bring our Ronan home safely,' Father Fogarty added at the end. And they all said 'Amen' to that.

Later on Ma showed her a letter that had just arrived from Ronan. He'd been promoted to lance corporal and was now second in command of his section. Lillie and Ma wondered if this mightn't put him in more danger.

'Not at all,' Dad said. 'In fact, I'm sure he'll be a lot safer.'

But Lillie wasn't so sure.

Back in Sydney after a quiet Christmas with the family, she worked hard at her jobs, which she had managed to get back, before she was to commence her English literature course at Sydney University. She missed Seamus heaps and wrote often. At first he wrote back with glowing words of love and told her how much he was missing her. But for the last few weeks she hadn't had any letters at all. At first she didn't fret, however as the weeks went by she worried he was losing interest. This really upset her as she realised how much he meant to her.

Then she discovered she was pregnant.

***

Lillie had always been like clockwork with her periods. When she missed the first one she put it down to the long trip home having mucked her up. Also she'd been working hard and getting nervous about university and not eating all that well. On missing her second period, she suspected something was wrong. When the doctor in Manly confirmed that she definitely was pregnant, she was so devastated she spent the next two days walking around in a stupor. With no letters from Seamus, Lillie's mind was clouded with doubts. What if he'd met someone else? When she'd left him at Shannon to come home to Australia, he was heading back to Drominderry House for Christmas. In his last letter he'd said he was going up to his flat in Merrion Square in Dublin, which he'd bought with money his grandfather had left him. But she knew the flat had no phone, so she couldn't ring him. She sent a telegram, saying she had urgent news. There was no response.

Being a Catholic, it was against Lillie's morals to have an abortion. Even if she wasn't a Catholic, she'd be unable to kill the tiny being cocooned inside her womb that she and Seamus had made with such love on the shores of Kenmare River. She sat down and wrote a letter to his Dublin address, but she knew it would take an age to get there. In the end she decided to bite the bullet and make an overseas trunk call to Maisie at Drominderry House to see if by chance he was still there.

When Maisie answered the phone, Lillie could hardly get her words out.

'Lillie, is that you?' Maisie asked down the crackly line. 'What's the matter? Has someone died?'

'No, nothing like that. It's just that I was wondering if Seamus definitely went back to Dublin?'

''Tis what he said he be doing.'

'Oh!'

'Have you not heard from him yourself?'

'No. He's stopped writing to me and I've something important to tell him.'

'And what would that be?'

Lillie blurted out that she was pregnant.

'Sure, don't these things happen,' Maisie said in her matter-of-fact way. 'I'll see if Charles can be tracking him down.'

It was as if Lillie had told her she wanted to find Seamus in order to tell him dinner was ready. Then Lillie asked the question that persisted in the back of her mind, waking her at night and making her toss and turn.

'Maisie, do you think Seamus has met someone else?'

There was a moment before Maisie answered. 'Wouldn't he write to tell you if he be doing that?'

Lillie fiddled with the telephone cord. 'Yes. I suppose you're right.'

All the same, Lillie wasn't so sure. He was a darn attractive man. And she had left him there in Ireland, where there were thousands of gorgeous Irish girls floating around looking for a man like him. He'd begged her to stay and she'd refused. What made her imagine he'd wait for her?

In the end Lillie had to come to terms with the fact that Seamus had probably forgotten her and met someone else. Otherwise, wouldn't he still be writing? She looked at the Claddagh ring on her finger, touched it with her lips, and took it off.

***

Freddie and Marcus were the first in the family to find out about Lillie's baby. They'd come down to Sydney for a weekend visit when she'd started to show.

'You've put on a bit a weight,' Freddie said, giving her a kiss. 'It suits you,'

'She's pregnant, you dolt!' Marcus pointed out, looking at Lillie's swollen belly. 'Any fool can see that.'

Freddie's eyebrows shot up and he looked at Lillie.

'Yes. I am.'

'Wow,' Freddie said.

Although she swore Marcus and Freddie to secrecy, there was no way she could hide her pregnancy from her parents forever. But they would probably try and make her give the baby up for adoption. However at this stage Lillie didn't think she wanted to do that. It would, of course, interfere with her work and university studies. On the other hand, she could do most of her assignments at home. Fortunately she hadn't spent all of her savings and with the money she was still earning she would have enough to get her over the first few months. Then she would put the baby in a crèche and find a part-time job.

The next hurdle was to go up to Eureka Park and confess to her parents what had happened.

***

'My, you look well,' her father said when he picked her up from the train in Tamworth. 'You've put on a bit of weight. Suits you.'

Lillie waited until they were on the road out past Gullumbindy before she told him she was pregnant.

He turned and looked at her with a long, hard stare. Then he pulled the car over to the verge of the road and jerked it to a halt. 'You're *what*?' he exploded. 'Please tell me I didn't hear you say that.'

'No, Dad, you did hear me. I'm pregnant. It happened when I was in Ireland. It's Seamus's. The fellow living at Drominderry House I told you about. The one I was getting the letters from.'

James reached for his pipe and then his tobacco pouch. He filled the bowl and put the stem to his mouth. Lillie had never seen Dad look so cross. For a dreadful moment, she thought he was going to shove her out of the car and make her walk.

'Why didn't you take more care?' he demanded furiously.

'It only happened once.'

'Well, my girl, even you should know once is all it takes.'

He fiddled with his lighter and lit the tobacco, took a long draw and exhaled. It was obvious he was trying to control his emotions. After a few minutes sitting stranded in silence, he put the pipe in the ashtray and started the car again.

It wasn't until they reached the entrance to Eureka Park that he spoke again. 'What does the father think?'

'I don't know. I can't contact him.'

'Well if you haven't got a man to marry you, you'll have to look at adopting it out. There's no way you can keep it.'

'Dad. Please. I want to keep it. Truly I do.'

'And how do you plan to cope on your own?' A long pause. 'There may not be another me around the corner, prepared to take you in. Like I did with your mother.'

Lillie looked at him in horror. 'You loved Ma. That's why you married her. Surely.'

James pursed his lips and took a breath. 'It hasn't always been easy, as you well know. Your mother married me because she was pregnant. Her true love, Dermot, had died.' When he glanced over at her, Lillie saw great sadness in his eyes. 'Sometimes that's a hard pill to swallow.'

'She loves you now, Dad. I know she does.'

'Yes, well... that may be so. I hope it's love. Not just gratitude. In any case, your situation will undoubtedly bring back memories for her. As it did when Ronan dropped the bombshell that he was to marry Clara and she found out Dermot was Clara's father.'

'As it brings back memories for you?'

'It can't help but do so.'

Lillie placed her hand on his arm. 'I'm sorry, Dad,' she said. 'Truly I am. I didn't mean it to happen this way.' She paused. 'And despite what you think, I know Ma loves you deeply.' A long pause. 'You do love her, don't you?'

James brought the car to a stop outside the homestead. 'Yes, of course I do. Very much so. Now,' he said, taking the key out of the ignition and sounding cross again, 'we'd best go on up and see what she has to say about the situation you've got yourself into.'

When Kathleen came out of the front door of the homestead, Lillie remained sitting in the car for a few minutes, unable to move.

James sighed. 'No good hiding in here. Best go face the music.'

Eventually Lillie got out of the car and stood by the passenger door as if cemented to the earth. Her mother said nothing. Not even that she'd put on weight. As normal, she gave her a kiss and reached for her small bag. 'Here, I'll take this. You must be starving and dying for a cup of tea.'

When they got inside and went to her bedroom, Lillie turned to her. 'You know, Ma, don't you?'

Kathleen nodded. 'You forget I've been through it four times.' She came over and gave Lillie a kiss. 'Have you heard from Seamus? I presume it's his.'

Lillie nodded. 'I've written and sent a telegram. I haven't heard back. I even rang Maisie at Drominderry House to see if she or Charles knew where he was. They don't know.' She started to cry. 'Dad said I should give it up for adoption. Will he make me?'

'Nonsense,' Kathleen said, placing a consoling arm around her. 'Imagine how tragic it would be if I'd done that with Ronan. You're old enough to make up your own mind. I'm not saying it'll be easy. But I'll be there to help.'

'What about Dad?'

'Leave him to me.'

'And Grandma?'

'Let's not tell her just yet. I think she's had enough shocks for a while.'

Lillie gave her a small smile. 'I know it'll be hard. But I definitely want to keep it.'

'Well, in that case,' Kathleen said, standing back, 'we'd best be getting Ronan's room ready for the new arrival.'

'Have you heard from him this week?'

'Yes. He said it'd been a busy time. He's got a few days of R&R and he's heading down to Vung Tau.' She moved forward and wiped Lillie's eyes with her fingers. 'You'll give up work, I imagine. Come back here.'

'What will everyone think?'

'Who gives a damn fig what other people think?' It was the first time Lillie had heard Ma come anywhere near swearing. 'Did you tell Deb?'

'Yes. I rang her.'

'And what was her reaction?'

'She sounded sorry for me, but said she'd be there for me.'

'Well, there you go. Now,' Kathleen said briskly, 'let's have that tea and then we'll go for a walk down to the stables. There's a new foal, Cosmo, who I just adore.' She smiled. 'Nearly as much as Shannon Boy. Arthur thinks he's got great potential.'

'How is Arthur?'

'Just the same. He's got a girlfriend. Lovely lass. She spends a bit of time out here.'

'Living with him?'

'Only the odd weekend. It appears times have changed. So we have to turn a blind eye.'

Lillie smiled. 'I look forward to meeting her.'

Down in the paddock Ma showed her Cosmo, who was running around, his tail frisking in the wind, his proud head looking around excitedly.

'He is gorgeous,' Lillie said.

'I think he's even more loving than Shannon Boy was.'

'I'm so pleased for you, Ma.'

Lillie was relieved Ma had taken her pregnancy so well and understood why she wanted to keep the baby. Lillie should have realised that's how she'd feel, having been in more or less the same situation with Ronan. What if Ma had given in under pressure? Had an abortion? Or given him away? Lillie couldn't imagine her life without Ronan. And although she was terrified of what the future might hold, she was proud that she'd decided to keep her baby.

***

Three weeks later when Lillie had packed up her things in Manly and come back to Eureka Park, she could see her father was still annoyed with her. Often he was abrupt with her. Her morning sickness made her tired when she was trying to study her uni course by correspondence and she often woke up at 3 a.m. in a panic. How was she going to cope? Once she had the baby she couldn't live here with her parents for the rest of her life, even though she was studying and helping out in the stables to earn her keep. She tried writing one more letter to Seamus. Nothing. Often she cried for no reason at all, just feeling so sad that Seamus had thrown her over like that.

One day when she was sitting on an upturned bucket talking to Arthur down at the stables, complaining that Seamus had dropped her like a hot potato, Arthur came and squatted next to her.

'How you know something mightn't have happened to him?'

'What do you mean?'

'It sounds to me like he was hooked on you. To go off you like that seems kinda odd.'

Lillie shrugged her shoulders. 'He must've met someone else.'

The hardest thing was seeing Arthur and his girlfriend, who had luminous dark eyes and a mass of shiny black hair, so happy. One weekend the two of them went riding up into the hills with their saddlebags bulging with stuff to cook on a campfire.

'Why don't you come with us?' Arthur called as they were packing up to go.

Lillie placed her hand on her belly. 'Don't reckon I should.'

It wasn't that she was frightened of hurting the baby. It was because she didn't want to be a gooseberry. At times she was so depressed she wondered if she shouldn't have had an abortion after all and just not told anyone she was pregnant in the first place. If she'd done that at least her father wouldn't be treating her like a leper. It was almost as if her mother was being overly nice to compensate.

Marcus never mentioned the baby, but every now and then Freddie would come and put his hand on her belly and say 'I'm sure I can feel it moving.' And he'd grab Lillie's hand to make her feel as well. Whenever he saw her looking sad, he gave her a hug and tried to cheer her up. And so did Deb when she was back from Armidale and Lillie told her how she was having second thoughts about having kept the baby.

'You did the right thing,' she said when they met up at Allen's milk bar in Gullumbindy. 'You can decide later if you want to adopt it out or keep it.'

'So you don't think I should keep it?'

'I didn't say that. It'll be hard. That's all I'm saying.'

After this conversation Lillie spent hours wondering if she shouldn't give her baby up for adoption after all. Despite what Deb said, she obviously thought as much. She desperately wished she could talk to Ronan about it, but she hadn't written to him yet to tell him what had happened. When she asked Ma whether she should or not, Ma said it was up to her. So far, Lillie had chickened out. Not just because she was to be an unmarried mother, but also because in the back of her mind she thought it might remind Ronan of what he had missed out on with Clara. And she didn't want him dwelling on that while he was in Vietnam. But sooner or later he would have to know.

***

It was a warm Tuesday afternoon when Lillie sat with her mother on a rug under the maple tree having a cool drink. As she fiddled with the collar around Dingo's neck and wondered when her morning sickness would ease up, she heard a car drive up to the front of the homestead.

'You expecting someone?' she asked Ma, as Dingo broke free and rushed out to see who was there.

'Could be the vet for the mare that's foundered, but surely he'd go down to the stables.' Lillie heard a car door bang shut and footsteps going up to the front verandah.

'I'll go and see who it is,' Kathleen said. 'I had an Avon woman call in last week. Maybe this is her dropping off what I ordered.'

A few minutes later Kathleen returned. By her side was Seamus.

Lillie's eyes nearly popped out of her head. Where in God's name had he come from? He looked so handsome standing there next to Ma. His hair was longer and he was wearing a pair of cream moleskins and a bottle-green corduroy jacket that almost matched his eyes.

'What the hell are you doing here?' she exclaimed.

'Isn't that a grand way to be welcoming a poor sod who's travelled across the globe after his gorgeous lady left him to pine away in Ireland.' He looked at Kathleen. 'I must say I got a far better welcome from your beautiful mother.'

'Why didn't you answer my letters?' Lillie demanded. 'Yours had stopped coming before that anyway.' She knew her tone was sharp. She couldn't help it. Did he think he could waltz in here and expect her to be all over him? Like Dingo had done. She was pregnant with his child, for Godsakes, and he'd more or less abandoned her. He should have written. 'And how did you know I was here?' she asked. 'And not in Sydney?'

'I rang Drominderry House and spoke to Maisie. She told me you'd been trying to contact me. Said your mother had written and you were up here.'

Lillie pressed her hand to her stomach. 'Did Maisie tell you what I told her?'

'She did. And I thought to myself, what a lucky man you are, Seamus Flaherty! You're going to be a dad. You'd better hightail it across the world and see how your gorgeous wife-to-be is.'

Lillie shook her head. 'Why on earth should I marry you? I'd more or less given you up for dead — and I want to finish my degree anyway.'

'You'll marry me because you love me. And,' he added with a wink, coming over and giving her a passionate kiss on the lips, 'I happen to be in love with you. I'll even help you with your degree. So you'll need a darn good excuse to get out of a wedding. Is that not right, Mrs O'Sullivan?'

Kathleen nodded. 'Yes, that sounds perfectly right to me, Seamus. Though I must correct you on one thing. You can drop the Mrs bit, particularly if you're to be my son-in-law. Kathleen will do fine.'

'Ma!' Lillie exclaimed.

'I'll leave you two to catch up,' Kathleen said, ignoring Lillie. She looked at Seamus. 'Is that car out the front a hire car?'

'I picked up a Hertz in Sydney. They kindly said I could drop it off in Tamworth when I'm finished with it.'

'I presume you'll be staying the night, then.'

Seamus turned his gaze to Lillie. 'I hope so.'

'It depends on what you tell me,' Lillie said. 'Why did you stop writing?'

When Kathleen had gone inside, Seamus sat down on the rug next to Lillie. He picked up her hand and kissed it gently. Then he stroked her hair and tilted her face towards him. 'I'm sorry, but I didn't get your last letters. You see, after Christmas when I went back to Dublin, I was having a bit of writer's block. I thought a change of scenery would do me good. So I went to Paris.'

'Couldn't you have had your mail forwarded?'

'I was only going for a week or so. Then it sort of got under my skin. And I decided to stay around a bit longer.'

'But your letters stopped.'

'So I gather. I've heard the French postal system's the worst in the world. And that's before the strike they had. I can only presume they're winging their way across the skies right now.'

Around them the afternoon light was fading. Birds swooped and dived and there was the continuous mantra of cicadas. A soft breeze blew and deep shadows were forming where they sat under the maple tree. Dingo got up from where he'd collapsed in a heap under the bottlebrush by the fence and sauntered over. First he put his head on Lillie's knee for a pat. Then he nudged Seamus, who tickled him behind the ear.

'I need time to think about what's happened,' she said. 'I got a shock to see you, that's all.'

'I can understand that.'

Lillie looked past him to where the breeze was shifting the leaves in the weeping willows. She looked back at him and sighed.

'Would you mind if I went for a walk down to the river? On my own. I can always work things out better down there.'

'Of course. And while you're there I might wander along and take a look at the horses I passed on the way in.'

Lillie nodded. 'You might meet up with Dad. Or Arthur, the head stable hand. They'd probably be at the stables.'

'You sure you wouldn't like me to come with you?'

'No, Seamus. I need to be on my own.'

Down by the river Lillie paced up and down. Her emotions were churning in her stomach. On one hand she was still annoyed with Seamus, despite the fact he said he'd written. And was he only asking her to marry him because she was carrying his child? On the other hand, he had flown across the world to see her. She could go on being angry with him. Or she could do what her heart was telling her to do: believe that he really did love her and accept his proposal. Apart from the fact she loved him with all her heart, there was also their baby to think about. To bring up a child without a father, when that father had offered to marry her, would be a huge burden to carry if she refused him because of pride. She sat down on the riverbank and fiddled with a piece of wood, pulling the bark off in strips and throwing them into the water, watching them float downstream like rickety canoes.

Ten minutes later she went back up to find Seamus.

When she found him he was leaning over the fence of the front paddock, talking to Cosmo.

'I caught up with your father and Arthur,' he said. 'They're tied up with a vet down at the stables. So I'm getting to know this little fella.'

'His name's Cosmo,' Lillie said, patting the horse on the nose. 'He's been great for Ma. After Shannon Boy went.'

Seamus looked at her with a worried expression. 'So what's the final decision? Am I to stay? Or hightail it back to Ireland without my lovely bride?'

Lillie reached her hand out and caressed his face. 'If your letters turn up,' she grinned, 'I might consider marrying you. If they don't… Well… I'll have to think again, won't t I?'

'So the state of my poor heart is going to rely on the postal system?'

Lillie laughed. 'Looks like it.'

'In the meantime,' he said, rustling in his pocket and handing her a small black box. 'I have a wee offering.'

Lillie turned the box over in her hands. 'What's this?'

'Look inside.'

When she opened the box she gasped as she saw a stunning emerald ring set in gold nestled on a black velvet cushion.

Seamus leaned forward and took hold of the ring. 'I found it in Paris. Even before I heard you were expecting my child I knew I wanted to buy you this ring. I thought I'd hold onto it until you came back to Ireland for Christmas like you said you would.'

When he placed it on her finger it was far too big and swivelled around. 'There,' he laughed. 'It'll give time for my letters to arrive while we get it adjusted.'

'Thank you,' Lillie said, leaning forward and giving him a kiss. 'I love it.'

***

Fortunately for Seamus, his first letter arrived in five days' time and Lillie's flatmate sent it on. The next day another one turned up.

'Just as well,' Lillie said, fiddling with the emerald ring, which they still hadn't got adjusted, but instead had managed to get an insert put in, as Lillie felt her fingers would swell later in her pregnancy, 'otherwise I'd have to give this back.'

At first Lillie wasn't so sure whether Dad had taken to Seamus or if he was just relieved his wayward daughter wouldn't have a bastard child after all. However, the longer Seamus stayed at Eureka, sleeping in Ronan's room, the more she realised the two men liked each other a lot, and often sat on the back verandah together enjoying a glass of port after dinner. Marcus and Freddie took him fishing and rabbit trapping with Arthur and once they all went camping overnight. Ma loved him and spoilt him rotten with lots of biscuits and cakes and showed him how to develop photos in her darkroom. Lillie wished Ronan was here to meet him; she was sure they'd get on too.

After the banns of marriage had been announced each Sunday for a month, she and Seamus were married on a bright sunny day at the small church in Gullumbindy with Father Fogarty officiating and Deb as Lillie's bridesmaid. Arthur, who had shown Seamus how to skin a snake and make fire out of stone, was roped in as his best man. Lillie wore a cream silk shift she'd found in a David Jones catalogue that fell loosely over her bump. And Ma made her a garland of flowers for her hair. She and Deb had done a wonderful job with the flowers in the church with a bunch of gardenias attached to each pew and huge vases of white lilies at the altar.

'Lilies for Lillie,' Deb had laughed when Lillie saw them the evening before the wedding when they had a rehearsal at the church. There were more bunches in the sink in the sacristy waiting to be put in vases.

Although at six months pregnant she felt as fat as a porpoise, Lillie did feel pretty. And immensely happy.

'You look gorgeous,' Deb said as she'd helped her get ready at Eureka before the drive into Gullumbindy.

Deb had finally met Seamus one lunchtime at the Telegraph Hotel. 'He's a real spunk,' she'd gushed, 'and charming to boot. Maybe I should head over to Ireland to find a bloke like him.' Deb had had a few boyfriends, but none had quite measured up to her wish list, which Lillie knew included Ronan. Lillie was chuffed to know she thought Seamus was all right.

'He's a good man,' her father whispered in her ear as they waited at the back of the church to walk down the aisle. 'Your mother and I know he'll look after you and the babe.'

'Thank you, Dad.' Lillie smiled up at him. 'And thank you for everything you have done for me.'

He squeezed her arm. 'Come, Seamus is waiting.'

When they passed Ma, Marcus and Freddie on the way to the altar, Lillie found it difficult to stop the tears. At the altar Father Fogarty gave her a warm smile. Right through the mass she could hardly concentrate, she felt so happy. All those years ago when she first met Seamus she had no idea that they would end up in a fairytale like this. When he took the simple gold band they'd chosen together from the Angus and Coote catalogue and placed it on her finger next to the emerald, Lillie could no longer stop the tears falling down her cheeks.

'I love you, Lillie,' Seamus said, wiping her tears away with his finger.

Lillie was sad that Ronan wasn't there to share her joy. She'd had a lovely letter from him wishing her good luck and saying how much he was looking forward to meeting his brother-in-law.

Mind you, he wrote, *I hope the poor bloke knows what he's let himself in for.*

She also wished Grandma was there. Last month she and Seamus had rung her to let her know they were getting married. Taking a deep breath Lillie had also told her that she was pregnant. There was a long silence on the end of the line before Grandma said, 'Well, I'm sure you'll have a beautiful baby, darling. And I'm very pleased you and Seamus are getting married.'

As she looked at Seamus, she was so glad that Grandma had encouraged her to stay just that bit longer in Ireland. Although her pregnancy had been a shock at first, now she wouldn't wish it any other way. Taking hold of Seamus's hand, she squeezed it so tight that he gave a mock wince. Then he leant down and gave her a long lingering kiss and her heart soared with joy. Joy for her and Seamus. And joy for the little being inside her.

She saw the happiness in her parent's faces as she and Seamus walked down the aisle together as man and wife. Even Marcus looked delighted, and Freddie's grin was so large she thought his face might crack.

After the wedding ceremony there was a small party in the garden at Eureka Park. Lorna Medlow gave Lillie a kiss and patted her stomach. 'I hope your new arrival gives your parents as much pleasure as our little Margo does.'

The day after the wedding, Lillie and Seamus left for a honeymoon at Noosa. They took a small flat on Hastings Street and swam at the beach every day.

'If this is what married life's like,' Seamus chuckled, falling down on the sand next to Lillie on their first day there, 'well, I think I'll manage to cope just fine.'

Lillie placed her hand on her swollen belly. 'You'd best enjoy it while you can. Soon it'll be a screaming baby. And lots of nappies to wash.'

'Ah,' Seamus said. 'Won't that be grand?'

With the sound of the waves breaking on the shore and a warm breeze ruffling her hair, Lillie thought how fortunate she was to have Seamus. If only Ronan was back from Vietnam, life would be complete.

Chapter 49

Lillie and Seamus were not long back from Noosa when the phone rang one Thursday morning. Kathleen went down the hallway to answer it, and a moment later let out a piercing shriek of anguish. What she dreaded had happened.

'Oh my God,' she spluttered down the phone, making the sign of the cross. 'Ronan… Ronan...'

'I'm so sorry,' said the Catholic padre on the other end of the line. 'So very sorry. And that I have to tell you this sad news over the telephone. We would have got your parish priest, Father Fogarty to come and tell you, but he's away on a retreat.'

Kathleen tried to swallow the huge boulder in her throat. Her head was racing and she felt faint. 'How did it happen?' she managed.

'A mine in a paddy field. Your son was behind the poor bloke who stepped on it. That's when he was hit by flying shrapnel.'

Kathleen had read about those deadly mines and had feared that Ronan might be injured by one.

'I'm afraid I can't tell you much more, Mrs O'Sullivan,' the padre said. 'That's really all I know. He was picked up by an Iroquois and taken to the field hospital at Vung Tau. A Hercules will evacuate him to hospital in Sydney in the next day or so. You should be able to see him then.'

Kathleen remembered another time like this. A telegram. Now it was his son. And both had been in Vietnam. How could God allow this to happen twice?

'Is he conscious?' she asked.

'I'm sorry, Mrs O'Sullivan. I don't know that.' There was a long pause. 'I'm saying a mass here in Holsworthy shortly. I'll ask the troops to pray for him.'

'Thank you,' Kathleen said. 'We would appreciate that very much.'

She asked for the address of the hospital where they would bring Ronan, and put the receiver back in its cradle. Then she collapsed in tears on the floor. Curling herself into a ball she rocked back and forth, sobbing as she had never sobbed before. Not even when Dermot had died.

This is where Lillie found her. 'Ma,' she screamed, rushing down the hallway. 'What's the matter?'

When Kathleen told her she gasped. 'No… no…!'

'Oh Lillie… it's my fault…'

Lillie knelt down. 'Ma. It's not your fault… it's a horrid, horrid war.'

Kathleen wiped her nose on the sleeve of her shirt. She couldn't get the image of Ronan's broken body from her mind. When Dermot died he'd been burnt beyond recognition and his remains had been brought back to Calcutta from Vietnam. She'd stood beside his grave as a bugler played 'The Last Post' and his coffin was lowered into the ground at Bhowanipore Military Cemetery. What she didn't know then was that she was carrying his child. Please, please God, don't let that child die.

'Shall I go and get Dad?' Lillie asked, placing her hand on her shoulder.

'Yes, please do,' she said, wiping her eyes.

'Will you be okay here?'

Kathleen nodded. 'Thank God Marcus and Freddie are up at school.'

'But we'll have to let them know.'

'Not until I've seen Ronan.'

'Mum. It might be in the papers. Someone could tell them.'

'Yes,' Kathleen said. 'You're probably right.' And imagined the horror in Freddie's eyes. Marcus's, too. Oh, Ronan, she inwardly cried. My darling Ronan… please, please have the strength to pull through. For all our sakes.

***

Once the Hercules arrived in Sydney, Ronan was placed into an ambulance and taken to hospital. When Kathleen and James entered the ward, he was lying unconscious with drips in his arms; around him machinery blinked and beeped.

'Oh Ronan… what has happened to you?' Kathleen whispered, moving to take his hand.

His beautiful face was as pale as the sheets that covered him and his eyes were closed. James put a hand on her shoulder.

'He's lucky he's fit,' the doctor said as he came into the room.

He beckoned Kathleen and James outside. There he told them that the main damage to Ronan — apart from a severe blow to the head, which was why they were keeping him in an induced coma to see if there was any brain trauma — was extensive damage to his right leg, which had taken the full force of the shrapnel.

'Will he be all right?' Kathleen asked, afraid what the answer might be.

'As I said, it's lucky he's fit. So I have no reason to believe he won't pull through.'

Kathleen let out a sigh of relief. 'Will he walk again?' she asked.

'We don't know,' the doctor said. 'Time will tell.'

Kathleen looked desperately at James. 'Oh my God!'

The doctor put a hand on her arm. 'We should be grateful he's still with us. He was lucky there was a medic close by. Otherwise it could've been a lot worse.'

'It's just that he never should've been there in the first place…'

'None of those young men should be there, Mrs O'Sullivan.'

***

Ronan tried to focus. He looked at the machinery by his bed and the blurry figure of the woman sitting beside him.

'How can I rest when you're here, Clara?' he whispered.

'You must,' she said.

Ronan tried to work out how he had got here. And why. But none of that mattered. All that mattered was that Clara was sitting here by his bed. In Vietnam he'd thought of her constantly. He loved her more than any human being had a right to love another. It wasn't something you could expunge from your heart, it wasn't like rubbing a line of chalk from a blackboard.

'Where am I?' he asked.

'In hospital in Sydney,' she said.

Now it came back to him. A paddy field. A woman. A baby. An explosion. Pain, dreadful pain.

The night before it happened, Clara had come to visit.

'Ronan,' she had called out, rushing into his hutchie in the jungle. 'It's all a horrid mistake. You're not my brother after all. We can get married. Oh, Ronan… can you believe that?'

She had lain down beside him and kissed him on the lips. He felt the pounding of her heart on his own pounding chest. Her tongue inside his mouth. For so long he hadn't allowed himself to think of her like that. Every time an image of their entwined bodies came into this mind he shoved it away, believing it was a crime to

485

recall such ecstasy. But now she was there with him in his hutchie, and they were no longer brother and sister, it wasn't wrong at all.

It was so, so right.

'Clara,' he now said as she sat by his bed. 'Clara…'

Again she told him to rest.

When he'd woken up in his hutchie in the jungle, Clara wasn't there. He remembered the emptiness as reality hit. She had never been there. And here he was lying alone on his sodden ground sheet in his putrid jungle greens in the steaming heat as part of this godforsaken nightmare of a war where the impenetrable jungle was riddled with Viet Cong guerrillas, booby traps, ambushes, a shocking assortment of poisonous spiders, snakes and Christ knows what else. And the ground was littered with mines. Early the next morning he had gone on patrol as if on automatic pilot. There was a torrential downpour and he did not much care whether he lived or died. Without Clara life was hardly worth the fight.

His platoon came to a small paddy field and saw a woman lying injured in the middle of it. Her baby was crying. Was it a set up? Many were. Yet the baby's crying was too hard to ignore. It was as he and a fellow soldier were creeping across the field to try and help them that the mine went off. It blew the other bloke clean into the air and Ronan felt the shrapnel hit him. He lay on the ground in such pain he thought he would die. In a way he was pleased about that. What followed was a blur of stretchers, padres, drips, aeroplanes, and ambulances. Now he was here. And Clara was at his side. It wasn't a dream this time.

'Would you like a glass of water?' she asked.

'Yes, darling, please.'

When she handed him the water he smiled at her. This time the blurriness lifted. It was Ma sitting beside him. Not Clara.

'Where's Clara?' he asked. 'She was here.'

Kathleen smiled gently. 'I'm sorry, darling. She's not here.'

'Where's she gone?'

'She was never here.'

'But I saw her. I heard her.'

'It was just me, darling.'

Ronan noticed the worried expression on Ma's face. Her eyes red-rimmed from lack of sleep, her hair even greyer than when he last saw her. How could he have mistaken her for Clara?

'I think it's the drugs,' Kathleen said. 'They've affected your mind.'

Ronan turned away. An image of Clara projected itself onto the wall opposite. It was when she had first arrived at Eureka Park and they were down by the river. She was wearing her white bikini and laughing. Beside her was Dingo. Next to Dingo were Marcus and Freddie. Lillie was there, too. And Dad and Ma. He remembered how much he had tried not to look at Clara, when all he wanted to do was stare and stare. She was so beautiful. All too clearly now he saw the truth: Clara had never been to his hutchie in Vietnam. She had never been sitting beside his bed. She had disappeared from his life a long time ago. But without Clara, why was he still here? What was the point?

Some time later he focused on Ma again. The mother he loved so much. The mother who had given him life. His gaze wandered back to the wall; the image of that afternoon by the river was still so clear. Clara was no longer there, but Lillie was. So was Dad, Marcus and Freddie. Even Dingo. Most of all Ma was there, laughing, telling Freddie to stop teasing Clara. Ronan took a deep breath that made his chest hurt. His life might no longer have Clara in it, but it did have the rest of his family. He owed it to them to pull through. After a moment he tried moving his right leg. There was no feeling in it at all.

'Don't try to move, darling,' Kathleen said, and he could see the tears shining in her eyes. 'I'll go and get the doctor.'

Shortly afterwards the doctor arrived and bluntly told Ronan what his injuries were. Which was the way Ronan wanted it; no bullshit. When he'd gone Ronan asked Ma to leave him for a while. It felt as if a thick veil had been thrown over his determination to pull through. What was the point? Not only did he not have Clara, the damage to his leg was so severe he might never walk again without crutches.

'If I'd given in when your father died,' Ma said when she came back some time later, 'I wouldn't have you. If you give in now, you'll be letting me down.' She took a deep breath and put her hand on his. 'We'll get through this, darling. I know we will. And you'll soon be up and about.'

'That's a load of baloney, Ma,' Ronan said. 'Don't belittle me by lying.'

Silence pervaded the room. Ronan tried to come to terms with the life ahead of him. Bad as he felt, he knew if he gave in now, Ma, who had gone through so much, would be grief-stricken. For her sake he should try to pull himself together. He saw his father come in carrying two coffees. For his sake as well he should snap out of it.

He took Ma's hand and gave it a squeeze. 'I won't give in,' he said to them both. 'I promise.'

And he meant it.

***

But it wasn't easy. He went through two operations on his leg and it was weeks before he was able to get out of bed. Lillie came down to see him the first week and brought Marcus and Freddie with her. She looked so distraught to see his condition that Ronan found he was the one trying to cheer her up.

'You sure you not having twins?' he said. 'Seems a huge bump for just one.'

Lillie patted her stomach. 'Seamus thought he'd wait to come down until you feel a little better. He didn't want to intrude.'

'I'm not all that keen on joining the Army now,' Freddie said. 'Not if I can end up like this.'

Marcus stood by his bed and scoffed. 'Stupid idiot for getting hit like that. Should have been more careful.'

Good old Marcus, Ronan thought. You never change.

But he had to admit Marcus was spot on. When Ronan was finally released from the hospital, he had to stay in Sydney for rehabilitation. He was pleased when Ma found a small house close to the hospital, big enough for them both and for the rest of the family to visit. Sometimes Dad came down and relieved her. Or it might be Lillie and Seamus, who Ronan thought a decent bloke.

'You sure you know what you're in for with my sister?' Ronan said with a grin when he first met Seamus. 'She's pretty bossy.'

Seamus laughed, placing his arm around Lillie. 'I've got a fair idea. But I daresay I'm in for a few surprises.'

Ronan went to outpatients every day, where the physios worked so hard with him that after six weeks he was able to shuffle about with the help of crutches, before graduating to a stick. One Saturday his friend Dave was down for the weekend and insisted he come out for a drink with him at a nearby beer garden.

'Dave's thinking of going to New Zealand over the summer,' he said to Ma the next day. 'He's told me to get better so I can go with him.'

'That's a great idea, darling.'

'A mate of his owns a deer farm. Seems to be doing well. With all this time on my hands I've been trying to work out what to do with my life.'

'There's always Eureka.'

'Yeah, I know. But maybe I can get a piece of dirt of my own at some stage. Deer farming might be the thing if I find the right spot. I'll get a bit of compensation from the Army to keep me going till it's up and running.'

'It gives you something to work towards,' Kathleen said. 'First New Zealand and then we can look around for a small farm or something.'

So that's what Ronan tried to focus on when he woke in the night, worrying what would become of him.

Then one morning the physio said to him, 'We can do no more for you here. The rest is up to you.' He looked at Ma. 'He might as well go back to Eureka Park and continue his exercises there.'

Two days later his father drove down and collected them. As Ronan sat in the back seat of the car looking out over the countryside, he remembered when they had first driven up in the Holden in 1963. So much had happened since then, not least of which was this bloody leg of his. He tried not to think about Clara. But it was impossible. He only had to feel the pain in his leg to remember why he had gone to Vietnam.

Chapter 50

Lillie almost cried as she watched Ronan hobble around the garden and down to the stables when he first came back to Eureka. She also suspected it wasn't only his external injuries he was trying to come to terms with and that Clara was still causing him immense pain. Once she had asked him to play his guitar, but he refused. Was it because it would remind him of Clara singing with him?

'Do you think we should let Jessica know that Ronan was injured?' she asked her father not long after Ronan had arrived at the hospital in Sydney. 'I'm sure Clara would want to know what's happened. Maybe Jessica's got some idea where she is. I know Ronan said he and Clara didn't really want to keep in touch. But if I were in her shoes I'd want to know. She must still care about him a lot.'

Eventually her father nodded. 'Yes, you're probably right.'

But when Lillie rang Jessica's number, another woman answered the phone. Jessica wasn't there. She told Lillie she was Jessica's friend Mary Archer.

'I've been living with Jessica to help her with the rent. Can I pass a message on?'

When Lillie explained who she was and how Ma and Jessica had been friends for years and Clara had been out to stay with them in Australia, she said: 'Jessica told me all about your family. I'm sure she won't mind me telling you that she's in hospital. Cancer. All that smoking caught up with her in the end. It seems to have taken a hold.'

'Oh. How awful,' Lillie said. 'Does Clara know?'

'Not that I'm aware of. Jessica and I have tried to find her. A bit like looking for a needle in a haystack. If you want to get lost in London it's so easy. Not that we know for sure if she's still in London.'

'I suppose she could be anywhere.'

'Exactly.'

'Could you give me Jessica's address at the hospital? I'm sure Ma would like to drop her a line.'

'Of course… I'll get it.'

Lillie and James agreed that Ma should be told, but when Lillie rang her down in Sydney she said she was far too concerned about Ronan to be worried about Jessica.

'What if Clara gets in touch with her?'

'Well, if you've got Jessica's address, maybe you could drop her a line.'

So Lillie did. But the family hadn't heard back.

One afternoon when she was sitting on the back verandah while Ronan was doing his rehabilitation exercises nearby, Seamus strode across the lawn and sat down beside her. He put his hand on her belly.

'And how's that baby of mine this afternoon?'

'Kicking and shoving as though it wants to get out. Now.'

'Well, perhaps we should take a stroll down to the horses and that might get things on the move. How about you, Ronan?'

Ronan shook his head. 'You two head off. I'll work here a little longer.'

Lillie was pleased that Ronan and Seamus got on so well. They both loved rugby and when Ronan was still doing rehab in Sydney Seamus sent him books on Irish history, which Ronan devoured. Seamus had ditched the book he was writing on the Crimean War to write another about the uprising in Ireland, which he had called *The Chalice,* and he gave Ronan the manuscript to read.

'Rathgarven features in it a great deal,' he'd said to Lillie, when he first arrived at Eureka Park and gave her a copy. 'Well, I don't call it Rathgarven in the book. I call it Ballymont. I didn't want that Donoghue man getting any spin off out of it if, by chance, it became successful. Which,' he laughed, 'is highly unlikely. Mind you, I put all the right ingredients in — sex, lies, betrayal, violence. The lot. As you well know, it was an explosive time back then.'

When Lillie finished it she thought it was one of the best stories she'd ever read. Ma and Dad thought the same.

'You've captured the burning of Rathgarven so well,' James said. 'I was only very young but I do have certain memories.'

'But you've never seen Rathgarven,' Lillie said to Seamus.

'Ah, but your descriptions were enough to fire my imagination.'

'Well, it's very good,' Kathleen said. 'Congratulations.'

'Ah, you're all biased,' Seamus had chuckled, sounding chuffed all the same.

***

It was now coming close to the time when Lillie and Seamus had to make a decision about where they were going to live. Seamus couldn't stay in Australia forever. He had a bit of money saved from the earnings of his last book, and he had some dividends from shares, which they were living on. He'd sent his manuscript of *The Chalice* to his agent, but hadn't heard back.

'I'll need to go see him and give him a push when we get back to Dublin,' he said to Lillie.

Fortunately when the Australian government heard that his wife was pregnant, they gave Seamus an extension on his visa, but that would run out in a few months. Since their honeymoon, he and Lillie had been living together in the manager's cottage — Arthur had decided to take a year off and travel around Australia with his girlfriend. Although James had employed another head stable hand in Arthur's absence, he lived at Gullumbindy and travelled out each day, meaning the manager's cottage was free. Lillie had decorated it with seagrass matting and cane furniture, making it feel homely.

'I could get used to this,' Seamus proclaimed one balmy evening as they sat on the verandah looking down on the river. On the far bank the cattle were milling as they usually did at this time of the day. 'If I didn't have a flat in Dublin I'd suggest we make your parents an offer and live here forever. It's a grand spot for a writer.'

'I know you could apply for residency,' Lillie said. 'But you wouldn't survive without Ireland. And Ireland wouldn't survive without you.'

'Your family has coped.'

'That's different,' Lillie said.

But she wondered if it was much different after all. Lillie knew her father missed Ireland. There wasn't an Irishman in the whole world who didn't dream of his homeland. No matter what success they'd had in their new homes, Ireland, with its emerald fields and haunting music, would always hold their hearts. Much as Lillie loved Australia and would miss her family, she too was missing Ireland. And she would like to be closer to Grandma before she got much older and frailer. The only cloud was that she wouldn't be able to go back to Rathgarven. But at least she could visit Drominderry House and see Maisie and Paddy and gaze down on the beautiful Kenmare River.

'How soon do you think we can fly after the baby comes?' Seamus asked.

'Maybe if we plan to go back when it's around four months. If you like I'll ring Qantas and see if we can get a reasonable fare then.'

'That sounds like a good idea,' Seamus said, getting up to give her a kiss. 'Mind you, my freezing cold flat in Dublin will be a lot different to this.'

Lillie looked down to the river with the last of the sun shimmering across its smooth surface. Seamus was right. It certainly would be different.

***

'Oh my God,' Lillie screamed. 'I don't think I can do this. Can't you give me anything? Gas or something?'

'You've had enough, love. If you have any more you won't be able to push,' the officious white-clad nurse said as she wiped Lillie's brow with a wet cloth. 'A few more hard pushes and you'll be there.'

The pain was so excruciating Lillie thought she was going to die. Her mother had gone through this four times. How had she done that?

'Push,' the nurse urged again, standing at the end of the bed. Now the door opened and the doctor came rushing in.

'I think it's about to come,' the nurse said to him.

Sure enough, just as Lillie thought she couldn't cope with the agony a second longer or push any more, she felt her baby slide out from between her legs and she heard a loud bellowing cry.

'Oh my God! What is it?' she stammered.

'A girl,' the doctor said. A few minutes later he handed a messy bundle to her. 'A beautiful, perfect little girl.'

Lillie looked at her daughter and felt such a rush of love she immediately forgot the pain she had just endured.

When Seamus set eyes on her he declared, 'She's a bonny wee lass. Like her beautiful mother.'

They decided to call her Gemma simply because they both liked the name and she would always be their little gem. For her second name they settled on Alice, which delighted Lillie's parents.

When Marcus and Freddie saw her they thought she was the funniest thing they'd seen in a long while. When Ma looked at Gemma she burst out crying.

'She looks so like you,' she said to Lillie. 'I don't believe it.'

'Nothing of me at all then?' Seamus asked. 'Not a smidgen?'

'I can see she's got your eyes,' James said diplomatically.

As Gemma had been born with blue eyes — as nearly all Caucasian babies were — and Seamus's joyous eyes were so obviously green, both Lillie and Ma laughed.

The next day Ronan came in with Seamus. For some reason Lillie got a shock when she saw him walking with his stick. With all that had happened over the last day or so, she had more or less forgotten about his injuries. Although she could see he was genuinely happy for her, she was sad for him. This is what he thought would happen when he had proposed to Clara.

***

On a brisk morning with a stiff wind blowing and everyone rugged up in warm coats, Father Fogarty christened Gemma at the church in Gullumbindy. Deb and Ronan were godparents. Outside the church afterwards the family stood on the steps posing for photographs. Gemma was screaming her little head off, causing Freddie to exclaim, 'She doesn't like having her photo taken, so we should stop doing that right now!'

Lillie soon realised that being a mother was no piece of cake. She seemed to be forever sitting with Gemma attached to her breast, trying to pacify her, or washing bucketloads of dirty nappies and hanging them on the line to dry. It was as if a Martian had dropped down from the sky and taken hold of her life and turned it upside down. In fact Lillie wasn't sure how she would have coped without Ma during those first few weeks. It wasn't only the lack of sleep, it was the feeling of hopelessness when Gemma screamed, kicking her legs in the air and flailing her little arms.

'It's only wind,' Ma would say, placing her over her shoulder and burping her.

And sure enough Gemma would settle down until Lillie was ready to feed her again. However, if Lillie tried to mimic Ma and lay Gemma over her shoulder to burp her, she would continue to bellow.

'She must sense you're an anxious new mum,' Ma said one day when Lillie came to the homestead bemoaning there was no way she could stop Gemma crying. 'I had the same problem with Ronan. That's when Alice was such a help.'

In some ways Seamus seemed frightened of Gemma. 'What if I drop the wee thing? And she breaks in two?'

And he certainly was no good at changing nappies.

The one who was best with her was Freddie, who spent ages sitting by her bassinet talking to her and trying to calm her down. Lillie was pleased to see Ronan was getting out and about a bit more with his walking stick. His friend Dave often came out to Eureka and they would go off for the day in Dave's car. Ronan told her he had made a firm commitment to go to New Zealand with Dave where Dave's family friend had a deer farm.

'I daresay they'll find me some sort of job,' he said, glancing at his walking stick. 'Even if it's bookwork. Gives me a bit of breathing space before I decide what to do next.'

Lillie thought that was a great idea. He needed to get away from Eureka. In New Zealand he might be able to get over the trauma of Vietnam and forget Clara for a while. He may even meet someone else.

Chapter 51

It was late November 1969 with Gemma now nearly four months old. Lillie and her mother were sitting on a rug in the garden letting her little legs get some sunshine when Lillie picked up the newspaper Ma had been reading. On the front page was a report that Winifred Black had been acquitted, the judge and jury believing her account of Finn's murder and that it was self-defence when she killed her husband. Lillie knew the police had been out to Eureka when she and Seamus were away on their honeymoon to collect evidence and get Winifred to show them exactly what had happened.

As she laid the paper down on the rug, Ma picked it up: 'I hope that poor lady manages to get her life back in some sort of order. I can't imagine what she's been going through.'

'Going through what?' Ronan asked, flopping down on the grass beside them.

Although he still had a dreadful limp, his face had filled out and Lillie thought he seemed reasonably happy. He was looking forward to going to New Zealand with Dave in a few weeks' time.

Lillie showed him the paper. 'We were talking about this again.'

Ronan read the article. 'He must've been a brute of a man.'

'And got what he deserved,' Lillie said.

'True. And it's good she's been acquitted. Anyway,' he added, putting the paper down and pulling himself up, 'I'm heading in to Gullumbindy to post this letter to New Zealand. There's a fishing lodge Dave and I want to visit while we're there. You want anything?'

'No thanks,' Lillie said.

'Me neither,' Ma added. 'Drive safely.'

Lillie watched him head towards his car and move off down the driveway. Now that he could drive again he was so much more independent. 'He does seem a lot better, doesn't he, Ma?'

'New Zealand will do him good. I bet he comes back with all sorts of ideas about running deer or setting up a fishing lodge.'

'If only we still had Rathgarven he could do that there. A fishing lodge on the island would be wonderful.'

'It would, wouldn't it?'

They sat on, enjoying the afternoon, then just as the sun disappeared behind the hill on the other side of the river and they were thinking of going inside, Seamus came rushing through the gate.

'Would you believe this? Guess what Ronan picked up at the post office when he was in there?'

'Haven't got a clue,' Lillie said.

'Lo and behold this telegram I'm holding in my hand.'

'And…?'

'I told you that my grandfather had started a trust that was to mature when I turned 21.' He looked at Ma. 'He did that after my father was killed in the war. With part of that I bought my flat in Dublin. I gave quite a bit of the remainder to a friend of mine who's a stockbroker in London to invest in a portfolio of shares. I must admit I didn't take much interest, apart from receiving the dividends each month. What I didn't realise was that many of those shares were in a nickel company here in Australia, Poseidon.'

'I read about Poseidon in the newspaper late last week,' Kathleen said. 'The shares skyrocketed when they found that nickel site. Along with everyone else I wished we'd invested in it.'

Seamus's smile was so wide that Lillie thought his face might crack. 'My good friend tells me in this telegram that he sold when they were at their peak. He made a whopping profit on my behalf and is waiting to see what I want to do with the money.'

'My God!' Lillie exclaimed.

Seamus held up the telegram again. 'Put it this way, the amount he's made is enough to put a hefty holding deposit on your beloved Rathgarven for you. With the sale of my flat in Dublin we should be able to come up with the whole amount.'

Lillie gulped. 'Rathgarven?'

'Yes! I didn't want to say anything before and get your hopes up. But when you were last in Ireland I saw how much you missed the place and how sad you were when you heard it had gone downhill. I could see how much it meant to your Grandma, too. And,' he said, touching his heart, 'the story she told me about the role my father played in rescuing the chalice from the ashes got to me. So I asked Charles to see if he could find out how much Donoghue wanted. When he told me, I thought I'd never in my wildest dreams be able to afford it. Even so, I rang the real estate agent and went and had a look. And like you all,' he grinned, glancing at Kathleen, 'I fell in love with the place. How could one not fall in love?'

'So that's how you could write about it in your novel,' Lillie exclaimed.

'Quite true.' He waved the telegram in the air again. 'And with this I can well afford it. All we have to hope for is that it's still on the market. In his letter last week Charles said it was, so I can't imagine someone's snapped it up in the meantime.'

'Oh my God,' Lillie cried, jumping up and throwing her arms around his neck. 'How could you not have told me you went to have a look?'

'Because if I had you would've been asking all sorts of questions, which I'd have had to give you answers for. It would have broken your heart to hear how Donoghue had let it all go. But now   well, hopefully — we can bring the old girl back to her glory days. What's more your lovely Grandma can visit us as often as she desires. And Ronan might come and help us run it for a while when he's back from New Zealand. For a farmer I am not.

And you, my sweet, will be far too busy finishing your English literature course. And then teaching little brats and producing a heap more wee Flahertys.' He laughed at Kathleen 'What do you say to that, my lovely lady?'

'I think it's marvellous news,' she said, tears in her eyes.

'Would you like to come there to live?' Lillie asked. 'You and Dad, I mean. And Marcus and Freddie.'

Ma shook her head. 'No darling. That's very kind of you. However, Dad and I decided long ago that Eureka Park's our home now. But to think Rathgarven might come back into the family makes me happier than I could ever imagine. And, as you say, maybe Ronan could come over for a while and give you a hand.' She checked her watch. 'So what are you waiting for? You know where the telephone is, Seamus. Go and see if it's still for sale.'

And it was. With a holding deposit from Seamus it was taken off the market. Three weeks later the real estate agent in Dublin had found a buyer for Seamus's flat, and Ronan had agreed to go to Ireland with them for a while after he came back from New Zealand.

'You never know, I might pick up a few hints in the shaky isles that could make the old place viable.'

The thought that Ronan would be coming back with them to Rathgarven made Lillie very happy. It wouldn't be forever, though it would be lovely to have him there for as long as he wanted. She wondered if he was sad it wasn't him who had been able to buy it back. At least this was something.

***

When it came time for Lillie, Seamus and Gemma to leave for Ireland, Lillie found it incredibly hard to say goodbye to the family. Ronan had already left for New Zealand, but it nearly broke her heart kissing Marcus and Freddie and Ma before getting in the car with Dad behind the wheel. She was also sad to leave Deb, who she had farewelled the day before with a lunch together at the Telegraph Hotel.

'I'll miss you heaps,' Deb said gloomily. She gave Lillie the Akubra hat she had brought as a farewell present. 'I thought you'd look dapper in that when you go hunting in Kerry.'

'You've got to come and visit,' Lillie told her. 'I won't take no for an answer.'

'Wild horses won't keep me away,' she laughed. 'Particularly if you have another Seamus waiting there to sweep me off my feet.'

Now the car was moving down the long driveway, and she could see Cosmo and the rest of the horses, including her Muffin, grazing contentedly behind the post-and-rail fences, and Dingo barking his farewells as he ran alongside the car. Lillie tried to curtail the tears flooding her eyes. There were so many things about Eureka Park she would miss. So many things about Australia. The wide-open spaces, the warm sun on her face, the smell of gum trees and wattle. And the people she had met. But as she looked at Seamus sitting beside Dad, and then at Gemma on her knee, she knew she had made the right decision. Particularly as Ronan would be joining them next month. And Ma and Dad had assured her they would come over when she and Seamus were settled at Rathgarven.

Nearly twenty-four hours later as their plane neared Dublin airport, Lillie looked down to where the choppy Irish Sea met the hotchpotch of green and gold fields divided by stone walls. She could see tiny specs in the fields, which she was sure were sheep grazing happily. The blue-grey waters of Dublin Bay spread out towards the Wicklow Mountains. Lillie took Seamus's hand and gave it a squeeze.

'Thank you,' she said. 'Thank you for making this happen.'

'You better wait until you see Rathgarven before you say that. There'll be so much work to do you may rue the day we bought it.'

'Oh, I doubt that very much,' Lillie said, giving Gemma a bounce on her knee. 'No matter what it looks like.'

Straight off the plane they caught a taxi to pick up Seamus's car from his friend's flat and headed to Grandma's hotel. She was so delighted to see them and to meet little Gemma that Lillie felt guilty it would be another two weeks before she could come down to Rathgarven to visit them. Lillie wanted to make sure her room was ready for her arrival — and, as much as she could, the rest of the house.

After overnighting at Jury's Inn in Dublin, they drove down the steep winding road from Moll's Gap and through Sneem. Lillie smiled happily as Seamus turned into the tree-lined avenue leading to Rathgarven, where snow-drops and winter heath lined the side of the road. Stretched out before them were the choppy waters of the Kenmare River and the rolling Kerry Mountains in the distance. Lillie felt a huge rush of excitement knowing this would be her new home.

When Paddy wandered out from the orchard to greet them, she was sure she would burst with happiness. She looked at the familiar gabled stone house with smoke billowing from two chimneys. She wondered where Maisie was. Probably in the kitchen getting dinner ready. When Maisie and Paddy had discovered Lillie, Seamus, Gemma and Ronan were coming back to Rathgarven, they immediately asked Charles Fitzpatrick if he would mind if they joined the household there again. Lady Fitzpatrick had died a few months ago and Charles was now engaged to a wealthy society girl from Dublin, Annabelle Stratton. They were to be married at Christchurch Cathedral in the autumn, followed by a reception at the Shelbourne. Just the way he and Clara were supposed to do.

Maisie and Paddy had finally decided they belonged together. They were now married and living in the small whitewashed cottage near Rathgarven's front gate. Lillie had no idea what Rathgarven had looked like when Donoghue had it, apart from what she'd been told, but now she looked around in astonishment; it didn't look that different to when the family had left for Australia. Fortunately all the big trees were still there and Paddy, with the help of some workmen Charles Fitzpatrick had insisted on lending him, had the gardens and hedges looking like a million dollars. Lillie glanced down to where she used to wheel Grandma to sit by the cove; a rowboat was tied to the end of the jetty. It was the same one that she and Ronan used to take fishing; Seamus had made sure it was part of the deal.

To the left of the house, the walled garden with the fruit trees was still there, and in the front garden was the oak tree Lillie could remember sitting under with Uncle Finn on his last trip to Ireland. She saw the trees Marcus and Hugh used to climb and shoot their bows and arrows from, and remembered Clara showing Freddie how to tie a string to Mandrake's shell last time she was here.

The house itself was still covered in ivy vines, even though it wasn't out, and the conservatory was still there, where Grandma loved to knit or write in the sun. That she would soon be sitting there again was very gratifying.

They got out of the car and the front door opened and Maisie came rushing out, oohing and ahhing at Gemma and hugging and kissing Seamus and Lillie.

'Welcome home,' she declared with a smile from ear to ear. She was even wearing the very same apron covered in shamrocks and harps that she used to wear when Lillie was a child. 'I've got the room next to the top landing all ready for you two. And,' she added, tickling Gemma under the chin, 'the room next door to that is for this little pixie. Ronan can be having his old room when he comes. Isn't it grand he'll be here for a while.'

'All sounds good to me,' Seamus said placing his arms around Lillie. 'May I have the great honour of carrying my lovely bride over the threshold?'

'Honestly, Seamus,' Lillie protested, 'we've already done that with the little cottage at Eureka.' But when she saw how disappointed he looked, she said, 'Well, go on, then,' and let him pick her up and carry her towards the front porch. When he plonked her down inside the front door, he gave her a long lingering kiss.

The hallway and the two front rooms, like much of the rest of the house, was furnished with bits and pieces that Lillie and Seamus had had delivered after poring over a Broderick catalogue, plus some items Seamus had managed to buy back from Donoghue.

'Aren't we the lucky ones?' he said, looking around.

It seemed funny to see the new pieces they had chosen gracing Rathgarven's hallways and rooms alongside the family portraits and landscape paintings — not to mention the wonderful harp, which Uncle Finn and Ronan had played — that Grandma had managed to have stored in Killarney. These, along with the chalice, were the family treasures she had refused point blank to give up.

'One day one of you might come back and want them all,' she had said, patting the chalice. 'There's no way that I'll let this go to anyone else. Let alone to that man Donoghue. He might have got the rest of the furniture, but not this precious piece and not our paintings.'

As Lillie walked into the study and saw the chalice — lovingly polished by Maisie, who had collected it from the bank's safety deposit box — sitting proudly on the mantelpiece, she thought how right Grandma had been. When they moved along the hallway and she saw the portrait of Dermot O'Sullivan hanging on the wall in its usual spot, she thought how strange it would be for Ronan to look at that picture knowing he was his father. More than ever she wondered how Ronan would cope being at Rathgarven, knowing it should have been his one day.

'A damn handsome blighter, is he not?' Seamus said, standing back and looking at Dermot. 'Pity he doesn't know the chaos he left behind him.'

Yes, Lillie thought, studying her uncle's steady eyes staring out from the portrait. You are extremely handsome. And I can quite understand why Jessica was smitten and why Ma loved you so very much. But I'm sure you'd be horrified to know the turmoil you've caused in their lives.

And your children's.

Chapter 52

Kathleen was going through the mail at Eureka Park's front gate as she waited for the bus from Quirindi to arrive with Freddie, who'd been staying with a friend during the term break. She was hoping for a letter from Ronan in New Zealand and one from Lillie in Ireland — Lillie had promised to send photos of Rathgarven. There was a letter addressed to Kathleen, but she didn't recognise the writing. When she opened the envelope there was a letter and then another envelope. The letter was from Mary Archer, the woman who had been living with Jessica before she went into hospital. Mary wrote that Jessica had sadly passed away.

Kathleen stiffened. Even though she had been expecting this news, it was still a shock. When she had heard Jessica was so ill she had written to her in the end, but hadn't heard back. She looked at the date of Mary's letter. It must be at least three weeks since Jessica died. Mary said Jessica had asked her to post the letter enclosed on to Kathleen in the event of her death. She had no idea what was in it, as it was sealed and she had promised not to open it. Sure enough, there was her friend's familiar handwriting on the front of the envelope, and there was a seal of red wax on the back. She searched in the glove box to see if there was anything there to slit the seal with. She found a screwdriver and slid it under the wax, pulled out the letter, and started to read.

Dearest Kate,

I was so sorry to hear about Ronan. I can't start to imagine what pain you've all gone through. And what pain there is ahead for Ronan with his injuries. To think that what happened to him was as a result of my actions.

As you know the dreaded cigarettes have finally got to me and the grim reaper's waiting like a rapacious eagle, ready to snap me up in its claws. In fact by the time you get this it'll have carried me away. But before it does, I have to make a dreadful confession. Although I haven't had the courage to tell you the truth in person, I felt I had to write it down while I still have the strength. So that you can try to rectify the awful damage I've done.

A confession and plea from the grave, you might say.

If only I'd been able to find Clara I may have been able to tell her to her face what I'm about to tell you. But, much as I've searched, I'm unable to find her anywhere. I even put a notice in the International Herald Tribune, *asking her to write to me or my solicitor. But alas, to this moment she hasn't been in touch. After what I've done, it was the least I could do to tell her to her face that I made it up.*

Yes, Kate, I made the whole thing up.

I didn't sleep with Dermot at all. It wasn't his baby I was carrying. Clara's father was the colonel in charge of the Garrison Headquarters you and I worked for. Married, of course. A pillar of the military establishment, a nice man, you might remember, and long since dead. Someone I turned to when I realised Dermot had fallen for you, breaking my heart.

Holding the letter in her shaking hand, Kathleen tried to breathe, but couldn't find any air. She hurled the letter onto the dashboard, opened the car door and threw up on the side of the road.

Desperately she tried to stop the *boom boom* in her head, which was threatening to explode. It was impossible. Wiping her lips with her sleeve, she stood and stared across the road at their neighbour's herd of Santa Gertrudis that were calmly chewing their cud under the wattle tree. How could the world go on when this had happened?

'Oh, Ronan!' she cried out in anguish, tears streaming down her cheeks. And Clara, she thought. What has your pitiable mother done to you both? She looked at the letter lying on the dashboard. Slowly she moved back to the truck and picked it up.

I made up the lie because I was desperate, Kate. Frightened, too, for I'd just learnt I had terminal lung cancer. I'd been in a relationship that had finished. As he was paying my rent, that then stopped and I feared I'd be out on the street. As you know Charles Fitzpatrick, lovely man that he is, had promised me the use of the flat at the side of Drominderry House after he and Clara were married. What you didn't know was that he'd promised me an allowance as well. When Clara said she was staying in Australia and living at Ronan's digs I thought it might have been because of him she had broken off with Charles. That was when my mind flipped and I came up with the idea of Ronan being her brother. For quite frankly, my sweet, if I had managed to seduce Dermot, she may well have been his daughter. And God, how I wished that she was. You and he were so utterly in love and so joyously happy I could hardly look at the two of you together. I felt you had stolen the happiness that should rightfully have been mine. To find out after his death that you were carrying his child was more than I could bear.

Ultimately all I wanted was for Clara to come to her senses. To return to Ireland and marry Charles. He had so much to offer her. And me. As it is, I now know that I destroyed her life. And Ronan's. Forgive me, Kate. And

<blockquote>forgive me for not telling you until now. Courage was never my forte. Please also ask James to have mercy on my soul. Now that I'm gone I'm sure he'll tell you the heinous thing I did to him over the years.</blockquote>

Kathleen gasped. What did she mean? What had she done to James?

<blockquote>And please, please try and find Clara and show her this letter. I know I don't deserve forgiveness, but please beg her to try. Ronan too.</blockquote>

For a long time Kathleen sat unmoving, her anger so raw she felt it might kill her. *You might be dead now, Jessica, but Ronan and Clara were at the beginning of their lives. Their love. How could you?*

To calm herself she took long deep breaths. As she did, she tried desperately to imagine why Jessica had done such a thing. It was obvious that she had loved Dermot with all her heart, and that in her mind Kathleen had stolen him from her, and the loss had destroyed her. And then her marriages didn't work out. For someone like Jessica, captured by a false value system that put appearances above everything else, including her own daughter's happiness, getting older, losing her attractiveness to men, was terrifying. Was that what made her so pitiable? So manipulative? Clara marrying Charles Fitzpatrick was her last hope. And Ronan had spoilt that. Then to discover she was dying on her own. All of that, added together with the medicine she was on for her illness may have finally turned her mind. Surely that must have been it. It was too hard to believe that her friend was really evil. Yes, she was self-absorbed, vain and shallow at times, but Kathleen had never really known her to be evil. Even so, she found it impossible to forgive her for what she had done to Clara and Ronan. And what had she done to James? She had always felt James had disliked Jessica — what had she done to him?

She tried to collect herself as the bus rattled to a stop. Freddie jumped off and ran across the road and into the truck beside her. He took one look at Kathleen and held his nose.

'You smell like vomit and you've been crying.'

'Oh Freddie,' she cried, holding him so tightly he could hardly breathe. 'Oh Freddie, my darling, darling Freddie. We've got to ring Ronan as soon as we get back to the homestead. And we've got to find Clara.'

'Why?'

'I'll tell you when I've spoken to Dad.' She was shaking so much there was no way she could hold onto the steering wheel. 'Now,' she said, trying a smile, 'do you want to drive?'

'Me? Drive?'

'Yes, and don't tell me you can't. I know Seamus used to let you drive back from the gate all the time. He said you're very good. And I don't think I could possibly handle driving right now.'

'Really!' Freddie grinned broadly at the prospect, his whole face lighting up. 'Well, okay, then. If you insist.'

So Kathleen moved to the passenger seat and Freddie slipped behind the wheel and they had a bumpy ride up the road between the horse paddocks.

When they arrived at the homestead, Kathleen told Freddie to go inside and find the buttered scones she'd left on the table for him. She leapt out of the truck and rushed down to the stables to find James.

***

James was trying to fix the water pump when he saw Kathleen come flying around the corner, holding a letter in her hand.

511

'James! James!' she cried, rushing over. 'Read this. It's from Jessica. She wrote it before she died.'

James wiped his hands on a rag. 'Jessica's dead?'

Although he'd known she was sick, and indeed had wished her dead many times, it was still a shock.

'Yes. But oh my God, James…' Kathleen didn't seem to be able to get the words out. 'James… She says Dermot's not Clara's father after all.'

James gasped. 'What on earth do you mean?'

'She made the whole thing up. Here… see what she says.'

James took the letter and began to read, swallowing hard as he did so. Jessica was unstable, but he'd had no idea she was as bad as this. He looked up from the pages in front of him and held Kathleen's eyes. All he could think of was Ronan and Clara.

'We'll need to let Ronan know as soon as possible,' he said, taking a deep breath.

'What if he can't find Clara? What if she's married someone else?'

James sighed, endeavouring to come to terms with what he had just read. 'That's why we need to try and find Ronan as soon as we can.' He held the letter tightly; he had no doubt that Ronan would want to read it with his own eyes.

Kathleen looked at the pages over his shoulder. 'But what does Jessica mean by this… the bit about what she did to you?'

James waited a long time before answering, all the time staring at the letter in his hand. 'It's something I should have told you. Now this has happened I will. Come,' he put his arm around her and beckoned for her to step over with him to where they could sit on some upturned logs. When they were sitting down, he told her the whole story.

Whenever Kathleen tried to interrupt, he put his hand up, forcing her to listen to the end. When he finished she stood up and paced up and down, not looking at him. Finally she came and stood in front of him.

'My God, James,' she said, 'you're telling me we lost Rathgarven because Jessica threatened to tell the whole world that I had fallen pregnant out of wedlock to your brother. That Ronan wasn't your son.'

He nodded. 'You could say that.'

'But James — How could you? I mean you should have told me.'

'To begin with it felt like a small price to pay to protect you and Ronan. But then as the economy got worse I should have refused. Ultimately I felt it was in Clara's interest to keep it going, for Jessica assured me she was using a lot of the money I gave her for her education. To stop it would hurt Clara more than Jessica. Or so I thought.' He sighed. 'But there is no getting away from the fact that I allowed her to take advantage of me. Of us, really.' He looked up and smiled. 'Maybe my love for you, my desire to protect you and Ronan clouded my judgement.'

Kathleen sat down beside him, squeezing his arm. 'Oh James… I'm so sorry. After all you did for me and then this…'

He smiled and put his hand on hers. 'It was also my concern for what the scandal would do to Mother, and her standing in the community and the church. But ultimately it was for you. And Ronan. As it happened he found out anyway.'

'But the time that sent us over the edge, when she demanded that extra money and you tried to get it gambling at the Killarney Races, what was that for?'

He paused. 'Jessica agreed that if I gave her a lump sum that would be enough to cover the pickle she was in, and also enough for Clara to finish school, she wouldn't worry me again.'

'What sort of pickle was she in? She had a husband, Phillip, for God's sake.'

'She couldn't ask him.'

'Why ever not?'

'She was pregnant to another man.'

Kathleen's eyes opened wide. 'James, don't be so silly.'

'I'm not. It's true.'

Kathleen's eyes opened even wider. 'Who on earth was she pregnant to?'

'A reasonably high-up Indian civil servant she met at the Tollygunge Club. That's why she came back to England. For an abortion. As she hadn't slept with her husband, Phillip, for over a year she knew the baby would be half-Indian and Phillip would throw her out. Totally cut her off. Her reputation would be ruined. And Clara would never forgive her.'

'My God! But you could have dobbed her in to Phillip. That would have stymied her plan.'

'I could have, yes. But if I had, she would most likely have found a way to disclose our secret. And Clara would have found out that her mother had aborted a half-brother or sister. That didn't worry me for Jessica. But it did for Clara. And, apart from everything else, it could have got us into a bit of hot water for fudging Ronan's birth certificate. If she decided to announce to the authorities, or the church for that matter, that he wasn't my son and we had said he was, that could have caused a scandal on its own.'

'But why keep what she was doing a secret from me for so long? Even after we came here? After what happened with Clara and Ronan?'

'If you'd known what she was up to, I couldn't trust you not to confront her. If you had, all bets would have been off, and apart from anything else, it would have been awkward for Mother back in Ireland. In any case, Rathgarven was gone. I saw no point in giving you more heartache by telling you what your friend had done. For, as we know, she was a good friend to you for many years. Particularly when your parents died. And then Dermot. And I know how much that friendship meant to you. Let's just say that life got the better of her. It didn't turn out quite the way she imagined it would. From you stealing Dermot from under her nose and Guy Preston losing all his money… then her other failed dalliances and Phillip turning out to be a philanderer and …'

'I know… but...' She gave a deep sigh. 'If only I'd been involved in the finances at Rathgarven, like I am here, I might have noticed that money going out. And put a stop to it.'

'You wouldn't have known. I did it through Declan at the bank. And that was where she wrote to me.'

'And Declan never asked what it was all about?'

'He was always a great one for telling people to mind their own business. If he did wonder, he never said.'

'But James, we've got to tell Ronan and the others what happened. The real reason why we lost Rathgarven.'

James thought for a moment. 'No, he said adamantly. 'There's a small possibility that Ronan and Clara might have a life together if he can ever track her down. And if he does, she'll have enough on her plate learning her mother lied about her father. Let alone that she had aborted her sister or brother and blackmailed me.'

'But you will tell your mother?'

'What's the point? All it might do is cloud her feelings for Clara. No, it's best to let sleeping dogs lie. You and I know. That's the main thing.'

'But what about Finn paying her all that money? It's quite possible that was why he wasn't able to honour his debts here before he died.'

'That's best forgotten too. He would have paid his debts in the end. He was just a slow payer. And Finn was fond of Jessica. Despite everything he didn't want to see her in a pickle. I'm just sorry that I didn't have the chance to repay him.' He sighed. 'One of the reasons I've been determined to make a success of Eureka Park in a way is to repay him.' He took Kathleen's hand in his.

'The best thing we can do is help Ronan find Clara. If we do that, then at least something might be retrieved from this sorry mess.'

James refolded Jessica's letter and handed it back to Kathleen. Again he thought how important it was that Ronan read it himself, not hear the contents second-hand from his parents. 'We'll need to show this letter to Ronan of course.'

'And if he asks what Jessica did to you?'

'I'll tell him it was when we were young and stupid. Long since forgotten. For that's how I see it.'

And, James reflected, that *was* how he saw it. What was the point of Ronan knowing it was Clara's mother who had not only destroyed his life with Clara, but also caused James to lose his inheritance?

***

Ronan never did go to live at Rathgarven with Lillie. When his mother tracked him down at the deer farm near Taupo on New Zealand's north island and told him what was in Jessica's letter, he had to grab a stool to sit down in case he keeled over.

'Are you sure you're reading it correctly?' he gasped, terrified Ma had got the wrong end of the stick.

'Both your father and I have read it many times. There's no getting away from what Jessica meant. She made up the whole thing. She never slept with Dermot at all.'

'So how do we know that she hasn't made this up as well?'

'This time I'm sure she's definitely telling the truth. And in a way it all makes sense. I always knew she had a soft spot for Dermot, but what I couldn't understand is why he never told me that he had an affair with her. It seemed so out of character.'

After he hung up Ronan tried to come to terms with it all. He paced around and around the small office where he'd taken the call. The enormity of what his mother told him sank in. If Clara wasn't his sister, there was nothing to stop them being together. Unless, of course, she had met someone else, which Ronan didn't even want to think about. Over the coming days he rang his parents again and again to get their assurance that they believed Jessica was telling the truth. He even rang Lillie in Ireland.

'You've got to believe it's the truth,' she said. 'And you've got to find her, Ronan.'

'How?'

'I don't know. But don't give up until you do.'

Dave said the same thing when they went into Taupo for a beer. Ronan had never told him about Clara being his sister. As far as Dave was concerned Clara had decided to break it off and go back to England. But now Ronan told him the whole story.

'Gees, mate,' he said. 'Why the fuck didn't you tell me?'

'I suppose because you knew I'd been sleeping with her. I felt I owed it to her not to tell.'

Dave nodded. 'Well, bloody hell mate, you better make up for lost time. I saw how much you fancied her. And she's a bloody good sort. I often wondered how you let her get away.'

'So where do you suppose I should start looking?'

'Where you last knew she was. England.'

'You reckon they'd mind it here if I took off?'

After visiting the fishing lodge on the Motueka River, they had been working on the deer farm for over a month. The owners were clearing out the thick, tangled woods down by the river to allow the deer to roam more easily. Ronan had been driving the tractor and Dave and another fellow had been doing the groundwork.

'I think the work's finishing up here anyway. The other bloke and I can do what's left.'

Ronan thought for a moment. 'Do you think I'm mad to go looking for her?'

'Hell no, mate. Imagine if she found out that you knew this and hadn't told her. She'd be forgiven for skinning you alive.'

Dave was right. What was the point of trying to make a go of the rest of his life without at least trying to find Clara? Sure, she may well be with someone else. Or he may never find her. But if he didn't try he'd never know if they had another chance. It was a risk he needed to take. And the sooner he took it the better.

Chapter 53

Three days later Ronan flew to England. He booked himself into a hostel in central London, and Ma forwarded Jessica's letter to him there by express airmail. When he read it he had no doubt that she was telling the truth. First of all he went to find Mary Archer at the place she had shared with Jessica. In fairness to Jessica he didn't go into details as to why he wanted to find Clara, except to say it was extremely urgent. He left her his phone number at the hostel in case she heard anything. Frantically he placed advertisements in a number of newspapers. He even went to Clara's old school to see if they could put him in touch with any of her friends. But no one had any idea where she was. It was as if she had evaporated like the morning mist. Until Mary Archer rang one morning to tell him a letter had arrived addressed to Jessica. She suspected it might be from Clara so had opened it.

'Do you want me to read it to you,' she asked. 'Or would you like to come and get it?'

'Please read it,' he said, unable to wait.

'*Just letting you know I'm okay and living on a beautiful island off Papua New Guinea,*' Mary read out. '*Don't try to find me, Mummy, please. One day I might forgive you, but not now.*'

'Is that it?' Ronan asked.

'Yes, and the postmark's so faint I can't make it out. And by the looks of the envelope it's been a long time getting to England.'

Mary didn't ask what it was that Clara couldn't forgive Jessica for. And Ronan didn't say.

'Can I come around and get it?' he asked her.

'Of course.'

Within a couple of hours Ronan had Clara's letter in his hand. And yes, Mary was right. Hard as he looked the postmark was indecipherable.

Watching him read the letter, Mary said, 'She obviously means a lot to you.'

Ronan smiled. 'Yes, she does.'

'Well, off you go then. Go and find her.'

Knowing Clara was probably somewhere in Papua New Guinea was enough for him to set off in pursuit. He quickly organised a ticket and flew to Port Moresby. And there began his long and arduous search of the islands of PNG. Everywhere he went he showed a photo of Clara, which he kept in his wallet.

Each time he got the same answer, whether it was in English from the expats or pidgin from the locals: 'Sorry, mate. Never seen her.'

For weeks he battled the heat and his bung leg. He travelled by trading boats to the islands, including Manus, Samarai, New Britain and New Ireland. Gutted that his search was proving fruitless, he finally arrived on the island of Bougainville and repeated the steps he'd taken on all the other islands: he first sussed out the district commissioner's office, which was in Arawa and proved to be a thatched building, close to the beach and shrouded by a scarlet dazzle of bougainvillea. The commissioner was away in Moresby, but his ADC, a bloke from Townsville who sported an immaculately ironed khaki shirt in contrast to Ronan's rumpled checked one, was there. He raised his lanky frame from behind a steel desk. Behind him a push-out window framed a group of native women standing waist-deep in the ocean, fishing with nets.

He looked at the photograph Ronan handed him. Turned it over in his hand. Glanced at Ronan and then at the photo again. 'I know that face, mate,' he said, lighting a Rothmans and scraping his chair on the wooden floor as he sat down again. 'How could one forget it?'

Ronan took a deep inward breath and tears threatened his weary eyes. 'Where did you see her?' he asked, trying to control his excitement.

'On the island of Kiriwina in the Trobriands. I was staying at the small guest lodge there. An English couple own it. One evening we were having sundowners on the verandah overlooking the lagoon. The girl in your photograph was there. She teaches the kids in the village school. I must admit I was rather taken with her.' He grinned. 'She wasn't interested. I figured she must have a boyfriend already.' He fiddled with his neatly trimmed moustache and blew smoke rings into the muggy air. 'I presume you're not him or you'd know where to find her?'

Ronan shook his head, hoping that he was wrong about Clara having a boyfriend. 'No, I'm not,' Ronan said.

'Why you want to track her down then? For, quite frankly, mate, if she's camped way out there in the Trobriands, maybe she doesn't want to be sussed out.'

'Her mother died not long ago. I need to let her know.'

'Well if that's the case, that's where I reckon you'll find her. Give her my regards when you see her. And the couple who own the guest lodge. Can't for the life of me remember their name, but they were good hosts.'

'Thank you,' Ronan said, shaking his hand. 'You've been a great help.'

***

Three days later Ronan found a trading boat that would take him from Arawa to Kiriwina and stumbled into a small village of thatched houses with pitched roofs near the town of Losuia. A circle of native men sat cross-legged chewing betel nut, while

521

another man hacked into a coconut with a bush knife nearby. Beyond them, bare breasted women squatted on the ground shaping carvings out of wood and polishing shells, their children playing close by. Chickens pecked in the dirt next to a ring of rocks containing the remains of a smouldering fire. A few scrawny dogs lolled in the shade of a frangipani tree that held a couple of rainbow coloured parrots in its branches. It was the same scene Ronan had encountered in nearly every island village he had visited. Now his attention was drawn to where a few teenage boys were playing cricket with makeshift bats. Beyond the cricketers a group of younger children were gathered in a circle under swaying palms.

And there she was, sitting on the ground helping the children make necklaces out of shells. It took all his self-control not to rush over. If he did, he would not only frighten the school children, he would also alarm Clara. He couldn't get over how beautiful she was. Her hair was still long and she was as brown as a berry from the hot New Guinea sun. She was wearing a red skirt and a white t- shirt. Now one of the children saw him and tugged on Clara's sleeve. She turned to look at him and her eyes opened wide.

'Oh my God, Ronan! Is that you?' she called, standing up and shading her eyes against the sun. She came over and stood before him, the whole time looking him up and down. It was as though he was a vision that had appeared from the sky.

He nodded and touched his beard. 'Yes, it's me. A bit worse for wear. But it's me all right.'

She glanced at his walking stick. 'You're injured. How did that happen?'

'Vietnam. A mine.'

'My God! You went to fight that horrid war?'

'I did. It seemed a way out at the time.' He touched his leg. 'Until this happened.'

'Oh Ronan… I'm so sorry. You wouldn't have been injured like that if I hadn't gone to stay at Eureka Park. It was all my fault.'

'No it wasn't.'

Now there was a long and awkward pause as neither of them could decide what to do next. 'You shouldn't have found me,' she said.

Ronan smiled. 'Yes, I should.'

'Why? What good can come out of it?'

He looked to where the little children had stopped making their necklaces and were staring at the two of them.

'Can I talk to you? Please?'

After a moment Clara nodded. 'Let me give the children something to go on with.' She pointed to a log near the lagoon. 'I'll come over in a minute.'

Ronan wanted to take her in his arms. Here and now. With great difficulty he held back. 'I'll be there waiting.'

As he walked slowly with his stick towards the log, he wondered how she had ended up here in this tiny village. He saw the schoolhouse set in among the trees. It was made out of woven palm and had a small verandah to the front, which looked down over the lagoon. Further along the bank was what looked like a small guest lodge. It was built of timber and had a thatched palm roof and a large, vine-covered verandah wrapping around all sides. Surrounding it was a beautiful garden of native bushes and plants and there was even a cassowary, which seemed tame, strolling around. Behind him were ornate yam houses perched on wooden stilts. Two happy-looking pigs were digging in the mud and through the pandanus trees he could hear the women working among the yams. He sat on the log and put down his rucksack. Picking up a small stone, he threw it into the water as he had done so many times at Rathgarven and Eureka Park. He smiled when he remembered Clara asking if there were crocodiles in the river at

Eureka Park when she first arrived. There would certainly be saltwater crocodiles in this lagoon, he thought. He opened his rucksack and pulled out the letter Jessica had written to Ma. He had thought so often of how he would handle this moment. Should he tell Clara what was in the letter? Or should she read it herself? In the end he decided he'd give her the letter and she could read it quietly on her own.

There were footsteps behind him and he turned around. 'So you're not afraid of crocodiles anymore?' he said, smiling up at Clara.

She grinned. 'It's certainly not the place to be faint-hearted. Sadly, we can't swim in the lagoon here. Further along we've made a sort of pool out of fence posts and wire netting, which we hope will keep them out.'

He looked across the lagoon to where another village stood on the opposite shore. The happy sounds of children wafted on the humid air. In front of them fish jumped in the water and a fat eel slithered along beneath the surface.

'Despite the crocodiles,' he said, 'it's certainly a beautiful spot you've chosen.'

'I know. I never want to leave. The guesthouse belongs to a friend of mine. She and her husband have run it for a couple of years. They took over from her parents as her mother's ill and had to go back to England. When I told her I wanted somewhere to find myself she suggested I come here. It took me a while to decide. Now I can't imagine why I took so long. Freezing cold London. Or,' she laughed, 'here in paradise.'

'I don't know either.'

'But why are you here?' she asked again.

'Because I had to find you.'

'Why?'

'To show you this.'

He handed her the letter.

'It's Mummy's writing but it's not for me,' she said, studying the front of the envelope. 'It's for Aunt Kathleen.'

'All the same you should read it. While you do, I'll go back and see how those kids are getting along with their necklaces. When you're ready, come over and rescue me.'

She fiddled with the letter. 'When did she write this?'

'Just before she…'

'She's dead, isn't she?'

He nodded. 'Yes. She died of lung cancer.'

'Oh!' He could see that despite everything her mother had done to her, Clara was visibly upset. 'All those cigarettes. I knew they'd get to her in the end.'

He got up and touched her on the shoulder. 'Take as long as you like to read her letter.' He smiled. 'Now that I've found you I'm not going anywhere. Not without you.'

Clara gave him a puzzled look. 'But…'

'Read the letter. Please.'

***

Ronan sat with the children and watched Clara open the envelope and read. Saw her stand up and run a hand through her hair. Sit down again. Pick up the letter and re-read it. It was as though she was trying to take it all in. Trying to believe what she was reading. He gave her some privacy and turned his attention to the children, who were delighted to show this unexpected playmate their necklaces.

Half an hour later she sought him out. His fingers were shaking so much he was having difficulty threading the fishing line through the shells of a little girl's necklace. Smiling at the children, she beckoned for him to follow her back to the lagoon, where they sank down on the bank.

'Night after night I dreamt you'd turn up one day and tell me that it had all been a huge mistake,' Clara said, turning the letter over in her hands. 'That we weren't brother and sister after all. Often, when I woke in the morning and discovered it had been a dream, I'd find it really hard to get through the day.' She looked back towards the children. 'It was those children who helped me go on. Without them I'd have given up long ago. Now to find out what I'd dreamt of so often is true.' She sighed. 'Oh Ronan… Did she hate me so much to do what she did?'

'I don't think she hated you at all, Clara. When she found out she was dying I think she was so mixed up she didn't realise the consequences. She must have thought you'd get over me and marry Charles Fitzpatrick after all and she'd be looked after.'

'If only she'd told me she was dying.'

'Would it have made any difference to how we felt? We still would have got married. No, she had to come up with a reason that would definitely stop us.'

'You're probably right.' She sighed. 'I tried to think of Dermot O'Sullivan as my father. I know I should've felt something, but I didn't. The only role he played in my life was to destroy it.' She looked away and back again. 'I always thought Guy Preston was my father. Now… Well… Now to find out it was some colonel in charge of Garrison Headquarters. God, Ronan. I'm so confused. Why for heaven's sake didn't Mummy tell the truth? If she'd done that right at the beginning it would've saved so much heartbreak.'

'I suppose she didn't want to upset the apple cart. All hell would've let loose if it'd been discovered her boss had got her pregnant.'

'She should've dobbed him in.'

'It was a different time then. Not only wartime, but also a different kind of society. She may have been shunned. When Guy

Preston asked her to marry him, she must've thought it was a way out.'

Clara sighed and took Ronan's hand. 'Despite all the horrid things Mummy did, the only thing that matters now is that the love we shared was never wrong. That's what turned my mind. And,' she said, squeezing his hand, 'it must have turned yours as well. I didn't contact you because I could never think of you as a brother. Every time I looked at you I'd think of us making love. No matter how hard I tried, your face was there every night when I went to sleep. Every morning when I woke up. Every hour of every day.'

Ronan held her gaze. 'As yours has been with me.'

'I'm sad that Mummy died. But I'm so, so angry with her.' She fiddled with the letter. 'I'm just grateful she told the truth in the end.'

'So am I,' he said.

'But what was the heinous thing she did to your father?'

'I don't know. Both he and Ma said it was when they were young and best forgotten.' He smiled. 'I didn't take it any further. I daresay they're entitled to some secrets.'

For some time they sat in silence before Clara stood up and tore the letter into little pieces. 'I want to get rid of this.' Ronan watched her throw the pieces into the air where they fell like large snowflakes into the lagoon. 'Having thrown that away, I can pretend Mummy never tried to ruin our lives. If I read her letter again, it'll make me so cross. And all I want is to be happy.'

She did a twirl and let out a shriek of loud, joyous laughter, which made all the children drop their necklaces and look at her in astonishment. Even the birds and the butterflies seemed to stop in mid-flight. She dragged Ronan to his feet and for some time they stood there as he caressed her face, her hair and touched her lips to his. Then she put her hand out and beckoned for the children to come over and join them in a dance. As they danced, she held onto Ronan's hand to stop him putting pressure on his leg.

'*Yupela hamamas, yupela hamamas*,' one of the little girls cried out, clapping her hands.

'Yes, Vavina,' Clara said, kissing Ronan fully on the lips and dancing for joy. 'We are happy. Very, very happy.'

Ronan pulled her close to him and held her tight. He could feel her heart beating against his chest. As long as he lived he would never let her out of his sight again. Although, like Clara, he was angry with Jessica for what she had done, he was grateful that at least she had tried to make things right before she died.

He couldn't imagine how he would have coped if he'd never found Clara. Or if she had married someone else. He wanted to ask her to marry him right now. The only cloud on the horizon was his injuries. Could he saddle her with a cripple?'

'What if I'm stuck with this stick forever?'

Clara laughed. 'I think it's rather distinguished. Besides, who knows… maybe you'll be able to throw it away one day.' She became serious. 'Ronan, I'm so sorry that those injuries happened to you,' she said, stroking his cheek. 'But we can't let a mere walking stick stop our happiness.'

Ronan sighed with relief, and his face broke into a wide smile. 'In that case, will you marry me, Clara?'

'Oh Ronan… I love you so very, very much.' She stood back and grinned. 'So, yes, I daresay I'll marry you. How could I not?'

'That's so true. This time we'll make sure it happens.'

With Clara by his side, and the little village children looking on in wonderment, Ronan felt more joy than he had ever thought was possible.

Chapter 54

When Kathleen went into Gullumbindy to see Martha Hogan, she picked up the mail from the post office and saw there was a letter with a New Guinea post mark. She knew Ronan had gone there to try and find Clara. She opened it in the car, hoping it would have good news.

> *Dear Dad and Ma,*
>
> *I can't ring as we have no phone lines here. But I've found her. In the Trobriand Islands on the island of Kiriwina. She's great. Beautiful as ever. What's more she's agreed to marry me. In six weeks. Up here. Will you come? It's a fabulous spot. You'll love it. There's a terrific guesthouse run by a friend of Clara's and her husband. That's why she's here. She teaches at the mission school. She doesn't want to live anywhere else. Nor do I. We've agreed to lease the guesthouse from Clara's friend as her mother's very ill in England and she wants to go back home to nurse her. I can run it during the day while Clara's teaching. We'll run it together at night. Please say you'll come. Will write more later but wanted to get this on the plane leaving this afternoon for Lae. Love to everyone from us both, Ronan.*

Kathleen looked at the letter again and again, turning it over in her hands, which were trembling with excitement. She had dreamt of this moment for so long, now it had happened it was hard to believe it was true.

Looking up to the sky through the windscreen she said, 'Thank you, God. Thank you.'

She drove home quickly and made her way up through the paddocks to where she hoped she would find James with Arthur.

Arthur had got married and was now back and living in the manager's cottage with his wife. Kathleen found him with James doing some work on the horse shelters. When she told them both the news, James lit his pipe and stood there smiling.

'I'm so very happy for them.'

'Gees, Mrs O'Sullivan,' Arthur said. 'Good on Ronan for finding her.'

'What about the wedding?' Kathleen said to James. 'The boys will be in the middle of exams in six weeks.'

'And Arthur and I'll be getting ready for the William Inglis thoroughbred sales. You should go on your own. You can take lots of photos, so we'll feel as though we were there.'

'Ronan will be disappointed if we're not all there.'

'He'll be far more disappointed if you don't go,' James said. 'And it will do you good to get away from here for a while.'

In the end Kathleen agreed. And after a few more letters back and forth in regards to her travel arrangements, she was on a TAA flight to Moresby, and then flying on to Lae, where she hopped on a small Cessna. As they came in low over the Trobriand Islands, she could see the yam gardens set out in the villages. From the air they reminded her of the ratalu gardens in the villages around Calcutta. Ronan and Clara were both at the airport to meet her. Kathleen thought they were the happiest people she had ever seen.

'Aunt Kathleen, how wonderful to see you,' Clara said, giving her a warm hug and taking her small bag, while Ronan took the large one. 'It's so kind of you to come.'

'I wouldn't have missed it for the world,' Kathleen said, turning to embrace Ronan.

Kathleen glanced around the small airport. Everywhere she looked there were islanders clinging to the wire fence, calling out and waving to the arriving passengers. Little children clung to their mother's hems or were cradled in their arms. The women's bare breasts gleamed in the sunshine, as did their colourful skirts. Many of the men had painted faces and some even carried spears. There was the smell of heat, dust, human sweat and smoke in the air.

'It reminds me so much of India,' she said. 'Even the smells are the same. I can't wait to see the village where the guesthouse is. And where you teach, Clara. Ronan told me it's such a pretty spot.'

'Oh, it is, Aunt Kathleen,' Clara laughed. 'The most perfect spot in the world. That's why we wanted to get married there.'

'You've got a lovely room overlooking the lagoon, Ma. It's the best, isn't it, Clara?'

'How lovely,' Kathleen said. 'Thank you.'

Soon they were in the Land Rover, which Ronan told Kathleen he often used to collect guests, some arriving from as far away as Scotland.

'It's amazing meeting so many different nationalities,' he told her as they drove through thick bush interspersed with small, neat villages. 'They come to listen to the islanders' *sing sings*, fish in the lagoon and the ocean and explore the caves. Most of all they come to buy the ebony carvings the islanders are so famous for. We get a number of Germans and of course lots of Aussie expats living up here as well.' He laughed. 'They sure can drink.'

When they drove into the village Kathleen could see why Clara had been so taken with it. Ronan too. It was delightful. As she stood by the Land Rover taking it all in, it was as if she was back in Calcutta with the aroma of the villagers' cooking on open fires, the women squatting on the ground peeling vegetables, their little ones close by; stray dogs scavenged for scraps, baby goats bleated and the birds and bats in the poinciana and flame trees created their own cacophony. The familiar sight of frangipani, bougainvillea and the sweet perfume of jasmine made her feel nostalgic. Not only for Calcutta, but also for Dermot, who would have loved this place so much. She thought of the lifestyle Clara would have had at Drominderry House if she had married Charles Fitzpatrick. It was like comparing the Shelbourne Hotel to one of these village houses. There could be no comparison at all. Seeing the joy on Clara's face, it was clear that life here on Kiriwina with Ronan and her schoolchildren was the life that suited her best.

The guesthouse was delightful too. With its sac-sac palm roof, deep verandah and rambling garden a riot of colour rolling down to the lagoon, it was no wonder it was popular with guests. She wondered how they ever left. And Ronan was right — her room was in the very best spot with a beautiful view to the lagoon and across to the yam fields on the other side. It was furnished with rattan pieces and colourful rugs on the floor. The bed beneath a billowing mosquito net would prove to be one of the most comfortable Kathleen had ever slept in.

'Oh, Ronan,' she said, as she stood with him on the verandah the next day, watching a group of children playing with a cockatoo nearby, 'I can see why you're so happy here, darling.'

Ronan put his arm around her. 'I'm very lucky. And very glad you're here with us.'

***

The village chief was decked out in his traditional regalia, his face painted in vibrant colours, his proud head adorned with magnificent feathers, his neck and arms bearing shell necklaces and bangles as he walked Clara along the path to where a makeshift altar, covered in a splendid mass of flowers, had been set up. Behind it stood the missionary priest, ready to officiate. Clara wore a white sarong, her shimmering blonde hair cascaded down her back and a frangipani was tucked behind her ear. Three of her little schoolchildren in grass skirts, their hair in braids, walked proudly in front of her. She smiled at Ronan, who looked radiantly happy as he waited for her at the altar. Kathleen tilted her

532

white hat to shade her beaming face from the sun and watched them greet each other. She thought of Dermot. How proud he would be of his son. As James would be as well.

Lifting her camera, she took some more photos. She had already taken a heap since she'd arrived on Kiriwina. And some of Clara down by the lagoon before the ceremony. This moment was so special she wanted to make sure the photographs were perfect. Lillie and Seamus hadn't been able to make the long trip from Rathgarven, as Lillie was pregnant with their second child and the her doctor was loath to let her take such a long flight. She would be waiting anxiously for photographs, as would James, Marcus and Freddie when she got home. And Brian and Lorna Medlow, who had been such a comfort to Kathleen ever since Ronan had been injured in Vietnam. Then there were the Hogans, and Father Fogarty, and Arthur — all of them would be keen to see the photographs.

After the ceremony, as they gathered on the verandah of the guesthouse, Clara came up to her.

'It's funny,' she said, 'despite what Mummy did, I do miss her. She would have loved this, wouldn't she?'

Kathleen smiled as she thought of Jessica on the verandah of the Tollygunge Club surrounded by a group of admirers. 'Yes,' she said. 'She would have been in her element.'

'She might have complained about India, but I know she loved it. If she'd had a happy marriage maybe she would have stayed there.'

'You may well be right,' Kathleen said.

What would have happened if Dermot hadn't died? Would she still be in India? Although it was wartime when they met, Dermot had loved India as much as Kathleen did. But she was happy with her life the way it was. She loved Eureka Park and was looking forward to the future there with James. Marcus and Freddie were doing well at school and Cosmo was proving to be a great little horse — Tommy Brown had agreed to take him on as well as a couple of others they had decided to hold onto. She had another photographic exhibition coming up, this time in a small gallery in Double Bay in Sydney, which had come about when the owner had seen her photographs in Roger Mann's gallery in Tamworth.

As she watched Ronan grab hold of Clara and, despite his walking stick, twirl her around and around to the delight of the little children down below, Kathleen laughed out loud. She remembered the letter Dermot had written to her all those years ago. A letter she had not received until after his death.

If only I could hear your laugh… I would settle for that, he had written.

How happy he would be to hear Kathleen laugh with joy for their son and his wife, Clara. The girl he loved so ardently.

Epilogue

Kenmare River, 1970

'Where would you like this to go?' Lillie asked Maisie as she walked into the drawing room at Rathgarven. It was a sunny but chilly late summer's day; the leaves of the oak tree outside the window were blowing in the light breeze coming up from the river.

'Over there on the sideboard will be doing fine. We'll be covering it up so your Grandma can't be seeing it until she should.'

Lillie placed the birthday cake, which she and Ma had spent ages decorating yesterday, on the sideboard and stood back. 'I think Grandma will love it. Don't you?'

'Ah to be sure now I do. Haven't the two of you been doing a grand job.'

'It's going to be such a lovely day for her, isn't it? The only pity being Ronan and Clara aren't here.'

'Yes, it is,' Kathleen said, coming into the room and carrying a vase of wildflowers for the table. 'But they'll be here in spirit.'

She was wearing a blue cashmere sweater, linen slacks and had her hair in a French roll. Lillie was amazed at how quickly Ma had seemed to fall back into the way of life at Rathgarven and the way of dressing. It was as if she felt Grandma, and possibly even Maisie, would disapprove of her wearing jeans and an open-necked shirt as she mostly did at Eureka Park. Even Dad, who had left the running of Eureka Park in Arthur's hands for the three weeks they were to be away, appeared to take on a different persona here, becoming more of the country gentleman, whereas in Australia he seemed to be one of the stable hands rather than the squire. Lillie was pleased that when they had lost Rathgarven to Donoghue in 1963, Dad and Ma had invented the lie of selling to him. It made it so much easier. Not only for Lillie and Seamus, but also for Ma, Dad and Grandma to return here.

When Lillie had asked Ma how she felt about being back at Rathgarven she had smiled. 'It's wonderful to be here, darling, and to see the old place. But Eureka Park's our home now.' She leant forward and used the poker to push a piece of wood back into the roaring fire. 'And I must say you've done her proud. We'll be forever grateful to Seamus for buying her back. As is Alice.'

When she first came down from Dublin to stay, Seamus had just received an offer from a publisher for *The Chalice*, and Alice had said to him, 'Of course it was my advice to you on the plot that got it taken up,' and laughed. 'Without my input it might still be languishing in your bottom drawer.'

Now Freddie came bowling into the dining room with Lillie's dog Bonnie in hot pursuit. 'What time's lunch?' he asked. 'I'm famished.'

'Me too,' Marcus said, following him in with Hugh in tow. 'We've been out in the rowboat. I reckon I'll catch a heap of salmon this afternoon.'

Lillie smiled. Her brothers were certainly enjoying being at Rathgarven and having Hugh close by at Drominderry House. If Marcus caught any more salmon Lillie and Seamus would have to buy another freezer. She wondered how Ronan's fishing was going on Kiriwina. She knew how much he loved fishing on the Kenmare River. And in the river at Eureka Park. But she also knew how much he loved the lagoon opening to the wide, open sea where he was now.

She grinned at Marcus, who had grown a good five inches taller than her. 'I reckon you're nearly as good a fisherman as Ronan now. You might even be better.'

'I was always better,' Marcus said.

'You *were* not,' threw in Freddie, who was also taller than Lillie by quite a few inches.

Lillie smiled. Some things would never change.

In the conservatory yesterday evening Lillie and her mother had looked through Ronan and Clara's wedding photos.

'They do seem so happy, don't they?' Lillie said. 'And I must say Kiriwina looks divine. I'm so glad they've negotiated to buy the guesthouse. And that Ronan's building a house for them down by the lagoon.' She had glanced out of the window to the river where a strong wind was whipping up the water. Beyond the river, the mountains rolled into the distance amidst the clouds. 'I could do with some of that warmth,' she shivered. 'Even on a summer's day it's freezing, isn't it?'

'But that's the beauty of Kerry. It might be freezing one day, glorious the next.'

And Ma had been right. For today, Grandma's birthday, although it was cold it was as clear as a bell. It was as if Grandma had put in a special order, which had been met with merriment from above.

'Charles is coming for Hugh shortly and lunch will be at one,' she said to Marcus and Freddie. 'In the meantime do you mind occupying Gemma? Dad's looking after her in the drawing room. No doubt he wants relieving so he can finish reading the *Irish Times*. He's loving catching up on the local news.'

'Where's Seamus?' Kathleen asked. 'I haven't seen him this morning.'

'He's down with Paddy. One of the stags got its horn caught in a gorse bush.' Lillie was amazed how Seamus had taken to farming. And how much he loved those deer. Although she missed Ronan, she was grateful that his advice to breed deer at Rathgarven had paid off. They now had quite a herd, and a young man from Sneem helped Seamus look after the animals. Together with Seamus's writing and Lillie's part-time teaching at the primary school in Kenmare while she finished her degree, they had a good income and were managing so well financially that they were able to put in a new central heating system and upgrade the wiring and plumbing. In fact, Rathgarven was now so warm during the winter that Grandma had once complained that it was too hot.

'Honestly, Lillie, we'll all be roasted like chestnuts if you don't turn it down.'

***

An hour later the family gathered around the table with Grandma seated in the middle and Gemma in her high chair between Lillie and Seamus. First of all Maisie brought out a silver platter with a huge salmon Marcus and Hugh had caught, surrounded by potatoes and greens from the walled garden. And when that was all gone, Lillie went over to the sideboard and uncovered the cake and lit the nine candles representing each decade of her grandmother's life.

'What a glorious cake,' Alice said, when Lillie put it in front of her. She clapped her hands in delight at the miniature gold chalice in front of a miniature Rathgarven on top of the cake. 'You really are very naughty to go to all this trouble for an ancient old bird like me.'

'Not at all,' James said, standing up to give a toast. 'Happy birthday, Mother. You've been a wonderful example to us all. And hugely loved by us all as well.'

'Hear hear,' reverberated around the table.

'And,' Lillie added, 'to the best Grandma and Great-Grandma in the world.'

'Thank you, darling,' Alice said. She glanced up at the portrait of her late husband, Eoghan, hanging above the fireplace where a turf fire was burning in the grate. 'We should also remember those who are no longer with us, yet are thankfully here in spirit. Particularly,' she added, looking at James and Kathleen, 'Dermot. Who has left us so much to remember him by, including our darling Ronan.'

538

No sooner had she said that than Maisie came in and handed her a telegram that had just arrived.

Lillie opened it and nearly jumped out of her skin. *Happy Birthday, Grandma. We wish we were with you. Great news. Clara and I are having a baby. Due in six months. All my love, Ronan.*

'You'll never guess!' she exclaimed in delight, looking around the table.

'Guess what?' Freddie asked, staring at the telegram in her hand.

'Ronan and Clara are going to have a baby.'

Lillie went over to her parents. 'Isn't that wonderful?' she said, giving them each a kiss. Their smiles and the smile on Grandma's face made Lillie think that there could be no better birthday present for Grandma. Or anything that could give the whole family more happiness.

Her father put down his pipe and lifted his glass again. 'To Ronan and Clara,' he said, beaming from ear to ear. 'And the new little O'Sullivan on its way.'

'Hear, hear,' Seamus declared, leaning over a beaming Gemma to give Lillie a kiss and a hug. 'And to the new wee Flaherty on its way.' Seamus took her hand in his and looked around the table. ''Twas a mighty grand day when I married into this fine O'Sullivan family.'

How lucky I am to have married such a man, Lillie thought. And to be sitting here at Rathgarven with my family. Even though Ronan isn't here, I couldn't be happier for him and Clara and their imminent baby.

She lifted Seamus's hand to her lips. 'And 'twas a mighty fine day when I sat next to a budding Brendan Behan on the school bus all those years ago.'

'It was indeed,' Seamus said with a wink, as the rest of the family burst into laughter.

Lillie caught Ma's eye. Although her hair was now grey, and there were deep wrinkles around her hazel eyes, she still looked beautiful. Her gaze then rested on her father, who was filling his pipe with tobacco. Behind him the harp Uncle Finn and Rory used to play stood next to the fireplace.

Her parents had trod a long, hard road in the seven years since they had left Rathgarven for Australia. Now, with Ronan and Clara's news, that road had turned another corner.

Author's Note

Many times I have revisited Ireland, the land of my birth, and where my parents returned to live in their later years. On one of those occasions I took my mother to County Kerry to visit Parknasilla Hotel on the banks of a rocky cove on Kenmare River where she stayed as a teenager in the 1920s. I loved the area so much that I thought then I would like to write a novel partly set there. Recently I returned to Kerry with my husband, Rob, to refresh my memories and edit this book. From the porch of our small cottage looking across Kenmare River to the Kerry Mountains I found the scenery just as rugged and spectacular as I remembered.

Although this novel is a work of fiction, I have drawn on historic events in my family's past.

My grandmother, Eily was a descendant of the O'Sullivans of Beare and Bantry. Despite having seen her last when I was seven years old there is no doubt that I have inherited her love of writing. And hence I have used the O'Sullivan name for the family in this book. Today in Kerry there are still many O'Sullivans related to the original chief, Eoghan (Owen) O'Sullivan of Dunkerron Castle. Nonetheless, the O'Sullivan family in my novel is entirely fictitious.

Rathgarven and Drominderry House are the work of my imagination, but my family's 'big house' in County Wexford was burnt down in the Irish Civil War of the 1920s and later rebuilt. The 1770s Georgian home on the shores of Lough Derg in Tipperary, where my father, Owen Esmonde, and his family lived during the Civil War as a young boy was spared and still stands. He regaled us with stories of how he and his young brothers hid in the attic as his mother pacified soldiers at the front door. It is where my parents and my siblings, Deborah, Gill, Eugene, Viv and I resided before moving to Australia.

My mother, Eira Mackenzie, lived in India for a time during the last days of the Raj before she married my father and moved to Ireland. Her memories of that time in Calcutta have always intrigued me.

Although Gullumbindy and Eureka Park near Tamworth in the New England area of New South Wales are fictitious I have drawn on my memories of this area from my many visits to my sister, Gill Rosewarne, who lived there for many years. Ever since I was a child my siblings and I have ridden horses, so, of course, they had to play a part in this book.

In the 1960s and 70s Rob and I spent five years in Papua New Guinea where Rob was an officer with the Pacific Islands Regiment. During that time I visited the Trobriand Islands, staying in the rustic timber lodge on the island of Kiriwina, the memories of which I have used in this book.

About the Author

Rosie Mackenzie was born in Ireland and moved to Australia when she was seven years old. After a successful business career in Tasmania, she now spends her time, writing, sailing and with her family. She is married to Rob Peterswald and they have two daughters and five grandchildren. She and Rob have published eight photographic coffee table books on sailing, seafood and wine together. She has adopted the pen name, Rosie Mackenzie for her historical fiction to honour her mother. When not in Australia, she and Rob are on their boat exploring the world. Rosie has also published a memoir, *Can My Pony Come Too?* under her name, Rosemary Esmonde Peterswald, and *Bird of Paradise,* a novel set in Papua New Guinea.

Love in a Far Place was released in 2023.

Acknowledgements

I could not have written this book without the help of a number of people.

Firstly I would like to thank Selwa Anthony who has represented me for many years. Her guidance, acumen and friendship have meant so much to me. When I first started writing in Tasmania after many years in the hectic world of business it was the author and tutor Rosie Dub who encouraged me to keep going. I thank Nicola O'Shea and Linda Funnell for their wonderful editorial advice.

The renowned award-winning author, Annie Seaton has been an inspiration to me and guided me through the layout and cover design of this new edition of The Homestead on the River, which was originally published by Harper Collins.

Every day I give thanks for my daughters Charlotte and Georgie and my five beautiful grandchildren who have given me inspiration to write.

Finally, a big thank you to Rob Peterswald, my soulmate for many, many years and who has offered me constructive advice and helped me with my research.

www.ballynastraghbooks.com.au

www.ingramcontent.com/pod-product-compliance
Lightning Source LLC
Chambersburg PA
CBHW020239120726
47904CB00001B/21